The Ghost Writer

A HAUNTING ROMANCE

Michaela Andrews

Grosvenor House
Publishing Limited

This book is published by
Grosvenor House Publishing Ltd
Link House
140 The Broadway, Tolworth, Surrey, KT6 7HT.
www.grosvenorhousepublishing.co.uk

A CIP record for this book
is available from the British Library

ISBN 978-1-78623-104-8

Chapter One

Stella parked her little red car outside what was to be her new home. A two-bedroomed end of terrace house in the village of Little Welborough. The removal van had not yet arrived so she allowed herself a moment to sit and collect her thoughts. The divorce had knocked her confidence and taken its toll on her bank balance, but hopefully that was all behind her now. She closed her eyes, enjoying the warmth of the sun on her face and the sense of peace that descended upon her. She was petite with red-blonde shoulder length hair. Her eyes were a deep blue and her skin was pale, too pale her friends had been telling her lately. Hopefully the strain of the last year would fade as she became involved in village life. No more arguments over who had bought what and no more insults. To be in her own home, with only herself to please was a luxury she was looking forward to. Her mum had wanted her to move back home with her, but that would never have worked. Stella needed to be able to do things her own way. If she felt like spending a Sunday in bed or stretched out on the sofa, she would. No more Sunday mornings at the gym or lunches with Gary's so-called friends. She could do what she liked when she liked. Except for going to work of course, but at least she had a week to get herself settled before starting her new job. Her stomach tightened into a knot at the thought of her new job, she wouldn't think about it yet she decided. She would just concentrate on moving in and finding her feet in the village before she thought about work. Her stomach churned again nervously. 'Oh God what have I done' she thought, 'new house, new job and new area'. It had seemed like a good idea at the time, but as a cloud passed over the sun causing her to feel a chill, she suddenly felt alone. This was a new start she reminded herself taking a deep breath. It was going to be exciting, meeting new people and having new challenges. She had never lived in a village before and she was looking forward to the change; maybe she would even grow her own vegetables! Just then the removal van turned the corner and slowly drove the short distance towards her down the narrow road. This was what she needed, something to keep her busy and take her mind off her anxieties. As the van parked, and the men climbed out of the cab she plastered a smile on her face and smoothing her hair in place stepped out of her car to meet them.

"That's the lot then," Derek said two hours later as he stepped through her front door for the last time.

"Thanks for everything," she called as he walked down the path to the waiting van. 'Her path' she reminded herself, to her house!

She watched the van manoeuvre cautiously passed a dustbin that had been left out and an overlarge hedge and drive away, before closing the door and let out a sigh of exhaustion. The whole thing had gone quite smoothly. There had been a moment of panic when she had thought her box of kitchen appliances had gone missing, but they had turned up after a brief search in what was to be her bedroom. The house looked a mess. There were boxes everywhere, but at least she was in. She looked about her, where to start she wondered?

First things first, she decided she needed a cup of tea to fortify herself before she tackled the unpacking. The table her mother had given her had been put in the kitchen, and on top of it stood the box with the kettle in it. Taking it from the box she filled it at the sink and switched it on. Now came the task of finding a cup. There were several boxes on the floor with the word kitchen written on the side. Stooping down she opened the first box she came to which she discovered, contained plates and bowls. The second box contained casserole dishes and cutlery. She looked around; there should be another box with her cups in, where was it? Stella shut the box she had just searched through, frustrated that she couldn't find what she wanted and stood up for a better look. It wasn't on the counter tops. She opened a few of the cupboards to see if it had been put inside one of them. No luck there either. She was just about to start searching the other rooms when she spotted a box tucked behind the kitchen door. Bingo; opening the box she grabbed the cup on the top and unwrapped it. It was her Disney mug, she remembered it had come with an Easter egg inside it the year she had met Gary. He had found her taste for Disney mugs cute back then, but as time had passed he had called them childish. His friends didn't drink from character mugs oh no, they had proper grown up mugs. He had made her pack them away where they couldn't be seen. Well not any more she thought putting it on the side next to the kettle.

That memory, along with the lack of sleep over the last few days, and the stress of moving had tears filling her eyes. She looked about for a tissue then realising that she didn't have any, or if she did then they had not been unpacked, she wiped her eyes on the sleeve of her hoodie. Gary had hated her wearing hoodies too. He had thought them scruffy and that they were only suitable for teenagers or wearing to the gym. Well Stella liked to wear one sometimes, she had to dress smart for work and they were comfortable. Of course, Gary's *friends* didn't wear them, which was the real reason he hadn't wanted her to wear one. He was always so desperate to conform to what they did, and what they liked. They weren't real friends. *'Ryan's wife always looks smart'* he had told her one day when they had been getting ready to go to the pub for lunch, *'Just right for an executive's wife!* Well good for Ryan, she had thought bitterly to herself as she had changed into a blouse to avoid an argument. Not anymore, she thought. She could wear what she liked when she liked. She opened the back door and sat on the doorstep with her tea, listening to the birds in the trees. She let the peaceful sounds of nature and village life wash over her, soothing her jumbled thoughts. Eventually she started thinking about what she needed to do in the house. First, she would need to sort out her kitchen and bedroom, as they would be the two rooms that she would need to use most today. She would need to cook and she would need to sleep. Her toiletries for the bathroom were in a box in her car so they would be easy to find when she wanted them, she could just take the box into the bathroom and get bits out as and when she needed them. Tomorrow she would sort it out properly, and the other rooms. At that moment her stomach rumbled reminding her that she hadn't eaten since breakfast and it was now just after three. One of the boxes in the kitchen had tins and packets of food stashed in it, along with bread and a packet of biscuits. She contemplated rummaging around until she found the biscuits, then looking at her empty cup sighed, no point now there was nothing to dunk a biscuit in. Perhaps she should visit the local shop. It would give her a break from sorting through boxes and give her a chance to see what the village had to offer. When she had been offered the job in the village school she had been lucky enough to find the house quite quickly, and the sale had gone through relatively smoothly. She had liked the look of the village the first time she had visited it for her interview, but since then she hadn't really spent much time checking it out. Now was as good a time as any she thought, taking her empty cup to the kitchen and rinsing it in the sink before leaving it to drain on the draining board; she hadn't found the tea towels yet.

Stella opened her front door and jumped in surprise as she came face to face with a lady standing on her doorstep. Her hand was poised in mid-air ready to ring the bell. The lady was colourfully dressed in a multi-coloured T-shirt and turquoise cropped jeans, she laughed and apologised, "I'm sorry I didn't mean to make you jump, I'm Jo I live next door with Sebastian". She had long dark brown wavy hair and brown eyes that seemed warm and friendly. "I thought you might like these," In her hands she held a bunch of flowers and a cake tin. "They're a sort of welcome to the village offering, I hope you like them".

Stella felt touched that a stranger should make the effort to welcome her. "Thank you that's very kind," she replied taking the tin and the flowers. "I'm Stella, I was just on my way to the shop or I would ask you in," she explained.

"Oh, don't worry about that, I didn't expect you to be ready for visitors. You must have a lot to do today."

Jo reassured Stella. "How are you getting on with it all?" she asked.

"It's going okay, but a bit slow as it's just me, still I'm in no hurry as long as I can cook and sleep!"

"Well why don't you come to us for dinner later? It'll save you the bother of finding everything today and I can fill you in on the village gossip," Jo suggested.

Stella smiled, "thanks, I'd like that". Maybe this was going to be alright after all she thought, feeling more positive about her life again.

"I'll see you later then Stella," Jo turned and started to walk away. Then as she went through the gate she asked, "You're not allergic to anything are you? Only I don't want to put you in hospital or anything on your first night here?"

Stella laughed at the idea then said, "No I haven't found anything yet, unless you count ex-husbands that is?"

Jo laughed along with her before adding, "Don't worry I won't be serving any of those".

Stella took the flowers into her kitchen and stood them in the sink with some water until she could find something to put them in. Then she had a peep in the cake tin. Inside was a selection of cupcakes all beautifully decorated. Stella picked up a chocolate covered cake with flake sprinkled on the top, and bit into it. It was amazing, so light and chocolaty, Stella's cakes never turned out as well as the one she was now eating. What a great neighbour she mused as she finished off the cake and put the lid back on the top of the tin to stop them going dry.

As Stella pushed open the door to the village shop a bell jangled to announce her presence. A lady looked up from where she was stood reading the paper at the counter. It was positioned to the far side of the door with a good view out into the street. She smiled and then supposedly went back to what she was doing, although Stella felt as if she was being assessed from afar. The shop turned out to be a small building, but it was crammed full of all the essentials that you might need. It also contained things you didn't know you needed until you saw them. Stella strolled casually around with a plastic basket she had picked up just inside the door, selecting a few items from the shelves before arriving at the counter. There was no one else waiting so she was able to put her basket straight down beside the till before asking the lady for a bottle of wine. The alcoholic drinks were kept on the shelves behind the till. "I've not seen you in here before, are you just passing through?" The lady at the till asked conversationally. Stella guessed she was in her late fifties, the glasses she was wearing were attached to a chain about her neck and her short hair had turned quite grey.

"No, I bought a house in the village, I moved in earlier today," Stella replied.

"Oh yes, I heard someone was moving in, you must be number one, Lovedon Lane, next to Jo and Sebastian!"

"That's right," Stella smiled, her friends had warned her that nothing was private in a village. Now she could see what they meant.

"Nice couple," the lady continued. "She runs the local café and he's a car mechanic, works in the garage on the outskirts of town," she paused as she checked the total on the till. "That'll be eleven pounds and nine pence then please". Stella fished in her purse for the money and handed it over.

"I'm Grace by the way, everyone knows me, and you are?"

"Stella, Stella Martin. Nice to meet you Grace."

"Stella, that's a nice name, you don't hear it much nowadays. So, what do you do Stella?"

"I'm a teacher," Stella replied. "I'll be starting in the village school after half term." Ten minutes later Stella was at last able to leave the shop. She now knew that Grace's grandson went to the village school and that her daughter helped her out in the shop on Mondays, Wednesdays and Thursdays. Grace on the other hand knew that Stella had been married for two years, was newly divorced and an only child. She also knew that Stella was twenty-nine years of age, a teacher and a chocoholic. How did that happen she thought? Stella took a leisurely walk back through the village with her shopping, it wasn't heavy and she was enjoying the fresh air and sunshine. It was quite a large village with a pub, a village school, a hall, a café, a chip shop and a lovely old church. A river ran through the village near to the church with an old brick bridge crossing it at its widest point. The church however was on the opposite side of the village to the shop so Stella didn't have to pass it on her way home. The village had a nice feel to it and with a park, and a green where children were playing there was a strong feeling of community spirit. There were some older boys playing football on the farthest part of the green as she passed, and mothers with pushchairs and young children in the actual park. Stella turned left at the park and into Lovedon Lane where her house stood on the corner. Back inside Stella put her shopping away leaving the wine on the table ready to take to her neighbours later. Thanks to Grace, Stella knew what type of wine Jo liked to drink and that she worked in the village café, hence the lovely cakes Stella thought, opening the tin and helping herself to a dainty butterfly cake. The cake, as she bit into it, was just as lovely and light as the chocolate one she had eaten earlier. As light as a butterfly in fact so it was well named, and the icing was rich and velvety. Living next door to Jo could mean having to do some exercise after all, although she would be walking to work now even if it wasn't far away, so maybe that and doing a spot of gardening would do instead of going to a gym. She had never been one for going to the gym, always preferring to walk or swim for her exercise. Stella spent an hour opening boxes and organising her belongings before she washed and changed into a casual skirt and a blouse. Picking up the bottle of wine from the kitchen table she headed out of the house and down her garden path. She was just shutting her gate when someone called her name, "Stella, coo-ee!" She turned around expecting to see someone she knew only to come face to face with a total stranger.

"Hi Stella, I'm Sophie," the stranger announced holding out her hand expectantly and a big smile plastered across her face. Stella shook the proffered hand and Sophie continued, still managing to smile as she spoke. "My mum told me you'd just moved in" as if this explained everything.

Stella looked at Sophie puzzled. Noticing the puzzled expression Sophie laughed, "Sorry, Grace Watkins who runs the shop is my mother", she explained at last.

Realisation dawned on Stella, "Oh nice to meet you Sophie," Stella returned Sophie's rather over enthusiastic smile with a friendly one of her own.

"We have a book club that runs on a Thursday evening if you're interested in coming," Sophie continued. "We take it in turns to host it. You're welcome to join us if you'd like, what with you being on your own.

A bit of company will do you good and it would give you a chance to meet people."

Having given her invite she waited expectantly for Stella to agree. Stella however didn't fancy joining the book club, especially as Sophie was implying that she was desperate for company, but on the other hand she didn't want to start village life by offending anyone. "That's very kind of you Sophie," Stella hesitated, "I'll have to see how it goes. I'm very busy at the moment sorting the house out and once term starts…" her voice trailed off. She hoped it didn't sound too much like an excuse, even though that was exactly what it was. A book club was really not her thing.

"Oh, that's okay. I know how busy you must be at the moment." Sophie replied kindly then added, "When you're ready just let me or mum know and we'll let you know the details. Bye for now," she waggled her fingers and continued on her way, crossing the road and heading back towards the park before Stella could explain that she wasn't interested in joining the book club now ***or*** in the future. Stella sighed, she could see that she would have to be a bit blunt in the way she dealt with some people, or she might unwittingly get signed up for all sorts of things. Jo was stood at her front door laughing when Stella pushed open the wooden gate.

"I see you've just met Sophie," she chuckled.

"Yes," Stella frowned. "She wants me to join the book club."

"The gossip club more like, I take it you're not keen? Come on in." Jo stood to one side to let Stella pass. "She tried to get me to join when we first moved in too, don't worry she'll get over it".

Jo and Sebastian's house had the same layout as Stella's she noticed, although it was a mirror image. But that was where the similarities stopped. Stella's house although small, was light and airy and felt spacious, whereas Jo and Sebastian's house was an eclectic mix of patterns and designs that gave the house a smaller, cosier feel. There were ornaments and fabrics from foreign holidays decorating the walls and tables, and the colours were very exotic. Large cushions were arranged in the corner of the room perfect for laying back to watch television. It was like stepping into a Bedouin tent. It wouldn't have been to Stella's taste but it seemed to work, and the whole feel was relaxed and inviting. Jo and Sebastian turned out to be fun and the evening passed very quickly. Stella left with the feeling that she had friends nearby, and that she wasn't completely alone after all. It was comforting that already she was beginning to feel like she was part of a community, and not just another cog in a wheel. All in all, it was a good start to her new life, and it convinced Stella that she had done the right thing moving to Little Welborough.

Chapter Two

The next morning was Sunday and Stella awoke to the sound of church bells ringing in the distance. For a while she felt disorientated, not sure where she was and then realisation kicked in and she remembered moving into her new house. The sun was streaming in the window through the flowery curtains and making sunny patterns on the walls. Stella stretched and pulled the covers up a bit higher; all she needed now was someone to bring her breakfast in bed. Gary hadn't been the breakfast in bed type, he always wanted to be up having his super juice smoothie before he had headed off to the gym. Stella wasn't against being healthy, far from it, but it was nice sometimes just to wake up slowly and daydream a bit before starting the day. She thought about all the unpacking still to be done and sighed. She had plenty of time. It was half-term so she had a whole week to get herself sorted before she had to go back to early mornings and marking children's work. She would be teaching the year one children in the village school. She hadn't taught that age before so it was a little daunting. Every time she thought about it, her stomach churned with anxiety, but she would manage. She had to, she was committed to it now and anyway she thought, it would be good to try something new. At least the old teacher had already established the children's routine for her. By the time the new intake came in she would be used to teaching the younger children, and she would be more prepared. At least she hoped she would anyway. When she had met her class a few weeks earlier, they had seemed lovely and eager to please. That wouldn't last long Stella knew, but it was a good place to start. It was going to be a new challenge, something to stop her brooding on the past. It wasn't that she was still upset about the breakup exactly, things hadn't been right for a long time but she felt like she had failed. All she had really wanted was for them to settle down and have a family, but Gary had become more interested in keeping up with his colleagues. Looking back now she thought he had only married her because having a wife was expected of him, and her job gave her long holidays. Gary had been a friend of her housemate's boyfriend and somehow, they had always ended up together. Eventually they had started going out without their friends and it had ended in marriage, with the help of their families nudging them in that direction. It had been comfortable to slip into the relationship, but thinking back now perhaps it had been too convenient. Neither of them had really considered what each other had wanted or expected from the future. To start with it had seemed perfect.

They had married at the end of the summer term and Gary had loved coming home to cooked meals and Stella fussing over him. When the term had started again in the September, and she had been busy marking schoolwork in the evenings, the meals were often late or rushed and that had been when Gary had started to become critical of her. He had started comparing her efforts at housekeeping with what his friends' wives apparently managed to do, even though most of them didn't work. He didn't see housework as a job to be shared by two working people, he thought it should all be done by Stella and that her job wasn't as important as his was. Then he had gotten a promotion and he had become snappy. At first Stella had let it go as he was working hard to learn the new job and fit in, but as time had gone on she had had enough of the constant criticisms. She had started to feel insecure and had then made more mistakes, often burning the dinner and becoming indecisive over her choice of clothes. She had thought more and more about having a family and could see that it wasn't high on Gary's plans for their future. One morning when Gary had been telling her how wonderful his colleague Patrick's wife was, how she never stayed in bed resting on a Sunday morning, Stella had finally snapped. They had had an almighty argument and Gary had stormed out. They had only been married for eighteen months and Stella had found herself thinking that if it was like that now, what would it be like in another ten years?

When Gary had come back later that morning they had talked properly, something they should have done before they got married, and they had decided they should call it a day. They both wanted different things and being together wasn't working. Stella had moved in with her friend Katy until the house was sold, and then after that she had rented a pokey flat on the outskirts of London. Gary had said it wouldn't look good to his boss if he had to sleep on a mate's sofa, it would ruin his image in the company. It had been up to Stella to make the sacrifice as usual, and move out. Secretly Stella thought it was more likely that no one was willing to put up with him and his 'OCD' tidiness.

He was always so uptight, everything had to be put back just so. Initially when he had picked her clothes up after her Stella had thought it was sweet, by the end of the marriage it was just annoying. He expected the house to be perfect when he got in from work and huffed and tutted if things weren't where he liked them. When Stella put things down he would move them, or adjust them until he was satisfied with their position. If she left her car keys on the hall table he would come along behind her and hang them up on a hook by the door. Her dressing gown couldn't be left on the chair in the bedroom; it had to be hung back in the wardrobe. Sometimes Stella found herself deliberately moving cups so the handles' all faced different directions because she knew it would annoy him, and he would have to rearrange them. She got a perverse pleasure in messing things up so he would spend hours sorting them out again. Looking back on it she could see that it was childish, but it had made her feel better about all the times he had demoralised her with his criticisms, and the fact that he expected her to do all the housework. It had allowed her to get her own back in a small way. Still, Stella smiled to herself, those days were gone.

When she had seen the advertisement for the year one teaching job in Little Welborough the thought of moving away and starting afresh had been like a dream come true. Then while visiting the school, she had been lucky enough to find a house that she could just about afford in the same village, and it had seemed like fate. She had put an offer in on the house the same day that she was offered the job, and it had been accepted. Now she had actually moved in. She had her own home, in what appeared to be a charming village. Stella rolled onto her side and looked at the clock. She was surprised to see that it was nearly ten o'clock. At that moment her stomach began to protest that it was empty, rumbling loudly. Flinging back the duvet she decided it was probably time to get up.

In the kitchen Stella filled the kettle and put bread in the toaster. While the kettle boiled she checked her phone for messages. There were three. The first one was from her mum, 'Hi darling. Hope the move went ok. Can't wait to see the new place, let me know if I can help bye', Stella smiled. Her mum was great but Stella wanted to get the house straight before her mum visited and tried to organise it for her. The second message was from her friend Katy, like Stella's mum she was checking that the move went smoothly. The third message was from Argos to let her know that the wardrobe and chest of drawers she had ordered, would be delivered on Monday between seven and twelve. Great she thought sarcastically, that meant an early start in the morning after all. Still it would give her time to put the wardrobe together and fill it with clothes. The house had a built-in wardrobe, but Stella had felt that it wasn't quite big enough to take all her things so had bought one cheaply in the Argos sale. It came with a chest of drawers, which Stella had intended to buy anyway, so she could easily justify the purchase to her mother. Not that she needed to, but it made her feel better that she could.

The sun was still shining so once she had replied briefly to the messages from Katy and her mother, she took her tea and toast into the garden. An old wooden bench stood under a cascading rose bush, a relic from the previous inhabitants. It was a bit weathered but it looked sturdy enough so she sat herself down, gingerly to start with in case it gave way. Once she realised it was quite safe she settled herself properly, putting her feet up. At the end of the garden near the fence was an overgrown vegetable patch. Nestled in amongst the weeds Stella could see strawberries growing, although they hadn't turned red yet as it was too early. It would be lovely to eat home grown strawberries when they eventually ripened. Over the fence Jo and Sebastian's garden was a riot of colour, much like their house. They also had a vegetable patch; theirs however was in much better condition and looked to be abundant with tomatoes, raspberries in a cage type structure with runner beans and some other plants that Stella didn't recognise. Whatever the fruit or vegetable was it hadn't appeared yet so it was impossible for Stella to tell. An expert would know by the shape of the leaves, but she definitely wasn't one of those. Further down the row of terraced houses Stella could hear a child squealing with delight, and a dog barking. It was a lovely leisurely way to start a Sunday morning. Once her tea and toast was finished Stella reluctantly went back inside, she might not be in a hurry but she really did need to get on with the unpacking and organising her house.

* * * *

Next door Jo was sat on the side of the bathtub trying not to cry. She had woken up with a familiar ache in her lower back and knew exactly what it meant. She and Sebastian had been trying for a baby for nearly a year now with no luck. Each month that came and went, Jo was finding it harder and harder to stay positive about the possibility of becoming a mum. To make matters worse, it seemed that more women than usual were coming into the café with young babies, or very obviously expecting them. It was like rubbing salt into her wounds. A tear rolled silently down her cheek. It wasn't that she begrudged them their families; it was just that she wanted one of her own. She knew Sebastian would make a great dad. Even the characters in her favourite soap on telly had just found out they were going to be parents. She wiped away the tear. If she had fallen pregnant straight away she would be holding a baby of her own by now. Another tear dripped onto her lap. Instead she was stuck with a bad back and a growing desperation that she would never have a child of her own. Sebastian knocked gently on the door.

"Are you ok in there?" He called. Jo wiped the tears away and unlocked the door. As she opened it Sebastian took one look at her sad face and pulled her into a hug. "No luck again huh?" Unable to speak through the lump in her throat, Jo just shook her head. "Don't worry it'll happen for us soon," he soothed.

"But what if it doesn't?" tears began to pour down her face soaking his chest.

"We'll cross that bridge when we come to it," he said rubbing her back, then trying to console her he said, "How about we give it a bit longer, then go and see the doctor if nothing's happened?"

Jo nodded her head. "Okay," she sniffed back the tears, trying to pull herself together. After all, at least they had each other. A niggling voice in her head added, 'but a baby would make it perfect'. She tried to ignore it.

"Come on," Sebastian coaxed. "It's Sunday lets have breakfast in bed, my treat."

Jo managed a watery smile, "Okay, can I have croissants with chocolate spread?"

Sebastian laughed, "You can have whatever you like".

Chapter Three

It was nearly four o'clock in the afternoon and Stella had been busy all day. At last she was pleased with how things were looking. The place was beginning to look like a home. All the furniture was where she wanted it, at least for the time being. The cupboards were filling up, which meant the boxes were emptying. Stella finished folding up the box she had just emptied ready for the recycling bin, and with a sigh of satisfaction glanced around her newly organised lounge. It was light and airy but with a cottagey feel to it, which she liked. Her light flowery Laura Ashley sofa looked good against the pale peach walls. The room was bright and had a warmth to it that made it feel cosy, especially with the sun streaming in through the windows. Her pictures were set out and her ornaments sat on the windowsill. Stella stretched out her back, it ached from all the bending and lifting.

The sun was still shinning outside, maybe some fresh air would do her good. Perhaps she would go for a walk and stretch her legs a bit she thought. She could even pick up fish and chips on the way back if the chip shop was open. Stella brushed the dust off her jeans and collected her bag. She was pleased with what she had managed to achieve so far, and was now looking forward to exploring the village. The prospect of getting chips was a rather nice one too and made her smile. It was quite warm for May so Stella didn't need a jacket.

As she walked along the path she saw several people in their gardens, weeding or mowing the lawn. It was a very tranquil sight. Most of the people nodded politely and smiled, or said hello in a friendly undemanding way as she passed by. It was something that would never have happened where Stella had lived before. Everyone had kept their heads down and passed by without so much as a glance, always in a hurry, not wanting to get involved in what was happening around them. It was a refreshing experience to feel part of a community.

Stella decided to head towards the church. She hadn't been that way yet as it was right at the far end of the village. The village was shaped a bit like a pointed oval, with smaller roads or lanes leading off from the two main ones. The two main roads eventually met at the church and then from there a lane led into the woods. One of the roads leading to the church carried on into the town of Winchester. It was about four miles away according to an old, off-white milestone that was falling sideways and half covered with a blackberry bush. If she headed towards the church she would be able to wander on into the woods, or pass the river and come back on the other road, which passed the shops and the pub. Stella's house was nearer to the shops and pub than the church, and not far from the school. It meant she would be able to walk to work and save money on petrol or train fares. As she drew closer to the church there were less houses, and the ones that were there were spread out with big gardens, high hedges and large trees. From what Stella could see as she passed each gateway, they looked old and very expensive. The road opened out as she approached the church, leaving space for several cars to park outside the lynch gate, although there were none parked there now.

An old stone wall ran around the churchyard. In some places it was chest height, but because the church was stood on a slight hill, in other places it was much lower, allowing her a good view of the church itself. She stopped and rested her elbows on the wall to enjoy the way the sun was shining on the stained-glass windows. She imagined that inside the colours would be splashed all over the pews and the stone floor. To the side of the church where the wall was at its highest, a bench stood in the shade of some ancient Yew trees. At that moment Stella noticed a man sitting on the bench watching her. She couldn't see him very clearly from where she was stood, as the shadow from the wall and the trees was obscuring her view. If he hadn't been wearing a white shirt she might have missed him altogether. He was sat sideways on the bench, with his arm resting along the back, and his long legs stretched out in front of him. He looked very relaxed. As she met his gaze across the churchyard, Stella felt her heart do a somersault and her pulse quicken making her catch her breath. The moment was soon ruined though as a car drove passed hooting its horn and making Stella jump. She turned around just in time to see Sophie, Grace from the shop's daughter and book club organiser. She was waving frantically at Stella from the driver's seat. Stella smiled and waved back somewhat less enthusiastically than Sophie.

When the car, which happened to be a little blue mini had gone, Stella looked back at the bench expecting to see the man, but he had gone. Her eyes quickly scanned the churchyard to see where he was, but there was no sign of him anywhere. It was as if he had just vanished into thin air. Puzzled she looked again at the bench expecting to see another gate behind it that he could have left by, but there was only the wall. The doors to the church were closed so he couldn't have gone inside. It was as though she had imagined him, and yet her pulse was only just beginning to return to normal. A cloud passed over the sun making Stella shiver at the change in temperature; all interest in the church had faded along with the sun. The churchyard, now cast completely in shadow, looked sad with its lichen covered headstones and long shadows. Stella, feeling a bit deflated decided to carry on with her walk. Passing the church, she saw the Vicarage across the road. It was a whitewashed Georgian cottage built in 1742 according to the plaque on the wall. It even had red roses growing over an arch round the door. Quintessentially English, a typical rural image.

Beside the church, down a long secluded driveway was an old Georgian farmhouse. It looked much bigger than the vicarage but it was difficult to see it clearly as it was hidden behind a high hedge. Some very large trees and shrubs had also been allowed to grow giving it a sleeping beauty kind of appearance. The dappled light, as the sun broke through the trees, teased with glimpses of what was probably a very beautiful property. Stella crossed the bridge near the vicarage and walked along by the river. Two butterflies flew passed casting a shadow on the water, like lovers dancing. Stella found her thoughts drifting back to the man in the churchyard, and her insides fluttered as if the butterflies were now dancing in her stomach. She was curious where he had gone and why. She wasn't really interested in him she assured herself, just curious.

The mystery of his disappearance intrigued her, an interesting distraction that took her mind off her jumbled thoughts of moving and her new job. She hadn't even seen him clearly as he had been sat in the shadows. But one thing she couldn't deny was the fact that he had made her pulse race. Even from a distance she had felt drawn to him, like a magnet he had unwaveringly held her gaze. What would have happened if Sophie had not distracted her she wondered? Would he have spoken to her, or would he still have disappeared like a ghost into the shadows? Stella sat down on an old tree stump and watched the water tumble and splash over the boulders. Occasionally a fish would dart by, making ripples on the surface. The sunlight made them appear like a flash of lightning under the water before they quickly swam away. A gentle breeze rustled the leaves on the trees. If she closed her eyes she could almost believe she were sitting on a beach, and that the sea was lapping on the shore. The noise the leaves made as they gently brushed against each other sounded very much like the sea crashing gently onto the sand.

Stella opened her eyes again and found her gaze wandering back towards the church. She was just in time to see someone in a white shirt disappear behind a large gravestone. She waited, holding her breath watching for him to appear again and was disappointed when he didn't. Perhaps he was laying flowers on the grave she thought, although there had been no evidence of flowers when she had seen him earlier. Stella suddenly felt guilty, as if she was intruding on someone else's pain and decided it was time to move on. She didn't want to be caught watching something as personal as another person grieving. She stood up and started walking back towards the centre of the village. Back to the houses and the sounds of people enjoying the early evening sunshine.

The smell of fish and chips made her stomach rumble as she opened the door to the chip shop. Luckily the only other occupants she could see was the lady serving and a female customer. They were busy chatting and didn't appear to hear her enter, or the noise that her stomach had made. The conversation paused briefly as the lady serving turned to scoop some chips into a little paper bag, she brought them back to the counter to put in another bigger bag along with the rest of the order. Stella waited patiently pretending to read the menu so it wasn't obvious that she was listening to their conversation.

"He always comes home late from the office now and he seems distracted all the time," the short, dark haired customer was saying, "Do you think he's seeing someone else?"

"I'm sure he wouldn't!" The lady serving tried to reassure her friend, then glancing at Stella added, "Try not to worry about it, how about we meet at the café tomorrow? We can discuss it properly then if you like," she suggested sympathetically.

"Ok," the dark-haired lady replied with a sigh. "Is 9.30 alright for you?" The lady serving nodded and handed over the bag she had filled with her friends' order.

"See you at 9.30 then. Bye."

Stella let the lady pass and then stepped up to the counter. "A large portion of chips and a pea fritter please," she said smiling at the lady serving whose name badge suggested that she was called Carly. Carly tapped the order into the till and Stella handed over the money. Five minutes later Stella was back outside and carrying a warm bundle against her chest. It was a bit like cuddling a hot water bottle but with the smell of warm chips coated in salt and vinegar wafting up under her nose. By now most of the people she had seen earlier in their gardens had retreated back inside their homes, and were now having dinner or watching the telly. She heard the title music of *'Escape to the Country'* as she passed one house with its windows wide open, and it made her smile. 'That's what I've done,' she thought, 'escaped to the country'. As she passed the Red Lion pub with its door open she could hear someone playing on the fruit machine and the gentle murmur of conversations. It was still quite early for the pub to be too busy; the evening crowd hadn't arrived yet.

Before long she was passing the playground and turning into her road. As she opened the front door and stepped inside she realised it was already beginning to feel like home. She felt comfortable and relaxed in the place; it wasn't just her house now it had become her home, her sanctuary. She left the chips in the paper on the kitchen table and put the kettle on. Then, while it was boiling she sat down at the table and ate the chips straight from the paper. She liked them best that way because it reminded her of when she was a child having fish and chips sat on the beach with her mum and dad. Of course, fish and chips at the seaside have their own unique flavour somehow, but the ones she was now eating were very tasty. They had been able to sweat just long enough on the walk home, soaking up the salt and vinegar to give them a very satisfying flavour. It didn't take her long to finish them.

Once she had finished them she scrunched up the empty paper into a ball and threw it straight into the bin. Of course, eating out of the paper also had the added bonus of saving her from the washing up. It was another one of those things she had never been allowed to do when she was with Gary, it wasn't proper to eat out of paper according to him. Stella washed her greasy fingers and then made herself a cup of tea. Taking it through to the lounge, she sat on the sofa and put her feet up. She thought back over her day. She had done quite well getting the house sorted out. She was gradually beginning to find places for everything and the overall effect was very cosy. The lounge could do with a lamp or two and perhaps a nice picture for the wall. She would have a look she decided, when she went into the town. But those were the fun things, buying little items that added that finishing touch to a place. The village seemed very nice and the people had been friendly when she had been out on her walk.

Thinking about her walk reminded her of the incident at the church before Sophie had driven passed and disturbed her. There was something about the man she had seen in the churchyard that fascinated her. When their gazes had met, even over a distance she had felt... well an excitement. It was like an instant attraction, although she reasoned it clearly wasn't that. But then Sophie had drawn her attention away, and when she had looked back he had disappeared. She had felt disappointed for some reason, which seemed silly when she thought about it now. He was a complete stranger, she knew nothing about him. He could be married or living with someone.

Developing feelings for someone who was already involved with someone else was not a good way to make friends in a village. She didn't want to get involved with anyone anyway she reminded herself, not yet. She wanted to sort herself out and get established before she started thinking about meeting someone new. It would complicate things at the moment, she had a new job to start and that was enough for her for the time being. At that moment Stella's phone rang. She could tell by the ring tone who it was and settled herself more comfortably with her legs tucked up beneath her for a long chat with her friend Katy.

Chapter Four

Katy checked her watch. She had half an hour before she was expected to be at the preliminary meeting with the director and the rest of the design team. She put her sketches in a large flat case and checked her appearance in the mirror tucked in the corner of the room. Smoothing down her glossy black hair inherited from her Spanish father, and reapplying her mascara to accentuate her green eyes inherited from her English/Irish mother she gave herself a smile of encouragement. She wanted to look her best for the meeting as it helped to make her feel more confident. With a heavy sigh she reflected that she needed all the help she could get these days. Once she was satisfied with her appearance she headed over to the wardrobe department. She wanted to show the sketches to Frank before the meeting began.

Frank was the director at the New Prince Albert Theatre just off Sloane Street. The theatre was known for its big productions and elaborate sets. Katy had been working for the theatre as a resident designer for over a year now and loved her job; or rather she ***had*** loved her job. Frank had joined the team recently from a much larger theatre and seemed to think he was better than everyone else. He had caused tension amongst the designers; always making them check with him before submitting ideas, which led to them doubting their abilities.

Katy was rather pleased with her latest sketches, but she wasn't sure what Frank would think when he saw them. She had read the script thoroughly and knew the angle the director was going for. The play was a modern take on *Romeo and Juliette* by an up and coming writer. It could be really good if it was done well. Katy loved the whole atmosphere of the Theatre; the smell of stage makeup, the perfume that seemed to linger in the passageways, the laughter. There was always a buzz of excitement at the start of a new production that helped generate a free flow of ideas for the characters and the costumes. If only Ray hadn't left life would be perfect. He had held everything together, firm but fair that was his motto and everyone respected him for it.

Since Frank had been with them life had changed, and it wasn't for the better. Even though he wasn't a designer he seemed to think he knew best what materials should be used, which often caused problems. Some of the materials he chose just weren't right for the type of costume, but he wouldn't be told. Katy had already had several disagreements with him. She was not used to people meddling in her department. She didn't mind the brain storming ideas, or people making suggestions, but she was the expert when it came to cloth and design, and he should listen to what she had to say. The trouble was, his obsession with every tiny detail was interfering with the rest of the teams' work.

On top of the work stress, Katy had noticed that Alex, her boyfriend had been acting strangely recently. Unfortunately, she had been so busy trying to get her basic sketches right for Frank that she hadn't had time to wonder about it too much. She knew that Frank had been giving him a hard time too. He worked as a lighting technician and Frank had criticised the lighting in the last performance of a *Midsummer Night's Dream*, telling him that the lights had been too slow following

Oberon on the stage. Alex had had quite a row with Frank outside one of the dressing rooms after the show. Frank was even more difficult now, especially with her. She supposed it was because she was Alex's girlfriend. Katy pushed open the door to the wardrobe department and put her case with the sketches in on the table. The wardrobe department had the biggest room and was where all their meetings were held. Katy used to enjoy the preliminary meeting where they all had a chance to thrash out ideas and begin to work out the list of costumes that would be needed. Frank was already there, making himself a cup of coffee with his back turned to her. He glanced up at her as she entered but didn't bother to offer her a coffee while he was there, not that that surprised her.

"Well what have you got then?" he asked abruptly as he strode over to a chair like a prime peacock, cup in hand and a derisive smile.

It made Katy want to slap his arrogant face. She bit her tongue to stop herself from answering him in the same abrupt tone he had used on her, and opened the case drawing out her sketches.

Frank picked one up, "Who is this one for?"

He was holding up the design she had done for 'Imelda', the Juliette of the show.

"I thought that would be for Imelda's first appearance," she said nervously, hating the way he made her feel so intimidated. She was better than that; she didn't need to take it. Ray had never found fault with her drawings, sometimes he had made suggestions but on the whole he had always been pleased with her work. It annoyed her that Frank made her feel like a naughty child who had been sent to the head for misbehaving, always having to justify what she had done. She was beginning to think the real Katy didn't exist anymore. The feisty fun-loving person that she had once been was gradually being beaten down by the constant criticisms.

"It needs to be longer and I don't like this bit here, change it," he ordered.

"If the dress is any longer she will get the heels of her shoe caught in the material and it will affect her performance," Katy tried to explain without letting him hear the wobble in her voice.

"Who is the director here?" he snapped, then without waiting for her to answer he tossed the sketch carelessly onto the desk. "I want it changed, the rest of the sketches had better be good," he glanced at his watch. "Where the hell is everyone else? They should be here by now."

He paced irritably over to the window and looked out into the dark alley that ran between the theatre and the building next door, a greasy spoon café that had been a meeting place for the staff in happier times. Katy picked her sketch up and studied it, trying to see if she could make part of the dress longer as a compromise to Franks wishes. She wasn't going to let him get to her she told herself, he wasn't worth it. With her face burning with resentment she found a chair and sat down. There was nothing wrong with her design, but even as she thought it she took out a rubber and began erasing the faint lines she had spent hours perfecting.

'Bastard!' she muttered under her breath, determined that he was not going to make her cry. She wished he would go back to where he had come from, but they probably wouldn't take him and were glad to be rid of him. If only Ray hadn't left. The atmosphere in the theatre had changed completely in the time Frank had been there. Where once the design team had felt like a big extended family who were happy to hang out together, now they just did the job and left. The atmosphere backstage wasn't the same anymore, there were arguments all the time where people were stressed and several of the gang had left. If it weren't for Alex, Katy would be tempted to leave too.

Alex had been working as the lighting designer and technician for several years. They had hit it off straight away when she started working at the theatre and before long he had asked her to move in with him. Everything had been going so well, and then Ray had announced that he was leaving. He had been there for donkey's years and was the glue that held them all together. On his last day, the cast and the crew had all gone out to the pub to give him the send-off he deserved. The evening had been a riot, too much drink, loud music, thespians and crew all trying to outdo each other for the most memorable story. Katy had loved everything about it. Sadly, life had changed considerably since then. What with Frank arriving and then Alex's behaviour changing too. She had thought at first it was because Frank was meddling in the lighting arrangements, but now she wasn't so sure.

She had some uncomfortable suspicions that she hadn't looked at too closely. She didn't feel ready to deal with them yet. The week before when Katy had been having a moan about Frank, Alex had actually said, 'he isn't that bad, you need to '*lighten up*', then he had laughed uproariously at his little joke. Of course, he hadn't found it so funny when Frank had complained about his timings for the lights. Oh no, it had been a different story then. Katy sighed, nothing was the same anymore. Sometimes she felt like packing it all in. Stella sounded so much happier now she had moved away and started afresh. The trouble was Alex wouldn't move, she knew that because she had half suggested it the other night. He had been shocked at first, and then outright furious. It wasn't like they owned the flat where they lived, they only rented it. It would be easy enough to find a flat somewhere else, but he wouldn't even consider the idea. He had started going out more on his own too. Katy knew she should check out her suspicions but at the moment she just didn't have the energy, and she couldn't face the fact that there might be something going on that she didn't want to find out. She knew she was burying her head in the sand, and that eventually she would have to face it, but it would have to wait until she was ready.

There was a noise outside the door; Katy glanced up as Martha the wardrobe lady arrived slipping into a chair as unobtrusively as possible. They shared a nervous smile as she sat down. The room soon filled up with the rest of the design team. Tony the musical director arrived at the same time as Alex, and Peter the set designer. They all sat waiting for Frank to start the ball rolling. Kyle the choreographer was late as usual. She watched Frank check his watch again and tut angrily. This was usually where they all put forward their ideas for how they thought their particular department would work for the new play. They had all read the script by now and made notes, or in Katy's case sketches to present to Frank. What had once been a fun, energy filled flow of inspiration had now become a chore to be got through. Katy thought again about her conversation with Stella. She envied the way she had settled into her new life. Maybe not her reasons for feeling that she needed to move on, but the result. It would be nice to visit her when she got the chance.

Katy pulled out the rest of her designs ready to show them at the appropriate time. She couldn't help casting a critical eye over each one of them in turn. Was Frank right? She sighed heavily; she was in serious need of a break as she was losing faith in her ability to get anything right these days. A quick glance at Martha and she knew that she was feeling the same. It was about time someone put Frank in his place and if he kept pushing, that someone would be her. As it was she kept her mouth shut and listened to what the others had to say; she had bills due next week and couldn't afford to let her temper fly. Frank went through the number of characters and the amount of costumes that would be needed, while Katy and Martha each made notes in a book.

Then Frank spoke to Tony about the musical composition. As Frank knew very little about music Tony wasn't questioned as much as everyone else. Frank discussed the moods he wanted to create for each scene and moved on. Poor Kyle suffered the worst. The fact that he had been late didn't help. He rushed in all red in the face and panting, he apologised explaining that the tube had been delayed due to an accident but Frank didn't want to hear any excuses. Once Kyle had at last sat down and explained how he thought the dancer's numbers should go, Frank turned on him. Frank wanted him to change most of the suggestions he had made, making him look incompetent. If Kyle became any more deflated, Katy thought he might cry. When Frank turned his attention to Alex, Katy put her hand on Kyles arm and asked quietly if he was alright. He nodded but she could tell that he was just putting on a brave face. At the end of the meeting they all breathed a sigh of relief. If they thought it was bad before the play began it was nothing to what Frank would be like once the actors were being put through their paces. God help them Katy thought as they all shuffled miserably out of the room.

Chapter Five

Wednesday morning arrived and Stella decided it was time to venture into the town of Winchester. The house was more or less sorted and she wanted to fill her freezer before she started work on Monday. She could also look out for some lamps or a nice picture to hang in her lounge. Jo had told her over the garden fence one afternoon while she was hanging the washing out on the line, that Wednesdays and Saturdays were market days in Winchester. The Market apparently had several specialist stalls that Stella thought would be worth a visit.

After a leisurely breakfast she set off with a list of things to get and a desire to browse. Driving passed the church she couldn't stop herself from having a quick look to see if there was anyone in the churchyard causing a little flutter of anticipation. There wasn't of course and for some strange reason she couldn't help feeling slightly disappointed. The drive into Winchester didn't take long, as she had missed the early morning traffic when there would have been people heading into the town for work. She followed the one-way system round to the main car park and found a parking space on the upper parking level, nearest to the shops. As she rode up to the shops in the glass lift she noticed a display of roman remains that according to the description, had been found during an excavation when the car park was being built. The actual town of Winchester was quite small with a main high street and several smaller streets leading off from it. Stella liked the mix of old Tudor buildings wedged in between the newer more modern structures and decided that on another occasion she would check out the museums, the round table and the old west gate to the city.

The gateway consisted of a stone structure that would have held the old wooden gates and a tower above where the gatekeeper would have lived. The tower was now a small museum. Stella spent the next hour looking in shops, trying on clothes and smelling perfumes. At the bottom of the town in one of the larger shops that sold material, gifts and curtains she found a painting of the seaside and decided to buy it to go on the wall in her lounge. It was now lunchtime so she headed back up the high street and into Starbucks. Having bought herself a tall caramel frappuccino and a panini, she sat down on a big brown squashy sofa in the window and watched the other shoppers passing by.

Once lunch was over it was time to tackle the food shopping. The Sainsbury's supermarket in the town was quite small but there were three large supermarkets on the outskirts of town and as she wanted to fill her freezer, she decided to make a detour on the way home to visit one of them. She spent another hour and a half walking up and down isles picking up items and filling her trolley before at last she was finished and set off back to the village. She was pleased with her day, it had been fun to explore the town and her picture was going to look good hanging over the fireplace. It had made a nice change from organising furniture and crockery, which had been occupying her days lately. She pulled up outside her house and popped the catch on the boot. It was quite warm and Stella was keen to get the shopping put away so she could sit in the garden with a drink and enjoy the peace and quiet. Although Winchester wasn't manic like some towns it was still nice to get back to the sights and sounds of village life that she was already growing to love.

She could hear the gentle distant rumble of a tractor in one of the fields behind her garden. Her garden was actually a good size, not too big and not too small. Eventually she would sort out the vegetable patch, which at the moment was overgrown. She hoped it would produce a few vegetables when she got around to it. The rest of the garden was set out as lawn, a small patio with flower beds to the sides and several bushes and a couple of small trees. At the bottom of the garden was a wooden fence and beyond that were some fields. Two of the fields had wheat growing in them and one had a horse, which always seemed to be leaning over the hedge and looking into the lane. Stella had noticed the previous day while looking over the fence that another tall plant was growing at the side of the field behind her garden and when she had asked Jo about it Jo had told her that it was corn on the cob, although there was no sign of the yellow corn cobs yet as it was too early. The farmer who owned the fields also reared pheasants, and sometimes Stella saw them strutting about from her bedroom window.

As Stella opened the front door and bent to pick up a bag of shopping she had left on the doorstep, she noticed her post sat on the mat. She picked it up and held it in her teeth so she could still pick up her shopping, and stagger down the passage to the kitchen. Dumping the shopping bags on the kitchen floor she put the post on the table to read later. She filled the kettle with water and switched it on to boil while she finished bringing in the rest of the shopping. By the time the kettle had boiled and the tea had brewed, Stella had just finished putting the shopping away; the painting she had left in the passage ready to hang the following morning. She took her tea and her post into the garden and sat on the bench to relax. Setting the tea on the ground beside her she began sorting through the post.

The first two letters were just circulars which would go straight in the recycling bin. The third letter was for the previous owner, which she would have to send on or return, and the fourth was for her. It was written in a handwriting style she recognised only too well, very precise and tidy. With some trepidation to find out what was written, and curious why he felt the need to contact her now she ripped the envelope open straight away. Her hands were shaking slightly and her heart was beating hard in her chest. It hadn't occurred to her that she would hear from Gary. They had barely spoken over the past few months except to sort out legal matters, and as she hadn't given him her new address she couldn't help wondering who had. To suddenly get a letter from him was not only unexpected but unwanted. It felt like an invasion into her new life. She steadied herself and pulled the letter from the envelope. *'Dear Stella'* she read, *'your mother gave me your address I hope you don't mind'*. It's funny she thought, how her mother had omitted to mention that fact when they had spoken on the phone. She hoped her mum wasn't harbouring any thoughts of a reconciliation between her and Gary because there was more chance of hell freezing over than there was of that happening. *'Getting the decree absolute on our divorce a couple of weeks ago hit me quite hard and made me think back over the good times we had together, and they were good, for me anyway.'* A lump formed in Stella's throat. Yes, she conceded, it had become a nightmare from which she was glad to have woken up, but at the start they had had fun. Feeling guilty that it might have been her fault that the marriage hadn't worked, and longing for the happiness that had eluded her in her marriage made Stella feel uncomfortably nostalgic. With a tear forming in her eye she read on. '*Well I thought that I should let you know before someone else tells you, because of what we had before, that I'm getting married again, to Helen. I'm sure you remember her.*'

Stella stopped reading. The joy had gone out of her day. A cloud was passing over the sun, causing her to shiver and casting a shadow over the garden just like Gary's letter had done to her heart. It was as if the weather were reflecting her mood. The letter was causing her to have very mixed emotions. Her relationship with Gary was over, it had been over even before they had finally separated but somehow it still hurt that she had been replaced so quickly; with Helen no less. She had never liked her, and now that she thought about it Helen had always been hanging about Gary. Always ready to help him when Stella had been busy with parent's evenings or school concerts. Stella felt the tears that had filled her eyes earlier threatening to fall. How could he do that to her, stir up happy memories only to douse them by informing her he was in love with someone else. She had been happily getting on with her life and then he had to go and ruin it, she didn't want to sit in her lovely idyllic garden anymore, the moment had been spoilt. She gathered up the letters and her half-drunk mug of tea and went back inside. Putting the post beside the kettle she walked aimlessly into her lounge, moving ornaments a fraction then putting them back as they had been before, her mind elsewhere. Thoughts of

Gary and Helen filled her head as if they were taunting her. She felt claustrophobic all of a sudden, like a caged animal. She stopped her pacing at the window and looked out into the street, she needed to get out for some fresh air, she needed to walk the hurt away. She knew she wouldn't be able to concentrate on anything until she had got the pain of humiliation out of her system.

Her keys were on the kitchen table where she had left them after her shopping trip. A good walk in the fresh air was the answer, away from the post, from the phone and away from any possible visitors. With her mind made up she strode purposefully off to the kitchen, grabbed her keys and set off. She hoped the peace and quiet of the village would help restore her spirits. She hurried down the garden path and through the gate. Now where? She considered her options. She didn't want to bump into people and have to make polite conversation, even if it was only to say hello so she turned away from the path that would lead to the shops and playing fields and headed towards the river. To begin with she walked quickly, the anger that he could brush what they had aside so quickly, and the upset of hearing that he was in a serious relationship with Helen pushing her on. She was completely unaware of the scenery about her as she found herself wondering again if there had been anything going on between the two of them before her marriage had been over.

Had he and Helen been seeing each other behind her back, if so had his friends known about it? She marched on considering the possibility. She didn't think he was the type and surely someone would have told her if he had, wouldn't they? She thought it was more likely that Helen had seen her chance to console him as a way to win his affections. Stella snorted inelegantly at the idea of Helen waiting like a vulture for the right moment to pounce. Gradually her feelings of pent up misery began to subside and so did her pace. After all it was bound to happen at some time, Gary meeting someone else. It just felt a bit soon and a bit like he couldn't wait for her to be out of his life so he could start again, and that hurt. It wasn't because she still wanted him, she didn't. It was just, well it all seemed so final, like the decree absolute had done. When she had received the letter telling her that her marriage was officially declared over it had left her feeling like a failure. Maybe that was the cause of her upset now? She considered the idea carefully as she walked along. She felt confused. She had loved Gary once and she didn't want him to be unhappy. Maybe she was just jealous of him finding someone else.

By now she had reached the church and the storm of emotions that had driven her to set out on the walk had now left her feeling tired and listless. She had never considered herself to be a jealous person before. Spotting the empty bench in the churchyard shaded by the trees she decided to rest for a while before heading back home. The metal gate groaned as she swung it open and then clunked as she shut it behind her. The bench stood sideways on from the gate and against the wall, which meant there was a modicum of privacy from anyone passing by. Not many people walked that way anyway unless they were going to the church or to see the vicar, all the amenities were at the other end of the village. A few dog walkers and the occasional child throwing sticks in the river was about all that was usual, and at this time of day there wasn't even anyone doing that, which suited Stella. She walked slowly across the lush grass to where the wooden bench stood waiting. She read the metal inscription that had been screwed onto the backrest before she sat down. *'In loving memory of Hugh, loving husband, father and grandfather, gone but not forgotten.'* A tear rolled silently down Stella's cheek for the family's loss, and for what she might have had if things had worked out differently with Gary.

She hadn't been sat on the bench long when she heard a twig snap under someone's foot. She looked up in the direction of the sound and found her gaze drawn to the man standing in the shadow of the church. Her heart started pounding hard in her chest from surprise. It was the same man she had seen before. Her heart skipped a beat as she realised he was watching her intently.

"You look upset, are you okay?" he asked. His voice was deep and gentle like rich warm chocolate on a cold day, and made goose bumps appear on her arms. He wore a loose white shirt with the top buttons undone and casual black trousers. Stella found herself thinking that he looked like a pirate stood in the shadows with his dark, slightly long messy hair. A very handsome pirate! She felt her cheeks warming as the thought flittered across her mind.

"I'm okay thank you," was all she managed to say through her now dry throat.

He regarded her for a while leaning against the wall with his hands in his pockets, and then quietly he pushed himself off the wall and moved forward, sitting down casually on the grass in front of the bench. She could almost see the ripple of well-toned muscle beneath the fabric He leaned back against a convenient gravestone with one leg bent and his arm resting absently on his knee. He looked very comfortable in a careless sort of a way, so sure of himself but not arrogant.

"You look sad," he said looking up at her and his eyes seemed to convey sympathy. "You can tell me about it if you want too, I won't tell a soul."

His eyes were a dark blue, like the colour of the deepest sea, and Stella found her own eyes drawn to his as if she was in a trance. It took her a while to process what he had said and then, for some inexplicable reason she found herself telling him what had brought her to be sitting morosely on the bench.

He listened patiently until she had finished and then said. “It’s understandable that you would feel hurt like that, but it will pass. You are not a failure. The marriage was just wrong, it takes two to make a marriage work”. He looked at her thoughtfully his head tilting on one side as he tried to gauge her reaction to what he was saying before adding very softly, “You mustn’t blame yourself for it all. You are moving on and so is he, it’s just his way is different from yours, and I don’t think you are jealous, so stop giving yourself a hard time,” he paused then added, “It’s just come as a shock”.

In that moment, hearing him say what she had so badly needed to hear, she felt a weight lifting off her chest. They continued to talk a while longer. He made her see that Gary finding someone else was not a negative reflection on her, and that her own life was better now. She could move forward without him. There was a pause in the conversation while Stella thought about what he had been telling her, then in his deep resonating voice that almost felt like a whisper across her skin he asked, “What’s your name?”

“Stella,” she replied a little breathlessly, “Stella Martin”.

“Well Stella Martin, I had better go. It was nice to meet you,” he stood up ready to leave, his hands casually tucked back in his pockets.

“Thank-you,” Stella said. “For listening to me and for making me feel better”.

He smiled at her then, it was a smile that lit his whole face, as if he were really pleased that he might have helped and it momentarily took Stella's breath away. He slowly sauntered away with his head bent as he picked his route carefully through the gravestones, Stella came to her senses and called out to him, "What's your name?"

He stopped in his tracks as if surprised by the question, paused a moment and then partially turned to her and answered over his shoulder, "Jack Davenport," then he continued on his way. She watched him strolling towards the back of the churchyard before she checked her watch to see what time it was. Six thirty already, wow! The time had flown past. She glanced back to where she had last seen Jack, but he had gone. Her eyes scanned the churchyard but he was nowhere to be seen. A smile crept across her face. She liked Jack, she hoped she would see him again, but for now she had to get home. She walked back towards the gate happier than she had been when she had come through it earlier, and took one last look behind her for any sign of Jack. The trees moved gently in the breeze, and the late evening sun was shining on the bench where she had been sat, but the churchyard was now completely empty!

On the way back to her house Stella made the decision that she would finish reading her letter from Gary when she got in. She would deal with it today and then put it behind her. It sounded easy in theory with the echoes of Jacks voice ringing in her ears; the reality however was a little harder. She found the letter where she had left it in the kitchen and sat down on a chair to read it. Okay she thought taking a deep breath, so he's going to marry Helen, well good luck to them. She read on a bit further and began to laugh. He wanted her to go to the wedding, really…! Surely there was some mistake. She re-read the last part of the letter but sure enough in black and white he was clearly inviting her to his wedding. What was he thinking, and more to the point did Helen know he was inviting her to their wedding? She mulled the idea over in her head. What would Helen say if she turned up? Would she be surprised, annoyed, afraid that she would make a scene, or quite probably all three? Stella pondered on it for a while, imagining the different scenarios and then stuffed the letter in a drawer and closed it firmly shut. She wouldn't think about it yet, it was all still too new. Maybe in a week or two she would consider what her answer should be and whether she wanted to see her ex-husband getting remarried, even if it was just to see the look on Helen's face. There was plenty of time to decide how best to reply to the letter when she was over the shock.

She found herself walking over to put the kettle on and gazing out the kitchen window at the view. Stella could see Jo in her garden, furiously digging and then wiping her face as if she was crying. The action jolted Stella out of her contrary thoughts of Gary and Helens pending wedding. The idea that her neighbour might be upset surprised her. Jo and Sebastian always seemed so happy. Maybe something had happened to a relative? Stella felt torn between going out to see if she could help and leaving Jo to her solitary digging. She bit her lip as she considered what to do. After all she may not want company and they hadn't known each other long. At that moment the kettle boiled and this seemed to give Stella her answer. Jo had been very good to her since she had moved in. The least she could do would be to offer her tea and sympathy. If Jo didn't want to confide in her she wouldn't push it, but she could at least give her the opportunity. Decision made Stella poured out two cups of tea and carried them into the garden. "I thought you might like a drink, you look like you've been working hard". She offered one of the cups over the fence tentatively and waited for Jo to either take the cup or excuse herself by saying she was too busy. In the end she did neither. She dropped the spade and covered her face with her hands and cried, heart-rending sobs that made Stella wonder if she had done the wrong thing.

Stella felt unsure how to respond standing on her side of the fence with a cup in each hand watching, she hadn't anticipated this reaction. Her instinct was to offer comfort but she wasn't sure how Jo would respond. She hesitated for a while undecided, then instinct won and so putting the cups on the ground beside her, she pulled Jo closer to the fence and gave her a hug.

"What's wrong?" she asked as gently as she could.

Minutes passed before Jo eventually sobbed, "It's not fair!"

"What's not fair?" Stella asked confused. Jo was silent for a moment as she gathered herself to reply.

"We really want a baby and... it's taking so long," She gulped on her words before stuttering on, "Why is it that it seems to be easy for everyone else? They just have to decide they want one and then they find out they're having one. Sometimes they don't even actually want one and they get pregnant and it's not fair because I can't". Jo started crying again.

Stella could understand Jo's pain, even though she and Gary hadn't tried for a baby she had really wanted one and he hadn't. She had had to watch other people getting excited about their babies while she had longed to have one of her own, to be a proper family. Now of course she was glad that they hadn't had one, but she could still sympathise with how Jo felt.

"Why don't you come around and we can talk properly?" Stella suggested.

Jo looked at her hopefully, as if she had all the answers. Stella gulped, she hoped that wasn't what Jo was thinking or she was going to be very disappointed. All she could offer was comfort and to be able to listen, she hoped that would be enough. Instead of going through the house to the front door as Stella expected her to do – neither house had a back gate, Jo went over to her patio while Stella watched her slightly confused. Picking up a white plastic garden chair she carried it over to the fence and put it down. Stella thought she was going to sit on it on her side of the fence and wasn't sure what to say, but then Jo stood on the chair and jumped over into Stella's garden.

Stella picked up the mugs of tea and handed one to Jo. They made themselves comfortable on the bench sipping the tea and then Stella tentatively asked, "How long have you been trying for a baby then?"

Jo wiped her face, smearing dirt from the garden across her cheek. "It seems like forever but actually it's been about a year now. Sebastian says if we give it a bit longer and nothing happens we can go and see the doctor, and I was coping knowing that until today."

"What happened today?" Stella gently coaxed. Jo began to cry quietly remembering what had happened, Stella didn't think she was going to answer, but then she took a deep breath and confided in a tremulous voice. "A lady came into the café with a baby. It could only have been a few days old and she gave her to me to hold her while she used the bathroom. The toilets in the café aren't big enough to take a buggy in," she explained. "So I offered to hold her. I knew it was silly but what else could I do? Well anyway, holding the baby was so lovely but it reminded me, as if I needed reminding that is, what I'm missing and it hurt. Now I can't get the image out of my head and it's making me feel worse than before."

"Oh Jo, I'm not surprised. When one of my colleagues where I used to work brought her baby son in to show him off to everyone, I felt a bit like you do."

When Jo looked at her questioningly Stella added, "Gary didn't want to have children and I'm afraid I did. Now I look back on it I'm glad we didn't have any because it would have been so much more difficult when things didn't work out, but at the time it hurt".

"Maybe it would have worked if you'd had children," Jo suggested, but Stella shook her head. She knew Gary was wrong for her and having his children would have pushed an even bigger wedge between them. She could see that now. Perhaps Helen was right for him after all. She just had to find her Mr right and then everything would be okay. As the thought entered her head the image of Jack Davenport sprang to mind but she quickly pushed it aside. She wasn't ready for a new relationship yet and Jack was basically still a stranger. Realising that Jo was waiting for her to carry on she said, "It would never have worked, we were too different, but I'm sure if you give it a bit longer you and Sebastian will be lucky."

The look Jo gave her said that she was not convinced. Thinking quickly Stella added, "One of the mums at my last school took a while to have her second child but they got there in the end, and at least Sebastian seems very supportive." Jo smiled a watery smile,

"He is, I'm very lucky. I suppose I should be grateful for what I have and I am, really I am." She wanted Stella to know that she knew she was lucky especially after hearing what Stella had said about Gary not even wanting children, she didn't know how she would cope if Sebastian didn't want them. But she couldn't help adding, "A baby would just make it even better, it would be someone else to share our love with".

Stella sympathised, she understood what Jo meant and her heart went out to her. She hoped they would get good news soon.

"You won't tell anyone what I've said will you?" Jo asked hesitantly, "It's just that no-one knows, and it's hard enough to deal with without people keep asking you if there's any news all the time".

"Of course I won't," Stella reassured her while making a mental note not to ask in future if there was any news. Sebastian who had just got in from doing overtime at work chose that moment to stick his head over the fence. "There you are, I wondered where you had gone!" Jo had pulled herself together now. Having shared her misery with someone seemed to have helped her get it out of her system a bit, and knowing Stella understood in a small way was a comfort. She knew she would have someone to talk to about it again if she wanted to. "Oh is that the time already. I'd better start the dinner," turning to Stella she said, "Thank you for the chat and if we can help you with anything let us know".

"Thank you," Stella smiled then watched Sebastian lift Jo back over the fence and the two of them headed off into their house. Their arms around each other's waists.

'That's what I want,' Stella found herself thinking. Not the baby problem obviously, but the type of relationship that Jo and Sebastian had. They were very comfortable with each other and gave each other support. It was obvious how much they loved each other. It had never been like that for her and Gary but it was only now, watching Jo and Sebastian that she realised how empty her life with Gary had been. It had never been a shared journey, it had always been Stella doing things for Gary, cooking, cleaning, ironing his shirts and supporting him in his work. She had spent many an evening encouraging him that his job would get easier when he was feeling less than confident. She had replaced his mother she realised, not become his partner, and now at last she was moving on. Helen was welcome to him. She could do all his washing for him and mother him if that made her happy. Good luck to them. With that she picked up the now empty mugs and carried them back into the house. The idea of Gary marrying Helen didn't seem to matter so much anymore.

Chapter Six

The weekend came and went and before long Monday morning arrived. The alarm clock on Stella's bedside table began a shrill beeping sound. It was like the sound a bus makes when it is warning you that it is reversing. She stirred, groaning as the horrible noise forced her awake and she sleepily switched it off. As reality gradually asserted itself Stella felt her stomach flip nervously, today was her first day in her new job. She threw back the duvet and staggered sleepily off to the bathroom for an invigorating shower before breakfast.

She had managed to achieve a lot in her week off, getting the house organised and registering with a new doctor and dentist. Hopefully she wouldn't need either for a long time, but it was better to have everything in place for when she did need them. The first part of the week she had been so tired in the evenings that she had fallen into bed and gone straight to sleep. A couple of the evenings she had spent chatting to her neighbour Jo which she had enjoyed, but as the weekend had arrived and all her unpacking had been done she had found herself at a bit of a loose end and a bit lonely.

During the day it was alright because she kept herself busy, but once the evening drew in she found even watching television on your own could become lonely. It was the not having anyone to talk to that she was now finding hard. She knew she could ring her mum for a chat or her friends of course but it wasn't quite the same as having someone there with you. Jo had been good and had told her she could pop around to see her if she wanted company but she didn't like to keep intruding, especially as she knew her neighbours were trying for a baby. The last thing they needed was for her to be a fly in the ointment. Occasionally was fine, but she couldn't do it every day.

On Saturday night she had found herself reading a book with the telly on for company and talking to the adverts. When one advert had asked, 'is your boiler old and worn out? Would you like to save money on your heating bills?' She had found herself answering the questions as if they had been asked to her directly, just so she could talk to someone. It would pass eventually she hoped. In time she would get used to the silence and her own company. The trouble was, she was used to having someone around in the evenings and it would take a while to adjust to her new way of life.

She had moved out of home to live in University halls as a student where there was always someone about. From there she had met Gary and they had soon moved in together, getting a flat in a busy part of London until it had all gone wrong. After that she had stayed with her friend Katy and her boyfriend Alex, the two friends had spent the evenings chatting or taking it in turns to each cook the evening meal. When Katy and Alex had gone out for nights on their own they were infrequent and she had always known that they would be coming back. Then she had seen the teaching job on line one evening. She had been drawn to the idea of getting away and starting again somewhere else. The age group she would be teaching was different to what she had taught before and she thought the challenge of trying something new would help her to move on. It had all moved quite quickly once she had applied for the job.

The day she had gone to sign her contract she had spotted the house for sale and gone straight into the estate agents. She had bought her house with some money from an inheritance and the money from her share of the flat she had lived in with Gary. Everything had progressed quickly and smoothly as the previous owners had moved abroad with work, and the house was already empty. Stella liked to think that it was all meant to be, an omen to tell her it was the right thing to do. She wasn't really superstitious, but it had felt right the moment she had stepped over the threshold to view the house. And then miraculously her moving date had turned out to be perfect for starting her job. It had to be fate she had surmised.

After her shower Stella made herself some toast for breakfast and her usual cup of tea. She put the portable television that her mum had given her on in the kitchen to watch the news as she ate her breakfast. It gave her chance to see what was happening in the world and a clock that would let her keep an eye on the time. Her first day at school was to be an inset day, so she was starting a little later than she would normally start. Hopefully it would give her chance to get to know the other members of staff before her first actual day of teaching. The inset day was going to be about children learning English as an additional language, which had been very common in her previous school. She hoped it would give her an advantage and make her first inset day in a new school easier. Once they finished the day's activities she was going to set up the role-play area in her new classroom. The topic for this half of the term was going to be castles. Stella had kept some of the cardboard boxes from her move and painted them to look like castle walls and a drawbridge. She would use the time to create a castle with a moat, which she was making out of a blue sheet.

At half past eight she collected the castle props, a briefcase with a note pad and pens inside it and her handbag and set off for the village school. It didn't take her long to walk to the school, although she had to keep stopping to rearrange her castle walls as they were large and kept slipping. Cursing her decision not to take her car because the distance was so short, she struggled on, gradually becoming more hot and flustered with each step. The school, when she arrived was quiet. A few cars were parked in the car park to the side of the building, which was a mixture of the old original village school and a new modern extension. The old stone building, which had once been the entire school, housed the reception and the staff room and the modern extension contained the classrooms and the assembly hall. Stella stood her cardboard castle walls down beside the door so she could open it, and then wedged it open with her foot so she could pick her props up again. Having managed to get inside this first door she found the inner door was on a security lock and as she didn't yet have the code for it she had to push a button for assistance. Mrs Ashworth the head teacher arrived to answer the door and smiled warmly when she saw that it was Stella.

"Hello dear come on in, we're all gathering in the staffroom for a hot drink before we get started." Mrs Ashworth was a tall lady in her late fifties. She was wearing navy blue smart trousers with a thin pale blue jumper and a multi-coloured blue floaty scarf about her neck. Her once brown hair was mostly grey but framed her face in a soft flattering style. Stella got the impression that although she could be quite firm she was actually very kind and had liked her immediately.

"I've brought some props for my role-play area," Stella explained, indicating the mass of cardboard she had lugged through the door. "I thought I would get it all set up before I go home later."

"Oh jolly good, well I'll see you in a jiffy then if you want to drop them off first," Mrs Ashworth smiled again and then set off for the staff-room leaving Stella to find her way to her classroom. Stella struggled down the corridor into the modern part of the building and pushed open the door to her classroom. She dumped her bag and briefcase just inside the door and carried her cardboard props over to the role-play area. She would sort them out when the inset day was officially over. She glanced around the classroom imagining how it would look once she had prepared it, and then picking up her bags from where she had left them, went in search of the staffroom.

The door had been left open and she could hear the voice of Mrs Ashworth talking to whoever had come to give the talk on 'ELA' (English as an additional language). She was asking the person where they would like to set up the display for the first part of the proceedings. As Stella nervously entered the room they both turned around to see who was coming in before carrying on with their discussion. A blonde-haired man, who was sitting on one of the armchairs in the corner reading the paper also looked up. Putting the paper down on a table beside his chair he got to his feet. Stella remembered him from her visit. He was the only male teacher in the school and taught the year five children.

He held out his hand, "Hello, you must be Mrs Martin, I'm Mr Robertson". He smiled warmly as she shook his hand, "you can call me Scott".

"Hello Scott, nice to meet you. I'm Stella."

"Welcome to Little Welborough Primary School Stella. Can I make you a tea or coffee?"

"A tea would be nice thank you," The tea making facilities were stood on the table near the armchair he had been sat in. She found herself a seat nearby and sat down while he made the tea for her. He was quite tall with broad shoulders. She guessed he was a little bit older than she was herself. He was casually dressed in jeans and a T-shirt that showed off his muscles, he obviously worked out she thought.

"Did you find your classroom again alright?" Mrs Ashworth asked. Having now finished her discussion with the lady presenting the inset day topic she wandered over to join Stella.

"Yes thank you," Stella replied looking up at the headmistress.

The lady who had been talking to Mrs Ashworth plonked herself down heavily in the chair beside Stella. The buttons on her dress strained as she sat forward to put her handbag on the floor.

"Are you new here then?" she asked

"Yes, I've just moved into the village and this is my first day in the school". Scott, who had just given Stella her cup of tea, asked her when she had moved into the village.

"A week ago, I'm just about sorted now so it will be good to get back to work again". At that moment two more members of staff arrived and after greeting Mrs Ashworth and Scott, introduced themselves to Stella and Vanessa Jarvis who was giving the talk. Liberty Freemantle was about thirty-five, plump with shoulder length curly brown hair. She taught the reception children and had a very motherly nature, which Stella thought the younger children would really like.

Janet Symons was the year two teacher and taught the key stage one children like Stella, although her class was obviously older than Stella's year ones. She was forty-two and had two children of her own who were ten and twelve she told Stella. "It's been hectic this morning I need a coffee," she announced after the introductions had been completed. Gradually the last three teachers arrived along with the teaching assistants and sat themselves in armchairs chatting about what they had done during their week off. Although the school only had one class for each year group it was a lot of names to remember in one go, and Stella was glad when Vanessa Jarvis asked them all to wear name badges so she would know who she was talking to. Bryony Hughes took the chair beside Stella that Vanessa had vacated when she had gone to get the name badges for everyone. Bryony was thirty-seven and Stella recognised her as the teaching assistant that would be working in her classroom. Her bleached blonde hair was cut in a modern choppy style and her long fingernails were bright pink. She delved into her oversized bag and produced a packet of biscuits, which she offered to Stella before taking one for herself. "This is my breakfast," she confessed. "I had to drop my husband off at the station this morning before leaving the kids with his mother and I was in a bit of a rush." Bryony accepted the coffee that appeared on a tray and dunked the biscuit into the drink before pushing the whole of the soggy disc into her mouth in one go. "So, how did your move go?" she asked once she had swallowed a gulp of the coffee.

"It went really well actually, I've just about got everything sorted," Stella was touched that Bryony had remembered that she was moving and had asked about it. On the whole the staff all seemed pleasant enough, although from experience Stella realised that there was bound to be one or two that could be difficult. She had liked Bryony when she had visited the school for her interview and they had chatted later in the staff room before she had left. That had been when Stella had told her about the move. Bryony had told her that she lived in a newly built estate about a mile or two outside the village, and usually caught the bus to work.

Stella was beginning to relax listening to all the chatter as they all caught up on each other's news and then Mrs Ashworth quietened everybody down so she could speak. "Well now you have all had a drink let's get started, it's lovely to see you all back and eager to take part in our inset day," she announced. Stella noticed a few people raising their eyebrows at this last remark before Mrs Ashworth continued, "I'd like to introduce Vanessa Jarvis who will be leading today's sessions. Vanessa would you like to begin?"

Vanessa stood up and straightened her black and orange dress as she moved to the side of the room where she could see everybody. She started her talk by explaining how difficult it is for children when English is not their first language to understand what is being said to them, and how it might take them longer to read and understand text. To demonstrate this she gave everybody a sheet of paper with text written in Spanish and asked them to work out what it said. Having let them struggle for a while she then gave them a shorter text with pictures to show how it was easier when there were clues to help them. She talked for about an hour explaining ways of helping children cope with the difficulties they faced and then handed out some bilingual books and resources for them to look through. They chatted amongst themselves about the resources and what they had been told, and then it was time for a coffee break. Scott joined Stella and Bryony who, having stretched their legs had just found themselves a seat to sit and have their drinks. He pulled his chair sideways on so that it was at a better angle to chat comfortably.

"Did you have many children coping with more than one language at your last school?" he asked.

As he spoke a couple of the other members of staff who were still waiting to make their drinks stopped to listen to Stella's reply. Stella had, until that moment stopped feeling nervous about being new, but now having suddenly been thrown into the spotlight she could feel the colour flooding her cheeks.

Just focussing her attention on Scott as he had asked the question she said, "There were quite a lot, although they all coped really well and often they would help each other."

A rather glamorous lady with long black wavy hair joined them, crossing her long legs elegantly in front of her and flicking her hair away from her face with a casual shrug. Stella who couldn't remember the ladies name, gratefully read the name badge while she had the chance. Monique sipped her coffee and then stood it carefully on the table beside her.

"So," she said with the merest hint of a French accent, "What do you think of Little Welborough Primary School? Do you think you are going to like it here?"

"Yes, I'm looking forward to getting started, it will be a nice change from the city."

Stella was enjoying getting to know the people she would be working with. She found out during the coffee break that Monique taught the year six children. Although very glamorous she seemed friendly enough, and it was interesting listening to her talk about the children in her class. Once the coffee break was over they were all asked to split into groups to make a list of the top ten things they would find hard if they were having to learn English as their second language. Stella, Bryony, Scott and Monique ended up in one group as they were already sat together. Monique took out her personalised Parker pen and a stylish flowery notepad nominating herself to be the person who wrote the list of ideas. To start with all the suggestions were sensible, and then Scott started making silly comments, which made the others laugh. Vanessa came over to see what they were finding so funny and checked their list by glancing over Monique's shoulder to see what they had written. "You've started very well but I think you could come up with some more yet," she told them with a frown on her face. She was clearly not impressed with their childlike behaviour. Feeling like chastised school children themselves, they giggled a bit before getting back to the task they had been set. After ten minutes Vanessa gathered them all back together so they could discuss what they had written. Stella listened to what each group had to say, making notes on her own basic supermarket note pad when they mentioned something her group hadn't thought of.

By lunchtime they were all ready for a break again, Mrs Ashworth led them to the dining hall where the catering staff had lunch waiting for them. They had a choice of jacket potatoes with various fillings or pizza. Stella chose a jacket potato with cheese and beans and found a seat near the window. Liberty Freemantle the reception teacher was already sat down with a plate of pizza and salad in front of her.

"That was quite intense, wasn't it?" She said as Stella sat down.

"Just a bit," Stella replied. "Especially when we got told off for messing about."

Liberty laughed. “I bet that was Scott’s fault! I worked in a group with him at the last inset day and the same thing happened to our group then.”

Stella looked over to the lunch queue where Scott was waiting to be served. He was chatting to the lady beside him who Stella thought was called Hannah and who taught the year three children. Hannah was laughing at what Scott had just said.

“He’s a bit of a joker our Scott, you must watch it on April fool’s day because you never know what he’s going to do,” Liberty told her.

Janet Symons joined them at the table with her lunch, along with Tessa, a learning support assistant who worked in Janet’s class. They chatted about school life for a while and then Janet’s phone rang. She wandered outside to answer it and Bryony took her vacated seat at the table. After lunch the afternoon session started with a talk on the statistics that on average ‘ELA’ pupils need an extra three minutes thinking time to process what they are being told as they have to translate the information in their heads as they go. Although the talk was interesting Stella found herself feeling sleepy after lunch, and listening to someone talking was making it hard to stay focussed and to stay awake. An image of her falling asleep and sitting there snoring popped into her head and made her want to giggle.

Trying to distract her thoughts she glanced around the room at the rest of the group. They all looked as if they were feeling the same and Stella thought it would have been better to have had the talk in the morning before they had eaten the lunch. Her mind wandered and she started thinking about the preparations she would be making to the classroom once the inset day was over, and she began to doodle in her notepad. Scott who had sat on her right-hand side started writing something in his notebook which he discretely passed to Stella to read. '*How about a drink later?*' it read.

Stella wrote back, 'maybe, I have to prepare my classroom for tomorrow first,' she checked that no one was watching then carefully passed the note back. He read it quickly then added, '*I'll help if you like,*' at the bottom of the paper. Rather than risk passing another note to her he turned the paper sideways so she could read it from where it rested on his notebook. Having first checked no one was watching Stella read the note and nodded her head in agreement. Vanessa who was still talking saw Stella nod and thought she was agreeing with what she had just said.

"If you have experience of this sort of thing would you like to share it with us Stella?" Vanessa asked.

Stella felt her mouth go dry as she heard her name mentioned. What had Vanessa been talking about? She looked across the room at the white board hoping there might be some clue as to what Vanessa had been discussing, but sadly it was as blank as Stella's mind had suddenly gone. Everyone was waiting for her to speak. She was sure they all knew that she hadn't been paying attention and were secretly enjoying her discomfort. It was adding a bit of interest in what was otherwise a very dull afternoon. Thinking quickly Stella eventually said, "I haven't really got anything new to add I was just agreeing with it all in principal," she could feel her face burning with embarrassment and hoped that what she had said, made some sense. Vanessa seemed happy enough with her answer, smiling brightly at her before she carried on with the thread of her talk.

Stella breathed a sigh of relief and vowed to pay more attention. As she caught Scott's eye she could see him grinning. He knew she had just made up what she had said on the spur of the moment because it was his fault she had not been listening. Sucking in her cheeks to prevent her own grin, she looked pointedly back at Vanessa trying to concentrate on what she was now saying. After five minutes her attention wandered off again and she found herself studying the other members of staff. Now that the momentary excitement of Stella's discomfort had passed they were all looking a bit like they were in a boredom induced trance, with the exception of Mrs Ashworth and a teaching assistant called Pam. Pam had short spikey black hair and large rather wide eyes that made her look permanently surprised. She didn't wear make-up, or at least she wasn't wearing any today and the jeans, checked shirt and boots she wore would have been more suited to a man than a woman. She worked in the year six classroom with Monique and this made the contrast seem even more noticeable as Monique was very definitely a feminine woman. Stella found herself wondering about Pam's life, whether she was single and if not what her partner looked like until she suddenly realised that Pam as if drawn by the force of her thoughts was now watching her. Self-consciously she looked away, her face flushed with embarrassment.

Her eyes wandered over to the clock on the wall, this must be what it's like for the pupils she thought, desperate to get back outside and have some fun. Hannah had slipped one of her shoes off and it was dangling precariously on the end of her toes as she gently jiggled her leg up and down on her crossed knee. Stella found herself watching the movement, waiting and hoping for the shoe to be flung off into the air, as it would add a bit more life into the proceedings. Up and down it went and swinging sideways at the same time. It was a stiletto heeled shoe and Stella wondered, if it shot off her foot whether it would fly like an arrow and impale itself in the wall. This idea made her smile, if it was a comedy film that was definitely what would happen she decided, especially if it was Mr Bean, although Mr Bean probably wouldn't be wearing high heeled shoes. The enforced silence while Vanessa talked was making her want to giggle. She looked at the clock again, trying to regain her wayward thoughts and then noticed that Hannah had just done the same thing. Hannah smiled at Stella and raised her eyebrows as if to say what a drag. Stella smiled back. As far as first days in a new job went, this one had gone quite well so far. At last Mrs Ashworth stood up indicating that Vanessa had finished her talk, and began thanking her for her time and the insights into learning English as an additional language. Everyone started getting up and stretching their limbs as they began to talk to each other again. It was a relief to be able to move about once more.

"You got out of that well," Scott remarked grinning.

"No thanks to you," Stella laughed. "I didn't have a clue what she'd been talking about," she added quietly while checking that she couldn't be overheard. They started to gather up their belongings and made their way out of the staff room. Stella found her way down the gloomy corridor, which seemed even darker now having come from the brightly lit Staffroom, and arrived at her classroom ready to set it up with the props she had brought with her. Scott and Bryony followed slowly behind her chatting about one of the pupils in Scott's class. As they entered the classroom Bryony asked, "So what do you want us to do?" She was stood near Stella's desk with her hands on her hips ready to get stuck in.

“It’s very kind of you but you don’t have to help you know,” Stella replied already dragging out the blue sheet she had stuffed in a bag. “I know you’ve got children to pick up from your mother-in-law”.

“That’s alright it will be quicker with three of us doing it, and besides my mother-in-law loves having the children. She says it keeps her young. I don’t know how that works because I think they age me.” Stella laughed as Bryony had intended and they set about making the role play area look like a castle with a drawbridge and a moat.

Chapter Seven

Stella watched Bryony drive away as she waited for Scott to unlock his blue Vauxhall Astra. She wasn't sure if going for a drink with Scott was a good idea but she didn't want to spend another long evening on her own either. At least Scott seemed quite fun and easy going, it would be good to have a friend like him in the school. Opening the passenger door, she slipped inside and put her bag on the floor at her feet.

"Where do you want to go for this drink?" Scott asked.

"I don't mind I don't really know the area very well so I'll let you decide."

"The King and Crown is not far from here and it's quite pretty sitting by the river. How about if we go there?"

"Ok," Stella agreed.

"It's just far enough away that we are not likely to see any of the parents who have children in the school." He gave her a cheeky grin as he added, "We don't want them gossiping about you before you have even started teaching."

They drove through the countryside to the smaller village of Upton Marsh where the King and Crown pub sat nestled beside a wide, fast-flowing river. Scott parked the car in the car park at the side of the pub and they walked around to the front door. As they stepped inside the dark interior Stella could hear the noise of someone playing on a fruit machine in the corner, the sound of a coin dropping and the electronic jingle then the blip, blip, blip as the lights created a path on the screen. A few people were sat at the bar chatting but otherwise it was very quiet. They both ordered an orange juice, which they took outside so they could sit at a table by the river. A weeping willow had draped itself halfway across the river and from under its branches swam two swans. Scott and Stella chatted companionably about the inset day and then Scott told her about the school fete, which would take place in June.

"Each member of staff is supposed to take part in some way. I'm going to run the hook a duck stall, you can help with that if you like," he offered.

"Thank-you I might take you up on that," Stella replied. There wasn't much time for her to come up with an idea of her own and to arrange what she might need for it, but she was reluctant to say yes just yet. If she spent too much time with him it might give Scott the wrong idea and she didn't want to do that. He seemed very nice but if he was looking for a relationship she wasn't sure that she would be the right person for him. After all she hadn't been divorced long and she was just getting used to being on her own. Not that that had been a problem for Gary she mused, he was already embarking on another marriage.

Perhaps she was reading too much into Scott's offer she thought. He might just be being friendly and offering her some support, and if he was also on his own like her he might only want the company. She decided that it was best to wait and see how things developed rather than worrying about something that might not really be a problem. Sitting in the beer garden where the only sounds she could hear were the birds singing and the babble of water over rocks felt very liberating having spent the day being cooped up listening to someone talking. It really highlighted for her the need for children to spend more time doing activities, rather than listening for long periods of time. It was also very different from the area she had come from where there were rarely moments that were not filled with the noise of traffic or people yelling at each other. Not that where she had come from had been rough particularly, but it was quite built up with lots of people living very close together. When people were crammed together it often caused tensions and arguments she had found. Scott's company was easy going and Stella found herself relaxing as he told her funny stories about some of his teaching experiences.

When he dropped her off outside her house with a wave she realised she had enjoyed the afternoon and although she didn't want any romantic involvement with him, she hoped they would be able to go for a drink together again, as friends. During their conversation, Scott had told her that he had been single now for just over a year. His girlfriend had moved abroad having been promoted. Apparently, it was an opportunity she couldn't afford to miss and so she had gone, leaving Scott to sort out their joint mortgage and to send on her personal belongings when she had found herself an apartment. Stella had found herself wondering if his happy go lucky nature was a cover up for heartache or whether he was just naturally that way. She watched his car as it turned the corner and then walked the short distance down her pathway to her front door. The phone was ringing when she got in and she only just managed to answer it in time before the caller rang off. The caller turned out to be Stella's mum ringing to see how her first day at Little Welborough primary school had gone.

"I still remember your first day at school as a child," her mother reminisced, "You were so sweet with your hair in plaits and your solemn little face". Stella had heard the story many times and zoned out while her mother rambled on. She was mentally going through what she was going to make for dinner when she realised her mother had asked her a question. For the second time that day she was left wondering what she was supposed to say. "Um could you repeat that for me I didn't quite hear what you said?"

"I said darling, that it would be nice for you to invite your long-suffering mother for a visit."

"Oh!" Stella considered her options. She didn't want to upset her mother by refusing, but she did tend to interfere at times. She also remembered how lonely she had felt at the end of the previous week with no one to talk to in the evenings. Perhaps a little company wouldn't be a bad idea, and if her mother decided to rearrange her furniture for her while she was staying she would just have to be firm with her. With a resigned sigh she suggested that her mother come on the Friday and stayed overnight.

"Wonderful darling. I'll look forward to it."

They chatted for a while longer and then her mother rang off. Stella sat for a moment wondering if she had made a mistake inviting her mother to stay overnight, but then felt guilty because she loved her mother dearly. It was just that she was bound to go on about Stella finding someone new or about Gary, and she didn't really feel ready for discussing it all. Still it was done now, and the company She thought would be welcome at the end of her first week. It would be someone to share news with and talk over ideas for her garden. Remembering that the next day would be Tuesday and her first day *actually* teaching in Little Welborough made her suddenly feel nervous, she busied herself making her dinner so that she could relax watching the telly before having an early night. She wanted to wake up feeling refreshed and ready for whatever the day held.

* * * *

The first week passed in a blur. Stella enjoyed the short walk to work each morning, often passing the same faces that were also on their way to work. Some spoke calling out a cheery good morning, while others merely nodded looking harassed and in need of a few extra hours of sleep. Two men who she had seen working in their garden from her bedroom window passed her most mornings, cycling to work on their bikes. They lived three doors down from her and always waved or spoke depending on how far ahead of them she was. She knew they were a couple because Jo had told her about them on her first night in her new house. Their names were Tim and Rory. Tim's family knew that they were a couple and were content that their son was in a relationship that made him happy. Whereas Rory's family thought they were just mates sharing a house to get on the property ladder. Rory's father was in the army and Rory was afraid that his dad would disown him if he knew the truth. On Friday as they cycled passed, with their suit trousers tucked in their socks so they wouldn't get caught in their bikes peddles, they stopped to invite Stella to a party. Handing her a formally written invitation with the time and date on it, Rory told her in his faintly Scottish bur, "You're welcome to bring a friend of course".

“The more the merrier,” Tim added. Stella smiled and thanked them for the invite “Is the party for something special like a birthday?” she asked wondering if she should take a present with her. Tim and Rory looked at each other both grinning mysteriously and told her she would have to wait and see. ‘Obviously not a birthday then,’ she thought as they cycled away, ‘but a celebration perhaps’. She carried on her walk to work pondering what sort of a celebration it might be. She considered the idea of an engagement or maybe a promotion at work. She would take a bottle of something she decided; that should cover whatever type of celebration it was.

She watched as they cycled out of sight and wondered where they worked. Jo hadn’t told her that piece of information. She would ask the next time she saw Jo and find out if she and Sebastian were going to the party. It would be nice to have someone going that she would know. She could take a friend of course but who could she take, Katy perhaps? She could invite her to stay for the weekend and it would give them a chance to catch up properly on their news. If Katy couldn’t make it, dare she ask Scott, or would that give him the wrong idea? She checked the date, it was several weeks away yet, she still had plenty of time to decide. She opened the heavy, metal school gate and swung it noisily shut behind her. Although there was still half an hour before the pupils were due to arrive there were always some that turned up early and were left to amuse themselves, the parents were obviously in a rush to be somewhere else – work most likely.

In the city, the school that she had worked at had had a breakfast club for parents to drop off their children early. It enabled them to get to work on time and the children could have breakfast and play with their peers. Little Welborough's primary school was much smaller and Stella supposed there wasn't the same call for a breakfast club, which meant sadly that the children were left unsupervised. Although it wasn't strictly her responsibility she often found herself keeping an eye on them from her classroom window as she prepared for her day of lessons. One child in particular caught her eye as he was there every morning when she arrived. As he was earlier than the rest of his classmates he sat on his own at a bench, his head resting sadly on his arms. It made her feel sad to see him sat there all alone.

She crossed the playground to where he sat hunched over the bench, "Would you like to come and help me set up my classroom this morning?" She asked. "I could do with an extra pair of hands," she added quickly seeing his frown, she didn't want to make him feel like a charity case. He nodded but remained silent as he swung his little legs over the side of the seat and followed her towards the entrance.

"What's your name?" she asked trying to draw him out of his silence as he shuffled along beside her, his hands stuffed firmly in his pockets and his backpack hanging off his back.

"Henry," he answered quietly. As Stella opened the door and walked in Henry hovered by her desk unsure of what to do, and waiting to be told.

"You can put your bag down by my desk Henry and then you could set out the pencils for me. One pot with each colour in it on all the desks," she explained. Henry completed the task that she had asked of him quietly and efficiently and then, unsure what to do next approached her desk again, his head down and his chin resting solemnly on his chest. "Would you like to sit and look at a library book now until your friends arrive?" she asked.

Henry shrugged his shoulders without speaking. Stella felt so sorry for him, he seemed so lost and she couldn't help but wonder why. She guessed he was in year four from his height and decided she would have a quiet word with his teacher, Nicole Watson, when she saw her in the staff room. For now, as he seemed reluctant to look at a book she suggested that he could play with the modelling clay.

She watched as he carefully pulled some clay from the tub she had offered him and began moulding it into a shape. The tension in his shoulders seemed to relax and he became absorbed by the activity, squeezing and rolling the clay until he had it the way he wanted it. Gradually more teachers arrived and Stella could hear them talking to the classroom assistants as they headed to the staff room to have a quick coffee before they began teaching. When the bell rang to announce that the children should stop play and enter the school, Henry gathered up the clay and put it carefully back in the tub. Handing it back to Stella he quietly asked, "Can I help you again tomorrow?"

Stella smiled kindly, "It's Saturday tomorrow," she reminded him, "But you can help again on Monday if you like, I can always do with a helping hand". Henry smiled tentatively, then swung his backpack up over his shoulder and strolled off to his classroom. The room steadily filled with noise as the children began to arrive talking loudly as they hung their bags on their pegs and found somewhere to sit on the mat. Bryony followed them in carrying a half-drunk coffee in one hand and the register in the other. She handed the register over to Stella before stowing her handbag in the cupboard behind the desk. Stella sat on the teacher's chair in front of the children waiting for them to settle down so she could read out their names and check them off.

Stella was on playground duty at break time. She walked slowly around the perimeter of the grass field where they played in summer when it wasn't wet, and where they played football and rounders'. It was also where the school fete was to be held which reminded Stella that she would have to decide if she was going to help Scott with his hook a duck stall.

Janet Symons, the year two teacher was on duty with her and they both cradled a hot drink in their hands as they walked around watching the children at play. Janet's own children were ten and twelve she told Stella, and her twelve-year-old son was definitely beginning to be a typical teenager, even if he wasn't officially one quite yet. Stella listened as Janet confided in her, stories of door slamming and the difficulty she had getting him off of his mobile phone.

While she listened, Stella kept her eye on Henry. She could see him sat on his own in a corner of the field with a *Star Wars* action figure. A group of boys were playing close by, seemingly unaware of Henry left out on his own. Stella wanted to go over to them and insist that they let him join in with their game but didn't feel it would be the right thing to do. When the boys moved closer to Henry he stood up and walked away, not keen to be part of what they were doing. Stella watched him go with a lump in her throat. 'She really must speak to his teacher at lunch time and find out why he was so quiet' she thought.

* * * *

When Stella entered the staff room at lunchtime she made herself a cup of tea and took it over to where Nicole Watson was sat eating her packed lunch. "Hello, could I have a quick word with you about Henry, I believe he's in your class?" she asked tentatively.

"Of course, what's he done?" Nicole queried frowning.

"Oh nothing, nothing bad anyway," Stella reassured her. "It's just, I'm a little concerned about him, is everything alright at home do you think?"

Nicole sighed, she was aware of how quiet Henry had become lately. She was keeping an eye on him herself and knew that his mum was having to drop him off early for school now that his dad was unable to do it. She explained his situation to Stella. "His mum and dad have just split up and I think he's finding things a little difficult at the moment. The trouble is he seems to be shutting himself off from people and doesn't want to talk about what is happening."

"He came in to help me in my classroom before school this morning and asked if he could do it again next week. Is that okay? I don't want to tread on your toes as he is your pupil. It's just that I seem to get in quite early and I don't like to see him sitting outside all alone," Stella told her.

Nicole smiled, "No that's fine. If he talks to you about anything that's concerning him though will you let me know? All the changes must be upsetting for him".

Stella agreed that she would keep Nicole informed of anything Henry told her and they began to discuss the upcoming fete.

At nearly five o'clock, with all the children gone home for the weekend, Stella was just finishing off some marking before she too packed up to go home. Her mother was arriving at six o'clock and Stella wanted to get in and put the dinner in the oven so she could spend the time talking to her mum and not fussing in the kitchen. She was going to make shepherd's pie because it was nice and easy, and once it was made all she had to do was put it in the oven and forget about it until it was time to eat. Scott caught her just as she was shutting her classroom door. "I'm glad I didn't miss you, I wondered if you wanted to go for a drink tonight to celebrate your first week here?" he asked.

"I'm sorry I can't tonight, my mother is coming to stay for the night, maybe some other time?" she offered glad that she had a genuine excuse. It wasn't that she didn't want to go out for a drink exactly, or that she didn't like his company, it was just that she didn't want it to become a habit or to give him the wrong idea. Scott walked out of the school with her, chatting about his plans for the weekend. He was coaching a football match on the Saturday. "You should come along one weekend, we could do with some supporters."

When they reached his car, he offered to drive Stella home which made her laugh as she lived so close to the school, but having turned him down for the drink Stella didn't feel she could say no again and graciously accepted. In less than five minutes he was pulling up outside her house.

"Thanks for the lift, I'd better get on, I need to make sure everything is ready for when my mum arrives." She gathered her bags together and climbed out onto the path. "I'll see you next week."

They both said goodbye and he drove away leaving Stella feeling guilty for not offering him a coffee. She was beginning to think that he was a bit lonely and didn't want to go back to an empty house. That was something Stella was beginning to understand too, but she didn't want to end up in a relationship just because she felt sorry for him, or because she too was lonely. It would be very easy to slip into a relationship that way. Having a drink after work, sometimes a meal and before you know it they would be a couple. That was how her relationship with Gary had started. They had ended up together when their friends had started seeing each other. They had often gone out as a four and from there they had drifted into the relationship. Admittedly Scott was much more easy going than Gary, and she always enjoyed the time she spent with him but that wasn't enough This time she wanted to be absolutely sure of her feelings before getting involved with someone. She wanted to find somebody that would love her like Sebastian loved Jo, someone she could love equally in return.

Chapter Eight

Stella's mum arrived dead on six o'clock. Stella found herself wondering if her mum had been parked around the corner just so she could arrive at the exact time she had said she would, which bought a smile to her face. The smile was still on her face as she opened the door and welcomed her mum in with a hug.

"Hello darling, how are you?" her mum asked, then without waiting for a reply added, "I've bought you a bottle of wine and a cake your auntie Lucy baked, she said to say hello by the way. So, this is your new house then?"

She followed Stella into the kitchen where Stella put the wine and the cake on the worktop before filling the kettle. "I expect you're ready for a coffee after driving all this way?"

Stella's mum lived in a three-storey terraced town house in Frithville Gardens, Shepherds Bush. It was very different from the village of Little Welborough. Stella's mum agreed that she was definitely in need of a coffee and stood looking out into the garden and at the fields beyond.

"Where are all the shops?" she asked, "I think I only saw one on my way through the village!"

Stella laughed at her mother's question. "It's a village mum, not a town. You don't get lots of shops in a village."

"Oh Stella, your so cut off from everything. What will you do with yourself?" she seemed genuinely worried about the lack of amenities in the area, which had been one of the reasons that Stella had not been in a rush for her mother to visit.

"It's fine. I do my weeks shopping in Winchester, which is lovely by the way, I'll show you tomorrow, and if I run out of anything there is a village shop that is very well stocked as well as being very friendly."

Stella's mum bit her lip only partially mollified. She couldn't imagine not having big stores on your doorstep waiting to sell you anything and everything at all hours of the day.

"I don't know what you're going to do to fill your time here, and how are you ever going to meet someone new stuck in the middle of nowhere like this?"

Stella took a deep breath before answering. She didn't want to have an argument with her mother, Joyce, before they'd even had chance to sit down.

"Firstly, I work every day Monday to Friday, so I'm quite busy during the week, and secondly I'm not looking to meet anyone else at the moment." She put her hand up to stop Joyce from interrupting, "And I am not in the middle of nowhere, you must have noticed that there is a whole village out there with lots of people living in it. I have already been invited out to dinner, for a drink, twice, and to a party in the short time I have been here, so if I was looking for someone there would be plenty of opportunities!"

Joyce's face brightened considerably with this last bit of information. "Oh how exciting, who have you been for a meal and a drink with? Do tell, what's he like?"

Stella sighed with frustration, she hadn't meant to tell her mother anything about Scott because she knew that she wouldn't let it go and would start trying to encourage her into a relationship that she didn't think she was ready for or want. On the other hand, she didn't want her mother to carry on needling her about finding someone new either. Her mother, who was now sat at the kitchen table with her coffee cup in her hand waiting expectantly for news smiled encouragingly.

In that moment Stella decided it might actually stop her mum from interfering if she thought there was something going on with Scott. A small white lie to stop her worrying, and so taking another deep breath, she quickly thought about what she could say that might keep her mum happy, but that wouldn't actually be a complete lie.

"I have been out with someone called Scott Robertson if you must know, he's a teacher at the school where I work. We've been out for a drink and seen each other quite a bit recently." Stella crossed her fingers behind her back at the slight deception and felt her face heat up at what she was implying. They did see each other every day at work so she did see him quite a bit, and therefore it wasn't exactly a lie. "The meal was with my neighbours next door who are really lovely."

Her mother watched her waiting for more than the little bit of information Stella had given her. Stella fidgeted uncomfortably aware of her mothers' persistence for news of a new relationship that didn't really exist. Having tried to ignore the hope in her mother's eyes Stella eventually added, "I would have been seeing Scott again tonight, but I wanted to spend my time with you instead".

It wasn't really a lie because he had invited her out for a drink. The fact that she had had no intention of accepting the offer was irrelevant under the circumstances. Her mother didn't have to know that and besides, if her mother hadn't come she may have accepted his offer, she couldn't be sure that she would have said no.

"Oh darling you shouldn't have turned him down for me." Joyce patted her daughter's hand fondly then her face suddenly lit up as she had an idea. "I know, why don't you ring him, he could have dinner with us and it would give me a chance to meet him?"

Joyce smiled happily at her plan. Stella's heart sank and she nearly choked on her tea. What could she say? She couldn't tell her mum that she didn't have his number or her mum would know that there was nothing in this supposed relationship. "He's made other plans now, I think he is seeing his mother."

"Oh, what a shame! Still if he's seeing his mother that shows what a considerate young man he is."

Stella's smile was strained, hopefully that would be the end of that conversation and her mother wouldn't feel the need to push her into meeting anyone else. Once Joyce had finished drinking her coffee, Stella took her mother upstairs with her overnight bag to the spare bedroom. Stella had spent the last few evenings sorting the room out so that it looked presentable and pass her mother's critical inspection. The last boxes of items Stella had not gotten around to unpacking had been left in there until her mother's visit, but they had had to be opened and cleared to stop the room from looking like a storage space. It was probably a good thing Stella conceded, or she might just have left them unopened for months. It had mostly been mementoes of her late fathers who had died just as she had finished at University. She could still remember the policeman standing at the door as if it were yesterday. She had been at home for the summer before she started her job in the September. When she had answered the door, and saw who was on the doorstep, she had known at once that something awful had happened. Her mother had come up behind her and invited the policeman and woman into the sitting room.

Mother and daughter had sat on the sofa holding hands waiting for the fateful news to be broken. Her father had been in his car on his way home from work when another car had shot out of nowhere and collided with him. He had been killed instantly. It turned out later that the other driver had gotten away with only minor cuts and bruises, being so drunk they had not tried to save themselves. Stella could still remember the sounds of her mother crying herself to sleep at night and had worried about moving out and leaving her to start her job, but her mother was strong and had insisted that she still go. She couldn't help wondering if her mother was lonely still and if that was why she was so interested in what was or wasn't happening in Stella's life.

Going through the boxes had bought back happy memories of the times they had all shared, and pain at the realisation that her father would never see her house. She had left out his paperweight that had sat on his desk for as long as she could remember and a beer mug she had bought him for his fortieth birthday. The room now looked bright and fresh with new lilac and white broidery anglaise bedding on the bed and fresh flowers in the beer mug on the chest of drawers.

The chest of drawers was a remnant from her life with Gary and so had been relegated to the spare room. Stella had bought new for her own use. She was quite pleased with the way the room had turned out, a feminine country cottage look. Just right for the countryside. Joyce stood her bag on the floor by the bed and went to look out the window. "It's very pretty for a holiday, but I would go mad living here all the time. There's nothing to see!"

Stella stood beside her mother at the window enjoying the view of the corn blowing gently in the evening breeze, rabbits were hoping about eating the grass at the edge of the fields and in the distance a man and a woman were walking their dogs. How could her mother say there was nothing to see?

"I'll leave you to unpack while I see to our dinner," was all she said in response. There were some things she would never see eye to eye with her mother on and that was one of them. It wasn't worth trying to make her see it from any other point of view, Stella already knew she would be wasting her breath. She left the room and headed down stairs. She could smell the dinner and knew it was nearly ready to serve.

* * * *

Stella was up early the next morning so she was ready to make breakfast for her mother when she emerged. At the moment though it was peaceful, and she was enjoying her first cup of tea of the day sat outside in the early morning sunshine. She marvelled at the way the scent of the flowers always smelt stronger in the mornings and the evenings, and how serene she felt listening to the birds singing. Perhaps she should get up early at the weekends more often. She thought about it for a while and then decided not. She had to get up early Monday to Friday that was enough. She could enjoy the flowers and the birds then. She could see some early risers already out walking their dogs across the fields and a lady on her horse bobbing up and down as she passed by the hedge. This was a much better start to the day than listening to car horns blasting and the continual drone of traffic.

At that moment Stella heard her mother's footfalls on the stairs. Stella got up off the back-door step where she had been sitting and headed over to the kettle.

"Good morning how did you sleep?" she called over her shoulder as her mother appeared in the kitchen.

"It took me a while to get off actually, it was so quiet, and so dark! Haven't they heard of street lights around here?" Stella smiled, that was one of the things she liked about living here,

"You get used to it," She replied cheerfully, "Coffee?" she asked as her mother sat herself at the kitchen table.

"Definitely I need something to wake me up properly," Joyce yawned. "What's for breakfast?" Usually she had grapefruit and Jordan's cereal but she didn't expect Stella to have that in as she had only invited Joyce to stay earlier in the week, and she didn't believe she could have got her usual cereal at the village store, let alone the grapefruit. She was pleasantly surprised when Stella opened a cupboard and offered her the familiar box, a bowl and a jug of milk. This visit was going better than she had expected. She knew her daughter sometimes found her a little pushy, but what did she expect? She was her *only* daughter and she wanted her to be happy. She knew how lonely it could be on your own and she wanted to see Stella settled with a family of her own.

The other benefit of that would be that she would herself be a grandparent, and then she could have her grandchildren to stay. It was something to look forward to, she hoped it would stop her feeling so alone and make her feel useful again. It had been hard when Stella's dad had died, not financially he had left her quite well off, but emotionally it had been hard. They had been together from the age of seventeen and married young. Together they had got through the many ups and downs of married life, the financial hardships, the loss of a baby, which had left Joyce unable to have any more children and all sorts of other things in between.

The one thing that had kept them both going was their love for each other and that had been cruelly snatched away from her when David had had his accident. Stella was a thoughtful girl and had offered to give up the job she was about to start so she could stay at home to look after her, but Joyce couldn't do that to her daughter. She had a right to live and continue on the path she had chosen. Joyce had been so happy when eventually Stella had married Gary. She had hoped that Stella would find the same happiness in married life that she herself had had, but only two years later it had all ended when they divorced. Joyce had worried that when she arrived here in the village she might have to push Stella into getting back out into the world, to encourage her to find herself a new man, but had been delighted to hear that Stella had actually met someone already. It was funny though, how she hadn't said anything about it over the phone when they had talked Joyce thought, but perhaps she had wanted to wait and tell her in person.

Joyce took a sip of her coffee, life looked like it was picking up again. She had bumped into Stella's friend Katy only a week before, and she had told her when pushed for information, that Stella hadn't been interested in starting any relationships while she had stayed with her. That was one of the reasons that she had wanted to visit Stella, to encourage her to move on. That and the fact that she loved spending time with her daughter of course, even if they didn't agree on everything. When Stella had split up with Gary, Katy had offered her a bed in her flat which she shared with her boyfriend Alex, Stella had accepted it as it was closer to where she worked than Joyce's home, it made practical sense even though Joyce would have liked the chance to mother her daughter for a while. The day before when she had been driving through Little Welborough, she had been afraid that Stella was shutting herself away in a sleepy little village, but now she felt much more reassured. She had gone to bed happily knowing that Stella was now dating someone called Scott.

Chapter Nine

Stella parked her car in the Brooks car park having collected a ticket at the entrance on her way in. Once she was satisfied that she had everything she wanted, keys and her foldaway shopping bag, she led Joyce to the glass lifts where they pressed the button and waited for one of the two lifts to arrive. When one did arrive, they had to wait while a harassed looking lady with a pushchair loaded up with Argos bags and a toddler struggled out. Once inside the lift, it glided smoothly up to next floor where it stopped to let more people in. One of them was an old man wearing a jumper with holes in it. He stood unnecessarily close to Joyce which made Stella giggle, "I think you've pulled mum" she whispered when they were finally back on solid ground and heading towards the exit and the main high street.

Joyce grimaced, "His breath was awful, I don't think he'd cleaned his teeth for weeks. Imagine waking up to that every morning". She shuddered at the very idea making Stella laugh. They passed a pleasurable morning looking around the Cathedral and at the round table, which was hanging on the wall of the Great Hall. It was a medieval hall with a recreated medieval garden outside one of the side doors called Queen Eleanor's Garden. They were both impressed by the size of the round table and as they headed back towards the high street to find somewhere to eat for lunch, wondered if it could really be King Arthur's round table.

They were just passing Boots on their way to Starbucks, where they had decided to have lunch, when a man stepped out of the shop looking at a list he had in his hand causing him to nearly collide with them. Stella's heart nearly stopped from sheer panic as she realised the man was Scott. The last thing she wanted to do was to introduce them having led her mother to believe that they were in a relationship. Scott smiled unaware of the pounding of Stella's heart as she tried to think of a way out of the potentially embarrassing situation she was now faced with.

"Stella! I didn't expect to see you today."

She smiled nervously back, aware of her mother standing expectantly beside her, waiting to be introduced. When no introduction was immediately forthcoming Joyce took matters into her own hands. "You must be Scott how lovely to meet you," Joyce held out her hand, a broad smile on her face. "I've heard so much about you."

Scott took her proffered hand, slightly baffled at how warmly he was being greeted and wondered what Stella had been saying about him. He glanced at Stella who seemed to be very interested in the paving slabs all of a sudden and when she looked up at him, she had gone red.

"This is my Mum, Joyce," she said quickly before her mother could say anything else and drop her in it any further, "Mum this is Scott". To Scott she added, "I've been telling mum about work," hoping this would explain her mother's comments but knowing she would have to come up with something better on Monday morning when she saw him.

"We were just going to have lunch, why don't you join us Scott and it will give me chance to get to know you better?" Joyce offered. Stella suddenly felt faint.

"Well…." Scott began, wondering if perhaps Stella had confessed to liking him and her mother was being indiscreet about it. That would explain her red face.

"I thought you were coaching some would-be footballers today?" Stella hastily grabbed at an excuse for him to leave.

Scott decided to take pity on her. Whatever was going on he didn't want to cause her any further embarrassment. He liked Stella but he didn't want to rush her. He got the feeling if he agreed to have lunch with them she would not be pleased, and if he was to stand any chance with her it was probably best to beat a strategic retreat. Hopefully then she would feel she owed him an explanation over a drink.

"Yes, sadly I'm rather busy this weekend, another time maybe," Stella's smile showed relief. He had definitely done the right thing; wickedly he added, "I'll look forward to talking to you on Monday then Stella".

Her face was a picture. He knew she would spend the rest of the weekend wondering what he would say on Monday. He said goodbye to them both and left with a mischievous smile on his face. Stella was grateful that he had turned down the invitation, but knew he was expecting an explanation for her mother's behaviour on Monday. She was already dreading it. The night before when she had told her mum about Scott it had only been to stop her pestering her to meet someone, she hadn't expected them to actually meet each other. It was meant to be a harmless exaggeration to let her mum think she might be starting a relationship, one that she could back out of at any time. But now it seemed her mum believed it was much more than that and somehow, she needed to backtrack slightly. Not too much or her mum would try and meddle, and she would feel pressured into it anyway.

They pushed the door to Starbucks open and made their way to the counter. Ordering food delayed the moment when her mother would question her further on Scott, which gave her a little time to think. She wasn't sure what else she could say to her about him. They sat at a table in the corner that had two squashy armchairs beside it.

"So that was Scott," said her mother at last. "He seems very nice, it's a shame he's busy this weekend."

Stella took a bite out of her Panini and nodded while she chewed.

"Perhaps next time I visit we could all go out for a meal?"

Stella really didn't want to lie to her mother about her relationship or lack of relationship, so she would have to be careful with what she said. Eventually, when she had swallowed her mouthful she mumbled, "Yes maybe," then quickly changing the subject asked, "So what do you think of Winchester?"

The trouble was she was pretty sure that Scott did want a relationship and she just wasn't sure if that was what she wanted yet. She didn't get the excited feeling in her stomach when it flip flops and your pulse quickens when she was with him. Her mind strayed to the memory of the man in the churchyard, Jack Davenport. He had made her pulse race and her stomach flutter with excitement. She had hoped that she might bump into him again in the village shop or while she was out walking, but she hadn't. Every time she drove passed the churchyard on her way to town she looked to see if he was there, her heart beating madly just in case, but so far, he hadn't been. It made her feel like a teenager with a crush.

Perhaps that was why she didn't feel anything special for Scott, because she was too busy thinking about Jack.

The silly thing was, she reminded herself, she didn't really know anything about Jack except for his name. He hadn't asked her out for a drink, or a meal or even given her his phone number. He had just chatted to her and tried to cheer her up, much like the vicar might have done. Stella froze mid thought, oh my god was he the vicar? That might explain why both times she had seen him he had been in the churchyard. As tomorrow was Sunday perhaps she should go to church and find out, her heart gave a lurch of excitement at the prospect of seeing him again. She wasn't quite sure how she felt about fancying a vicar but it did seem to fit. He had been kind and considerate while she had talked, letting her get all the hurt out of her system without judging her. The more she thought about it the more she thought he must be the vicar, a very sexy vicar at that. She would definitely have to go to church in the morning and find out for sure.

Her mum had by now finished talking and eating, and was looking at her curiously. She must have asked her a question and she had missed it while her mind had been occupied elsewhere. "Um.... Sorry did you ask me something? Only I just remembered something that I have to do and it distracted me."

Her mum smiled happily, assuming that Stella had been thinking about Scott. They finished in Starbucks and spent a couple of hours looking around the shops where Joyce insisted on buying Stella a mirror for her hallway and a new dress for her next date with Scott, which made Stella feel bad about the deception. The dress however was lovely and it was more expensive than she could have justified paying at the moment, what with moving and paying a mortgage on her own, so she accepted it gratefully and ignored her conscience.

On the way back to Stella's house they stopped for tea and cake in Jo's café. Jo was stood behind the counter wearing a rainbow coloured top and a pair of jeans with pink flowers down one leg. Stella introduced her mother to her neighbour and as it wasn't busy, Jo decide to take her break and joined them at their table.

Jo placed the tray with their order of tea and cakes on the table and sat down with a weary sigh. "It's nice to sit down. I've been rushed off my feet this morning. So, what have you both been up to?" she asked.

Joyce wasted no time in telling Jo that she had met Stella's new boyfriend, which caused Stella to fidget uncomfortably, and Jo to raise her eyebrows at Stella in surprise. She had the sense not to say anything that would cause Joyce to doubt that she had met Stella's boyfriend, but the look she gave Stella told her that she was looking forward to hearing about it when Joyce was safely back in Shepherds Bush. Stella fiddled nervously with the little fork she had been given to eat her chocolate cake.

Unable to meet Jo's eye she tried changing the subject. "Have you been invited to Tim and Rory's party?" she asked before she popped a delicious mouthful of cake in her mouth.

"Yes, it should be fun. I wonder what it's for? I know for a fact that it's not for either of their birthdays because Rory's already had his, and Tim's isn't until the end of the year. Are you going?"

She took a sip of her coffee and looked longingly at Stella's cake. She had made the decision to eat healthier in the hope that it would help her to conceive. Anything was worth a try but it wasn't easy when you were surrounded by cakes all day, especially when you had a sweet tooth. She concentrated on what Stella was saying deliberately avoiding looking at the cake or she knew her resolve would weaken.

"Yes I said I would. I was just hoping that you and Sebastian were going so I wouldn't feel like a lemon left on my own."

Joyce had been listening to the conversation as she ate her cream scone. "Perhaps you could take Scott to the party with you? I'm sure they wouldn't mind," she suggested. Stella nearly choked on the piece of cake she had just put in her mouth and began coughing.

Jo patted her back for her, "What a good idea, I'd love to meet him," she told Stella with a smile. Stella frowned back at her through watery eyes causing Jo's smile to broaden, and raising her eyebrows at her as if to say, 'it's your own fault'. Stella was dreading her saying anything else but luckily her mother unwittingly came to her rescue. "This scone is lovely did you make it yourself or do you buy them in?" she asked Jo.

Pleased with the compliment Jo replied, "I made it myself, I make most of the cakes myself actually with another lady called Amy, but she's not in today. I thought I might start doing some birthday cakes too, on an order only basis; what do you think?"

"That sounds like a great idea, I might be able to advertise it in the school newsletter for you," Stella told her, happy that the conversation seemed to have changed direction.

"Perhaps you could make a cake for this party your both going to as a sort of demo, you could take pictures of it to advertise yourself," Joyce suggested after she had wiped the cream from her fingers.

"That's a good idea. I might go and see Tim and Rory and see what they think, I could do it as a present as it will be my promotional cake." Jo was pleased with the idea and having now finished her coffee and her break, she picked up her cup and went back behind the counter to work on a possible design for Tim and Rory's cake.

When Stella and Joyce got back to Stella's house they unloaded their purchases and stood the mirror up against the wall in the hallway. "That will look lovely when it's up," Joyce remarked. "Perhaps Scott could put it up for you, he looked like he could be handy with a power tool, he had very strong looking arms. You'll have to ring him and ask him." Stella could feel her face burning with shame, the more her mum went on about Scott being her boyfriend, the guiltier she felt about letting her believe he was. The trouble was now that her mum believed it and had met him, the harder it was to now tell her the truth. If she did confess that he was just a friend she would be back where she started with her mum trying to play matchmaker with god knows who! And on top of that she felt sure that Scott might want to be more than just friends and she wasn't sure how she felt herself yet. She had stayed with her mum for a weekend a few months earlier and she had taken Stella to various dinner parties with friends who had single sons. It had been very embarrassing and was not something that Stella wanted to happen again. The thought of her mother on the phone every night to tell her of possible candidates was enough to keep her from blurting out the truth. Stella just couldn't face the prospect of fending off her mother's helpful suggestions, so she smiled brightly and found herself saying "I won't disturb him now. I'll ask him later". Then to try and salve her conscience a bit, she added, "We really haven't known each other long so don't go buying a new hat, it may not last".

Hopefully that would stop her mum getting too carried away, and at some point, she could announce that the relationship had just fizzled out if she wanted it to, and that they were just friends. As things were her mum could go back to London happily thinking that Stella was in a relationship, which just left Stella to think of an explanation for Scott. She pondered on the idea of telling him the truth, but as she really hadn't known him long she wasn't sure how he would react. She wanted time to get to know Scott with no pressure or she wouldn't be sure what her true feelings for him were. She wondered if she was put off Scott because he did seem keen on her, and maybe she was scared of getting involved again. Jack Davenport was safe in comparison because he hadn't shown any interest in her except to be kind, and he was elusive which made him interesting.

* * * *

Joyce left Stella's house at five o'clock because she didn't want to drive home in the dark, and she had said it was bound to be busy on a Saturday evening. As Stella waved her goodbye she breathed a sigh of relief, she had enjoyed seeing her mother but she didn't like deceiving her. She knew that she needed to tell her the truth eventually, but for now she would leave things as they were. Her mum was happy believing she wasn't burying herself away in the back of beyond, and it gave Stella breathing space to decide what she wanted.

Chapter Ten

As the alarm clock started beeping to announce that morning had arrived Stella sat bolt upright in bed, her heart pounding with panic. She felt disorientated from being awoken from a deep sleep, and was unsure what day it was. She only knew that if the alarm had gone off she should get up and get dressed. She staggered off to the bathroom to wake herself up with a shower, wondering if she had all her work organised. As the water splashed down on her head she gradually remembered that it was Sunday, and then what her reasons for getting up early were. She was going to church. Her heart did a somersault in her chest, if Jack was the vicar she would soon be seeing him again. The thought of sitting in church watching him give a sermon made her want to laugh nervously. Then she realised that if he was the vicar he might have a wife who would also be in the church and suddenly the idea of going didn't seem like such a good one after all.

Wrapping herself in her big white fluffy bathrobe – a new purchase she was rather pleased with, she headed downstairs for breakfast. Now she was up she might as well still go to church. At least she could find out if her suspicions about him being the vicar were correct. Perhaps it would stop her thinking about him so much if he was no longer a mystery to her. With her mind made up she ate her breakfast and dressed ready for her first visit inside Little Welborough church. She couldn't remember the last time she had been to an actual church service, with the exception of her father's funeral, and her own wedding.

Thinking back, it was probably when she was at school herself as a child. She had been taken to a nativity service by her mother while her father did some last minute Christmas shopping. She remembered feeling cold and sitting huddled up close to her mum on the pew. She had watched a man who was sat a couple of rows in front of her. He had had a big red nose with little tufts of hair hanging out of his nostrils. At the time she had found it fascinating. Each time he took a breath the hairs had danced in the breeze like flags on a windy day. She had tried poking her finger up her own nose to see if she too had hairs that might hang out and her mother had told her off for picking her nose in church. It had made it sound like it was okay to pick your nose, just not in church. So, the next week when little Tommy in her class at school had been caught picking his nose, she couldn't understand why he had been told off too. After all school was not the same as church, which she had been told was Gods house. She could understand God not wanting peoples' bogies in his house but school wasn't anybody's house, it was just school. The memory made her smile.

She grabbed her bag from where she had left it on the kitchen table and set off in the direction of the church. It was only just after nine o'clock and wasn't as warm as it had looked when she had first got up and dressed. She was wearing a pretty summer dress with a thin cardigan, if Jack was the vicar she wanted to look better than she had the last time she had seen him. There was a definite hint of rain in the air and now she felt cold and foolish trotting off to church to see if the vicar was actually Jack. If he was the vicar she wondered why he hadn't just told her that, but then she supposed she had asked him his name not his profession. It was a good job she hadn't told anyone else what she was doing, they would think she had gone mad. She wasn't even quite sure what she expected or wanted to happen if he did turn out to be the vicar, but at least she would then know where he lived and he wouldn't be a mystery. She was walking quite fast due to the chill in the air and the nerves that had settled in her stomach, and before long the church came into view. Her heart did another somersault of excitement at the prospect of seeing him again, but she was also worried that he might turn out to be a married man, and a vicar to boot.

"This is silly," she chided herself. She was a grown woman not an adolescent with a crush; she was just going to church along with a lot of other people. She didn't need to feel nervous, it wasn't as if she was interested in a relationship with him she reminded herself, even if he wasn't married or involved with someone. She was just going because she was curious. The fact that she had found herself thinking about him every day since their meeting was because he had been easy to talk to and he was a mystery to her; that was all she reassured herself.

There were several cars parked outside the churchyard as she arrived, and she could hear the melodic strains of the organ being played as the members of the congregation got ready to go in. A family arrived at the same time as her and she recognised the children from school. The boy, who was the oldest of the children smiled, but his sister hid behind her father's legs. Stella smiled back; she couldn't remember their names. The mum bent down to wipe toothpaste from her son's face and quietly asked him who the lady he had smiled at was. When he told her that Stella was the new teacher in his school his mother seemed to want to get to know her and fell into step beside Stella.

"It's a lovely day, isn't it?" she asked trying to make polite conversation.

"Yes, a bit chilly though, I thought it would be warmer," Stella replied.

"I gather you're the new teacher at Little Welborough, what do you think of it?"

"It's a lovely school, very friendly." By now they had reached the entrance to the church and the churchwarden was stood patiently at the large wooden doors handing out the order of service and the hymnbooks. Stella stood back to let the family enter first so they didn't feel obliged to sit with her. She would then be able to find her own seat tucked out of the way where she would be able to study the vicar in private. There were butterflies dancing in Stella's stomach as she accepted the order of service and a hymn book from the warden, a short elderly man in a light grey suit and with a brown jumper peeping out from his jacket. He smiled kindly but didn't chat, which Stella was grateful for as she passed through the doors.

It was much darker in the church and Stella shivered as the temperature dropped again. The warden had the right idea wearing his jumper under his jacket. He obviously knew what to expect and was well prepared. Stella was just about to sit herself in a pew near the back when a voice called out loudly into the muffled peace and quiet, "Coo-ee, Stella over here there's plenty of room with us!" Stella who had wanted to make an unobtrusive entrance so she could watch the proceedings, and the vicar, from a safe distance now found that the whole congregation had turned around to see who had entered. She could feel her cheeks turning crimson. Her desire to sit at the back unnoticed had been thwarted by Sophie, the daughter of Grace Watkins from the shop.

Unable to decline the offer without appearing rude, Stella made her way to where Sophie and her family were sitting two rows from the front. Stella plastered a smile on her face and joined them. Sophie introduced her husband, a tall thin man who had slightly hunched shoulders; Stella suspected it was from always having to stoop down to listen to people. Either that or he was totally cowed by the domineering Sophie, which was a definite possibility. He shook hands but was otherwise quiet leaving all the talking to his wife, something she was obviously very good at.

When she did eventually pause for breath Stella was able to look over the order of service so she would have some idea what to expect, and to hopefully stall Sophie from making any further conversation. Luckily Sophie had found someone else to pester in the pew behind them while Stella was looking at the order of service, leaving Stella free to look for the vicar. He was stood at the front of the church with his back to Stella. The light from the stained-glass window was streaming through on him making it hard to see if it could be Jack or not. The height looked about right although it was difficult to tell from a distance and with him wearing a vicar's robes. He was talking to a young woman with a baby. Stella wondered if she was planning on getting the baby christened and if that was what they were discussing, or whether it was the vicar's wife and child. She felt a stab of jealousy tighten her chest and looked down at her hands on her lap to gather her thoughts. The vicar finished his conversation and made his way to the pulpit to begin the service. The congregation quietened down and Stella with her heart beating fast in anticipation, glanced up to where the vicar was now stood waiting for quiet so the service could begin.

Stella nearly gasped out loud when she realised that the vicar, heavily clad under the robes, was in fact a rather tall dark-haired woman. The absurdity of the situation and the nerves that she had felt leading up to this point nearly made Stella giggle out loud. To think that she had considered the person with her back to her, to have possibly been Jack now seemed utterly ridiculous.

As the vicar started the service by giving announcements for a coffee morning and an evening prayer group, Stella struggled to keep a bubble of laughter from surfacing. She had geared herself up for the possibility of Jack being the vicar, and that he might have a wife or girlfriend but not that the vicar would be a woman. She had made herself get up early on a Sunday morning for nothing.

The vicar announced the first hymn and everyone stood up with their books open at the right page ready to sing. Stella was still fumbling, searching for her page when everyone else started. She had just found her page when she became aware of Sophie's husbands voice, loudly singing out of tune and slightly ahead of the rest of the congregation. The bubble of laughter that had threatened to come out earlier was now forcing its way into her mouth and as she opened her mouth to sing a snigger of amusement crept out instead. Once the laughter had started Stella found it harder and harder to stop. With tears in her eyes she bit the sides of her cheeks and tried to think of something else. She could feel her insides quivering, waiting for a chance to explode into full blown laughter and had to give in to a little chuckle as the singing reached a crescendo. After the first hymn, the children were gathered together to go to Sunday school while the adults listened to the sermon on being a good neighbour and Good Samaritan.

The sermon lasted about ten minutes and by that time Stella had just about managed to compose herself again. In an attempt to stem the laughter her mind had wandered onto the problem of what she was going to tell Scott on Monday when she saw him. The thought of which had set off a different sort of nerves in her stomach. After the sermon they sang another hymn and then it was time to take Holy Communion. Each pew took it in turns to kneel at the front of the church for the vicar to give them bread and wine, and to bless them. Stella searched each row as they went forward to see if Jack was sitting in one of them, but was disappointed not to see him in any. It seemed odd when both times that she had seen him, he had been at the church. When it was time for Stella's row to proceed to the front, Stella who had never taken part in Holy Communion before had to copy what everybody else did, holding out her hands as the bread was placed into them. When everyone was back sitting in their seats for a final hymn, the collection bag was handed around and the service was over.

The vicar stood at the door while the congregation left thanking them for coming and telling those who didn't know that there were refreshments in the hall behind the vicarage. Sophie was busy talking to someone so Stella took her chance to escape from her, and made her way quickly out of the church. She was still trying to see if Jack had been inside and whether perhaps she had missed him as she reached the door. As she handed back her hymnbook she saw Sophie heading purposefully towards her. Quickly she ducked around the corner and hurried along the side of the church intending to hide behind it until Sophie had gone. She kept close to the wall of the church, her heart now pounding with adrenalin. She wasn't sure how she would explain her actions if she were to get caught scurrying away. As she reached the corner she checked over her shoulder that no one had seen her and slipped behind the church bumping into a tall, warm body leaning against the back wall. Stella nearly screamed with fright, her emotions were all over the place at the moment but she was silenced by a gentle hand covering her mouth.

She looked up to see Jack smiling at her with a finger placed on his lips warning her to be quiet. When she nodded in understanding, he removed his hand and beckoned Stella over to an old doorway that was half covered with bushes. Jack sat on the doorstep and Stella squashed in beside him. Some of the tufts of long grass had already been flattened and Stella suspected that he often sat there.

"Who are you running away from?" he asked quietly but obviously amused.

Sophie breathed a sigh of relief that the whole ordeal was over. It wasn't that she hadn't enjoyed the service because she had, but the desire to laugh each time they had sung a hymn had been almost over whelming. To the point that Stella had thought she was going to choke on it or suddenly burst out laughing loudly at an inappropriate moment. Stella thought back over the whole thing, how she had thought that the vicar might be Jack, to Sophie's husbands appalling singing and suddenly the laughter that she had been holding in burst forth bringing tears to her eyes. She was so absorbed in her laughter that she even forgot that Jack was sitting next to her, waiting for an explanation. She clutched her side that was now aching, and wiped the tears from her face. The laughter died down to a chuckle and she leant her head back against the door.

"So, are you going to tell me what that was all about?" Jack asked in his deep husky voice, making her toes curl in delight. He was smiling at her; her laughter had been infectious and he had found himself laughing along with her even though he didn't know what she was laughing at. Stella now thought about her reasons for going to church, there was no way she could tell him that she had turned up to see if he was the vicar. Instead she told him about Sophie and how badly her husband sang. She told him about how much she had wanted to laugh and that because it would have been completely inappropriate, she had wanted to laugh even more.

"I was actually trying to escape Sophie when I came around the corner. She looked like she was going to invite me to something that I would rather avoid, and she's not easy to say no to."

Jack had laughed at her description of Sophie's husband's voice and seemed sympathetic to her wanting to avoid the pushy Sophie. In a moment of panic Stella suddenly thought, 'what if Jack is related to Sophie', after all she didn't know anything about him.

"Um, you're not related to Sophie, are you? Because if you are, I have just made a total fool of myself?"

Jack laughed again, "No thank goodness. She sounds like a nightmare".

The sun was warm shining on their little hideaway behind the church, and Stella closed her eyes for a moment, listening to the birds singing in the trees. She could no longer hear the voices of the other members of the congregation and guessed that they had made their way to the hall for refreshments. She became aware of the warmth of Jacks body close beside her, and her skin began to prickle as a wave of attraction flooded through her. She opened her eyes and turned to face him. Up close she could see the coloured flecks in his dark blue eyes as they sparkled with amusement. Neither of them spoke as their gazes became locked on each other. Jack reached forward and brushed a strand of her hair away from her face and tucked it behind her ear, sending shivers running down her spine. Her breath caught in her throat, she hoped he couldn't see how desperately she wanted him to kiss her. At that moment a reggae tune started playing in Stella's handbag shattering the seductive atmosphere. It was gradually getting louder the longer it was left unanswered. Stella fumbled with the zip on her bag with shaky fingers silently cursing whoever it was for interrupting, and withdrew her mobile phone.

"Hello!" she answered slightly breathlessly,

"Hello darling, I think I might have left my yellow cardigan at your house when I left, could you check for me?" It was Joyce, Stella's mother. As Stella started to tell her mum that she wasn't at home at the moment and that she would check when she got in, Jack got to his feet, waved and quietly walked away with his hands tucked casually into his pockets. Stella sadly watched him go, distracting her from her conversation. She wanted to call him back and ask him to wait.

"What was that you said dear, you seemed to have gone quiet?" Stella was disappointed that he was leaving and wanted to put the phone down so she could run after him. "Can I call you back mum, I'm a bit busy at the moment?"

By the time Stella had stood up to follow him, Jack had disappeared around the side of the church. If she wasn't quick he would be gone and she would miss her chance to invite him to Tim and Rory's Party. The idea had come to her suddenly as she listened to her mother talking.

"Okay don't be long though because if it's not at your house I will have to have another look for it here. I'm going out later and I had wanted to wear it".

Before her mother could say any more Stella had said "goodbye" and pushed the off button. Later she would have to apologise for being rude but if she didn't hurry he would be gone. Already on her feet she rushed around the corner, but Jack was nowhere to be seen. 'He can't have disappeared that quick!' she thought, trying to shove her phone back in her bag as she hurried towards the front of the church, carefully picking her way between the grave stones. At the gate she looked up and down the road but there was no sign of him. He should have still been in sight. It wasn't as if he had run when he left. He always seemed to walk slowly in a laid back unconcerned fashion, so she should be able to see him, but she couldn't. Puzzled she let out the breath she had been holding.

"Damn!" yet again she had lost him and didn't know how or when she would see him again. There was no point hanging about in the churchyard. She knew he wouldn't come back. With a sigh of frustration, she set off for home, the morning had not gone the way she had wanted at all. There was something about Jack that she felt drawn to. She felt she could talk to him about anything, and then of course there was the fact that he was very attractive. Stella smiled to herself, at least her early morning trip to church hadn't been for nothing. If only her mother hadn't phoned when she had, she might still have been sat with Jack now. She could have invited him to go to the party with her and they could have exchanged phone numbers. As it was she still knew nothing about him, he was a mystery.

Chapter Eleven

Stella went to bed early on Sunday evening, but rather than going straight to sleep she had spent several hours lying staring at the ceiling and thinking about Jack. Whenever she saw him he managed to get away without telling her anything about himself. She couldn't help wondering why she had found him behind the church and not actually inside it at the service, it seemed a strange way to spend a Sunday morning. Although he was a stranger she felt very comfortable in his presence, and as if she could tell him anything. What she didn't understand was how he always managed to disappear so quickly, and why he made her heart flutter when Scott who was clearly interested in some sort of relationship didn't.

Scott was perfectly nice, he seemed kind and he was fun to be with but there wasn't that spark of interest when she was with him that she felt when she was with Jack. She couldn't help wondering if some of the reason was because she knew that Scott was interested in her, and whether maybe she was a little scared of getting involved. Then she remembered the first moment she had seen Jack sitting on the bench in the churchyard, and the way he had made her pulse race. She hadn't even spoken to him then. Her thoughts went around and around and rather than getting an early night, she ended up going to sleep late and having strange dreams.

When Monday morning dawned, rain was pouring down the windows, and tapping repeatedly on the metal barbecue that was stood against the fence in her neighbour's garden. Stella forced herself to eat breakfast even though her stomach was tied up in knots at the prospect of facing Scott. She still wasn't quite sure what she was going to say to him about her mother's reaction to him. Every time she thought about it she felt her face burn with embarrassment. It was still raining when she left the house an hour later to go to work. She saw Tim and Rory cycle passed on their bikes with the hoods of their matching coats pulled up against the downpour. Putting up her umbrella and hitching her bags onto her shoulder she set off, trying to avoid the puddles that had already formed. The damp air was making her feel cold and despite her best efforts, her feet were beginning to feel decidedly wet. Although it was only a short walk she began to wish she had used her car.

'What a great Monday morning this is turning out to be,' she thought, and she hadn't even spoken to Scott yet.

She narrowly avoided being splashed by a car as it went speeding passed through a large puddle. Luckily Stella had moved further away from the kerb as she had just arrived at the school gate. She pushed open the gate that led into the playground and saw a little figure huddled against the wall. Henry was standing under the eaves of the school building, trying to keep dry. Stella's heart went out to him and she completely forgot her own wet feet as she walked towards him.

"Would you like to help me again this morning Henry?" She asked.

At the sound of her voice Henry looked hopefully up at her. Rain dripped off his nose as he nodded eagerly. Anything was better than staying out in the rain and he liked the new teacher, Mrs Martin.

"Come on then," she said briskly and together they walked towards the doors. She shook out her umbrella and left it standing in a bucket in the reception office to drip. "How was your weekend?" she asked once they were heading down the corridor to her classroom.

Henry shrugged, then after a few minutes realised she was expecting him to speak, so reluctantly said, "it was ok". He had spent most of it sitting in his bedroom. His mum and dad had had a big argument on Saturday morning, and he was pretty sure it had been about whose turn it was supposed to be to look after him. He had found his mother later, sitting on the stairs crying. When she had seen him, she had told him that his dad had had to go to work so he wouldn't be able to see him after all. He wasn't sure if his mum was crying because she hadn't wanted him to go with his dad, or whether she was upset that his dad hadn't taken him with him, so that she didn't have to look after him. She had given him a hug but she had seemed distracted. Henry didn't want to remember his weekend it made him feel sad and unwanted. As they entered the classroom Mrs Martin turned on the lights as the rain outside was making it seem dark.

The sudden brightness made him blink. He wiped the rain away from his face with the back of his hand and waited for her to tell him what to do. He watched as she took off her coat and hung it on a hook behind the door.

"Pass me your coat and I will hang it on the back of a chair near the radiator to dry."

Henry took off his coat and handed it over to her. She draped it over a chair and then picked up some books.

"Could you put these books about castles on the display table for me Henry?"

Henry took the books she was holding out to him and carried them over to the display table. He remembered learning about castles when he had been in year one. His life had been happier then, his mum and dad had still been together. They had taken him to look at a castle near the sea one weekend and he had pretended to be a king. He wished he could go back to those days. A tear slipped down his cheek. He felt Mrs Martin's hand on his shoulder and heard her asking him if he was alright, but he couldn't answer her. If he did he knew that he would cry. He swallowed back the lump that was in his throat and nodded his head. There was no point telling her about what was upsetting him, she couldn't change anything. She couldn't make his mum and dad live together again.

He finished setting out the books and found his bag that he had left on the floor by her desk. His gran had popped in to see him on Sunday and she had given him a book and a bag of sweets. He fished in his bag for the book and sat at a chair looking at it. If Mrs Martin thought he was reading it, she might not ask him any more questions. He peeped at her over the top of the book he was reading, she was sat at her desk looking through some work that the children in her class had done the week before. He could see her watching him out the corner of her eye but she didn't say anything, and he began to relax. His book was about *Star Wars*, he knew that his dad had been a fan of *Star Wars* when he was a boy. Maybe the next time he saw him, he would show him the book and they could play a game on his PlayStation together. At that moment Mr Robertson came into the classroom. He looked like he was about to say something to Mrs Martin but when he saw Henry he seemed to change his mind.

"Hello Henry, is that a *Star Wars* book? I used to love *Star Wars,*" he strode over to where Henry was sitting to have a better look. "Who is your favourite character?"

Henry thought about it for a while, then said, "I like the Jedi knights best". He wished he was a Jedi knight, he would use their mind control so he would be able to make his dad come back, and they could all be a happy family again. He didn't want to tell anyone else his reasons for liking the Jedi's though.

Mr Robertson smiled, "They are rather cool, aren't they?" then he turned to Mrs Martin and said, "I'll catch you later" he was smiling, but Henry noticed that Mrs Martins face had turned pink and he wondered why. Adults were strange; the things they did didn't make sense to Henry. Just before the bell went to tell everyone it was time to come in, Mrs Hughes arrived carrying two hot drinks. She gave one to Mrs Martin and then sat on one of the chairs near her desk.

"So, what are we starting with this morning?" She asked. Henry didn't hear the answer as at that moment the bell rang. He gathered up his bag and put his book away, then Mrs Martin Handed him his coat and smiled, "See you tomorrow Henry".

He took his coat from her mumbling a thank you and left for his class, getting swallowed up by the other children swarming the corridor. Stella watched him go and sighed, "I wish he would talk to someone about what's bothering him".

"He will when he's ready, at least he has somewhere to wait until school starts, and he knows he can come to you if he wants to," Bryony replied. Stella knew she was right but she felt so sorry for him, she just wanted to be able to help.

At breaktime Stella found herself on playground duty with Scott. He was watching some of the children playing football at the side of the playground. When the ball landed at his feet he kicked it back to them and walked on. When he saw Stella coming towards him he stopped and waited for her to catch up.

"I'm sorry about my mother on Saturday," she blurted out in a rush. She had been dreading this moment all morning. Taking a deep breath to calm her nerves she added more slowly, "It's just that she was worried I would be lonely and so I told her I had been out for a drink with you. She drew her own conclusions, and I'm afraid I left her thinking that she was right because I didn't want to disappoint her."

Scott wasn't going to let her off the hook that easily, "What conclusions did she draw then?"

He was amused to see Stella blushing and trying to work out what she would say next. Scott laughed, "It's alright I can guess".

Stella breathed a sigh of relief. She was glad to have dealt with it at last, "I'm sorry if she made you feel uncomfortable!"

"That's okay," Scott replied good-naturedly. "You can make it up to me on Friday, by coming for a drink with me."

"Okay." She conceded. "I'll follow you in my car though, it will save you having to drive me back home afterwards." It was a bit like playing a chess match. She may have been manoeuvred into going for a drink, but she had made sure she could leave when she was ready.

"Fair enough," Scott agreed. They walked slowly around the playground keeping an eye on what was going on. A group of girls were arguing over whose turn it was to hold the skipping rope and one of the year

R children had fallen over and cut their knee. They sorted out the argument and sent one of the older children in with the child with the cut knee to see the school nurse.

When they moved on again they found Henry sat at the bench reading his *Star Wars* book on his own. "Don't you want to play with the other boys Henry?" Mr Robertson asked.

Henry shook his head without looking up. He was sad and he didn't feel like playing. He just wanted to be left alone to think. Maybe if he was very good his dad would come back. If he were a real Jedi he would make his dad come back, and his mum would stop crying and be happy again. He turned over the page in his book. Ben Kenobi could make people do what he wanted; he used the force, if only he could use the force.

Scott and Stella watched Henry for a while and then moved on. Scott could see the look of concern on Stella's face. "Don't worry, parents evening is coming up next month, Nicole will get a chance to talk to his mum. He's just a bit quiet while he's coming to terms with his family's situation and in the mean time we can all keep an eye on him."

"I don't like seeing him so alone and sad though, if only he would talk to someone."

"He will when he's ready," Scott told her.

He was the second person to tell her that today. Bryony had told her the same thing when she had arrived that morning. Stella knew that Scott was probably right, and that Henry just needed a bit of time but it made her feel helpless not being able to do anything. Maybe when Henry felt a bit more comfortable with her she would try and coax him to tell her what was wrong. With that thought in mind she changed the subject and asked Scott about his weekend. He told her about the football match he had coached and about meeting up with some of his friends. They had gone out for an Indian meal in a restaurant on the outskirts of town. The bell rang then and it was time to head back inside for lessons to begin again.

At the end of the day Stella was stood in the playground with her class waiting as the parents came one by one to collect their children, she watched Henry leave on his own and wondered if he was going home to someone, or if he was going home to an empty house. As he crossed the road a black car pulled up and Henry got in the passenger's seat. When the car drove off Stella saw that the driver was a woman who looked very much like Henry. At least it seemed like he was going home with his mum she thought.

Chapter Twelve

Jo hurried in from work and put the kettle on. She wasn't sure that she actually wanted a drink, but she needed something to do while she thought about the conversation she had just overheard. One lady had been telling her friend about someone who had been to a reflexologist to help her cope with stress, and having believed she was unable to have children had later found out she was pregnant. Jo didn't believe in coincidence, she had overheard that conversation for a reason. Fate was throwing her a lifeline and she was going to take it. She paced her kitchen, opening cupboards without really looking inside them and then closing them again, her mind was awhirl. The question was what should she do now? She hadn't had the nerve to ask the ladies for the address of the reflexologist. For one thing she hadn't wanted them to know she had heard their conversation, and besides she didn't want anyone else to know that she and Sebastian were trying unsuccessfully for a baby.

She needed to talk it over with someone sensibly. Impatiently she tapped her fingers on the work surface wondering what she should do and looked at the clock, Sebastian was working late today, which would mean waiting another couple of hours. She couldn't wait that long she was so keyed up. She wandered into the lounge and fluffed up the cushions just as Stella appeared heading home from work. Jo rushed to her front door and called out to Stella just as she was opening her gate.

"Do you fancy coming in for a cup of tea? Only I could do with talking to you about something."

Stella shut her gate again and carried on along the path to where Jo was waiting for her. "Is everything alright?" she asked concern showing on her face.

"Come in and I'll tell you."

Stella followed Jo through to the kitchen where Jo set about refilling the kettle and switching it on to boil. Jo's kitchen was as colourful as the rest of the house. The Moroccan style tiles on the wall were in various shades of blue and there was a big yellow teapot and matching plates and cups on display on a dresser along with a vase of cerise pink and orange flowers. The white table and chairs stood in the middle of the room with yellow, green and blue seat cushions and a matching tablecloth. Stella sat on one of the chairs and waited for Jo to tell her what was on her mind. Jo busied herself making the drinks, Tea for Stella and a green tea for herself. She wasn't keen on the flavour but it was supposed to be good for you and she was trying to be more health conscious. Once they were both sat at the table Jo took a deep breath and asked, "What do you know about reflexology?"

"Um...." Stella looked at her curiously. "I know a couple of people who have tried it why?"

"I overheard these two women talking in the café today, about a lady who had been to a reflexologist for stress and then miraculously, having thought she was unable to have children she had found out she was pregnant. I wondered if I should give it a try, what do you think?"

Stella thought about what Jo had just told her, she didn't want to encourage her to spend money on something that may not work. It might give her false hope.

On the other hand, the people she knew who had had reflexology had both said how good it was, and how much it had helped them with other problems. She could see by the look on Jo's face that she really wanted Stella to agree that it was a good idea. It offered her the hope of conceiving that she desperately wanted. She considered carefully what she should say.

"Have you looked it up online to see if there's any evidence of it helping?" she asked trying to be practical.

Jo's face fell, "No, do you think I should?"

"Well I think I would check out what other people say about it before I got my hopes up."

"I suppose so, I was just so excited that I might have found something that could help. We've tried everything else, checking my temperature for when I ovulate and all the other stuff, this just seemed like fate, you know, when I heard them talking about it."

Stella hated seeing the look of excitement fading from Jo's eyes and knowing that it was her that had put the doubt there. "I'll tell you what," she said trying to be a little more positive, "why don't we look it up now. We can see what the reports say and take it from there".

Jo brightened up again and went to get her laptop. Flipping open the top she switched it on and waited impatiently for it to load. Once the home screen appeared Jo tapped in 'Reflexology and Conception', several articles came up so they clicked on one that was a newspaper report posted a week earlier. In it, the report described how reflexology had enabled some women who would otherwise have had to have fertility treatment, to conceive naturally. Stella read the report out loud, "*Practitioners claim that the soles of the feet are like a mini map of the inside of the body and are linked to the systems and organs of the body. This includes the fallopian tubes and the ovaries. Therapists claim that by massaging certain points on the feet they can unblock the energy pathways and allow the body to regain its natural balance, thereby helping some women who would otherwise have had fertility treatment.*"

The report went on to say where the research was being carried out and how successful it had been. Jo suddenly squeezed Stella's hand with excitement, "This is the chance I need I know it is! It was fate those women coming in and me overhearing their conversation. Now I just need to find out where there is a reflexologist I can get to".

Stella had to admit the research did look promising and Jo's enthusiasm was infectious. "Okay let's look up where the nearest reflexologist is," she suggested. They typed in reflexologists in their area and two came up. They made a note of the addresses and the telephone numbers.

"Oh god! What do I do now?" Jo's hands were shaking, the thought that a solution to her problem could be within her grasp made her suddenly feel nervous. What if she tried it and it still didn't work, what if she couldn't get an appointment for months. When she voiced her concerns to Stella, Stella was very practical and told her the only way she would find out would be to ring and ask. They both looked at the addresses again and chose the nearest one to ring. Stella held Jo's hand as she picked up the phone and made the call.

"Hello, I was wondering if you have any appointments available?" Jo asked in a shaky voice. The lady on the other end of the line checked through the practitioner's schedule "Let me see, ah yes she's had a cancellation for this Saturday at eleven o'clock if that's any use to you?"

Jo turned to Stella, "They've got an appointment on Saturday at eleven, what shall I say?"

"Say yes," Stella told her.

"But Sebastian is working, I don't want to go on my own and I won't have the car!"

"Don't worry I can drive you there and wait for you if you like," Stella reassured her.

Jo squeezed her hand again with gratitude. "Are you still there?" She asked the lady waiting at the other end of the phone. When the lady replied that yes, she was still waiting for her answer, Jo said, "I'll take the appointment then, thank you". Then with a little prompting from Stella asked, "How long does the appointment usually last?"

"It can take anything from thirty minutes to an hour," she was told, "and you will be asked a brief history of your health before they begin. If you have any further questions please feel free to ask them when you come, or if you think of anything beforehand just give us a ring," the lady told her in a friendly manner.

When Jo put down the phone she said, "That's it then, I've booked it. It was obviously meant to be".

Stella gave her a hug, "It all looks very promising but don't get your hopes up too high, just try and enjoy the experience and see what happens," She advised Jo.

Jo nodded, "I know but it gives me another chance, I feel like I'm doing something positive at last," she took a sip of her tea. "Yuck, this is cold and it wasn't too great hot. I'll make us another cup,"

She took Stella's half-drunk tea and tipped it away along with her own and made a fresh pot. In the cupboard she found a full cake tin and put some cakes on a plate.

"I know I shouldn't, I'm meant to be eating healthy but this is a celebration," she told Stella as she pulled the cake paper off of a chocolate cup cake.

Stella smiled, "Well I'm very happy to celebrate with you," and she too pulled the cake paper off a chocolate cake and began to eat.

"So, tell me about this boyfriend that your mother met," Jo asked when they had finished eating the cake.

Stella groaned, what with Henry and now Jo's dilemma she had forgotten that she hadn't had a chance to talk to Jo about her weekend yet. "It's silly really," she began to explain, "but when my mother turned up saying that I had cut myself off in this village, and that I would never meet anyone here, I told her that I had been out for a drink with Scott from work. Which is true, and she thought that we were going out and I just kinda... let her carry on believing it".

When Jo raised her eyebrows, Stella added in her defence, "It stopped her nagging me to meet anyone else. I didn't know that we would bump into Scott in town".

Jo laughed, then when she saw the look of anguish on Stella's face she asked, "What happened?"

Just thinking back over the events of that morning made Stella want to squirm. "Well I had to introduce them or it would have been rude. My mother told him she had heard all about him in a way that sounded like I couldn't stop talking about him, and then she asked him to join us for lunch."

Jo gasped at this last bit of news.

"And did he join you for lunch?" Jo wanted to know.

"No, I think he realised that I wasn't keen on that idea and made an excuse. But today I had to face him and try and explain, which wouldn't be quite so bad if I didn't think that he would like the idea of us seeing each other. I don't think I'm interested in him in that way."

"What do you mean you don't think you're interested in him in that way? Either you are or you're not; surely?" Jo looked confused by what Stella had told her. "I knew straight away that Sebastian was the one for me."

She stared dreamily into space for a while as she remembered their first meeting. She had been working in a café in town at the time, having recently finished a course on catering. He had strolled in for his lunch and teased her about the colourful harem pants she was wearing, but she had noticed his T-shirt peeping out from his mechanics overalls, which was equally as colourful as her trousers and had teased him back. Before he left he had asked her out for a drink and they had been together ever since. It had been fate that they had met, just like over hearing the ladies in the café talking about reflexology. As the thought of the appointment that she had made earlier crept back into her mind she felt the excitement build up in her chest, making her want to squeal with delight. By the end of the year she could be pregnant. Fate, that's what it was. She was a great believer in fate, so if Stella wasn't sure about Scott it probably wasn't right. Jo, back in the present concentrated on what Stella was telling her.

"I like Scott, he's a laugh but he doesn't make my heart leap like..." Stella stopped speaking, she had been about to say 'like Jack does', but she felt silly even mentioning Jack as she had only spoken to him twice and knew nothing about him.

Jo had noticed her slip though and wasn't about to let it go, "Like who? Who makes your heart leap? You're not talking about your ex are you?" Stella nearly chocked on her tea with shock,

"No of course not, no! I don't think I ever felt like that about him either, which is why I don't want to drift into a relationship with Scott. The trouble is I'm not sure whether I'm just scared of having a relationship. Maybe that is why I don't feel anything for Scott, because I know he's interested in me and it's putting me off". She paused, she might as well tell Jo everything. Let's face it, Jo had confided in her about the baby situation and she really needed to talk it through with someone. "Oh God this is going to sound silly but I met this man at the church the other week, and as soon as I saw him my heart beat was all over the place. We didn't even speak to each other, and then he sort of disappeared." Seeing the puzzled frown on Jo's face Stella explained, "I only looked the other way for a second and when I turned around again he had gone".

Jo was looking at her intently now, curious to hear the rest of the story, she was sure there was going to be more to it than she had heard so far. Stella continued. "We met again a few days later, it was the day you came over for coffee and told me about your problem; do you remember?"

Jo nodded of course she remembered. It had been good to have someone else to share it all with. It helped, like Stella helping her to phone the reflexologist and offering to take her there and back. Sometimes you needed the support of another woman, a friend. Stella was now carefully folding the cake paper she had discarded earlier absent-mindedly.

"I've spoken to him twice now, the first time was the day you told me about your problem, but I only managed to find out his name. I thought perhaps he might be the vicar because I had only ever met him in the churchyard... so, I went to church on Sunday..."

Stella paused as Jo began to giggle, "The vicar of our church is a woman," she said.

"I know that now!" Stella told Jo about having to sit with Sophie and her husband who couldn't sing in tune if his life depended on it, and how she had managed to escape at the end of the service, "I bumped into the man behind the church which seems odd doesn't it? I mean why didn't he just go to the service like the rest of us?"

By now Jo was laughing hard but managed to say, "Perhaps he's been before and had the pleasure of sitting next to Sophie and her husband, it might have put him off".

Stella and Jo were both laughing now at Jo's suggestion.

"So, what happened then?" She asked when they had finished laughing.

"My phone rang, it was my mother asking me about a cardigan she thought she had left behind, which she hadn't."

It still made Stella cross now when she thought about it. If only her mother hadn't rung when she had. "While I was on the phone he left, by the time I had rung off and gone around the side of the church to try and stop him, he had gone, vanished just like that." Stella snapped her fingers to emphasise the point.

"So, what's his name, this mystery man?" Jo asked enthralled by the story.

"Jack Davenport, do you know him?" Stella suddenly realised that maybe all she had to do to find out more about Jack was to ask. After all Little Welborough was a small village, everybody practically knew everybody. She watched Jo's face for signs of recognition and was disappointed when none was forthcoming.

Jo shook her head, "I've never heard of him are you sure he lives in the village?" Stella shrugged.

"That's the problem I don't know anything except his name, but I can't stop thinking about him, silly, isn't it?" Jo shook her head again making her hair that had been tied up on top of her head for work, come loose and fall about her shoulders in a dark brown cascade.

"Have you tried looking him up in the phone book?" Jo was now on her feet and heading for a shelf that held cookbooks, recipe cuttings from magazines and the telephone directory. She pulled it down off the shelf and put it on the table between them so they could look up the name. On page two hundred and seventy, where the DAV's began they found David's, Davidsons and Davis's but no Davenports.

"He must be ex-directory," Jo said shutting the book and putting it back on the shelf. "What about looking on Facebook?" she asked.

Although Stella wanted to know, a little part of her was scared she would find out he was married. Now she still had her dreams. He could be anything she wanted him to be. "I don't think I want to look just yet, I'll see if I bump into him again and ask him myself."

Jo wasn't willing to let it go yet; Stella obviously liked him but was afraid because of what had happened with Gary. "It would only take a minute to look," She coaxed.

Stella hesitated for a moment then said, "No, I'd rather him tell me himself"

"Okay if you're sure?" Jo checked, but this time Stella assured her that she wanted to leave it to fate, which of course Jo couldn't really argue with as she was a believer in it herself. Still it didn't have to stop her from making some discreet enquiries on Stella's behalf, but she would keep that to herself for now.

* * * *

Jo and Stella had just finished drinking their tea when the door opened and Sebastian came in.

"Hello ladies what are you both up to then?" he asked as he bent to kiss Jo on the lips.

Stella looked tactfully away. Jo turned slightly pink before saying, "Nothing really, just chatting". Then as an afterthought added, "about men mostly," and grinned mischievously.

"I'll leave you to it then while I get washed and changed," he returned her cheerful smile and left the kitchen, whistling merrily as he headed up the stairs for a shower. Although he always wore overalls at work, and cleaned up before he left he could still smell oil and exhaust fumes on his skin and clothes and liked to have a shower when he got in. He was pleased to see that Jo was getting on so well with their new neighbour.

"Are you going to tell him about your appointment? Stella asked when Sebastian was out of earshot.

"I will, but not yet. I want to try it first and see what I think of it and then I will tell him. Imagine his surprise if it works and I get pregnant. We'll keep it to ourselves for the time being."

Stella hoped that Jo wasn't going to get too carried away and that she wouldn't end up depressed if it didn't work. She would feel the guilt of it herself if that happened even though it hadn't been her idea, especially as she had agreed to take her to the appointment. She crossed her fingers under the table. 'Please let this work out for Jo and Sebastian'.

Chapter Thirteen

When Stella eventually arrived home, and opened her front door, a local paper was sitting on the doormat along with her post. She gathered it all up and looked through it briefly as she made her way to the kitchen to make dinner. Dumping her handbag and her bag of books to be marked on a kitchen chair she quickly read the postcard from her Auntie Pat in Canada. She was surprised to see that her usually quiet aunt and her husband had had a helicopter ride over the Rocky Mountains while they had been in Banff. They were now on their way to Jasper, Alberta having stopped en-route to visit a huge glacier. She stuck the postcard on the fridge door with a magnet. Once she had put the rice on to boil and the mince was bubbling away in the sauce she had made – chilli con carne was a quick option on a weekday, she sat down to read the local paper. One page had a list of advertisements, people selling unwanted furniture, toys and a lost and found section. Someone had lost their tabby cat and was desperate to find it, *'lost one tabby cat named Tibbles'* it read. *'Last seen in Woodburr Close on Friday. If found please contact Lee at the newspaper office.*

'If this was a film,' she thought, 'I could put an ad in the paper too, *'desperately seeking Jack, last seen in Little Welborough churchyard'*. Except this wasn't a film and, she reminded herself, she wasn't desperate to find him, just curious. Ha! Who was she kidding, she was more than a little bit curious. She thought back over her conversation with Jo. There was nothing to stop her looking him up on Facebook, after all looking couldn't actually do any harm. If he was married she would find out without anyone knowing she was even looking. People made searches all the time. It might just give her some of the answers that she had so far failed to find out by asking him, or not asking as the case may be. There was no harm in looking. She could just imagine their next meeting otherwise, "Hello Jack are you married, where do you live, have you got any children? She laughed, there was nothing like coming straight to the point to scare someone off. He would think she was desperate for sure then, and he would probably disappear forever after that.

The thing was, she reassured herself, she wasn't desperate, interested, yes, intrigued yes, but not desperate. If he didn't keep disappearing without telling her anything he probably wouldn't occupy her thoughts so often. The answer she decided was to do a little detective work and find some answers. Then she could dispel the air of mystery about him that intrigued her so much. She wasn't sure that it would stop her heart racing when she met him again, but at least she would know something about him, like if he was married or not.

When she had eaten her dinner and washed up she set her laptop up on the kitchen table and googled his name and the area in general. Thirty-five possible candidates popped up as she pushed the search button. She scanned through them all. Some had pictures and she was able to discard them straight away as she could see that they were clearly not her Jack. Two of them turned out to be businesses and on further investigation she was able to rule them out as well. 'Davenports of

Newbury, picture framing' didn't seem likely. She looked anyway just to be sure but the man had red hair so he clearly wasn't the right man. The other business was a computer company, 'Davenports Electronics and Computers'. A picture appeared of a fat bald Jeff Davenport smiling for the camera. She was left with nineteen more possibilities. The first one she clicked on was a man in his sixties, there was no picture but she was pretty sure she could rule him out. The Jack she had met certainly didn't look like he was in his sixties unless he had undergone some serious plastic surgery, and that didn't seem likely. She clicked on another five who all turned out to be living in New Hampshire America, so again she felt quite sure that none of them had hopped over to Little Welborough to sit in the churchyard.

She was now left with thirteen. 'Click', a boy of three who lived ten miles away; that was a no then. 'Click', 'click', 'click', a lady named Jackie, an actor whose surname was Davenport and who had played someone called Jack, someone called Jack who was in the export business, 'Click', 'click', 'click'. She had checked thirty-four of the names and none of them matched up to her Jack, either he wasn't on any social networking sites or she had over looked something. Jack remained a mystery. She had one last name to check. As she read the small piece of writing under the last name, she saw the words '*Little Welborough*' and she could feel the adrenalin suddenly coursing through her body. She clicked on the name and a newspaper article came up.

'It is thought that Jack Davenport of Little Welborough, Hampshire, formerly from Polperro in Cornwall, was one of the smugglers who got away with pearls and other jewellery items that

were being transported on a ship from Guernsey in 1798.'

Stella stopped reading and sat back in her chair. Jack Davenport from Little Welborough was a smuggler from the eighteen hundreds. Obviously, it couldn't be her Jack, but it might just be a relative. It was too much of a coincidence not to be. She read on.

'Most of the smugglers were rounded up by revenue men as they came ashore, but Jack Davenport tried to get away from them and was shot in the shoulder. It was later discovered that he had made his way to Hampshire leaving behind his girlfriend who he had been engaged to. He lived in Hampshire until his death in eighteen hundred and twelve at the age of thirty-four in a village called Little Welborough, a bachelor with no children.

The article finished, there were no pictures to compare the two men but Stella was convinced that they were related. Leaning her elbow on the table she rested her head on the palm of her hand as she considered carefully what she had found out. Interesting though the article was it didn't help her find out if her Jack was married or where he lived, although she was pretty sure now that he must live in the village. Suddenly she felt much brighter, if he lived in the village then it was reasonable to assume that she would bump into him again. When she did, she would have to remember to look and see if he was wearing a wedding ring, it wouldn't be conclusive proof that he wasn't married if he didn't have one – some men didn't, but it would be a start. If he lived in the village and had children the chances were that they would go to the village school too, unless they were too old.

She considered the possibility; he didn't look old enough to have children older than primary school age. She thought back to the way he had looked when she had last seen him. He was probably older than her but not by much, about thirty-five at a guess. If he had children of eleven or more he would have been quite young when they were born, so if he had any children they were more likely to be younger than that. She could check the school registers and see if there were any Davenports in the school. Of course, he might be rich and send his children to private school, in which case she would still be none the wiser. Still, she might as well check out what she could.

Thinking about school reminded her that she had some marking to do. So, with a weary sigh, she shut her laptop and dragged the heavy bag containing the history exercise books over to where she was sat and put them in a pile on the table. There was some interesting hand-writing and spellings to decipher but at least they were all trying hard. Several of the children had written that the castles had Merlins instead of merlons, which made her smile. As far as she knew there was only one Merlin and although he may have lived in a castle he wasn't part of the crenels.

* * * *

Further along the terrace at number five Tim and Rory were busy washing and drying up after their dinner.

"Invite them over this weekend Rory, or next weekend, I don't mind which one, but you are going to have to tell them before we tell everyone else. It's only fair!" Tim was trying to be reasonable and understanding but the time had come. He finished wiping the plate with the tea towel and put it away in the cupboard with all the other plates.

"Rory, I realise that it's hard, but you know I'm right. We've discussed it several times already. How do you think they will feel if they find out after we have told everyone else?"

Rory continued scrubbing the already clean saucepan. Of course, he knew Tim was right, but even the thought of telling his parents about his relationship with Tim was bringing him out in a cold sweat. There was no way his dad would accept them as a couple. The trouble was if they were going to have a civil partnership he would at least have to tell them. He knew that Tim was upset that he hadn't already invited them to stay so they could break the news to them.

"I'll phone them later," he told Tim at last.

Latching on to the small victory Tim picked up the phone and held it out to Rory, "Do it now or you won't do it".

Rory looked at the phone in Tim's hand. It was red to match the décor in their red, white and black sitting room. Now the colour seemed to be an accurate prediction of the colour his dads face would turn when they told him their news. Still putting it off again wouldn't make it any easier. He wiped his still damp hands on his jeans and took the phone. His hand shook as he punched in the numbers and the ring tone began. Tim gave him an encouraging smile and held his other hand for support. As the phone continued to ring Rory let out the breath he had been holding, perhaps he had been spared the ordeal and they were out. He was just going to hang up when he heard his mother say hello. He tensed up again and squeezed Tim's hand tighter.

"Mum it's me Rory," he paused while he listened to her telling him, how lovely it was to hear from him and that they had only been talking about him the other day, "We said we hadn't heard from you in a while and now here you are ringing," she gushed.

When she had finished calling out to his father in delight to tell him who was on the phone Rory continued. "The thing is... well I was wondering if you and Dad wanted to come and stay here for a weekend, maybe next weekend or the weekend after?"

"Oh, that sounds lovely, I don't think we're doing anything I'll have to check my diary. Should we bring our camping mattress as you only have two bedrooms, or will your friend Tim be away and let us use his room?"

Rory took a deep breath, this was his chance to tell them and it would save him having to do it face to face. "Tim will be here but you don't need to bring your camping mattress, you can use our spare room." There was a pause on the other end of the line as his mother took in what he had just told her.

"Have you... had an extension?" she asked puzzled and with an air of caution in her voice. Rory took another deep breath and continued, "No, Tim and I share the same room".

There was silence on the other end of the line, the only noise he could hear was his mother's breathing and the sound of his heart thudding painfully in his chest. Then he heard his father asking what was wrong. He closed his eyes and waited for the explosion. His mother was whispering something to his father, then he heard his father's voice telling his mum that she had misheard.

There was a clatter as the phone changed hands then the dulcet tones of his father's broad Scottish accent came down the line.

"What's this all aboot Rory lad?"

Rory tried to swallow back the lump that was forming in his throat so he could answer but it wasn't working.

"Rory are ya still there?" his dad asked. Seeing how pale Rory had become, Tim took the phone out of his hand and very calmly answered for him. "Rory was asking if you and your wife wanted to come and stay for a weekend?"

"Who's this, is that you Tim, what's happened to Rory?"

"I'm afraid he's not quite feeling up to talking right now, but if you could let us know your answer then we can sort things out. There is something we want to tell you when you do come, but I think your wife might have already guessed part of it".

There was a click as the connection was broken at the other end. Tim put the phone back in its cradle and gave Rory a hug.

"Well at least he didn't shout, that's better than we thought," he consoled Rory.

Rory considered the prospect of not seeing his parents anymore if they chose not to accept his way of life, and the lump in his throat got bigger. Despite their reaction they were still his parents and he loved them. The thought of not seeing them again hurt, the thought that he may have upset them or disappointed them hurt too and he began to cry. He hadn't wanted this moment to come but it had. Tim was his soul mate and he was allowed to be happy. They would have to get used to it. Now it was done hopefully the worst was over and they could get on with their lives without worrying about his parents finding out by accident. Everything was out in the open at last. They had plenty of friends who accepted them. Tim's family accepted them, maybe his parents would come around to the idea eventually. He didn't hold out much hope, but there was no going back now. It was up to his parents now to make the next move.

Chapter Fourteen

Stella arrived at school earlier than usual on Tuesday morning because she wanted to have a look through the registers and didn't want to have to explain what she was looking for. Although there was nothing wrong with looking through the registers, because it was for personal reasons she felt guilty. The receptionist was busy making herself a cup of coffee in the staff room so with adrenalin coursing through her veins she began her search. She started with the reception class and gradually went through each class until she had checked them all. She breathed a sigh of relief; there were no children with the surname Davenport. She had just picked up her own register to take with her to her classroom when the receptionist came back. Yvonne, who also doubled as the school nurse was surprised to see her. "You're keen aren't you, what are you doing here so early?"

"I didn't sleep well last night and woke up early this morning so I thought I would come on in and do some work," Stella told her. It was mostly true. She had slept badly. At one point in the night she had woken from a dream in which she had been searching for Jack but he kept disappearing, and Gary would appear in his place. That had definitely been her definition of a nightmare. The fact that she hadn't told Yvonne that she had planned to get up early and get into school anyway was her own business. She was starting the day knowing that Jack didn't have children in the school, which had put her in a good mood. When she saw Henry arrive in the playground she called out to him and asked if he would like to help her prepare her classroom again. When she saw the smile on his face at her question she felt a little glow of pleasure that she was able to make a difference in his life, even if it was only in a small way.

* * * *

Jo decided to stop off at the village shop on her way to work. What better place to start her investigations than at the hub of village life. Between Grace and Sophie, they seemed to know everything that went on in the village. Well, nearly everything she conceded. So far, she had managed to keep a few secrets from them, and there was probably the odd thing that escaped the duo, but not much. If there were any Davenports living in the village they would surely know. The only problem was going to be how to ask without arousing their suspicions. She picked up the loaf of bread which she had needed and which gave her a reason to be in the shop, and made her way down the aisle to the counter. Grace was stood at the counter in her usual pose of pretending to read one of the newspapers while she kept an eye on whatever was happening inside and outside the shop. She put it aside as Jo approached.

"How are you getting on with your new neighbour?" she asked.

"Stella is very nice thank you. What about you, how's your knee? You were having problems with it the other week as I remember?"

"Oh well, yes it's okay now, I give myself a little break now and then and have a sit down. Just to take the pressure off of it. The doctor thinks I twisted it badly while I was stocking the shelf".

"Oh dear!" Jo sympathised, wanting to keep Grace in the right frame of mind to chat even though she thought that it was more likely that Grace had injured her knee trying to be nosy. She paid for her loaf of bread and decided to start her detective work.

"We had a job application pushed through the door of the café the other day and I'm sure the surname was Davenport but the person didn't leave an address, do you know of any Davenports living nearby who might have left it?"

There was no way Grace would guess her real reason for asking with a question like that, it was perfectly possible. In fact, now she thought about it someone had done something very similar around Christmas time, it had turned out to be a student looking for some extra cash before the festive season began. Grace had her chin in her hand as she tried hard to think who it might have been who had been careless enough to forget their address.

"No, I'm sorry I can't think of anyone, not now. Of course, there used to be a Davenport living in the village years ago, but I'm talking a long time ago so it wouldn't be him".

"Really!" Jo tried hard to conceal her excitement, "Where did he live?" Grace thought about it for a moment and then said, "I think it was Rose Cottage, but it was back in 1800 and something, and he didn't have any children or relatives that I'm aware of. I only know that because Sophie nearly bought that cottage with her husband some years back, and they did a bit of research on its history."

Jo hadn't realised that Grace had meant *that* long ago and was disappointed, but she tried not to show it. "Oh well I'm sure if they really want a job they'll get back in touch," she casually brushed off the enquiry as nothing of importance.

"Do you want me to ask around for you?" Grace asked, always keen to get involved in whatever was happening in the village, but Jo declined the offer. "No, I was only wondering if you knew them, it doesn't matter."

She took the bag Grace handed her with her loaf of bread in it and left. Well that wasn't a very productive start. It was interesting that there had been a Davenport in the village though, even if it had been a long time ago she thought as she carried on through the village to the café. The café was still in darkness as it was her turn to open up and get everything ready. She unlocked the door and pushed it open. She liked this part of the day, the calm before the storm. Not that the café ever got that busy on Tuesday, at least not until just before school finished. Quite a few mums met up at the café before they picked their children up from school. It gave them chance to catch up and have a natter without the children around.

There was a small patch of grass beside the café with a swing on it and the river was at its most shallow there, running along the edge of the grass. Sometimes when the weather was nice, mums would let their children paddle in the water while they chatted with friends over a cup of tea or coffee. The children who were hungry when they came out of school would often come in and buy a cake to eat while they played which kept the hunger at bay until they got home. Jo liked working in the café and being part of what made village life thrive, offering a place for people to meet and have time out from the hustle and bustle of their busy lives. She loved baking and the café gave her chance to do all the baking she wanted without having to eat it all and get fat.

As she put her handbag and her loaf of bread away in the cupboard she gathered all the ingredients she needed to make her first batch of cakes. She washed her hands and donned her apron and wondered if there was any other way of finding out where Jack Davenport lived. It was possible that he didn't live in the village and was a tourist researching old family history or even visiting a friend or relative. The trouble was she couldn't think of any way she could ask Grace about that. The chances were that Grace would know if someone in the village had someone staying with them who might fit the description, but Jo couldn't ask because she was supposed to be being discreet. She had hoped that Grace would have known straight away who she was talking about this morning, and then she could have told Stella what she had found out when she got home. It would have been a nice surprise, assuming he wasn't married of course.

She would have to leave it for now she decided and hope that Stella managed to find out something herself. Even though Stella had said she would leave it in the hands of fate to discover who he was, Jo was sure that the temptation to find out would get the better of her. Jo put the first batch of cakes in the oven and wiped down the worktop ready to make scones. Amy arrived carrying two cake boxes just as Jo was finishing the scones.

"Mornin Jo how's it goin?" she asked as she deposited the cake boxes on another worktop and she too put her bag in the cupboard and tied her apron around her waist.

"Not bad," Jo replied, "I've nearly finished the scones and the vanilla cupcakes will be ready to come out the oven soon."

"I'll put the kettle on then shall I and put these cakes on display?" Amy asked.

Amy was a tall lady in her early forties with short dark hair that was just beginning to go grey. Her children were at college and she enjoyed coming to work, for the company more than for the money. Her husband had a well-paid job in London. Working in the café and helping to bake the cakes was more of a hobby for her than a job. Today she had brought in a chocolate cake and a banana and walnut one. They were both popular choices amongst their customers. Once she had put the kettle on she arranged the cakes in the glass fronted display counter ready to serve. Jo put the scones in the oven and took out the cupcakes. She left them to cool on a wire rack while she took the millionaires shortbread out of the fridge and cut it into thick squares. Her mouth watered, she would love to sink her teeth into one right now with a cup of coffee, but she had to be strong and keep to her healthy eating plan.

She was going to do everything in her power to make sure she was in tip-top condition to have her baby. She was reminded of her plans for the weekend. She hoped what she was doing was going to work. She didn't like the idea of having to go to the doctor and explaining that she couldn't conceive. It was supposed to be the most natural thing in the world, so why did it have to be so difficult for her. Without realising she let out a sigh.

"Penny for them?" Amy asked.

The last thing Jo wanted was to discuss it with Amy who wasn't good at keeping secrets, so she improvised. "I was just thinking about visiting my aunt, I haven't been for a while and I think I probably should go and see her again."

Amy seemed satisfied with Jo's explanation and handed her a cup of coffee. Luckily Jo was scheduled to have Saturday off so she didn't need to find anyone to cover her work for her. The door to the café opened as they were drinking their coffees and the first of the days' customers came in. It was the mums and their babies' brigade. They had dropped their older children off at school and were meeting for a coffee and a chat before they spent their days at the beck and call of their younger pre-school age children. Last week it would have been like salt in Jo's wounds but today with her secret appointment all booked Jo let the feelings of jealousy go. After all it could be her next year, sitting chatting with the mums about her own babies' first smile or the sleepless nights. They would compare methods of getting their babies to eat or sleep and how tired they felt.

Jo stopped herself from getting too carried away. Although she hadn't had the appointment yet she just knew it was going to work. It had to. She was glad Stella was going to go with her, she needed someone to talk to about it, but she wasn't ready to tell Sebastian yet in case he thought she was mad, or just plain desperate and tried to talk her out of going. He had told her to wait for a while longer before they sought any help but surely a reflexologist was different. It was more of a whole-body therapy, and besides she didn't want to get his hopes up as well in case by some horrible twist of fate it didn't work. At least this way it would only be her who felt the sting of disappointment. She took the orders for drinks and scuttled back to the kitchen. She wasn't as completely immune to the feelings of longing as she had at first thought. The sight of a downy haired head and big blue eyes would still bring a tear to her eye if she didn't keep a little bit of a distance.

* * * *

Stella was hanging washing out on her line when Jo got in from work. She could see her from the kitchen window. Jo opened her kitchen door and wandered over to the garden fence. She wouldn't have rushed around to Stella's house to tell her that she had found out that there had been a Davenport who had lived in the village years ago, but as she was in the garden she decided she might as well tell her. When Stella saw her coming she smiled and stopped what she was doing. Joining Jo at the fence she said, "I couldn't help myself, I looked on line last night to see if there were any Davenports in the area"

"And?" Jo asked, she wasn't surprised by Stella's confession.

"No luck I'm afraid, but I did find out that there are no children in the school with that surname, and a Jack Davenport lived in the village until eighteen hundred and twelve."

Jo looked impressed. "I found out about the Jack from the eighteen hundreds too, he used to live in Rose Cottage". Stella considered this extra bit of information Jo had told her.

"He must be a long-lost relative who lives in the area, in which case I'm bound to bump into him again at some point".

Jo nodded in agreement then suddenly had an idea, "I could discreetly ask the postman if he delivers to a Davenport if you like? When he brings in the post for the café I can drop it into the conversation casually. He usually stops for a Latte on a Wednesday morning".

Stella bit her lip, she didn't want anyone to find out that she was interested in Jack in case he turned out to be married. "I don't know, I mean I do want to find out but I'm not sure about you asking the postman. Won't he think it a bit odd?"

"No, I'll make up an excuse for why I'm asking don't worry. I won't let on."

With Stella reassured, Jo went back inside to make dinner so it was ready when Sebastian came home. She would use the same excuse she had used for asking Grace to quiz the postman. At least if the postman let slip to Grace that she had asked it would back up what she had already said, otherwise Grace with her nose for gossip would know something was going on.

Chapter Fifteen

When Stella finished work on Friday she waited in the staff room for Scott to finish marking his pupils work so they could go to the pub for a drink. She was actually quite looking forward to it. There was going to be a pub quiz and Bryony and her husband were going to meet them at the pub later to make up a team. It wasn't something that Stella had ever done before, but she was willing to give it a go. It was better than spending your Friday night on your own, or worse still ironing. She would just have to make it clear to Scott that she was only interested in being friends. Her obsession with Jack had made it obvious to her that there wasn't the spark of chemistry between her and Scott that was needed to form a lasting relationship, and she didn't want to make another mistake just because it was comfortable. Even if it didn't work out with Jack, it would be better for her and Scott not to start something if it wasn't going to go anywhere.

Bryony had already left to pick up her children from their school, she wanted to get them fed and bathed before her mother-in-law arrived to babysit them. While Stella was waiting, Mrs Ashworth came into the staff room to pick up a folder she had left on the side. She was closely followed by Nicole Watson who wanted to pin up a reminder of the stalls at the school fete, and a request for any unwanted books for her stall. Mrs Ashworth read the notice Nicole was pining up.

"Ah jolly good, how is the organising coming along?" She asked Nicole. Stella who had been flicking through the messages on her phone looked up to see what she was talking about and who she was asking.

"Not too bad" Nicole told her. "People are pretty much running the same stalls they ran last year with a couple of exceptions." Stella could feel her face turning red, she still hadn't put her name down for anything. Mrs Ashworth put on the glasses that hung around her neck so she didn't lose them, and began reading the list.

"I see your name isn't down here yet Stella, what are you thinking of doing?" She turned to face Stella, peering at her over the top of her glasses just as Scott came into the room to collect her.

All eyes were now on her and Stella suddenly felt under pressure to come up with something, "Um..." she looked at Scott, perhaps she should take him up on his offer to help on the hook a duck stall. While she hesitated both Nicole and Scott spoke up for her at the same time, "She's helping on my stall," they said in unison then they looked at each other, then at Stella. Stella jumped in quickly to rescue the situation before Mrs Ashworth guessed that she hadn't even thought about it yet.

"I agreed to help them both, to give them a break or an extra pair of hands when it's busy, whichever they need." Mrs Ashworth seemed happy with her answer and hopefully didn't notice that it was a spur of the moment decision.

"Jolly good, I like to see everyone getting involved. I'll leave you all to it then. Have a good weekend."

With that she smiled benignly at them all and left.

"Phew!" Stella sighed, "Thank you, both of you. I hadn't gotten around to thinking of anything yet".

Nicole laughed, "Sorry about that! I could tell from the look on your face you hadn't organised anything and I felt guilty for drawing Mrs Ashworth's attention to it. If I hadn't been putting up the reminder she wouldn't have thought about it to ask you".

"That's ok, I would have had to put my name down for a stall sooner or later, at least now I won't have to run one on my own," Stella reassured Nicole. She put her phone in her handbag and stood up.

"Are you ready to go?" she asked, Scott who was lounging in the doorway with an irrepressible grin on his face.

"Yep, I knew I would get you to help me out with my stall one way or another, and now Nicole has done the hard work for me."

"I'm helping Nicole as well don't forget," she told him, then, "You'll both have to tell me when you want help and what you want me to do".

They all left the staff room together and headed out to their cars. "I'll follow you," Stella told Scott. "I've got a rough idea of where I'm going but I'd rather not get lost. Once I've done the drive I'll be able to remember the way to get back".

By the time they arrived at the pub it was nearly six o'clock and Stella's stomach was in danger of rumbling loudly. Scott found a table in the corner near a fireplace that had a large flower arrangement filling the empty space. In winter it would have a roaring fire in it, but the weather was mild and a fire would have made the pub far too hot. There was a menu on the table and as neither of them had eaten, they decided what they wanted and then Scott ordered the food from the bar along with their drinks. Stella wanted to enjoy the evening, but she also felt uncomfortably aware that she would need to let Scott know gently that they would only ever be friends. It wasn't fair to keep seeing him and raising his hopes. The longer she left it the harder it would be.

She was playing nervously with the stem of a plastic flower, trying to pluck up the courage to say something when Scott returned to their table. There was always the chance that she had misunderstood his intention and then she could be about to make a complete fool of herself. Stella looked up and smiled as he sat down. Now would be a good time to tell him if she was going to, before Bryony and Lee arrived. Taking a deep breath she plunged on before she lost her nerve.

"Scott there's something I've got to tell you before the others arrive."

He took one look at her face and the way she had been fiddling with the flower, and he knew what she was going to say.

"Don't worry I think I know what you are going to say and I want you to know that I agree." Stella looked at him with relief, the surprise showing on her face, "You do?"

"Yes, you're worried you're going to be useless in this quiz, and you want me to know that it's only a bit of fun and it doesn't matter if we lose."

Stella's mouth dropped open, she didn't know what to say now. She hadn't even given any thought to whether she would be any good at the quiz or not. Scott started laughing when he saw her expression.

"It's okay I know that wasn't it really, I'm just teasing you."

He paused to check for her reaction, making sure that that definitely wasn't what she was going to say before he carried on. "You wanted to say that you just want us to be friends, and I agree. We should just be friends. I had hoped that we could be more than that to start with but, during the week I realised that as we work together it's probably better if we don't complicate things."

Stella let go of the breath she had been holding and sank back into her chair. It was like a great weight had been lifted off of her shoulders. "Thank you for being so understanding. I really like you but you're right, I only want to be friends. Now I know you feel the same way, I can relax properly."

At that moment their food arrived, Lasagne and chips for Stella and Chicken curry and rice for Scott. With the uncomfortable conversation out of the way, they chatted amicably while they ate their food. Bryony and Lee arrived half an hour later. Stella saw them enter and make their way to the bar. Bryony was scanning the crowd and the people sat at the tables, trying to spot where they were. Stella waved in her direction and Bryony smiled, told Lee where she was going and joined them at their table.

The pub was beginning to fill up now as people gathered into teams ready for the quiz to begin. Lee arrived with his and Bryony's drinks and Bryony introduced him to Stella. Scott had met him a couple of times before both in the pub with Bryony, and at school events. Lee was about average height with a bald head and a tattoo of a mermaid on his arm. Stella was surprised, from all the things Bryony had told her about him he wasn't what she had expected at all. The pub quiz turned out to be fun. Each team was handed a piece of paper and a pen and the pub quietened down as the questions were read out. Lee and Scott were like a double act calling out comments and exchanging friendly banter with the other tables. Stella couldn't remember the last time she had laughed as much.

At the end of the evening when the totals were added up, Stella's team had come third. It didn't matter that they hadn't won because they had all enjoyed themselves. While Stella was driving herself home, she found herself wishing that she did feel romantically inclined towards Scott because it would make everything so much easier. But it was no good; you just couldn't control your heart. She didn't get that thrill of excitement when she saw him or heard his voice that she got when she was with Jack. Before she went to bed Stella set her alarm for nine o'clock. She probably wouldn't sleep in that late, but she wanted to make sure she was up in time to get ready to take Jo to her first reflexology appointment.

* * * *

Jo was like a child before Christmas when Stella arrived at her doorstep on Saturday morning; all nervous excitement and a bit hyperactive. After Sebastian had gone to work, Jo had cleaned the house from top to bottom to take her mind off what she was hoping would eventually change their lives for the better. All the washing was washed and out on the line and she had picked the first batch of early strawberries from the strawberry patch. They were now sitting in a bowl in the kitchen waiting to be eaten.

"Are you ready to go then?" Stella asked as she watched Jo rush around gathering things to fill her handbag, her keys, a shopping list and a piece of paper with the directions of how to get to where she was having her reflexology treatment.

"Yes ready." She paused, "actually I think I need to use the loo again, I won't be long". Jo handed Stella her bag and rushed upstairs to the bathroom. She was so nervous, what if this didn't work?

Langley Manor turned out to be in a big old Victorian house on the outskirts of a village called Kingsclere. They had twice driven up a farmer's track, thinking that they had found the driveway to the centre, and had had to reverse back down the lane. The lane was full of potholes that they bumped through slowly and passed a bored horse that watched with interest, as they had to manoeuvre around an on-coming tractor. When at last they drove up the gravel driveway to Langley Manor they saw a big welcome board that advertised meditation sessions, a spa centre and cranial osteopathy as well as reflexology.

"We're definitely in the right place this time," Stella said as they took in the view of a group of people doing Tai chi or some other form of martial art on a partially hidden, well-kept lawn.

A large conservatory had been added onto the side of the building. In it they could see the shimmer of water in a pool through the shrubbery, which had obviously been planted to offer the guests privacy from any new visitors arriving.

"Wow I wasn't expecting this," Jo exclaimed, peering up at the imposing building. She could feel the nerves making themselves known again in her stomach, and a sudden desire to use the bathroom.

"Are you okay?" Stella asked seeing Jo's knuckles turn white as she gripped her handbag.

"What if this doesn't work Stella, what will I do then?"

"If it doesn't work... well you won't have lost anything will you? You will have just had a nice relaxing foot massage and you can go back to your original plan, to see what happens in the next few months and then talk to the Doctor if nothing has happened."

Jo relaxed her grip on her handbag and took a deep breath. "You're right, okay I'm ready to go in now." They climbed out the car and crunched across the gravel drive to the front door.

"Do we have to ring the doorbell or just go in do you think?" Jo asked as they stood in front of the duck egg blue panelled door.

Stella glanced around to see if there were any notices with instructions on, like 'please ring for assistance', or 'please enter'. She couldn't see anything so she tried the handle and the door opened. Inside was a large marble entrance hall with a grand staircase. To the side of the staircase sat a lady at a modern white reception desk. She smiled as they entered and said, "good-morning".

As Jo seemed to have lost the power of speech it was left to Stella to explain why they were there. "My friend has an appointment with the reflexologist."

"Okay, what's her name please?"

"Jo Loxley."

"Ah yes if you'd like to take a seat in the waiting room I'll let Mrs Clarke know you're here." The receptionist indicated some chairs in a room on her right and as they went to sit down they heard her phone through to the reflexologist. "Hello Gabriella, your next client has just arrived."

It was like waiting in a dentist's waiting room. The walls were a pale yellow with old comfy chairs set around the edge. There were low tables with old magazines for visitors to read while they waited, and it was reverently silent. Some might say that it was calm and peaceful, but when you were waiting for the first time and didn't know what to expect the silence was intimidating. Jo was busy studying the pictures on the walls when a lady came in wearing what looked like a royal blue dental tunic. If Jo hadn't seen the welcome board out the front, she would have thought she was in the wrong place. The lady introduced herself.

"Hello, I'm Gabriella Clarke the reflexologist, if you'd like to follow me we can get started".

Stella gave Jo's hand a squeeze for reassurance as she stood up to follow Mrs Clarke out of the room.

"Are you nervous about this?" Stella heard the reflexologist asking Jo.

"Yes, a bit" Jo replied.

That was the understatement of the year Stella thought to herself as she picked up a magazine and began to flick through the pages. She just hoped this was going to work. Jo would be so upset if it didn't. Gabriella Clarke took Jo up the stairs to a light airy room on the first floor. Soothing music was playing quietly in the background as they entered, and Jo noticed several large potted plants stood on the floor over by a desk. Standing in the middle of the room was a treatment chair that looked very similar to a dentist's chair. Gabriella, as she had told Jo to call her, sat at the desk and indicated that Jo should sit in the chair beside it so she could take some notes. Gabriella spoke to Jo in a quiet, gentle voice to explain what was going to happen and to put her at ease.

"Firstly, I'd like to take a brief health history, and then I'll get you to sit in the treatment chair and I will manipulate the pressure points in your feet. By massaging your feet, I will be able to unblock the energy pathways and help your body to regain its natural balance. Have you got any questions before I begin?"

Jo shook her head. Despite the fact that Jo had thought the room looked like a dentist's surgery without all the pictures of teeth when she first entered, the tranquil music and calm and restful way that Gabriella spoke was gradually helping her to relax.

"While I'm manipulating your feet it is possible that you will feel lightness, tingling in the body or you may even feel like crying, but it is all perfectly natural and nothing to worry about. If I find tightness or congestion in an area I will spend longer on that area. Okay?" Gabriella asked and Jo nodded again.

In the waiting room Stella had read through one or two of the magazines and was beginning to scroll through her messages on her phone. Jo had been with the reflexologist for nearly an hour when Stella heard the sound of voices in the reception and then she appeared in the doorway looking relaxed and happy. Stella put her phone back in her bag and they walked out to the car in silence. Once they were outside Stella asked how it had gone.

"It went really well!" Jo enthused. "The reflexologist thought there might be some congestion in my fallopian tubes and when she manipulated my feet, I felt this funny tingling sensation. The whole thing was so relaxing."

Stella and Jo had decided they would have lunch in town, followed by some shopping in the afternoon before they went home. While they were sat in the Slug and Lettuce eating their lunch Jo finished telling Stella about what had happened during her treatment.

"I can't believe I was so nervous before hand."

"Well if you want to go again I don't mind taking you, as long as it's not during school time of course," Stella offered.

"Thank you. Gabriella suggested that I have weekly appointments for about six weeks but don't worry I wouldn't expect you to take me to them all. Oh, by the way, I asked Chris the postman about whether there were any Davenports in the village when he came in on Wednesday..."

Before Jo had chance to finish what she was saying Stella quickly asked, "What did he say, are there any in the village?"

"No, well he said he hadn't ever had to deliver any mail to any, so there might be but they just haven't ever had any mail". Jo knew that it wasn't very likely that there were any Davenports if Chris hadn't delivered mail to any, but it seemed odd that Jack would keep visiting the churchyard if he didn't live nearby.

Stella looked puzzled; her mind was working along similar lines to Jo. "He must live fairly close or why would I keep seeing him there?"

Chapter Sixteen

Stella spent most of Saturday evening with the telly on but not really watching it. She kept pondering over the mystery of where Jack lived; it had to be close by. Maybe in another village that was in walking distance, because now she thought about it there had been no car visible when she had first seen him at the church, or on the second time she had seen him and they had spoken for the first time. For the second Sunday in a row she set her alarm clock so she could get up early and visit the church. This time she decided to time it so that she missed everyone going in, then instead of joining the service she would slip around the back and see if Jack was there again. So, on Sunday morning she set off half an hour later than she had the previous week. As she got closer to the church she could see some people still arriving so she walked passed and sat on the bank near the bridge where she could see when the coast was clear. Eventually when everyone had gone in, the warden who was handing out the order of service also went in and shut the door.

The moment had come, Stella stood up and made her way towards the gate. Before when she had met Jack, it had been by accident, but today when she turned up at the back of the church he would know that she had gone there looking for him. Suddenly her footsteps slowed. She didn't want him to think that she was chasing him. She hesitated at the gate, perhaps she shouldn't go in. She bit her lip as she dithered over her decision. If she didn't go in and he was there she would have let an opportunity slip by. It wasn't like she had ever seen him anywhere else in the village. If she didn't take the chance she might not see him again. On the other hand, she didn't want to look like a love-struck teenager following the object of her affections around.

Her hand gripped hold of the gate, should she go in, or shouldn't she? It was Sunday morning, she had gotten up early for this and now she was about to chicken out. What if she went home and then she never saw him again? She would always wonder what would have happened if she had been brave enough to take a chance. Decision made she quickly pushed open the gate and hurried through before she could change her mind again. She could hear the organ starting up for the first hymn. With her heart pounding in her chest as she prepared in her head what she would say when she saw Jack, she hurried passed the church doors. '*It's such a lovely day I thought I would sit outside this time*'.

No, he would know that she had come to see him if she said that. '*I didn't want to have to sit next to Sophie and listen to her husband sing again*'. That was definitely more believable. Perhaps she could tell him that she had arrived too late and as the doors were already shut she didn't want to disturb the service by opening them again. That was definitely a reasonable excuse, hopefully he wouldn't realise then that she had just come to see him. The dew on the grass was making her feet wet but she had nearly made it to the back of the church. As she got to the corner she took a deep breath and prepared herself to look surprised that he was there again. When she turned the corner and he wasn't there her heart sank like a lead balloon into the pit of her stomach. She had prepared herself for this moment, was ready with her excuse as to why she wasn't inside for the service and he had spoilt it by not being there. She had spent all the previous evening looking forward to seeing him again, had felt nervous about it and it had all been for nothing. She wondered what she should do now. There was always the possibility that he had just not arrived yet, and that he still intended to. After all she didn't know what time he had arrived there the Sunday before. If she was sat waiting when he arrived it wouldn't look like she was there to see him. She could be merely enjoying the service from the peace and quiet of the outdoors. The thought brightened her mood again and she decided to sit and wait on the back-door step where they had sat before. She was about to sit down when she noticed a scrap of paper pinned to the old wooden door. As she read the note her heartbeat began to accelerate once more. The note had to be for her she was sure of it.

'Meet me here at half past four
J

With shaking fingers, she pulled the note off of the door and reread it. It was definitely from Jack and he had obviously anticipated her coming. Whether he thought it would be to escape Sophie again or whether he guessed that she would turn up to see if he was there she didn't know, but he had left her a note and he wanted to see her. She glanced about the churchyard to see if there was any sign of him watching to see if she got the note, but there wasn't. Slipping the note into her handbag she retraced her steps and headed for home feeling light hearted and slightly giddy. He wanted to see her.

Did that mean he had been thinking about her all week like she had been thinking about him?

The journey home passed quickly and Stella was soon sat in her garden enjoying the sunshine with a cup of tea in her hand and a smile on her face. She didn't realise that Jo was in her garden too until she popped her head over the fence and spoke. "You look happy this morning"

Stella's smile turned into a broad grin.

"He left me a note, I'm seeing him at half past four this afternoon." At this news Jo gasped, she didn't have to be a mind reader to know who Stella was talking about.

"That's great. How did he find out where you live?" At this question Stella seemed puzzled until she realised that Jo didn't know that she had been to the church again. "He left a note pinned to the backdoor of the church where we were sat chatting last time".

"Oh, can I see it?" Jo asked.

Stella went back indoors to get it out of her handbag, then she took it outside and handed it to Jo. Jo read the note and then asked, "Um, I don't want to be a kill joy, but how do you know the note is for you?"

Stella's face fell.

"What do you mean? It's obvious it was for me because it was where we were sat."

Stella could feel her little bubble of happiness bursting. What if she turned up and it wasn't from Jack? She could come face to face with some other person. She would feel like a complete fool if that happened. It hadn't occurred to her that the note might not be for her. Now she was having second thoughts, she didn't know whether to go or not. Jo handed the note back to Stella. "I don't want you getting your hopes up and turning up only to find out it's the person who mows the grass wanting to meet the vicar or something."

Stella started to laugh. "Wouldn't it be awful if I burst in on a secret assignation between Grace and another member of the congregation?"

Jo joined in laughing with her.

"What, you mean like that Mr Neville with the big teeth and sweaty armpits?"

Both women began laughing hard at the thought of Grace with Mr Neville in a clinch behind the church.

"Or", Jo added, "what if it was one of the parents from the school, how embarrassing would that be?"

Stella's laughter petered out.

"Oh no that would be *soo* embarrassing."

She had another look at the note that she now held in her hand. Was it from Jack? She wondered. Jo accurately guessed what she was thinking. "I think it must be for you from Jack, just be a bit careful in case it turns out not to be," she advised. "If it is from Jack of course you'll have to tell me all about it. You can come for coffee after work on Monday if you like?"

Stella agreed and they both returned inside their own houses. She spent the next few hours alternating between being excited at the prospect of a date with Jack – the fact that he had invited her to meet him she decided constituted her calling it a date, and nervous in case the note hadn't been for her at all.

At ten to four Stella checked her watch and as she realised it would soon be time for her to set off, her heart lurched madly with a mixture of panic and excitement. She checked her appearance in the mirror her mum had insisted on buying, and tidied her hair nervously. She checked her watch again, realistically she knew it would only take her about ten minutes to get to the church. Wanting something to occupy her mind until it was time to go, she started sorting out her bag for Monday morning, checking she had everything that she would need. As she had already organised it earlier in the day it didn't take long.

She was checking her watch again when the phone rang causing her heart to almost leap out of her chest. Maybe it was Jack calling to cancel, was her first thought before she remembered that he didn't have her number so it couldn't be him. She was about to pick up the handset when she recognised the number and realised it was her friend Katy calling. If she answered it now she wouldn't get off the phone in time to meet Jack at half past four, and then he would think she wasn't interested. Her hand stopped midway to answering and as she waited the answer phone kicked in. She listened to Katy's message and promised herself that she would call her back when she got in.

Finally, she checked her watch and it was at last time to leave. With butterflies gathering in her tummy she set off. If the note hadn't been left for her she was going to feel such a fool. The walk to church passed in a blur and soon she was pushing open the gate into the churchyard, the fear of making a mistake nearly made her turn around and go home. It was only because she wanted to see Jack and she couldn't risk losing an opportunity that kept her feet walking in the right direction. With her heart thumping wildly, she walked along in the shadow of the ancient wall until she reached the back of the church. At the corner she peered cautiously around the wall to see if she was about to interrupt another couple, or come face to face with a complete stranger.

The space seemed empty at first glance and then she noticed a tartan picnic blanket on the grass. On it stood a big bowl of strawberries and a bowl of cream. Two glasses stood empty on a tray waiting to be filled. Stella stepped forward into the space and that was when she saw Jack. He was sat on the doorstep with a smile on his face. For a moment she thought that her heart had actually stopped beating, and then when it started again it was beating so hard she thought it would burst out her chest.

"You got my note then?" Jack asked in his rich, deep voice that made her toes curl with delight. He stood up and took her hand, walking her over to the blanket. When she sat down he offered her a glass of wine. "I'm glad you came I've been thinking about you all week."

Stella couldn't stop the smile from spreading across her face. "Have you?"

His declaration made her feel all warm and a thrill of anticipation made her blush.

"Yes. I hope you like strawberries. I thought it would be nice to have a picnic".

"I love strawberries." Stella took the glass of wine Jack had poured out for her and watched as he poured one out for himself. As they chatted Stella gradually began to relax. She told Jack about her job in the school and how it was nice to be able to walk to work because she lived close by.

"Um I was wondering actually... Do you live in the village Jack?" as she asked the question Jack suddenly seemed very interested in his drink. It was a while before he answered and Stella was beginning to think that he wasn't going to.

"Sort of, sometimes," he answered vaguely. Then before she could question him about it any further he changed the subject. "So, did you have to escape Sophie and her husband again this morning?" Stella felt the colour rush into her face. If she said no, then she had no reason to have found the note but she didn't want to lie. She decided to be brave and tell him the truth.

"Actually, I didn't go to church this morning..." She paused before adding, "I came here to see if you were here."

Jack smiled, pleased at her confession. Taking the bull by the horns she thought that now was as good a time as any to find out if he was married. "You're not married are you Jack?"

He frowned briefly before he answered in what sounded like a sad voice. "No, no I'm definitely not married. I nearly married once but..."

He stopped talking and Stella prompted him to continue, "But...? What happened?"

"Circumstances forced me to end my relationship with Anne abruptly. That's partly how I've ended up here, but it was some time ago and it's all well and truly behind me now."

"What about children?"

"No, I don't have any children either, I'm a bit old fashioned I suppose. I wanted to wait until I was married, and then it never happened." Jack reached for a strawberry and dunked it into the cream offering it to Stella. When she leaned forward to take the strawberry she noticed a small scar on the side of Jacks arm.

Before she ate the strawberry, she asked, "what did you do to your arm".

Jack turned his wrist over so he could see the scar. "Oh, that's nothing. I did it years ago when I was out on my boat. Do you like boats?"

"I've only been on a ferry to France to be honest, but I must admit that I rather liked the experience. I was fifteen and I was on holiday with my mum and dad".

It was Stella's turn for her face to cloud over with sadness. She found herself telling Jack about what had happened to her dad, and how she had been desperate to try and recreate the happy family life she had had as a child. "I think that's why I said yes when Gary asked me to marry him, I wanted to be a part of a family again."

It was funny, she hadn't realised that that had been behind her desire to marry Gary when she did, and why she had wanted to have children but it seemed so obvious now talking it through with Jack. The conversation turned to happier topics and then Jack noticed the time.

"It's nearly time for evening service, we should go before someone finds us." He stood up and drew Stella to her feet. I will walk you to the gate and then I'll come back and gather up our picnic."

In a moments panic that she wouldn't see him again Stella asked, "Shall I give you my phone number so you can call me?" She realised after she had said it how desperate it made her sound, but she had enjoyed the afternoon and didn't want it to just end with no hope of the possibility of seeing him again.

"I'm sorry I don't have a phone," Seeing the look on her face Jack said, "Honestly I don't! I do want to see you again, I'm not making excuses. I really don't have one, not right now anyway, but if you tell me where you live I can get in touch with you. Or I can leave you notes here if you would rather".

Stella brightened up again when she realised that he wasn't trying to fob her off so he didn't have to see her again. She told him her address and he held her hand as they walked to the gate, his fingers were warm as they interlaced with her own. He stopped at the gate and turned her to face him.

Looking into her eyes he said, "I've enjoyed today, I'll be in touch". Then he leant forward and kissed her on the cheek before turning around and walking back the way they had just come.

Stella watched him go feeling confused. She had enjoyed the afternoon having a romantic picnic, but it had come to a rather abrupt end. It seemed odd that Jack was worried about them being found in the churchyard having a picnic. It wasn't like the bit of grass behind the church was used for anything and it was unlikely that anyone would have found them anyway. As he disappeared out of sight she started walking home. At least she knew now that he wasn't married, and he had been thinking about her too. She was ridiculously pleased that he had told her that. Her face still tingled where he had kissed her. It was strange that he didn't have a phone though; everybody had phones these days, even children. It was a funny coincidence too how the Jack Davenport in the newspaper article had had to leave his fiancé and so had her Jack. She wished she had asked him what the circumstances were that had made him leave her, but he had quickly changed the subject and she hadn't thought to ask again. The two Jacks had to be related she thought, otherwise it was a very bizarre coincidence. She couldn't help thinking about the other coincidences between the two Jacks, her Jack had told her he had a boat, and the Jack from the eighteen hundreds had been a smuggler who had nearly been caught coming ashore from his boat. A love of the sea might run in the family she supposed. The similarities between the two were in some ways, a little unnerving. As she turned into her road she saw Rory in the garden cutting the grass and Tim trimming the hedge. Tim saw her and waved. She waved back, and was reminded that she had meant to invite Jack to the party, 'I'll have to do it next time I see him' she thought.

When Stella got in and saw her answer phone flashing she remembered that her friend Katy had phoned before she went out and she needed to ring her back. What she really wanted to do was to sit and relive her afternoon with Jack and imprint it indelibly in her memory but she reasoned, she could do that later when she was tucked up in bed.

Katy answered on the third ring, her voice sounded tearful and Stella wondered what had happened, and then felt guilty for not answering the call earlier.

Chapter Seventeen

When Stella finished work on Monday she called in on Jo at work in the cafe. It wouldn't be long before she too finished, as Stella had stayed late to do some marking and preparation for Tuesdays' lessons. They might as well walk home together she thought, as they were meeting for a coffee anyway, it would save Stella watching out for Jo to get home. She pushed open the door to the café and waved as she saw Jo talking to a lady at the counter. When the lady left with a piece of chocolate cake to take away and a cardboard cup of coffee, Jo couldn't wait to ask how Stella's date had gone. When Stella just smiled and said she would tell her when they got back to Jo's house, Jo checked "The note was definitely for you then?"

"Yes, it was." Jo shut the door to the café, turned the sign so the word closed was visible on the outside and put the bolt across. "I'll just sweep up and I'll be ready to go. Amy's cashing up today." Jo swept up quickly as she was eager to hear Stella's news and they set off. Once they were settled in Jo's kitchen with their drinks she prompted Stella to begin, "Well?"

"When I first got there, I didn't think anyone was there and then I saw a picnic set out on the grass. Jack was waiting in the doorway at the back of the church so I didn't see him straight away. We spent the whole time chatting, sipping wine and eating strawberries."

"Ah how romantic, so he isn't married I take it, does he live in the village?" Jo asked.

"I asked if he was married and he told me he wasn't. Apparently, he was engaged a long time ago but it didn't work out. When I asked him if he lived in the village he told me that he sometimes does".

Jo frowned, "What does that mean?"

"To be honest I don't know, he was a little evasive. I know he has a boat though, because he has a scar on his right arm. When I asked him about it he said he had had an accident when he was on his boat. Maybe he lives on the boat sometimes. He doesn't have children either because I asked him that too."

"So, did you arrange to meet again or is he going to ring you?" Jo noticed that Stella had started fiddling nervously with the spoon that was still in her cup. "Well?" Jo prompted, wondering why Stella was hesitating if the date had gone so well, and she knew it must have done because Stella was full of smiles.

That was of course until she had asked about them meeting again. Stella sounded unsure as she explained, "The thing is, he hasn't got a phone so he can't ring me. Do you think that's a bit odd?"

Jo was taken aback. It was definitely unusual that he didn't have a phone; it didn't seem very likely in this day and age.

"Did he say why he didn't have a phone?" she asked.

"No and I didn't think to ask that. When I'm with him he's so charming that I don't always think straight, and it all seemed so perfect yesterday. It wasn't until I got in and I was talking to my friend Katy on the phone, she has just split up with her boyfriend by the way because she found him cheating on her, that I started to wonder why Jack was so evasive about where he lives and why he doesn't want to talk about his past. Then I started wondering if my Jack was related to the

Jack Davenport in the newspaper article, but when I checked it again I noticed that he had died a single man with no children."

She paused fiddling nervously with the spoon again. "You don't think he's lying to me and he's really married, do you?" Stella sounded worried.

Jo thought carefully about what Stella had told her, trying to find a plausible reason for Jack to not have a phone and why he only sometimes lived in the village. "Well you might be right about him living on his boat mostly. That could be why he doesn't have a phone, maybe it doesn't get a very good signal so it's not worth having one. He would probably use one of those radio things they have instead. That would also explain why he only lives in the village sometimes wouldn't it?"

"I suppose so," Stella conceded.

Jo laughed, "It's a good job he hasn't got a bad shoulder where the Jack from the eighteenth hundreds was shot or you might think the two Jacks were really one and the same, what with all the coincidences and him not having a phone. After all a ghost wouldn't have a phone, would he?" Stella laughed as Jo had intended she should.

"So" Jo asked, "Are you going to see him again or was it a one-off meeting?"

"I'm going to see him again. He said he's going to write me a note and send it to me or leave me one at the church."

Jo couldn't help thinking it was all a bit cloak and dagger. It all sounded very secretive, like a clandestine relationship. She could understand why Stella had been having second thoughts about whether he was married or not, there was something suspicious about it all.

When Stella got home she flipped open her laptop, found the page with the article about Jack Davenport on it and read it again. If only there was a picture or a description of him, Jo's joke about her Jack being a ghost had sent a shiver of fear through her body. She knew it was silly but now the seed had been planted in her mind she needed to find some proof that Jo was wrong. Jack from the eighteen hundreds had been a smuggler, smuggling Jewels from the Channel Islands. Yes, he had had a boat just like her Jack had one. That was the first similarity. The Jack from the eighteen hundreds had left his fiancé behind when he escaped from the revenue men and had somehow ended up in Little Welborough. Stella's Jack had told her he had ended the relationship abruptly and had ended up in Little Welborough, another similarity. Neither of them had had any children. What were the chances of two people with the exact same name having so many similarities in their lives? The article said that in eighteen hundred and twelve Jack Davenport had died at the age of thirty-four, could her Jack be thirty-four? Reluctantly she had to concede that that was exactly how old he looked. What did it mean she wondered? She didn't believe he was a ghost. Surely, she would have noticed when he had held her hand, or when he kissed her. At least her Jack didn't have a bad shoulder, if he had that would just be too uncanny for words. As Stella was closing her laptop she heard the letterbox flapping. She went into the hallway to see what had been pushed through the door only to find a note. As she unfolded it she realised it was from Jack. She rushed out the door and ran to the corner of the road to see if she could catch him so she could invite him in for coffee. The road was empty, the only people she could see was the vicar talking to some mums across the road in the park. There was no sign of Jack either up or down the road, but she was sure there hadn't been enough time for him to disappear. With the hairs on the back of her neck standing up, she went back indoors and opened the note again to read what it said.

Meet me tomorrow at six if you can,
Same place
J

Stella could feel the butterflies fluttering in her tummy at the thought of seeing Jack again. Whoever he was she really hoped that he wasn't lying to her because she couldn't help the way he made her feel. For the first time in her life she had met someone who made her feel special, and who made her pulse race with excitement and desire. And for the first time in her life she wanted to carry on seeing him whether it was right or not, but she hoped to god he wasn't married because she didn't know how she would live with the guilt.

* * * *

Rory was busy cutting the grass. It had been a week since he had phoned his parents to invite them to stay for the weekend and he still hadn't heard from them. Every time he thought about it a lump formed in his throat that he struggled to swallow back. Poor Tim felt bad now for insisting that Rory tell them about the relationship between the two of them, but Rory knew that he would have had to tell them at some point. He had tried to reassure him that it wasn't his fault what had happened, but it was hard when yet another day passed without them being in touch. That was why he was trying so hard to put a brave face on it all. The last thing he wanted to do was to make Tim feel any worse. Rory was a disappointment to his father, he knew that, but he had hoped that at least his mum would have called. Twice now he had nearly picked up the phone when he thought his father would be out so he could talk to her and explain things properly, but the fear of rejection had stopped him.

At least if he didn't hear it with his own ears he could still believe there was a chance they would come around to accepting his relationship, and who he was. Tim was lucky that both his parents had accepted the news when Tim had told them about his relationship with Rory. They didn't make either of them feel uncomfortable or treat them differently because of it. If only his own parents could be so accepting. During the week, every time the phone had rung Rory had felt his stomach somersault with nerves wondering if it was it his parents phoning. Each time he had been disappointed. Tim had reassured him that they might just need a bit of time to come around to the idea, but Rory wasn't so sure. His dad was stubborn, and had set ideas about same sex relationships. The last thing Rory had wanted to do was to upset his parents, but he had. There was nothing he could do about it now, he just had to wait and see what happened. When he finished mowing the grass he put the mower away and offered to help Tim sweep up the cuttings from the hedge, "No its okay I can manage, but you could get us a drink, doing the garden is thirsty work in this heat".

He wiped his brow with a clean hanky and stuffed it back in the pocket of his jeans. Rory went inside to get them both a can of shandy from the fridge. As he walked passed the phone on the shelf in the passage, he noticed a light was flashing on it. Someone had left them a message. His palms suddenly felt damp as he nervously pushed the button that would play back the message. His heart was thudding so hard it was painful. Rory heard a rustling noise as whoever had left the message fiddled with their phone, and then a voice began speaking, "Hi Tim, Hi Rory, its Tess here. Pete and I got your invite and we would love to come to your party, see you soon bye". Rory began to breathe again and his pulse gradually returned to normal.

Tim was stood at the hedge talking to Jo from number two when he took the drinks outside. He wandered over to join them and Jo smiled warmly at him. He liked Jo and Sebastian they had always been friendly from the day they moved in. He found Jo's slightly bohemian choice of clothes a bit colourful and wacky but somehow it suited her. "Jo's offered to make us a cake for the party, she wants to start doing celebration cakes to expand the café's business, and our cake will be a promotional cake," Tim told Rory,

"That sounds like a great idea, thanks," They were lucky to have such nice neighbours Rory thought as he thanked Jo for the offer. Jo left and Rory handed Tim his shandy. "Tess and Pete left a message on the answer phone to say they can come to the party," He took a swig out of the bottle as Tim watched him thoughtfully.

"Are you okay Rory? I feel so bad about your parents but they had to know".

"I know, I'm fine", Rory tried to smile but his heart wasn't in it. Tim sipped his drink and watched as Rory went back inside the house. He hated seeing Rory so upset, there must be something he could do to help. He considered the possibility of ringing Rory's parents again and talking to them, but what if he made things worse? He knew Rory had been putting on a brave face to save his feelings. But the truth was he knew him too well for that to work, and so now both of them were hurting. Tim because it had been his fault that Rory had told them, and Rory because he felt rejected by his parents for something that he couldn't help. He wasn't a bad person he had just fallen in love with the wrong person as far as his parents were concerned. Why couldn't people understand, love was love, you couldn't help who you fell in love with and just because they were both men didn't make their feelings any less important or real. Tim sighed, he would have to try and get in touch with Rory's mum, see if he could talk her around. At least if she would talk to him it would be a start.

Chapter Eighteen

When Stella awoke on Tuesday morning a feeling of excitement washed over her. She was going to see Jack again at six o'clock and despite her doubts about whether he was telling her the whole truth, she couldn't help looking forward to it. First though she had to go to work. An hour later she was hurrying through the school gates as the first spots of rain began to fall. As she was shutting the gate behind her she saw Henry huddled up against the gatepost crying. She finished shutting the gate and stooped down so she could speak to him.

"Henry what's wrong?" she asked in a gentle voice.

When he didn't answer she tried again, "Are you hurt? Unwell?"

He still didn't speak but his crying grew less. She laid her hand gently on his back to offer him comfort and to let him know she was there for him.

"You don't want to sit out here in the rain, why don't you come in with me and have a glass of water."

Slowly he raised his tear-stained face and looked at her. He looked so young and vulnerable.

"Do you want to come in with me?" She asked.

He nodded his head and wiped his nose on the sleeve of his jumper.

"Come on then." Stella stood up and started walking towards the school doors. Henry followed slowly behind her with his bag slung carelessly over his shoulder and his head down. Yvonne was sat at the reception desk when they entered, she was about to say hello when she spotted Henry following Stella and she could see that he had obviously been crying. She mouthed 'what's wrong?' to Stella, who shrugged her shoulders in reply. Stella and Henry carried on along the corridor with Stella talking calmly about the children's topic on castles and how it was progressing. Once inside the classroom Stella left the door open and turned the lights on. Then she found a glass from her cupboard so Henry could have a drink.

"Come and sit over here and have a drink," she told him pulling out a chair.

When he sat down and took the glass she held out to him, she pulled out another chair and sat down beside him.

"Are you feeling a bit better now?" she asked.

Henry sat with the glass on his lap staring solemnly into it as if it had all the answers, but said nothing.

"What's wrong Henry? You can tell me and we can work out how best to help you".

Henry started crying again. "No-one can help me, they hate each other and it's all my fault!" He put the glass on the desk and buried his head in his arms as he sobbed.

Stella rubbed his back, "Is this about your mum and dad?" she guessed.

When Henry nodded, she went on, "None of it is your fault Henry, sometimes adults argue just like children do, but it's not because of you".

"It *is* because of me," he sobbed then in a rush he added, "My dad was supposed to come and look after me yesterday but he didn't come, and my mum was mad because she wanted to go out somewhere without me, and when my dad turned up late she yelled at him and it was all because of me. He stormed off and my mum looked at me and cried. They don't want me!"

Stella handed Henry a tissue from her box on the desk. "It might have seemed like it was because of you, but I'm sure it wasn't. Adults say and do things they don't mean sometimes when they are upset and it sounded like they were both very upset, but that doesn't mean that it was your fault. Why don't I talk to your mum and see if I can help you to sort this out?"

Henry's eyes were red from tears but he looked at her with hope. Taking his silence as a sign of agreement she took him to reception so Yvonne could keep an eye on him while she made the call to his mother. Yvonne let him lay on the bed that was usually reserved for the children who were sick while they waited for their mums to come and pick them up. Henry lay on the bed with his back to the office. He didn't want anyone to see him and he didn't want to talk to anyone. He could hear the other teachers arriving, and the whispered voices as they asked what was wrong with him. Soon they would all know that his mum and dad didn't want him. He wondered what would happen to him then. Perhaps they would let him go and live with his grandparents, at least they always seemed pleased to see him. He found the thought of his grandparents comforting, and it took his mind off the fact that Mrs Martin would actually be speaking to his mum at that very moment. He was trying hard not to think about what was being said.

When Stella managed to get through to Henry's mum at the office where she worked, she told her about her conversation with Henry.

"He thinks that it's all his fault and that you don't want him," she finished off by saying. Henry's mum had sat silently listening to what she was being told, her heart breaking as she realised how the arguments with his dad must have sounded to her innocent little boy. Tears ran silently down her cheeks, she felt so guilty.

"Can I come and talk to him?" she asked when she found her voice again.

"Of course you can, he needs to know that you still love him and that he's not to blame for what has happened."

Stella felt sorry for the whole family. They were all going through a tough time, but her main concern was Henry.

Henry's mum nodded in agreement even though Stella couldn't see her, then she said, "I'll let them know here that I need some time off, and I'll ring his dad and tell him what has happened. I will be as quick as I can. Tell him I'm on my way will you, my poor little love."

The conversation came to an end and Stella went back to the reception to find Henry. She sat down on the bed beside him and spoke gently to him. "I've spoken to your mum Henry, and she is going to come and see you. She's very sorry that you thought it was all because of you, and she wants you to know that it isn't, Okay?"

Henry was still laying on his side with his back to her but he nodded his head. Stella got up again and went to speak to Yvonne. "Henry's mum will be here shortly to speak to him. I'm going to go and explain what has happened to Nicole, is she in her classroom yet do you know?"

"Yes, I think so I saw her heading that way with her coffee five minutes ago."

Stella set off in the direction of Nicole's classroom. Nicole was putting up the finishing touches to her display board as Stella knocked politely and walked in.

"How's Henry?" Nicole asked.

She had seen the little boy laying on the bed in reception when she arrived. Yvonne had told her that Stella had found him crying in the playground and was talking to his mother.

"He thought his parents' arguments were about him, and that was why they had split up. His mum is on her way here now to speak to him. I thought it was best to get straight on with it, I hope you don't mind?" Henry was Nicole's pupil and she didn't want her to think that she was butting in.

"Of course not. I'm just glad that he has told someone at last what was wrong. I've tried a few times but he just clams up. Now we know what is wrong we can all help him to deal with it."

Henry's mum was out of breath when she arrived. She had been in a rush to get to him and try to make him understand that he was not to blame. When she saw him lying on the bed with his back to everyone, looking lost and alone she wanted to cry for him.

"Ah, Mrs Quinn come through," Yvonne told her when she approached the desk. Yvonne opened a security door and let Henry's mother in.

"Henry your mum's here," the receptionist told him. Henry's mum sat down on the bed beside him and gathered him into her arms. "Oh Henry" she cried rocking him in her arms. "None of this is your fault. Your dad and I both love you and we're really sorry that we've hurt you like this."

Henry was crying again now but his tears were a release of all the misery he had been bottling up inside. It was good to feel his mum's arms around him, soothing his fears and comforting him.

* * * *

It had been a good day Stella thought as she walked out the school gates on her way home. After Henry's mum had finished talking to him she had spent some time talking to Nicole and Mrs Ashworth, the head teacher. Henry had looked much happier when Stella had seen him at lunchtime, he was even joining in a game with some of the other children from his class. As she walked along the pavement she glanced anxiously up at the sky. It was looking a bit grey; she hoped it wasn't going to rain. She hurried home so she could change before she met Jack at the church. She must remember to invite him to Tim and Rory's party this time. The phone was ringing as she opened the door, dropping her bag in the hallway she picked up the receiver wondering who could be calling. She knew it wasn't her mother because she had programmed a special ring tone into the phone that played when her mum rang.

"Stella I'm glad I caught you in, I didn't want to ring your mobile in case you were still at work."

It was her friend Katy. Stella checked the time on her watch. As much as she liked talking to her friend she was in a hurry to get ready so she could go out.

"Hi Katy, what can I do for you? Or were you ringing for a chat? Only I have to go out in a minute."

"Oh yes, hot date huh?" Stella blushed. She didn't want to tell Katy about Jack yet. Not until she was sure about him, and that he definitely wasn't married. He was quite secretive and it still worried her why that might be.

"I'm going to church actually".

"Really?" Katy sounded surprised. "The vicar must be really hot, that's all I can say."

Stella laughed, because initially she had thought that Jack was the vicar and if he had been, Katy would have been right. Her guess was a little too close for comfort, but at least Stella could reply honestly to that query. "Actually, the vicar is a woman!"

"How disappointing! Anyway, getting back to why I phoned, I was wondering if I could stay with you for a few days? I've quit my job and I need to get away for a while. I really need to think things through; decide what I'm going to do next."

"Oh my god, why did you quit?" Stella was shocked; Katy had always loved her job designing and making costumes for shows.

"It's a long story which I won't bore you with now as you are going out, but can I stay?" Katy pleaded. She was usually so bubbly but having split with her boyfriend and now this, Stella wasn't surprised that she needed to get away for a while.

"Of course you can stay. You will have to amuse yourself most of the time though, as I will be at work."

"That's okay. I've got some things to sort out here first so can I come on Friday about five?"

"Yes that's fine, if I get held up with marking or you arrive earlier than you expect there's a café in the village which does fantastic cakes. You can tell me all about what's been going on when you get here." Stella checked her watch again. "I'd better go now but I will see you on Friday."

She said goodbye and hung up. Then dashing upstairs to get changed, she threw open the wardrobe doors and began rummaging inside for something to wear. She had to be quick because she only had an hour before she was meant to be meeting Jack. She pulled out a navy-blue dress and a red cardigan and held it up against herself as she looked in the mirror. Too dressy, she didn't want it to look like she had tried too hard. Tossing it on the bed she rummaged through the rest of her clothes until she found a pale blue dress that was just right. If she wore it with flat shoes it would look nice but not as if she trying to impress him too much. She pulled the dress on over her head and did up the buttons at the front. Then giving her hair a quick brush and re-applying her lipstick she was ready to go.

The phone call from Katy had put her behind and she realised she would have to hurry if she was going to get there on time. She picked up the bag she had dropped in the hall earlier and left. As she hurried along Stella started to wonder how long Katy would want to stay and how it would affect her seeing Jack. She was happy to help her friend, especially as it was Katy who had put her up when she had split up with Gary, but seeing Jack was important to her too. Still she was getting ahead of herself. She would have to take it a day at a time. For someone who hadn't wanted a relationship, she was becoming a little obsessed with Jack.

* * * *

As Stella approached the gate to the churchyard she checked to make sure no one was about. It was silly really she thought, she had nothing to hide, but it seemed important that nobody should see her. She was a little out of breath from hurrying and took a moment to calm herself before she pushed open the gate and went inside. The grass must have been cut recently as it was much shorter than on Sunday when she had last been there. She wandered passed the gravestones and along the side of the church. As she got closer to the rear of the church she could hear music faintly playing. She was surprised to see that Jack had found an old wooden table and two chairs and set it up behind the church. The table was laid ready for a meal with a pretty tablecloth, a candle and crystal glasses. The music sounded like it was coming from inside the church. At that moment Jack appeared carrying a large tray with their food on it. His smile, when he saw that she had arrived, was slow and sexy, lighting a fire in her veins.

The ever-present spark between them warmed her skin and sent shivers down her spine. He stood the tray on the table and walked slowly towards her. Taking her hand, he guided her over to one of the chairs. "Your dinner awaits madam," he said as he pulled out the chair for her to sit down. Stella's mind had gone completely blank, all she could think of was Jack and the effect he was having on her pulse. She sat in the chair and he placed a plate of food on the table in front of her. As he pulled out the other chair for himself he winced as if he had hurt himself. "Are you alright?" Stella asked with concern.

"I'm fine, I just had a twinge in my shoulder."

As he sat down Stella felt the hairs on the back of her neck stand on end. When he saw her face pale with what he thought was concern he added, "It's nothing to worry about".

"How did you do it?" Stella had to know, there had to be a simple explanation she reasoned. It had to be just a coincidence. Jack seemed to be thinking carefully about what he should say before he answered. "I was trying to get away from someone quickly, like you did the other day after church". He changed the subject. "Would you like a glass of wine?"

Stella nodded and Jack poured the wine into her glass while she tried to rationalise what he had said about his injury. The sky was dark and overcast with unshed rain and the air felt cool against the warmth of her skin. Jack lit the candle that stood in the centre of the table and it flickered in the early evening breeze. Stella put the incident with Jacks injured shoulder out of her mind as he gazed into her eyes from across the table.

"I've been looking forward to seeing you all day," he told her in a husky voice. Stella felt all warm and fuzzy inside, and felt a rush of pleasure at the thought of him thinking about her. It was quiet in the churchyard except for the gentle sound of music playing. She enjoyed listening to him speak as the rich timbre of his voice washed over her, sending ripples of awareness skittering over her skin. Jack asked her about her family and Stella told him about her mother, and her aunt who was having the holiday of a lifetime in Canada. He kept her talking about herself all through the meal and then as they finished eating Stella remembered about Tim and Rory's party.

"I've been invited to a party at my neighbour's house in a couple of weeks, will you come with me?" she asked.

He picked up her hand, which was resting on the table, and began playing with her fingers as he thought about his answer. "I can't Stella, I'm really sorry."

He could see by her expression that she was disappointed and he felt awful. "The truth is," he continued, trying to explain so she didn't feel like he was rejecting her, "I have a secret that means I can't be seen by anyone else." Seeing the look of shock on her face he hurried on, "before you start thinking the worst, I can promise you with all my heart that I'm not a married man cheating on my wife, but... my situation is complicated and I need you to trust me. I can't explain it anymore right now, but what we have is special, and I don't want to lose you."

He seemed so sincere that Stella felt her heart melt. She was pretty sure she knew what his secret was and didn't want to think about the implications of it just yet. She would deal with it later, when she had the time to think about it properly without any distractions. Right now, she wanted to enjoy her evening with Jack. She couldn't ignore the fact that she was falling in love with him. She had never felt that way about anyone before. At that moment the first spots of rain began to fall from the dark clouds. The few spots quickly turned into a downpour. Jack pushed back his chair and grabbed Stella's hand. Together they ran for shelter in the porch of the vestry door, laughing as they went.

Stella who was now quite wet, began to shiver. Jack wrapped his arms about her and pulled her close to keep warm. Stella could smell the musky scent of his aftershave, and feel the erratic beat of his heart as she laid her head against the comforting warmth of his chest. The air became heavy with an intense longing. As Stella slowly looked up into Jacks heavily lidded eyes and watched the rain dripping from his hair, she knew he was about to kiss her and her heart thudded madly in her chest. It was almost painful in its intensity. He brushed her hair gently away from her face sending shockwaves pulsing through her veins. As their lips met Stella could feel herself going weak at the knees and put her arms around Jack for support. She didn't care if Jack was a ghost, all she knew was that she loved him and being with him made her happy.

Chapter Nineteen

An hour later when the rain had finally stopped they said their goodbyes and she left him stood at the gate. Each time she turned around to check, he was still there watching her, a dark shadow against the churchyard wall with his white shirt standing out in the stark blackness of the night. There were no streetlights in that part of the village. She could see the silhouettes of bats flying silently overhead and hear the sound of crickets in the long grass. She wrapped her arms tightly about herself. Now she had lost the comfort of Jacks arms she felt cold. They had spent the last hour snuggled together in the porch watching the rain fall and the stars beginning to appear.

Jacks kisses had left her breathless for more but he had been a perfect gentleman and so they had eventually ended up sat on the step. They had sat companionably together both lost in their own thoughts. Jack with his arm around Stella and Stella with her head on his shoulder. She had felt completely at peace with the world and safe in a little cocoon of happiness. When Jack had finally told her that she ought to get home while it was still not too late she had felt bereft, but he had reassured her that it wouldn't be long before he saw her again. He had kissed her goodbye at the gate, a long lingering kiss that sent shock waves of desire through her body. She had felt like she was walking on a cloud, but as the lights of the village became brighter, reality began to reassert itself. What had she done? Had she really fallen in love with a ghost? The little glow of happiness that she had felt earlier now made her skin prickle. How could a relationship with Jack ever work out? There could never be a conventional future for them. No children? That had been one thing she had always wanted. She wasn't even sure if they would actually be able to live together. Could she give all that up to have a few stolen hours each week with Jack? He certainly felt very real for a ghost.

She could really do with talking to Jo about it. Telling someone about it might help her to put things in perspective she thought. There were no lights on that she could see in Jo's house when she got back, and she didn't want to intrude if they were having an early night. She would have to talk to her after work tomorrow. Later when she went to bed, she lay for hours staring at the ceiling, thinking. The evening spent with Jack had felt magical and special. When she was with him she felt so alive, which was ironic really if he was a ghost. Maybe she had got it wrong, maybe he wasn't a ghost at all. As she thought back over all the things he had told her, about his injured shoulder and how she was the only one who could see him, being a ghost seemed to be the only possible explanation, and yet she felt silly even thinking it. The fact that there were no known Jack Davenports living in the area also seemed to confirm her suspicions. Everything matched, if only she could find out the name of the Jack from the eighteen hundreds fiancé. It might be the last piece in the puzzle. If the names were the same she would have to accept that her Jack was a ghost. If they weren't she wasn't quite sure where that left her, still with a mystery she supposed.

After hours of trying to sort out how she felt about the situation she finally fell into a restless sleep. Her dreams were full of Jack who always seemed to be just out of her reach, a shadow she could only just see. A gentle voice in the dark, a shrill noise in her ear… She awoke abruptly to find that the shrill ringing was real, and that it was in fact her alarm clock. It was morning already, it only seemed minutes ago that she had finally dozed off. Now it was time to get up and get ready for work again. She stumbled out of bed feeling tired and lethargic. She wasn't even sure what day it was, but the alarm had gone off and that meant it was a workday.

She stepped into the shower and braced herself for the sting of cold water to hit her skin. She had turned the hot down low as she needed an extra hit of cold to wake herself up this morning. She gasped as the water cascaded down her back and snapped her out of her sleepy fog. The worries of the night before were replaced with the romantic memories of her evening with Jack. If only he weren't a ghost she sighed. Still she didn't know that he definitely was a ghost yet, after all it was a very far-fetched idea. She would have to try and do some more research and find out what the Jack from the eighteen hundreds fiancé was called. In the mean time she had to get to work. She was glad that Henry had finally confided in her what had been causing him to feel so sad so she could help him. Having spoken to Henry's mum about his confession, she hoped that Henry would be happier today. His mum had talked to him now and explained that the separation was not his fault.

As Stella emerged from her front door she saw Rory cycle passed on his bike. She frowned, it was unlike him to be cycling to work without Tim. They usually left together. She was about to call out and ask him if Tim was alright but he was cycling quite fast, and was already too far away.

Tim watched Rory cycle along the road from the bedroom window. He had arranged to start work later today so he could try and speak to Rory's mum while his dad was out. Tim hadn't told Rory why he was starting late or he knew he would be anxious. He had given the matter a lot of thought and felt that as he had pushed Rory into telling his parents about the two of them, it was up to him to try and sort out the upset it had caused. When Rory was out of sight Tim went downstairs and picked up the phone. He hoped he wasn't too early. Taking a deep breath, he dialled Rory's parent's number and waited. He heard the phone ring several times before a man's voice answered in a Scottish accent "Aye, who is it?"

Tim put the phone down quickly. He didn't think he would have much luck talking to Rory's dad. He checked the time. He would try again in half an hour, hopefully he would have left by then. To keep himself busy while he waited he decided to unload the dishwasher. He felt so guilty for the way Rory was feeling. If only Rory's family could be as accepting as his own. Surely they wanted their son to be happy?

Rory's mum came back from walking the dogs. "Who was that on the phone at this time in the morning?" she asked.

"A dinna ken. Whoever it was put the phone down when I answered it." He looked at his wife as if expecting her to offer up some explanation. When she didn't and carried on with the task of wiping the dog's feet and chatting quietly to them, he knew that she had nothing to hide. If she had she would have been flustered and she would have gone red. He guessed it was Rory trying to ring to win her over, to make her see things from his point of view, but had he thought about them and their feelings? No, he hadn't. How on earth did he think it would look to his work mates? He would be a laughing stock. They would never let him live it down. He glanced over at his wife, Lily. He knew she had cried herself to sleep every night since the phone call from Rory. She had longed to be a grandparent and now it looked like that was not going to be possible. She had spoilt Rory; she had always been over protective of him. That was probably the reason he had turned out the way he had. What neither of them realised was the pain it was causing him.

Despite what they might think he loved his son. Rory had always been a sensitive lad, kind and thoughtful. He hadn't always found it easy to fit in. They had moved several times while he was growing up, being the son of a soldier he was sure wasn't always easy. Watching someone you loved go away to war zones and never knowing if they would come back, must have been hard. Rory had clung to his mother, the only constant presence in his life. When he had grown up and gone to a college that was miles away from where they lived they had both secretly worried that he wouldn't be able to cope away from home, but he had.

Strange as it had seemed he had flourished, passing all his exams and making friends. When he had finished college he had found a job at a library near the college and he had been there ever since. He had started off by renting a room from one of his friends' parent's. Eventually he had met Tim and they had bought a house together, to get on the property ladder he had told them.

'Everyone did it nowadays,' he had said. But Tim wasn't just a friend it turned out, and as much as he loved his son he wasn't sure how to deal with the situation. He didn't want to lose touch with him but he didn't know if he could handle the alternative. Seeing his son with a man. He left Lily to wash up his breakfast plate and went to work. He would never be able to face his comrades if they found out. He left the house deep in thought. He didn't hear Lily's sigh. She had guessed who the phone call was from too. If she was right she hoped he would try again before his father got home. She wanted to know… no that was wrong; she needed to know that he was alright. It had been hard hearing Rory struggle to tell her about his relationship with Tim, but a part of her had always known really. She had always hoped for his sake that she had been wrong, and all the time no one mentioned it she had held on to that hope.

Her family was falling apart and she didn't know how to save it. Angus was her husband, she loved him and wanted to support him, but Rory was her son and she loved him too. A son that she had hoped one day would provide her with grandchildren. It was a loss but not the worst one. Losing Rory would be worse. She felt pulled in two, not knowing what to do for the best. If only he hadn't said anything they could have gone on in blissful ignorance. Even as she thought it she knew that it was wrong. Her son was entitled to happiness just the same as anyone else. If he loved Tim then surely it was his right to not have to be secretive about it.

She just had to get Angus to see that it was not the end of the world, and that was not going to be easy. He worked in a very masculine world. He was a man's man. He had been to war and survived, having to tell the men he worked with that his son was in a relationship with another man would be difficult for him. She washed up the plate he had left in the sink and a tear slid down her cheek. She loved them both, she didn't want to have to choose between them.

Tim had just finished putting the washing on the line. Half an hour had passed, he wondered if he should try again now or wait a bit longer. It was important that he get it right for Rory's sake. He didn't want to make the situation any worse. Feeling a knot of tension twisting in his gut he picked up the phone. He crossed his finger's hoping that Rory's father would be out. He listened nervously as the phone rang once, twice, three times. On the fourth ring it was picked up. With baited breath he listened to see whose voice he would hear. "Hello?" Tim let out a sigh of relief. It was Rory's mother, Lily.

"Hello Lily its Tim," he waited for her reaction hoping against hope that she wouldn't put the phone down on him. She didn't, that was the first hurdle over. "I wanted to talk to you about Rory".

Lily remained silent but he knew she was listening because he could hear her gently breathing on the other end.

"Lily?"

"I'm still here," she whispered through her tears. Tim could hear the pain in her voice and his courage nearly disserted him, but this was for Rory. He had to carry on. In a rush to say what he needed to while he had the chance he continued.

"Rory's really sorry that he's upset you both but you have to know that this isn't just a passing phase. We love each other and we want to be able to be honest with you. It will break Rory's heart if you cut him off. I'm asking you to consider his happiness."

Tim stopped speaking, he didn't know what else to say. He wasn't prepared for the hurt and the anger that Lily let loose down the phone.

"You've torn my family apart. How can you say you love Rory when you have done that to us? How am I supposed to choose between my son and my husband? Everything was fine until you came along," She shouted at him.

She felt guilty for saying it the moment it was out of her mouth but she couldn't stop herself. She had been holding it in for so long. The frustration, the hurt, the disappointment. She had needed to get it out of her system before she could begin to deal with it. It wasn't Tim's fault she knew that, but he was the one on the phone and she had to say it to someone. He had put himself in the firing line. If she showed how upset she was to Angus it would be harder for him to come to terms with it, if that was, he ever could.

She began crying again and Tim put the phone down. Listening to lily cry made him feel even worse than he had already felt. He swallowed the lump that was forming in his throat. He had achieved nothing by phoning. Realistically Tim knew if it hadn't been him, Rory would have met someone else, and eventually he would have still been in this situation but it didn't make him feel any better. Lily's words had hurt like a knife through his heart. Of course he loved Rory, how could she question that? She had dumped the responsibility of their family break up on his shoulders and it was going to be a heavy burden to carry. Now he had to decide whether to tell Rory about the phone call or not. He didn't like the thought of having secrets from him but at the same time he didn't want to cause him any further upset. Although he wasn't in the right frame of mind for work he knew he had to go, so reluctantly he gathered the packed lunch that Rory had made him that morning and set off. He could decide what to do next while he cycled in.

Lily was still sat by the phone ten minutes later rocking herself backwards and forwards. What had she done? She should never have said those things to Tim. She was hurting and had wanted to hurt him for causing it, but it wasn't his fault. When he told Rory what she had said it would probably push Rory further away. A fresh wave of despair had her eyes filling with tears again. It shouldn't be like this. Regret hung over her like a big black cloud. If only she could take it all back. If only things could go back to how they had been a few weeks ago. The day loomed ahead, bleak and empty. She just wanted her son to be happy and if that meant accepting Tim as his partner she would have to accept it. If only she hadn't let her emotions get the better of her on the phone. If only she could get Angus to see that it didn't have to be a problem. With a weary sigh she reluctantly pushed herself to get up and carry on with her day. Maybe she would be able to come up with a solution while she was helping out at the charity shop. At the very least it would give her something else to think about.

Chapter Twenty

Stella hurried along to the café after work to catch Jo before she finished. If she was lucky there might be some cakes left over that they would want to get rid of, and if that was the case she would be doing them a favour if she ate one or two. If she was very lucky there might even be a chocolate one. She pushed open the door as the last customers were gathering their belongings to leave. Stella loved the sweet smell of sugary treats mixed with the smell of coffee as you entered the café. Jo glanced up from her job of cashing up and smiled when she saw that it was Stella. Amy was busy sweeping the floor and Stella gave her a brief smile as she headed over to the counter.

"There's some cakes that won't last till tomorrow, I was going to throw it out but if you're hungry you're welcome to them." Jo told her as Stella stood her bags on a chair beside the till. "I would take them home myself for Sebastian, but I'm trying to be good and they would be too much of a temptation."

She was rewarded with a smile of delight from Stella. "Any chocolate ones?" she asked already opening the box on the side Jo had indicated.

Jo raised her eyebrows at Amy who had now finished sweeping the floor, and was collecting her handbag from the cupboard. "There might be."

Stella found a large piece of chocolate fridge cake at the bottom of the box. "I can't believe you were going to throw this away, it's criminal," she told Jo taking a huge bite. She really must pop in to see Jo on the way home more often she thought.

"I'll see you tomorrow then," Amy told them as she opened the door to leave, turning the sign on the door to 'closed' as she went.

"So, what brings you here, apart from the chocolate cake that is?" Jo asked when they were alone. She had finished the cashing up and was preparing the café for the following morning.

"I saw Jack again last night," Stella announced trying to hold back a grin.

"And? Did you find out any more about him?" Jo had turned now to give Stella her full attention. Stella had finished her cake and had a serious expression on her face. "What happened?" Jo asked.

"We had dinner together, in the churchyard again. He says he definitely isn't married and I believe him." Stella was fiddling with the napkin she had just used to wipe her fingers.

"But...?" Jo urged. There was obviously something still worrying Stella.

"I think I'm in love with a ghost!" Stella blurted out at last. "I know it sounds ridiculous but when he reached over to pick something up a pain in his shoulder made him wince, and when I asked him what he had done he told me he had injured it getting away from someone."

When Jo frowned 'about to say that doesn't mean he's a ghost' Stella continued. "Jack from the eighteen hundreds was shot in the shoulder don't forget, trying to get away from the revenues men."

"I admit that it is a funny coincidence especially with all the other stuff as well," Jo admitted, "But I'm not sure that a ghost would feel pain, there could be another explanation".

"Like what?" Stella asked desperate for Jo to be right.

"Well.... I can't think of one at the moment," Jo conceded, "but that doesn't mean there isn't one". Jo looked thoughtful, "We need to do some more digging, see if we can find out anything else about Jack from the eighteen hundreds. Something that will prove your Jack isn't his ghost".

"There's something else as well," Stella admitted.

"What's that?"

"When I asked him if he would come to Tim and Rory's party with me, he told me that no one else can see him. If he's not a ghost why would he say that?"

Jo had to admit that it was a strange thing to say. It would make sense of course if he was a ghost, but surely he couldn't really be one. Jo sighed, Jack was definitely a mystery and everything did seem to point to him being a ghost, being able to disappear, the fact that Grace from the shop didn't know him and all the other little things, poor Stella! "What are you going to do?"

"I think I'm in love with him," Stella's voice was almost a whisper.

"You think or you know?"

"I know I am. I just don't know what to do about it." Jo put her arm around Stella and gave her a hug. It would be awful to fall in love with someone only to find out they've been dead a good hundred years or so. She couldn't even begin to imagine how that would feel.

"We need to do a bit more investigating, see what we can come up with, just to be sure," Jo suggested. Stella nodded.

"Come on then," Jo grabbed her bag from inside the cupboard and switched the lights off.

They were walking slowly along the road that would lead them both home, discussing possible ways of finding out more about Jack when Tim and Rory cycled passed. Stella noticed that they were both quieter than normal and wondered what was wrong. Usually they would be chatting to each other as they passed and she would hear them coming. Today they were both silent with a faraway look on their faces. Something was wrong she was sure of it. Only that morning she had seen Rory cycling to work on his own, a first in the time she had lived there. She had thought that maybe Tim was unwell and that he wasn't going into work but clearly, he had. Perhaps they had had an argument.

"What do you think is wrong with those two?" she asked Jo who had stopped talking and was also watching their progress in silence. "Do you think they've had a row?"

Jo shook her head, "I doubt it. I think it's more likely to be because of Rory's parents".

Stella looked confused, "What have Rory's parents got to do with it?"

"Well Tim told me the other day when I went around and offered to do them a cake for the party, that they had invited Rory's parents to stay for the weekend so they could tell them about their relationship. Get it all out in the open, but they didn't take it very well. Now Tim feels bad because it was his idea and Rory is upset because his parents won't speak to him. It's all very sad. They're such a nice couple."

Stella watched as Tim and Rory disappeared around the corner into Lovedon Lane. Relationships were all difficult in different ways it would seem. Perhaps falling in love with a ghost wasn't so bad after all. Sebastian was working late so Stella invited Jo back so they could see if they could find out any more information about Jack.

As Stella pushed open her gate she saw a lovely bunch of flowers that had been left on her doorstep. With her heart fluttering like a butterfly trapped in a net, she stooped to pick them up. They looked like they had been handpicked from a garden and were beautifully tied together in a big bunch with blue ribbon. The ribbon looked the same as the bows that had decorated the pews in church ready for a wedding the previous week. Without even reading the card Stella knew who had sent them.

"Oh, how lovely! It looks like you have a secret admirer, unless it's your birthday?" a voice called from the car that had just pulled up at the kerb. Sophie climbed out and hurried forward so she could see when Stella picked up the flowers who had sent them. She couldn't wait to tell her mum what she had seen. It was just lucky she had turned up when she did with a box of books for the School fete.

Stella and Jo exchanged glances, why did she have to turn up now? The look had said. Sophie reached forward and pulled out a slip of paper. "Oh, look there's a note with them!" Without giving Stella the chance to react, Sophie had opened the note and began to read it.

"I met a lady in the meads,
Full beautiful a faery's child:
And that is why I sojourn here,
Alone and palely loitering.
Sunday, same time?
J

"Oh, how romantic!" Sophie declared having finished reading the note, "he's quoting you Keats. So, who is he?"

Stella looked at Jo hopefully, willing her to come up with an answer. "It must be that old man you helped in town on Saturday, he said he wanted to thank you for finding that book for him, didn't he? Jo quickly told Stella, sensing her panic.

The news would be all around the village by this time tomorrow, the best she could manage was to make it seem as mundane as possible to deflect Sophie's interest.

"Yes, that's right he did" Stella nodded playing along.

Sophie reread the note "But it says Sunday here?" she frowned. She had hoped for something a bit more exciting than finding a book for an old man. "And why does he want to see you again if you have already found the book for him?"

"He wanted to buy me a coffee to say thank you," Stella explained.

"Oh, the book must have been very special?" Sophie was desperate to find out as much as she could before she left. Stella and Jo both spoke at the same time, "It was a present for his wife"

"It had sentimental value." Sophie looked first at Jo then at Stella who were both looking guiltily at each other. "Which was it, a present for his wife or of sentimental value?" she asked eyeing them up suspiciously.

"Both really," Stella told her, "He had bought a copy for his wife years ago and it had gone missing and so he wanted to buy her another one for her birthday".

Sophie was thoughtful as she considered the possibility of whether she was being told the truth. It was possible but her gossip antenna was telling her that it was a story they had made up on the spot. Something fishy was going on and Sophie wanted to know what it was. She would have to keep her eyes and ears open from now on. Well she wasn't going to find out any more now, and she couldn't wait to pass on what she had seen so she might as well get back to the reason she was here.

"I've got a few books for you for the book stall, Danny said you were helping to run it so I thought I'd drop them off here for you." Danny was Sophie's son and he was also in Scott's class. Stella hadn't anticipated people bringing the books to her house. She didn't really want to store them when she still had a few unopened boxes of her own but Sophie was already opening her boot and carrying them up the garden path. "Where do you want them?" No way was Stella letting her through the front door.

"If you leave them there I'll find somewhere for them in a minute." Stella indicated a place to the side of the path and Sophie put them down. Her parting shot was, "Bye then, enjoy your coffee on Sunday with the *old* man", letting them know she was not convinced by the explanation they had tried to fob her off with.

"Damn! Why did she have to turn up then of all times?" Stella exclaimed. "And why do I have to store her books? Why can't she drop them off at the school like everyone else?"

Jo watched Sophie drive off with a smug look on her face. "You realise she will go straight to her mum and you will be the topic of conversation for the next few hours while they try to work out who 'J' is?"

Stella sighed, Jo was right and that was the last thing she needed, someone poking their nose into her private business. Trying to make light of the situation Stella said, "Well it wasn't a complete lie, if he is a ghost he is the oldest man I know," which caused Jo to giggle. "Come on let's go in, there's nothing we can do about it now".

Stella opened the front door wide handing Jo the flowers to take to the kitchen so she could carry the box of books in. Then fumed, "How rude of her to read my note before me anyway. The nerve of the woman!"

"That's Sophie for you, although it was nice of her to tell us the poem was a quote from Keats, I wouldn't have twigged otherwise, would you?"

When Stella didn't look mollified Jo continued, "Sophie has a nose for gossip but to be fair she does have a kind heart too. She's always doing things for charity and if you were in trouble she would try and help you".

Jo grinned, "Of course she would tell everyone all the details about it afterwards".

Stella couldn't help laughing. The whole situation was ridiculous.

"Well if she can find out more than us about Jack perhaps she will let me know."

Jo laughed then too. "You don't think those flowers are off someone's grave, do you?"

She asked once she had stopped laughing. She reached out fingering the pretty flower arrangement that Stella was busy admiring.

The smile faded from Stella's face as she examined the flowers, "No, he wouldn't do that. Would he?" She checked Jo's expression hoping to find humour in what she was suggesting.

"Well if he's a ghost he can't exactly pop to the shops to buy them, can he?" Jo reasoned.

"Eew, I hadn't thought of that," Stella pulled a disgusted face and put the flowers on the table. "He wouldn't do that, it would be stealing," she reassured herself.

"Well he was a pirate before he came here wasn't he? That was why the revenue men were after him, and why he got shot in the shoulder," Jo pointed out. They both stared at the flowers with a morbid curiosity. Could they have come from one of the graves in the churchyard? Stella didn't want to believe he would give her someone else's flowers but Jo was right, he couldn't very well go to the shops and buy them himself, so where had they come from? Wherever it was, they were very pretty and they would need to be put in water. Stella found a vase and filled it with water, slotting the flowers inside and retying the ribbon around the vase. She wasn't going to tell Jo that she had last seen the ribbon adorning the pews at the church or she would be convinced he had stolen them from someone's grave. It was the thought that counted after all, and no one had ever given her flowers before.

The box of books that Sophie had bought were now stuffed out of the way in the corner of the kitchen. "I'll put the kettle on if you want to start up my laptop," Stella suggested.

Jo sat at the table and switched it on. She tapped in Google and then when it came up, she typed in Jacks name and the dates they had found previously when they had been trying to find where he lived. "What am I looking for?" she asked.

"I don't know, anything that might give us a clue as to whether they are the same person I suppose." Stella stood the steaming Disney mugs of tea on the table and sat down, pulling her chair up beside Jo's so they could both see the screen. Jo was scrolling down the list that had come up. Most of the headings were irrelevant to their search but half way down they both spotted one that looked promising. It was a link to an article from an old local newspaper. There had once been a history group in the village and they had done some research on some of the earliest settlers in the village. Jack Davenport had been one of the more interesting characters they had discovered and there was a small piece written about him.

It is believed that Jack Davenport was originally from Cornwall. He was engaged to be married to a young woman by the Name of Anne Trevallyan. When Jack became mixed up with a group of smugglers, Anne supposedly informed the revenue men about the illicit proceedings and one night they lay in wait for the smugglers to return to shore. Most of the men were captured but Jack managed to jump overboard and swim to shore a safe distance from the revenue men. He was spotted however running away and one of the revenue men shot at him, hitting him in the shoulder. Jack kept on running and later turned up in the village of Little Welborough where he used his ill-gotten gains to build a small cottage. The cottage was called Rose cottage. Jack never married or had any children and died at the age of thirty-four. No other relatives were known of.

"I don't suppose you know the name of the woman your Jack nearly married, do you?" Jo asked when they had finished reading the article.

Stella swallowed but didn't answer putting her head in her hands.

"Oh my God it was Anne, wasn't it?" When Stella nodded, Jo exclaimed, "I don't believe it. I think you're right, the Jack who you are seeing, who wrote you those letters and who has sent you flowers is a ghost. What are you going to do?"

That was a good question. What was she going to do? Now Sophie was suspicious of her she was bound to keep more of an eye on her, which would make seeing Jack more difficult, and then there was Katy. She had forgotten for a moment that Katy was coming to stay on Friday. The letter Jack had sent with the flowers asked her to meet him again on Sunday, she would have to try and think of an excuse to slip out to see him. What a mess.

Chapter Twenty One

Katy had given herself plenty of time for the drive to Stella's house in Little Welborough to allow for any holdups on the motorway. Luckily the roads had been clear and she had made it in good time. She turned off the motorway and followed Stella's instructions leading her to the turning that would take her into the village. She drove at a fairly moderate speed with the windows down to let in the fresh country air, with her favourite CD playing at full volume. A big green tractor was heading towards her along the narrow road, she had to slow right down and pull over to one side to let it pass. The farmer frowned at the noise that was coming from her car which she had to admit, seemed louder now that the wind wasn't rushing in through the windows, so she turned the music down a fraction.

The rest of the journey passed uneventfully and she was soon pulling up outside Stella's front gate. She checked her watch, it was too early for Stella to be home so taking her advice, she decided to walk back the way she had come to the café. There was a bit of a breeze so she grabbed her extra-long black cardigan and put it on. With her jet-black hair, green eyes and long burgundy red nails she looked like a modern-day witch, only prettier. The flamboyant nature of her clothes only helped to add to the illusion. Walking passed the school and then the post office, where she could see an older lady peering out the window, she eventually came to the café. The door jingled the little bell that rested on top of the frame as she entered, and a young woman with brown hair tied in a ponytail looked up. Katy, aware of the looks she was getting from the other customers strode defiantly over to the counter. Her rather striking clothes meant that she stood out like a sore thumb amongst the elderly customers and the mums with muslin cloths and babies slung over their shoulders.

"You must be Jo?" She said with a smile. Jo realising that this just had to be Stella's designer friend smiled back and held out her hand.

"Yes, and you have to be Katy! Stella said you might come in. What can I get you?"

"A strong coffee and one of those apple crumble cupcakes please".

They looked heavenly. Stella hadn't exaggerated when she had said that Jo's café made delicious cakes. Jo poured out the coffee and put the cupcake onto a plate. "So how long do you think you'll be staying?" She asked making conversation as Katy took the money from her purse to pay.

"I don't know, it depends on Stella, and what I decide to do about work I suppose".

Suddenly the confident air that she had come in with seemed to have deserted her and Jo immediately felt sorry for her. It would be awful to find out that the man you thought was in love with you was actually having an affair, and then to lose your job as well. That was harsh. Although technically Katy hadn't lost her job she had walked out on it. The fact that she had lost her home too really sucked.

The doorbell jangled again and Sophie rushed in, she appeared to be looking for someone. When she saw Katy stood at the counter talking to Jo she made her way straight over to them. Jo couldn't hide the smirk on her face. It was obvious that Grace had phoned Sophie to let her know about the 'visitor' who had entered the café, and now here was Sophie to find out who she was.

"I'll have a Latte thanks Jo," she said when Jo was about to ask her what she wanted.

Sophie turned to Katy who had moved to one side to allow Jo to serve her. "I don't think I've seen you here before have I?" she asked.

Stella had told Katy all about Grace and Sophie, so it wasn't hard to guess who the new arrival was. She was going to have a bit of fun making it hard work for Sophie to get the answers she wanted.

"No, I don't think you have," Katy replied and wandered over to a table and pulled out a notebook she had brought with her effectively discouraging any further conversation. She started making some rough sketches for an idea she had had on the journey. If Sophie wanted to pursue her questioning she would have to follow her. Sophie stayed at the counter while Jo made her Latte, watching Katy and wondering how best to start a conversation with the newcomer. Katy was quite tall with her high-heeled shoes on, and the original clothing, dark hair and green eyes made her seem quite formidable. Sophie didn't want to disappoint her mum by returning without finding anything out however, so she tried again to engage in conversation. She skilfully manoeuvred a chair at the next table so it was at a perfect angle to scrutinize her prey and to be able to chat.

"Are you passing through?" she ventured trying to make the question sound casual. Katy fixed her with an enigmatic stare before simply saying, "No," and returning to her sketching. Frustrated Sophie tried to discretely see what Katy was drawing but she had deliberately tilted the book at an angle so that it was impossible for Sophie to see without getting up and standing behind her.

Amused Jo could almost see the steam coming out of Sophie's ears as she struggled to get the answers she wanted. Not to be thwarted, Sophie tried a more direct question. "What are you doing here then?" she tried not to make it sound as rude as it actually was. "I'm drinking coffee like you," Katy smiled closing her book and putting it carefully back into her bag again out of sight.

"Oh well I meant..." Sophie hesitated as Katy raised an enquiring eyebrow. "well..." she looked to Jo for help but Jo was busy wiping down the counter top and trying not to laugh. "Are you visiting someone in the village? If you're lost I could probably help you to find them," Sophie offered helpfully, trying a different avenue of questioning.

"Thank you but I'm not lost I know exactly where I'm going," Katy unwrapped the paper case from the cupcake and began wiping some of the icing off with her finger and licking it before taking a bite out of the cake.

Sophie looked disgusted, no one ate cake like that in public. She was desperate to know who this exhibitionist was. Jo couldn't help a little chuckle from escaping as she watched Sophie struggling to find another way to find out what she wanted to know. Sophie was stumped; there was no way she could ask any more questions without sounding extremely nosy.

"My names Sophie by the way, my mother owns the village shop." She smiled her friendliest smile, hoping Katy would at least supply her with a name. When she didn't, merely replying with a, "nice to meet you," before taking another bite of her cake Sophie was forced to give up.

She stood abruptly to her feet and said to Jo, who was now watching the exchange with interest, "I'd better get to the school then to pick up my son".

She gave Katy one last look hoping that she might say something before she left, but when Katy remained stubbornly silent Sophie was forced to leave having not learnt anything, her half-drunk coffee still on the table. Jo gathered the cup up as the bell on the door pronounced Sophie's frustrated exit.

"That has to be a first," she told Katy who had now finished her cake. "Sophie left without finding out who you are, I'm seriously impressed."

Katy smiled, "Well to be fair, Stella did warn me what might happen so I was prepared".

Jo carried the cup back to the kitchen and stacked it in the dishwasher. When she came back to the counter Katy carried her own cup over to save Jo another journey. "I don't suppose you know of any jobs going for a costume designer, do you?"

Jo shook her head, "I'm afraid not but I'll keep my ears open and let you know if something comes up".

"Thanks." Katy checked her watch, "I guess if Sophie has gone to pick her son up from school that means that school has finished for the day. I might as well head over there to find Stella. Bye for now, it was nice meeting you".

"Bye," Jo replied. The doorbell jingled again and Katy was gone, her high-heeled shoes click clacking on the pavement as she went. Stella hadn't been joking when she had told her that her friend Katy was bound to cause a stir in the village. Grace and Sophie would be beside themselves with curiosity until they found out who she was.

Katy walked slowly to the school. It was partly to give the school children time to leave before she got there, and partly because her fancy shoes were making walking any faster difficult. They were meant for posing in really, not actually walking any distance. She opened the school gate and with her long black cardigan fluttering behind her, she headed across the playground, which was now empty apart from a group of mums gossiping near the gate while their children played chase. One of the mums was Sophie, she was stood beside the gates telling a small crowd of fellow book club members all about the mysterious lady in the café. She fell silent and they all watched as Katy strode passed them without sparing them a glance in what appeared to be a confident manner. She opened the school doors with a flourish and went inside leaving them looking on with speculation.

Yvonne was busy at her computer when Katy entered. She glanced up and took a double take before coming to the desk to ask if she could help. "Is there something I can do for you?"

"I'm a friend of Mrs Martin is there somewhere I could wait for her?" Katy asked.

"Well if you would like to sign in as a visitor I can take you to her in her classroom." Yvonne pushed the visitors' book forward and Katy wrote her name in her usual elaborate style, the time and date and the purpose for the visit, which read 'To see Mrs Martin'. When she had finished Yvonne pushed a button on her desk and the interior doors opened to allow Katy to enter. Once inside Katy waited for the door to Yvonne's office to open and Yvonne herself to appear ready to take Katy to Stella's classroom. At that moment Scott arrived with a file to be put away, "Ah Yvonne just who I wanted to see, could you put this in the filling cabinet for me?" Yvonne hesitated before taking the file.

"I was just about to take Miss Ferraz here to see Mrs Martin, if you're going back to your classroom perhaps you can show her where to go on the way?" Scott noticed Katy for the first time. She was stood to Yvonne's right and partially hidden by the year four's display of poetry. She tossed her black hair back over her shoulder and Scott felt his mouth go dry. 'Wow!' where had she come from? Katy stepped forward and held out her hand.

"You must be Mr Robertson? Nice to meet you." She felt a shock of awareness travel up her arm as Scott automatically shook her hand and smiled. He continued to stare at her in stunned silence, his brain a bit slow catching up with the shock of seeing an exceptionally attractive woman in the school foyer. It must be because it was Friday afternoon, it had been a long week. Unaware of Scott's lack of focus Yvonne left them to return to her office and put the file away, shutting the door behind her with a click. When Scott didn't make any attempt to move, Katy asked, "So are you going to take me to Mrs Martin or do I have to find her classroom myself?"

"Oh right, yes of course come this way," Scott mentally kicked himself for his stupidity. She was stunning. The impact of seeing her for the first time had hit him like a punch in the stomach but he didn't know who she was or why she wanted to see Stella. Unusually for him he couldn't think of anything to say witty or otherwise, so they walked in silence along the corridor. Katy had been as surprised as Scott by the attraction she had felt on meeting him. Sadly this was the man that Stella's mum had told her Stella was going out with. Of all the people she could have met and felt that jolt of pure physical attraction, why did it have to be him?

At the door to Stella's classroom Scott stopped, "this is it," he stepped aside to allow Katy to enter. He waited awkwardly, wanting to say something else but not quite sure what, before finally turning on his heels and leaving.

"Thank you," she called after his retreating back, a pang of new misery tightening her chest. Stella was her best friend, she couldn't start harbouring desires for her new boyfriend. Surely her life couldn't get any worse.

"Katy!" Stella cried seeing her stood in the doorway, "Come in".

Katy fixed a smile on her face that she hoped didn't show her inner feelings of guilt, and went in.

"I'm nearly finished, have you just arrived?"

"No, I got here quite early so I went to the café like you suggested. That Sophie you were telling me about came in and tried to find out who I was but I kept her guessing. It was quite funny you should have seen her." Katy and Stella both laughed.

"I bet she's fuming now," Stella put the last of her marking away and picked up her bag. "Shall we go? We can pick up a takeaway later, and I've got a bottle of wine at home so we can have a nice long chat".

* * * *

Stella unlocked her front door and stood back to allow Katy to go in first with her bags. "Do you want me to show you your room first or shall we have a drink?"

"Let's have a drink first," Katy said taking off her shoes with relief and carrying them into the kitchen behind Stella. She sat at the kitchen table while Stella filled the kettle.

"So," Stella asked, "what happened to make you quit your job?"

Katy sighed, "It's a long story but in short..." she paused collecting her thoughts, "we got a new director who didn't appreciate my talents. Everything I did was wrong according to Frank, and what with finding out Alex had been up to no good behind my back, I just flipped one day and told Frank what I thought of him. Needless to say, it would have been impossible for me to carry on working with him, so I left." Katy hung her head, she wasn't proud of the way she had spoken to Frank but he had pushed her too far.

Stella placed the mugs of tea on the table and sat down. "So, what happens now?" she had never seen her feisty friend so down.

Katy shrugged, "I'll look for another job I suppose, and somewhere to live. I just need a bit of space to get my head together while I decide whether it's time for a change career wise".

"Well your welcome to stay here for as long as you want to," Stella offered, then remembering her assignation with Jack added casually, "The only thing is, I've started seeing someone so I might have to leave you on your own some evenings, I hope you don't mind? I'm seeing him on Sunday actually".

Katy felt a stab of jealousy at the thought of Stella going out with Scott but hurried to reassure her, "Of course I don't mind. I'll find something to do, you don't have to worry about me".

She hoped her feelings were just the result of all her emotional turmoil, because she didn't want to add jealousy of her friends' love life and the guilt it would cause her to her string of bad luck. If Stella was keen on Scott then she would have to combat her own feelings that had sprung up out of nowhere for him. After all she had only just met him, it should be easy to put him out of her mind.

And besides, Stella deserved some happiness after what Gary had put her through. She wondered if Stella knew that Gary was planning to get married again but chose not to ask her about it yet. She had only just arrived and had already developed a rather unfortunate attraction to Stella's boyfriend, the last thing she wanted to do was to cause her any upset by telling her about Gary's plans if she didn't already know about them, she wasn't even sure if it was true or who the unlucky lady was.

"Why do you think you want to change your career?" Stella was confused; Katy had always loved her job.

Katy thought back over the last few weeks and considered her answer carefully before she replied. "I love being able to design and make costumes but I think I want to have a bit more scope. Expand my horizons a bit. I've been thinking about starting up my own business." She watched carefully to gauge Stella's reaction to her statement.

"That sounds exciting. Will you still make costumes or were you thinking of designing clothes? You're very good at making eye catching clothes, the sort you don't see in the usual high street shops," Katy smiled at Stella's description of her choice of clothes. She had always wanted to be different, to stand out, so she had made her own clothes to wear. She supposed it came from being part of a big family. If you wanted to be noticed you had to be loud, bad or different, sometimes all three to get any attention.

"I was thinking I might make costumes for parties, and do my own range of clothes as a sideline. What do you think?"

"It sounds like a great idea," Stella encouraged "Are you going to sell on line or try and get a stall at a market or something? I would imagine a shop would be too expensive".

"I haven't got that far yet, it was just an idea I came up with on the way here," Katy grabbed her bag and took out the sketchbook she had been drawing in earlier in the café.

"I've made a few quick sketches of clothes I could make fairly cheaply that are unusual, but I think might sell. Take a look, what do you think?" she handed the sketchbook to Stella who studied the designs closely. She was impressed. Katy had toned down her slightly elaborate style to come up with something that was different but wearable.

"These are good. You should definitely go for it."

Katy took the sketchbook back looking at them again herself with a critical eye. It was good to hear Stella's opinion. She knew that she would always tell her the truth and Frank had made her start to doubt her abilities as a designer. If Stella thought they were good enough, then maybe she should go through with her idea. She could feel a glimmer of hope and excitement filling her deflated ego. Now all she had to do was come up with a business plan and get started. The bubble of excitement that had begun to build suddenly popped. There was one snag. She had nowhere to live now that she had split up with Alex. It was his name on the rental contract to the flat. She would have to find somewhere to live and that wasn't going to be easy without a job to pay the bills.

When Stella saw the light that had appeared in Katy's eyes starting to fade she was concerned. "What's up you look like you found a penny and lost a pound?"

"How am I going to start up a new business with nowhere to live and no way of paying my bills? I mean

I've got some money saved up but it won't last me long will it?"

"You can stay here until you get on your feet, and work from home," Stella offered.

"Are you sure? I don't want you to think that that's why I'm telling you this, or to feel obliged to have me," Katy worried.

"Of course I don't mind; you're my friend I want to help. Besides if I know you, you'll be making a fortune before long and be able to support yourself again."

Katy felt her heart swell at Stella's confidence in her abilities, but she still had her doubts. "But what if it doesn't work? You could be stuck with me for quite a while."

"If that happens then it does, but I have every faith in you. Let's get those chips now and we can have some wine and drink a toast to your new venture". Stella and Katy spent the rest of Friday evening catching up on other news and discussing Katy's new business. Stella had deliberately avoided the subject of her relationship with Jack as it was all too new, and she was still coming to terms with the fact that she had probably fallen in love with a ghost herself. Katy would think she had gone completely mad if she told her.

Chapter Twenty Two

Stella decided to invite Jo for lunch on Saturday morning after her appointment with the reflexologist, she thought it would give her chance to get to know Katy as she was going to be staying for a while. She hoped that they would become friends too. When she knocked on Jo's door to ask her, she had also warned her not to say anything about Jack when she came.

"I'm not ready to tell anyone else about him yet," she had explained. "And Katy has just broken up with her boyfriend so it would be unfair to go on about how lovely he is anyway."

When Stella got back Katy was having a rummage through the box of books Sophie had bought round earlier in the week. "Do you mind if I read one of your books? It'll give me something to do when you're out, other than working on my business plan of course."

"No, I don't mind," Stella replied then seeing which books Katy was talking about added, "those books are for the school fete though, they're not mine. But I'm sure it won't hurt if you read them first, after all they have been read once already".

"Great!" Katy picked up a thick hardback book with the authors picture in black and white on the back. "This is the latest Nathaniel Morgan!" Katy enthused, "I can't wait to read it, if you're sure it's okay?" she checked with Stella before hurrying upstairs to put the book beside her bed for later.

Stella was too busy getting the ingredients out for lunch to look at the book Katy had chosen. There were so many in the box if everyone was as generous the book sale would do well. Nicole would probably need her help more than Scott would with his hook a duck stall. She was surprised that he hadn't said anything when he had left Katy at her classroom door. It wasn't like him. She hoped she hadn't offended him in some way. He had taken it very well when she had told him that she wasn't interested in a relationship. She hoped that Sophie hadn't said anything about the poetic note from Jack to him when she had picked up Danny from school. He might feel hurt that she had turned him down only to find out that she was seeing someone else so soon afterwards. She bit her lip, perhaps she would get chance to talk to him on Monday and see what was wrong. She liked Scott as a friend and didn't want to think that she might have upset him.

* * * *

Jo was sat in the reflexologist's waiting room. Luckily Sebastian had not needed the car this week and she had managed to organise the work rota so she was off again, but she knew she wouldn't be able to keep having Saturdays off. It wouldn't be fair on the other staff. She would ask if she could have an appointment on a different day next week. If she made it for one evening she was sure Stella would give her a lift. A Friday would probably be a good day to choose. Stella might be able to take her straight from work and then they wouldn't have to explain where they were going to Katy. Jo sat nervously tapping her feet on the hard-wooden floor. She wasn't nervous about what the reflexologist was going to do anymore, she really quite enjoyed that part, it was the reason for her visits, and the fact that she hadn't told Sebastian that made her feel uncomfortable. She didn't like keeping secrets from him but he might not believe it could work, and then she would feel that she would have to stop coming.

She needed this to work. If it did she could be pregnant by Christmas and they wouldn't have to suffer the embarrassment of going to a doctor for invasive tests. The thought of being prodded and poked about to see which one of them had the problem was very off putting. She had heard other couples had fallen out when doctors had found out that one or the other was infertile, blaming themselves and becoming bitter. Then it sometimes caused a wedge between them because they both felt guilty about wanting to have children and not being able to. Jo loved Sebastian, she didn't want to risk that happening to them. If this didn't work she would have to try and come to terms with the idea of not being a mum. It was better than losing Sebastian.

At that moment Gabriella Clarke appeared in the doorway, "I'm ready for you now Mrs Loxley," she smiled. Jo stood up and followed her up the wide staircase again and into her treatment room. At least she knew what to expect now and they didn't have to go through her medical history again. Jo sat in the chair while Gabriella bathed her feet in warm water. Then she patted her feet dry and began manipulating the toes. Jo allowed herself to relax and enjoy the sensation, putting all thought of babies out of her mind. The next thing she knew, Gabriella was gently shaking her awake.

"I'll give you some time to get yourself reoriented as you come back to the present," she was saying in a quiet voice and placed a glass of water on a little table by Jo's right hand. "Take your time there's no rush."

Gabriella sat at her desk tapping some information into the computer. Jo wiped her hands over her face only to discover that it was wet.

Seeing her look of confusion Gabriella said, "You cried a little bit, during your sleep but don't worry it's all perfectly natural. I must have explained that to you on your first visit."

When Jo nodded she went back to her typing. Jo sat up slowly feeling very relaxed and drank the water. When she was ready she stood up, thanked Gabriella and went downstairs to make another appointment.

Jo stopped at the village shop on the way home to pick up a newspaper for Sebastian and some chocolates to share with Stella and Katy. She could almost feel the curiosity radiating from Grace who was keen to ask her about the visitor to the café.

"I don't suppose that lady told you why she was going to the School on Friday did she? You know the one with long dark hair, she was in the café? Only Sophie told me that was where she went after she left your place. Is she a celebrity that they are trying to get to open the school fete do you know?"

"I'm pretty sure she's not a celebrity, but I'll ask her the next time I see her if you like?"

"Ooh do you know where she's staying then?" Grace leant forward resting her folded arms on the counter ready for a good gossip. "Old Greg Thomas said he saw her arriving in a sporty looking car with music blasting loudly out the speakers, and frightening the horses in the field. I wondered if she was some kind of pop musician, she looked the sort that might be."

"Really? Well I'll definitely ask when I see her then, just to be sure," Jo picked up the paper and the chocolates and left before Grace could ask her anything else.

She should have realised that she would be interrogated if she went into the shop, but the reflexology session had made her feel so relaxed that it had put everything else out of her mind.

* * * *

Stella, Jo and Katy had spent an enjoyable afternoon chatting, painting their nails and demolishing the chocolates that Jo had brought. Grace and Sophie had suffered as the butt of several jokes but as they were unable to hear no harm was done. They had discussed the possibility of Katy's new business between them and Katy now felt much more confident about the prospect. Listening to Stella and Jo talking enthusiastically about the costumes and her clothes designs had made her feel that there might just be a future for her business after all.

Now it was Sunday evening and Stella was getting ready for her date. Katy was sat on Stella's bed flicking through a magazine as they chatted.

"I hope he's taking you somewhere nice?".

Stella felt her cheeks burning and she dived into her wardrobe to hunt for a pair of shoes to go with her lilac skirt and white top. When Stella didn't reply, Katy sat up straighter and looked at her more closely. She suspected that Stella had planned to entertain him in her house, and had changed her plans because of her, but was too polite to say.

"Is he picking you up here because if he is I can get out the way?" She made the offer sound as if it was for Stella's benefit, but really she didn't want to see the two of them together until she had got her reaction to Scott under control. She felt uncomfortable with the prospect of having to sit and watch them cuddling on the sofa.

Perhaps staying with Stella wasn't such a good idea after all. The trouble was she didn't have anywhere else to go and how would she explain her reasons for leaving to Stella. She frowned as she thought through the alternatives; she would just have to stay out of their way. She was sure that the attraction would eventually fade. Most of the men she had been romantically interested in had soon lost their shine, why should Scott be any different. 'Because' a little voice in her head argued back 'you've never had that reaction to a man before'. She shut the magazine up and put it back on the bedside table where she had found it. "I can always go out for a walk or to the pub if that's easier for you?" She offered, feeling bad about dumping herself on her friend and messing up her life.

"NO!" Stella exclaimed. "No it's okay I'm meeting him at his um... Well I'm meeting him in the... um, don't worry we were going out anyway, we haven't changed our plans because of you if that's what you're worried about?"

"As long as you're sure I'm not in the way? You must tell me if you want the house to yourselves ever, promise?"

"Definitely, I promise. But I'm sure that won't be a problem, he has his own..." Stella struggled for a way to describe where Jack stayed, she couldn't say lived because he didn't live. The thought of it made her feel quite faint. He was a ghost and she still hadn't quite managed to come to terms with the idea. She wanted to have a happy ever after life with Jack but the chances of that being possible would make her want to cry if she thought about it too much. There could be no real future for them, no family life, just stolen moments in a churchyard, and what would happen in winter? She wouldn't be able to have meals with him outside then. The more she thought about it the more impractical the scenario became. The trouble was, she was in love with him and she didn't want to give him up. She wasn't sure how it would work but she was going to have to try and find a way.

Locating the shoes she wanted at last, she pulled them on and made her way downstairs with Katy trailing behind like a lost puppy. She seemed very quiet all of a sudden.

"Are you sure you're going to be alright?" she asked. "You seem a bit subdued."

Although Stella wanted to be there for her friend, her time with Jack was precious to her and she was relieved when Katy faked a yawn, "Actually I'm quite tired. The last week has been draining," she explained. The yawn may have been fake, but what Katy had told Stella was most definitely true. Leaving Alex, quitting her job and moving out of the flat had all been very draining emotionally. Most of her stuff was being stored in her grandmothers small flat in Ealing, and for the time being at least that was where it would have to stay.

Satisfied that Katy would be okay without her, Stella set off for her rendezvous with Jack. She crossed over the end of her road and passed the far end of the park, intending to head in the direction of the church. As she got closer to the corner she became aware of footsteps getting closer and closer, and the familiar voices of Sophie and Grace chatting together. If she carried on in the direction she was going she would have to pass them and they would want to stop and chat. That would lead on to them questioning her on where she was going and heaven forbid they might even follow her. Looking desperately around for somewhere to hide, Stella turned and headed quickly back towards the entrance to the park. Her heart was hammering madly with panic; there was no way she could get to the gate in time. Frantically trying to come up with an excuse for where she was going in case she got caught, Stella shot through the hedge. A prickly bush caught on her sleeve as she went and she spent several valuable minutes trying to rescue it before she finally stood breathing hard on the other side of the bush. Once they had passed she would be able to continue on her way. A couple of children were playing nearby and they glanced up when they realised she had come through the hedge and gave her bewildered looks. Luckily, they were too old to go to the village primary school so they didn't know who she was. She rummaged in her bag for her phone to give her something to do so she wasn't just stood looking like a lemon in the playing field.

As her hand touched the phone she heard Danny begging to be allowed to play in the park. Stella's heart sank, how much worse could this possibly get She wondered as a dog ran over and started sniffing her feet.

"Shoo," she whispered, not wanting to be heard by either Grace or Sophie. She couldn't let them find her hiding. The dog, not understanding her need for discretion wagged his tail at her and began to bark. "Shoo," she whispered again gesturing with her hand for the dog to go. Unfortunately, he seemed to think she was about to throw something for him and began barking even louder ready for a game. All the time she could hear Danny trying to persuade Sophie to allow him some time in the park before dinner and Stella could feel herself breaking into a cold sweat.

"Go on mum just for a little while. Mr Robertson says exercise is good for you," he pleaded. Stella realised she couldn't afford to wait and see if he succeeded, she would have to find another place to hide or move on. She checked her watch; 'damn' she was going to be late if she didn't hurry. There was only one thing for it, she would have to walk to the church the long way around going passed the shops. At least she knew that Grace and Sophie wouldn't be there to see where she went. With her decision made she began to hurry along beside the hedge with the dog now running along beside her. She was nearly at the gate where she could get back onto the path when the dog's owner finally called him reluctantly away. She would have to be quick she realised, or she would still end up getting caught leaving the park. At least it would look like she had been in there for some exercise; she was probably red in the face from running. Although on second thoughts her clothes didn't look like something you would wear for exercising in realistically.

If they did bump into her at the gate she would have to come up with something better than that. Clutching her bag tightly to her chest she cautiously approached the gate. 'Please let me get there before they do,' she prayed over and over as she went. At the gate she quickly checked that the trio were not yet in sight, then she hurried out of the park and half walked and half ran along the path to get as far out of sight as possible. Every few steps she took she checked behind her to see if they had seen her. When she at last turned the corner without being spotted she began to slow down. She had a stitch in her side and her heart was still pounding hard due to her hurried exit from the park and the anxiety. It would take longer to reach the church going this way so she would have to keep the pace up for a while longer. As she hurried passed the fish and chip shop someone called out to her.

"Mrs Martin," it was Henry's mum and she was holding his hand as she crossed over the road to speak to Stella. "I've been meaning to see you to say thank you for helping Henry. His dad and I had a long chat after I spoke to you and he's been taking him into school again. It did us both good to talk things through properly, and although we're taking things slowly we might even get back together."

"That's great news, I'm really pleased for you," Stella was genuinely pleased, for Henry's sake more than anything else. She just hoped that if they did get back together it would work out this time, and that whatever happened Henry was not allowed to feel that it was his fault. She had noticed that Henry's dad had been taking him into school and that Henry had been a lot happier lately. Henry and his mum said goodbye and Stella was able to set off again. She hoped there wouldn't be any more interruptions. She still had quite a way to walk and she was already late.

By the time she reached the gate into the churchyard she was very hot and slightly out of breath. She pushed the gate open and ran along by the side of the church, stopping to catch her breath at the far corner. She couldn't see Jack when she first stepped into the space behind the church and thought that he had given up on her coming. Sadly, she leaned her back against the uneven stone of the church and closed her eyes as the pain of the stitch in her side, and the disappointment washed over her. If only Sophie and Grace had not been out for a walk she would have been there on time. She felt as if she were going to cry, all the feelings of expectation she had built up for the evening and he hadn't waited. Then as she opened her eyes again a figure emerged out of the shadows cast by the church steeple.

"Jack!" Stella cried rushing forward.

"I thought I had missed you".

He held her in his arms "I thought you weren't coming," he whispered in her ear then as he released his grip and their eyes met she felt a shiver of desire before his head slowly bent and he kissed her passionately on the lips.

It was a long kiss that left Stella feeling all warm and happy inside. She was aware of the strength of his muscles hidden beneath his shirt and the warmth of his skin as she rested her head against his chest. The blood was still thrumming through her veins. There was no way she would ever be able to give him up, he may be a ghost but he made her feel more alive than she had ever felt in her life.

Chapter Twenty Three

When Stella went out, Katy tried not to think about the fact that she was on her way to meet Scott, but the image of his face and the memory of the jolt of desire she herself had felt when she saw him was hard to shake. She needed a distraction, picking up her sketchbook from where she had left it beside the sofa, she tried making some sketches of clothing designs that she thought might sell. Five minutes later she screwed up what she had drawn into a ball when she realised that instead of designs, it had become a picture of Scott; what an awful friend she must be, harbouring secret fantasies about her friend's boyfriend. Annoyed with herself, she took the screwed-up paper and threw it in the bin. She decided she would read the book she had found in the box earlier. At least she would have to concentrate on the words on the page and not on her own thoughts. There was no point torturing herself over someone she had only met once.

She had left the book in the bedroom she was using so she climbed the stairs and settled herself on the bed. As she looked around the room she noticed that it was already beginning to be taken over by her possessions. She had a habit of spreading her things around wherever she went. Her long cardigan was hanging on the back of the door and the jeans she had worn the day before were supposed to be on the chair but were falling off. Her make-up was spread out on the chest of drawers and a couple of sketchbooks were lying open on the floor along with some material samples.

Stella's house was usually tidy but what you might describe as lived in. She hung coats on the back of chairs until she was ready to put them away, and had a pile of ironing sat waiting to be done in a basket in the passage upstairs. She wasn't obsessively neat like Gary had been, she was normal, that had been how it was prior to Katy's arrival. Katy was doing her best to contain her mess to the bedroom but it was only a matter of time before it would spill into the rooms downstairs and the bathroom. She didn't mean to be so messy, it just sort of happened.

It wouldn't be so bad if she had a room she could use as a studio because most of her mess was work related. She liked to spread out. Sometimes she would start a sketch or a job and get distracted, leaving whatever she had started out doing to be finished later. Or she would open a letter and get an idea that she really had to jot down so she didn't forget, and she would leave the letter on a side or in a chair, wherever she had last been. It would then stay there until she needed it again. None of it was dirty mess she consoled herself, just clutter.

She found the book under her nightdress. Having read nearly all of Nathaniel Morgan's books and enjoyed them, she couldn't wait to start reading. Two had been made into blockbuster films which she had been to see as soon as they had been released. It was lucky that she had found the book in the box before Stella took it into the school. His books were full of adventure with a main character who would make any woman swoon. It was a shame that Stella had never really had time to read his books; she would probably have enjoyed them if she gave them a chance. One of the films had come out in the cinema while Stella had stayed with Katy after her marriage to Gary had ended. Katy had tried to persuade her to join the group of friends when they had gone to see it, but Stella hadn't felt like socialising at the time so she had missed it. Stella seemed so much happier now, which was another reason why Katy had to put Scott out of her mind. If he was the reason for Stella's newfound happiness then she wasn't going to do anything to jeopardise it for her. Opening the book at the first page she began to read. She was soon lost in the adventure that was unfolding and the time passed quickly.

Further along Lovedon Lane Tim and Rory had just sat down to eat there Sunday dinner. It had been a quiet weekend and a bit strained as both Tim and Rory were trying extra hard not to upset each other. Rory was still feeling hurt that his parents had not tried to contact him since the fateful phone call when he had told them about his relationship with Tim. Tim was feeling guilty because Rory had only made the phone call because he had insisted that he should, and because he was worried that he had made the situation worse by trying to sort it out – although Rory didn't know about the last bit, which also had the effect of making Tim feel guilty for keeping secrets. It was a bit like walking on eggshells, the happy fun atmosphere that always filled their home was well hidden under a blanket of gloom.

On the surface everything seemed fine, they had still done their weekly shopping together, and gone to the darts match in the local pub as usual, but it all felt a bit flat. Rory had held on to the slim hope that once his parents got used to the idea they would get in touch with him, but so far it hadn't happened. Tim had been trying hard to cheer Rory up and he appreciated his efforts although he wasn't sure that he had shown that he was that grateful. Over the last few days he had begun to think that perhaps the time had come to let the hope go. To get on with his life before he spoiled what he had.

They were in the middle of eating their dinner, both lost in thought when the phone rang. Several people had rung during the week to accept their invites to the party or to politely decline, and Rory had given up expecting it to be his parents. They left the call for the answer phone to pick up as they didn't want the food to get cold. They could always ring whoever it was back when they had finished eating. After three rings the message he had recorded with Tim kicked in, "Hello we're doing something more interesting right now, please leave us a message and we'll get back to you when we can". There was a pause and then a high-pitched beep to signal that the caller should leave their message. Both Tim and Rory had stopped eating and were listening to see who was calling. "Rory… it's me. I'll call back another time".

It was Rory's mother's voice sounding tired and hesitant. As soon as he realised who was on the phone he pushed back his chair making it scrape loudly on the floor and rushed over to the phone. He scooped the handset off its stand and with his heart thumping said quickly "Mum!" but she had already put the phone down and all he could hear was the dialling tone. Tim was stood behind him waiting to see what Rory's mum had phoned for. His heart was racing madly in case she told Rory about the conversation he had had with her, or the things she had said before he had a chance to tell him himself. He hadn't wanted to cause him any further upset, but now Tim wondered whether he should come clean and tell him. If Rory heard about the phone call from his mother he might be cross that Tim hadn't said anything. On the other hand, it might make him start to think that his mother was right to say that it was all Tim's fault. Rory put the phone back on the stand but stayed staring at it as if he thought he could make her ring back by his own will power. What had she wanted to say? Tim wondered.

The meal they had been sharing was now forgotten. Tim put his hand on Rory's shoulder to offer his support and comfort but Rory remained motionless. It felt like a giant wedge had been pushed between them. If only they could rewind time and leave things as they had been. They would be busy planning their party full of enthusiasm; instead it had become the elephant in the room. It was the whole reason for coming clean and telling Rory's parents and it had spoiled what they had. Rory was often quiet now and didn't want to discuss the party, which meant that Tim was organising the whole thing himself. It was supposed to be their engagement party. A chance for them to show everyone how committed they were to each other, and to let everyone know that they were going to have a civil ceremony later in the year. They had been so excited when they had first begun the proceedings but it had all turned a bit sour because of Rory's parents.

Rory put his hand on Tim's where it was still resting on his shoulder. Despite what Tim thought none of this was his fault. Rory knew he would have had to tell his parents before the civil ceremony. If he hadn't told them when he did, he would only have been postponing the inevitable. The trouble was he couldn't bear to see the look of guilt on Tim's face every time the party was mentioned, so he had stopped talking about it. Tim had taken on the responsibility of organising the drink and the guests, even the food which Rory usually did. It was time for him to snap out of his self-imposed misery and take his life back before it pushed Tim away. Turning to face Tim he smiled weakly, "I'm okay. They will either come around to the idea or they won't. I don't want to put my life on hold any longer. Let's get on with making the plans for the party. We'll be happy with or without them".

Tim gave Rory a big hug. He hoped Rory's parents would learn to accept their relationship for Rory's sake, but he would help him through it no matter what. He loved Rory and he was so relieved that Rory wanted to be involved with the plans again. Maybe life would get back to normal now. The question was, should he tell Rory about the phone call he had made to Rory's mum and risk pushing him back into a depression or leave things as they were?

* * * *

Katy had nearly finished reading chapter three of the book when her mobile phone beeped alerting her to a text message. Without putting the book down, she manoeuvred herself sideways so she could grab the phone from the bottom of the bed where she had dropped it earlier. It was from Alex, curious about why he had decided to get in touch she read the brief message, *'I miss you, come back. I made a mistake forgive me,'* and he had added a sad face emoji. Katy gasped with shock the nerve of the man; he had got to be kidding. No way was she going back after what he had done to her. The humiliation of it, even Frank had known about Alex's affair with one of the dancers.

No wonder Alex had told her that Frank wasn't so bad when she had been having a moan about him. He was probably frightened that Frank would tell her what was happening, but he hadn't had he. She had found out for herself. She had been suspicious of him for a few weeks, as his behaviour had changed. It was funny really, but the thing that had convinced her in the end that something was wrong, was that he was being too nice. He had started complimenting her on her cooking, which was very good she had to admit, but Alex had never appreciated it before. One day he had even bought her flowers, Alex was never that nice. That was when she knew for certain that he was up to something and had started to snoop.

One day when he had told her that he was going to work early as Frank had been complaining about the lighting again, she had followed him. She didn't leave straight away; she gave him a bit of a head start and then set off. The streets had been busy so it was easy for her to follow him unseen, keeping a discreet distance behind. When he had actually gone into the theatre she had thought that perhaps she had got it all wrong. That perhaps he was going in to work early as he had said, and she had begun to feel guilty for doubting him. Then when she had looked for him in the lighting gallery and he wasn't there she had gone in search of Frank and Found Alex with Crystal.

Crystal was one of the dancers in the chorus but it definitely wasn't dance moves she was showing him. The look of shock on their faces when Katy walked in had been priceless. Alex had quickly pushed Crystal roughly away and used that old line, "it's not what you think". She wasn't stupid, of course it was what she thought and she wasn't going to put up with it. Alex wasn't worth it. The relationship hadn't been unhappy but it hadn't been wonderful either. The excitement had gone and it had become comfortable but not necessarily in a good way. Alex had begun to take her for granted. The funny thing was that she hadn't really noticed until it had all gone wrong. Finding him with Crystal had probably been the best thing for both of them as it had forced her to face the fact that she wasn't in love with him anymore.

She hadn't shouted or cried she had just walked out, back to the flat they shared and packed some of her things and left. It hadn't really hit her until she was sat in her car wondering where to go. She was more upset at leaving the flat than she was about leaving Alex. She drove to the only place she knew she would be welcome at such short notice that was still within easy reach of her job, her grandmothers flat in Ealing. It wasn't ideal as it only had one bedroom but she knew her grandmother would take her in without asking too many questions.

As the reality of the situation had begun to sink in she could feel the emotion well up inside. Alex had chosen someone else over her and that hurt. What was so wrong with her that he had needed to look elsewhere? Not only that, she could tell by the looks on peoples' faces that they had all known about it and pitied her. Her grandmother had been very understanding when she had turned up and so she had stayed with her temporarily until she could find somewhere else.

The commute to work took her longer than she wanted and sleeping on the sofa left her with a stiff neck. What with having to face Crystal draping herself over Alex at every opportunity as well, it wasn't surprising one day that she had lost her temper. Frank had been complaining about her designs again and she had finally had enough of it all and told him exactly what she had thought about him and his job, quitting on the spot. She had left in a hurry and had found herself crying in Cadogan Square Gardens. It was just after that that she had phoned Stella and asked if she could visit.

Katy deleted the text message and curled up into a ball on the bed. What a mess she had made of everything. No home, no job and here she was sat in her friend's house felling guilty for her reaction to her friend's new boyfriend. What a disaster. Still the last bit was only a problem if she allowed it to be one, and she vowed that it wouldn't be. Okay she couldn't help the way she felt, but she didn't have to do anything about it, did she? There was no way she was going to hurt Stella and certainly not over a man.

Chapter Twenty Four

It wasn't late when Stella got back. At only nine thirty-five it was just beginning to get dark. Katy was surprised when she heard the key in the lock, and assumed that Scott had returned with Stella, which made her wish she had stayed in the bedroom. After Alex had disturbed her she had ventured down stairs for a drink and had ended up in the lounge. She had assumed she would be safe for hours yet. When Stella walked into the lounge on her own and plonked herself down in the armchair, Katy wondered what had happened. She tried to ignore the little flare of hope that had lodged itself in her chest at the thought that maybe they had discovered that they weren't right for each other. It made her feel guilty again because that would mean Stella would be upset, or maybe she wouldn't. She didn't look upset.

Realising there was only one way to find out, she took the bull by the horns and asked, "How was your evening?"

She hoped that she sounded natural, not too eager to find out if they had decided that the relationship wasn't going anywhere. Not that she really hoped it hadn't gone well but she had to admit that she wouldn't be disappointed either. But only if Stella was okay with it, Stella was her friend after all, if it had been a mutual decision obviously. She wasn't a complete cow.

"I thought when you came back early that you had brought Scott back with you?"

Stella looked confused by the question. "Why would I bring Scott back?"

"Well... just thought..." Katy frowned did Stella know how she felt about him? Surely not. Changing the subject quickly she asked, "So, where did you go, somewhere nice?" That seemed like a safe enough question.

Stella looked uncomfortable for a moment, "We stayed at his..." she left the sentence unfinished. Jacks what? She couldn't say grave, could she? That would sound ghoulish. If she told Katy they had spent the evening in the graveyard she would think that it was a bit odd, and then she would have to try and explain why.

"So, did he drive you back then?" Katy asked unable to stop herself from trying to find out if Scott lived nearby.

"No, I walked". Stella thought back over the evening, and the drama it had been to get there without being interrogated by Grace or Sophie.

"I think I might drive myself there next time though." She began to laugh, it seemed funny now that it was all over, her hiding in the bushes to avoid Sophie.

"What's funny?" Katy asked. Stella told her about Sophie and how she had tried to give her the slip, which made Katy laugh too. At that moment Katy's phone beeped again. When she didn't pick it up to see who it was Stella guessed that Alex had been trying to get in touch with her.

"Is that from Alex?"

Katy glanced reluctantly at the phone and sighed. "He sent me a text earlier saying that he wants me back, and that it was all a big mistake".

"How do you feel about that?" Stella felt sorry for Katy.

Although she came across as very confident Stella knew her better, and knew that it was all a front.

Her flamboyant clothes were her armour as well as her passion for individuality. Katy had come from a large family and Stella knew that she had struggled to get the attention that she needed as a child. Often being overlooked because she was in the middle and didn't cause any real problems, unlike her siblings. Stella was sure that, that was why she had settled for Alex. Alex was ten years older than Katy and had been the first person to show her any real attention. When she had started working at the theatre her striking looks, a mixture of Spanish and English, had immediately caught his attention. He had been quick to sweep her off of her feet while she was still new to her job and unsure of herself. He had taken her under his wing and made her feel special.

The fact that he had worked there for some years and had plenty of experience was reassuring to an impressionable Katy. Katy was ambitious though, and good at what she did as well as being a hard worker. Feisty from years of defending herself from her siblings she had never backed down from a challenge, especially when it was for something she had wanted. She had soon gained the respect of her fellow designers and Stella suspected that Alex was jealous of her growing popularity. He had probably needed to boost his own ego and Crystal had been only too willing. Katy was definitely better off without him, she hoped he wouldn't use emotional blackmail to get her to go back to him. She deserved better.

"I told him it was over and I'm never coming back and since then he has been sending text messages telling me he never loved me anyway, and that I'm a bitch," Katy told her at last, trying to be blasé about it but not quite managing it. Stella was shocked that he had sunk to that level. At least she had never had to go through that with Gary. "How can he say that when he's the one who had an affair? He just wants to hurt you because he can't have what he wants. Ignore him, you can do better than him,"

Stella rushed over to the sofa and gave Katy a hug. She could see that she was trying so hard not to cry.

"I'm so glad I left the bastard, he can rot in hell," Katy said vehemently. "I know I'm better off without him. Now I look back I realise I wasn't really in love with him and maybe he knew that too and that was why he did what he did, but he could have told me. It would have been better than him cheating on me. It still hurts that he did that to me, why can't I find someone nice?"

"Oh Katy you will, believe me. I felt like you when Gary and I split up and I found out he was going to marry Helen."

"Helen!" Katy exclaimed, "You must be joking".

"No, he sent me a letter telling me about her, he's even invited me to their wedding."

The shock of hearing about Gary and Helen seemed to have the effect of bringing Katy out of her misery.

"Are you going to go?" Katy asked stunned.

"I don't know I haven't decided yet. Can you imagine Helen's face if I did? I'm not even sure she knows he's invited me." Stella began to laugh along with Katy. "That's how I met Jack," Stella confessed turning slightly red. She didn't want to say too much about Jack, but if Katy was going to live with her for a while she would have to know his name at least, in case he sent her any notes while she was out.

"Jack? Who is Jack? I thought you were seeing Scott, that teacher from the school."

"Whatever made you think I was seeing Scott?"

"Your mum told me," Katy explained, a glimmer of hope beginning to take seed. If Stella wasn't seeing Scott then she didn't have to feel guilty about fancying him herself. Life wasn't so bad after all, and a bit of flirtation would certainly help her get over Alex's infidelity.

"Ah well it's a long story. I sort of let her think that by accident and I don't want her to know about Jack yet, so don't say anything to her, will you?"

"Of course not, but who is Jack? You can tell me."

Katy watched as Stella began to fiddle with the hem of her skirt. She was wondering what she could say without telling Katy that he was a ghost. Katy was curious why Stella was looking uncomfortable about telling her about Jack.

"Oh my god he's not married is he? You have to end it if he is or you'll get hurt Stella. Not to mention the hurt you'll cause his wife if she finds out. It's horrible when someone does that to you and I would know."

Stella went bright red. She had thought he was married herself to begin with, that was until she had discovered that he was a ghost. "It's okay he's not married. I wouldn't do that to someone."

But could she really say that with conviction. What would she have done, feeling like she did about Jack, if that had been his secret? She liked to think that she would have ended it and she was ninety-five percent sure that she would, but there was a little part of her that wasn't convinced that she could. Of course she would, she chided herself. It would have hurt much more than leaving Gary but she would have done it, wouldn't she?

"I was upset when Gary sent me the letter telling me that he was marrying Helen and I went out for a walk," Stella explained. "While I was out I met Jack and we ended up talking. He made me see that it didn't really matter. I bumped into him again after that and we've been seeing each other ever since, but it's... well it's still new and I don't want anyone to know about us yet until I'm ready."

Katy thought the whole secrecy thing was a bit odd, but if that was how Stella wanted to keep it, then it was up to her. Stella braced herself for Katy to question her more about Jack and was surprised when she changed the subject.

"So, if you're not going out with Scott does that mean he's single?"

"Yes, he is. Why do you like him?" She could tell even without Katy saying anything that she did.

"Well I have to say I'm relieved that you aren't going out with him. He did kinda take my breath away when I met him on Friday, and I've been feeling guilty about it ever since. I wouldn't have done anything about it of course," she hurried on to reassure Stella, "it just made me feel really awful".

Stella smiled she knew Katy would never have done anything about her feelings if she herself had been seeing Scott, and now she thought about it, it would be great if they did end up together. Scott was a really nice guy and he would treat Katy much better than Alex had.

"I'm not in a rush to start another relationship you understand, it's just a relief that I'm not crushing on your guy."

Stella was sure that Katy was playing down her interest in Scott because she was scared of rushing into something. It was funny Stella thought, she hadn't been in a rush to meet anyone new either but she had met someone, and if she could help Katy and Scott get together she would. They both deserved to be happy. They were much better suited to each other than Stella and Scott would have been. She would have to find a way to contrive another meeting between them.

* * * *

Scott was surprised by his reaction to the woman who Yvonne had asked him to take to see Stella on Friday. Before he had left work, he had checked the visitors' book to see what reason she had put down for being in the school, but it hadn't been very helpful. It had just said, 'to see Mrs Martin'. That could mean anything. She might even be a parent, and the idea of that appalled him. You couldn't become attracted to the parent of a child in the school, it was wrong. She had signed in as 'K Ferraz. It didn't say whether she was a Miss or a Mrs leaving him feeling frustrated from lack of information. The door to Stella's room had been shut when he went passed too, so he hadn't been able to hear what they were talking about. He was pretty sure there were no children with the surname Ferraz in the school but that didn't mean anything. It could be the mother's name and not the fathers. On Saturday morning as he was finishing football coaching he had seen Bryony taking her children to the swimming pool. She had stopped to chat and he had tried to ask her casually who the woman was. "Do you have a child with a Spanish parent in your class? He had asked. Bryony had looked confused by the question. "No, not that I know of, why?"

"I was just curious. A lady turned up after you had gone and her surname looked Spanish, I didn't think we had any children with Spanish parents that's all, so I thought it was strange."

"We haven't so I don't know who that could have been, unless... We're supposed to be getting a new boy starting soon, it could be his mother. I didn't think they were Spanish though?" Bryony had added puzzled.

Then changing the subject, she had said, "We should do another pub quiz evening again, it was fun and I think there's another one coming up next weekend. What do you think?" Scott had agreed that it would be fun and Bryony had gone on her way saying she would arrange it with Stella. Stella hadn't told Bryony about Katy's visit so she didn't know that Miss K Ferraz was actually Stella's friend. Scott had packed away the footballs, said goodbye to the eager boys who had attended practice and went home. He hadn't been in long when his phone rang. It was his Sister Lucy, "Hi, I'm glad I caught you I want to ask a favour".

"What is it?" he asked.

"The choir I sing in are doing a concert in Winchester Cathedral and I need somewhere to stay for a couple of nights, so I wondered...."

"Of course I'll find you a hotel," he teased before she could finish asking the question.

"You idiot, I want to stay with you and you know it. So, can I?"

"It shouldn't be a problem, when is it?"

"The concert is next Saturday but we are rehearsing on Friday afternoon, so can I stay Friday and Saturday night? I'll get you tickets for the concert too if you like?"

"Okay as long as you don't mind joining in with a pub quiz on Friday evening. I'm making up a team with some friends." The teams varied in size but there was a minimum number of four and a maximum number of eight. Lucy joining them would boost the number to five so it would give them a better chance of winning. It might even give him the opportunity to ask Stella discretely about her visitor. He hoped she wasn't the mother of the new boy who was starting.

Still it would be nice to see his sister. They got on well and he didn't get to see her much since he had moved to Hampshire. He had gone to university in Winchester and had managed to get a job in the area as soon as he had graduated, moving in with the girlfriend he had had at the time. They had started off by renting a flat in the city centre but two years later he had changed jobs securing a position in Little Welborough primary school and they had bought a small two bedroomed house together in the newly built estate nearby. Everything had been great until she had been offered a promotion that had meant she had to move abroad. They had decided to end the relationship and he had taken on the whole mortgage himself. He had been out on a few dates but none of them had developed into anything serious, so he had been on his own ever since. When Stella had started working in the school he had liked her, and had hoped that it might develop into a relationship but she had turned him down. Realistically he could see that it wouldn't have worked out but at least they were still friends. It would be good to have an evening at the pub again.

Chapter Twenty Five

When Stella went to work on Monday she left Katy writing a list of the materials that she would need to start making the costumes and clothing for her new designs. Once she had finished the list Katy would drive to Ealing and pick up some more of her belongings that she had left with her Grandmother. Her sewing machine and other dress making equipment were at the top of the list.

Sophie was stood at the school gates when Stella arrived. She was pinning an advert for a paperboy/girl to deliver newspapers for the village shop on the school's notice board. When she saw Stella, she stopped what she was doing and hurried over to chat.

"Good morning," She said cheerfully. "I was wondering how your meeting with the old man went?"

She continued eager for gossip. She was sure that Jo and Stella had cooked up the story of the old man to hide the fact that Stella had met someone and didn't want to tell her. She was even more convinced she was right when Stella looked at her blankly. She obviously couldn't remember what she had told Sophie about the note.

"Um," Stella knew Jo had told Sophie something to throw her off the scent of her new romance but she couldn't remember what it was, so much had happened since then. Clearly it had something to do with an old man.

"It went very well thank you."

Hopefully that would cover whatever it was meant to be, she had to avoid being asked something else. She carried on walking trying not to look like she was desperate to escape, but Sophie wasn't ready to let the conversation end. "So, was his wife pleased with the book?"

Stella stopped and smiled, now she remembered what Jo had said. "Yes, she was, very pleased in fact which was why he wanted to buy me coffee."

"That's good. Which book by Keats was it? I wouldn't mind reading it myself." Damn the woman, Stella didn't have a clue what any of the titles of Keats books were called.

"Um, I can't really remember. He was looking for it on the shelf in the book shop but couldn't find it. My eyesight is better so I spotted it for him." That was plausible she thought. No one could argue with that.

"It's odd don't you think that he should send flowers and want to buy you coffee just for spotting a book in a shop. A shop assistant could have done the job and he wouldn't have felt the need to be so grateful."

Stella was lost for words. She knew Sophie was digging because she was not convinced by their story, but she was determined that she wasn't going to tell her anything else. She was just pleased that she had managed to avoid Sophie on her way to meet Jack on Sunday. Moving the conversation on for now as she realised she wasn't going to find out anymore by asking questions, Sophie drew Stella's attention to the box of books she had delivered to her on the day she had seen the note in the flowers.

"I do hope you are going to price them higher than the other books that people will donate, after all they are in tip top condition as I'm sure you could see. That's why I gave them to you before they went to the school fete, otherwise they will all be priced the same and they are worth more than a few pence." She looked at Stella hopefully awaiting confirmation that they would get special treatment.

"I'll see what I can do. I'll talk to Mrs Watson about the pricing later."

Seeing Nicole in the process of parking her car in the staff car park, Stella used it as her excuse to go, "There she is now I'll go and speak to her and see what she says".

Then before Sophie could say anymore she said a quick goodbye and hurried into the school. Sophie was left in the playground to wait for the other mums and dads to arrive with their children. Stella arrived at the main door at the same time as Nicole, she asked about her weekend as they walked to the staff room and then as Nicole finished telling her about her interfering in laws said, "Sophie gave me a box of books the other day that she insists should be priced higher than the other ones that we get for the book stall, so I told her that I would discuss it with you, what do you think?"

"Sophie is another interfering pain in the arse," Nicole complained, "but I suppose we'll have to price them a bit higher or we'll never hear the end of it, and she is a good fundraiser".

She sank heavily into a chair and took a sip of coffee. "Ah that's better. Have a look through them and if they are hard backs you can price them at a pound, all other books will have to be fifty pence, it is a school fete for God's sake not *eBay*."

Stella sympathised. Nicole had endured facing Sophie for parents' evenings the year before when Danny had been in her class. She had told Stella when they had been on playground duty together how relieved she was when the year ended and Danny had moved classes. Now that privilege was Scott's who chose that very moment to arrive. He was in time to hear Nicole finishing her moan.

"She has to get involved in everything, even when it doesn't concern her. If I see her coming I head the other way as much as possible."

"You must be talking about Sophie," he smiled. "What's she done now?"

"She wants the books she's donating to the fete to be priced higher than everyone else's, *because they're special*. The nerve of the woman, her books are in no better condition than some of the others we get given. It happens every year with something," Nicole continued.

Stella was beginning to wish she hadn't said anything.

"At least I'm not teaching her precious darling this year," Nicole stood up and taking her coffee with her went to prepare for her first lesson, leaving Scott and Stella alone in the staff room.

"Have you got an annoying parent as well or was that all just about Sophie?" He asked. It was possible that Stella might have been talking about her visitor on Friday and that may have sparked the conversation. If so it might help him to put the woman out of his mind if she was a seriously annoying parent.

"It was just about Sophie, she cornered me in the playground this morning," Stella replied. "I think Nicole 's weekend didn't go quite the way she planned either, something to do with her in laws."

She was wondering if she could bring up the subject of perhaps getting together for another pub quiz without making it look like she was after a date when Bryony came in carrying a heavy bag. "I can't believe its Monday morning again," She sighed, "I don't know where the weekends go".

Then "Have you asked Stella about Friday yet?" Stella looked from Scott to Bryony and then back to Scott waiting for an explanation.

"No not yet. I was about to when you came in," Scott turned his attention to Stella again, "We're going to do another pub quiz night this Friday and thought you might like to join us again, what do you think?" he asked.

"That sounds great." Stella enthused remembering that the teams weren't all the same size so it would be alright for Katy to join them. The bell rang announcing the start of school and they all headed off in the direction of their classrooms. Stella seemed very keen on the idea of the pub quiz Scott noticed. He hoped she wasn't having second thoughts about them going out together now or he would feel uncomfortable. Perhaps it was a good thing that he would be taking his sister with him. If she thought that he and Lucy were dating it might put her off without him having to have an awkward conversation. He couldn't go out with her now, not after his reaction to the woman he had met on Friday. It had proved to him that he and Stella weren't right for each other.

Stella dropped in to see Jo on her way home from work to let her know that she had told Katy about Jack, but not that he was a ghost. Jo looked very pale stood behind the counter and wasn't her usual cheerful self. "Are you okay?" Stella asked as Jo poured hot water into a teapot and put a chocolate cake onto a plate.

"I'm just tired, I could do with a sit down," she yawned.

"Why don't you join me and have a cake, it might give you a bit of energy," Stella suggested.

Jo poured herself a tea and sat down at a table with Stella.

"No cake?" Stella asked surprised.

"No, I couldn't face one right now, and I'm trying to be good anyway. I haven't eaten any cake for a week now at least."

"Perhaps that's why you're so tired, your body is missing its sugar fix,"

"Maybe," Jo agreed with a half-smile. "So, what's been happening with you, Jack and Katy?" she asked stifling another yawn.

Stella told Jo about how she had nearly been caught by Sophie on her way to see Jack, and about Katy being interested in Scott.

"There's another pub quiz on this Friday and Bryony suggested that we make up a team again, so I said yes. I'll take Katy with me, and then hopefully Scott and Katy will hit it off and my job as match maker will be done."

"Isn't it a bit soon after her break up with Alex to get involved with someone else?" Jo asked.

"Well, I did wonder that myself," Stella confessed, "But if she likes him it might do her good, assuming he likes her as well of course".

They finished drinking their tea and then Stella helped Jo close up the café. They walked back through the village together and stopped by their adjoining garden gates.

"Are you sure you're alright? You look very pasty." Stella was concerned, Jo looked really washed out.

"I'll be fine. I'll have a nice bath and a good sleep and I will be back to my usual self in the morning," she reassured her as she made her way down the path, walking parallel with Stella to the front door.

Katy hadn't been back from Ealing long when Stella got in. There were piles of material everywhere, a sewing machine and a dressmaker's dummy cluttering the hallway. Stella had to squeeze herself passed it all to reach the kitchen where Katy was stood at the cooker cooking.

"I see you got everything," Stella said as she went over to see what was boiling away in the saucepan. She picked up a teaspoon and tasted the sauce "Um nice, what is it?"

"It's dad's chorizo and lentil stew, I only started cooking it a little while ago so I hope you're not too hungry, it will be a while yet before it is ready. I'm sorry about the mess in the passage and the lounge too. I'll sort it out later but I thought I should start dinner first."

Stella hadn't looked in the lounge on her way to the kitchen but now that Katy had mentioned it she had a quick look. It was also a mess, and now that she had seen it she wished she hadn't. Part of her was beginning to understand how Gary must have felt when she hadn't put things away. Although to be fair she had never left the place looking in as much of a mess as Katy had left her house in right now. She had forgotten how untidy Katy could be with her work spread everywhere.

"Will it all fit in your room?" she queried although she already knew the answer to the question was going to be 'no'. Katy bit her lip.

"I can put most of it up there but then I won't have room to work. I was hoping you would let me work in the lounge," seeing the look of dismay on Stella's face she hurried to reassure her, "It won't be for long I hope, just until I can get a place of my own".

She looked so desperate that Stella didn't have the heart to object. Katy was her friend and had put her up when she had needed it. She would have to hope that Katy's new venture took off quickly, or that she could get a business loan for a workshop. Now she understood why Katy was cooking dinner. It was to soften her up. Oh well she would cope somehow. At least it wasn't as if she would be bringing Jack back, and it wasn't dirty mess, just clutter. Sitting down at the table to eat Stella told Katy about the pub quiz,

"Bryony from work and her husband are making up a team for a pub quiz, I said we would go and join them, its Friday is that okay?" Stella hadn't actually got around to telling Bryony about Katy joining them but she was sure that it would be okay.

"Yep sounds fun, who else is going to be on the team?" Katy piled Stella's plate with the Spanish stew and cut her a thick slice of shop bought bread that she had been warming in the oven.

The stew was good, Katy really was a good cook. It was probably another reason Alex suddenly wanted her back. He would be having to cook his own meals from now on.

"Scott will be on the team as well," she watched carefully to see Katy's reaction. Katy's hand stopped midway to filling her own plate. 'Shit,' Katy thought, she hadn't expected that. Part of her was excited, her stomach already aflutter. The other part of her was scared, was she ready to throw herself into the possibility of another relationship. She had never been one to stay on her own long before, always preferring to get straight back out there and find someone new. But that last someone had been Alex. Perhaps it was time to change, find out what she really wanted before she started seeing someone else.

Then she remembered her reaction to Scott when she had first seen him at the school, if she believed in love at first sight, then she had definitely felt it. Could she really afford to risk letting him meet someone else? Leaving Alex had hurt but not because she was madly in love with him. It had been her pride and losing her home that had hurt the most. She had never really had her heart broken because she had never felt that strongly about anyone before. If she started dating Scott and it went wrong she knew that she would be well and truly hurt. She toyed with her food as her mind went around and around the pros and cons. Should she go for it and risk getting hurt, or take the chance that if she didn't go for it he would meet someone else? Either way she could get hurt so she might as well throw herself into it wholeheartedly.

She let out a big sigh, "I shall need to wear a great outfit so he will have no choice but to notice me".

Stella smiled at that, there was no way that he wouldn't notice Katy even if she were to turn up in something as mundane as a pair of jeans and a T-shirt. Stella was more concerned about her frightening him off by being too flamboyant.

Chapter Twenty Six

Stella eventually remembered to tell Bryony that her friend Katy would be accompanying her to the pub quiz while they were waiting for the class to come in from break. "She's staying with me at the moment and needs a bit of cheering up".

"That's okay, we might stand a better chance of winning if there are more of us. My mother-in-law is having the children for the whole night too, so Lee and I will get a lie in for a change as well; heaven!"

Stella's class began to fill with chattering children as they found their seats and began fidgeting. One girl was holding a tissue over her knee, which appeared to be bleeding. "Oh dear Claire, what have you done?"

"I fell over Miss," a tearful Claire announced.

"Billy pushed her," her friend added accusingly.

"No I didn't, she ran into me," Billy told her defiantly putting his hands on his hips.

"Well sit down both of you, I'm sure it was an accident and we have a lot to get through this afternoon." She saw Billy poking his tongue out at Claire and her friend as he passed them on his way to his seat.

"Miss Billy poked his tongue out," Claire whined. Stella glanced at Bryony who raised her eyebrows in reply. It was going to be a long afternoon.

* * * *

Jo was passing the school on her way home when Stella eventually left. She had wanted to get all her marking out of the way so she could forget it over the weekend. She also didn't want to take it home in case it got lost under Katy's clutter. Jo still looked pale and when Stella checked her watch she realised that Jo had finished work early. "Are you okay?" she asked concerned.

"I don't feel too good today. I think I might be coming down with something." Jo's voice was shaky as if she were trying not to cry.

"What's wrong?" Stella tried again. Jo checked that there wasn't anyone behind her listening, before replying.

"I was alright yesterday, but today I feel so ill I might have to cancel my appointment tomorrow. When I go for those reflexology appointments I feel like I'm doing something practical to help me conceive but if I can't go it might stop it from happening. I need all the help I can get". Stella put her arm around Jo's shoulders and gave her a hug.

"You can't go if you're not well, and you never know you might be able to get an appointment in the week instead when you are feeling better. If it's late in the afternoon I can still take you so you don't have to worry. You don't have to miss a whole week," Jo cheered up a little bit at Stella's suggestion, then added.

"My sister has just announced that she is expecting her third child too and it hurts," at her last confession Jo began to cry again. Stella was at a loss what to say to cheer her up. It was good news for Jo's sister but she could imagine how painful it must be for Jo.

"I'm due on this week too, and I feel so weepy. I just want to sleep and forget it all."

"Oh Jo! Try not to let it get to you. You'll get to be a mum even if you have to go and see the doctor for help,

I'm sure it will all work out," Stella tried her best to make Jo feel better but it was hard.

If Jo hadn't been feeling so ill Stella would have suggested that she and Sebastian could join them at the pub for the quiz, but as it was she was probably better off getting a good rest. By now they had reached their front gates. Jo wiped her eyes and tried to pull herself together.

"So how are things going with you and Jack?" she asked wanting to have something else to focus on. Stella couldn't suppress the smile that the mention of Jacks name brought to her face.

"It's going well. I saw him again on Wednesday evening. The only thing is we can't go anywhere. I mean I'm happy wherever we are if we're together, but it would be nice to be able to go out on a proper date." Stella sighed, "I suppose if you fall in love with a ghost it's one of the sacrifices you have to make".

"Is he worth all the things you will have to give up?" Jo asked feeling that perhaps her life wasn't so bad after all. At least she could cuddle up with Sebastian every night and he was there for her whenever she needed him.

Stella didn't like to think too much about the future, she just wanted to enjoy what they had. She couldn't help the way she felt about him. He always managed to cheer her up when she felt down, he listened to her moaning about Katy's mess, and they laughed a lot together. Not to mention the fact that nothing seemed to matter but the two of them the moment he held her in his arms. Of course, she missed being able to go places together, and she didn't know what they would do when the weather turned cold, but she would have to manage.

"Yes, he's definitely worth it," she answered sadly before heading down her front path and opening the front door. "Let me know if you are still going tomorrow and I'll take you in the car, and if you can't go but feel like a morning in town we can do that instead."

The pile of dressmaking equipment was no longer in the hallway when she entered which was good, but it had only progressed as far as the lounge. Stella opened the lounge door for the third time that week to see the room littered with material and patterns that were pinned together. Katy was nowhere to be seen. Stella closed her eyes and counted to ten, trying not to let the despair for the pretty room she had once had get her down.

"I'm up here," Katy called from her bedroom. "I'll be down in a minute."

Stella could smell something burning in the kitchen and rushed off to find out what it was. She was just in time to recue what looked like lasagne from becoming charcoal. Smoke filled the kitchen as she opened the oven door and set the smoke alarms off. Stella opened the back door to let the smoke out and turned the downstairs alarm off. Katy turned the one off that was upstairs and hurried into the kitchen to check the lasagne. When she saw it sat on a heatproof mat on the table looking very dark she apologised.

"Sorry, I was going to turn it down when you were late coming in but I forgot. I 've found what I'm going to wear tonight though, so that's one thing sorted."

Stella poked at the lasagne to see if it was salvageable and decided that the underneath might just about be acceptable with a big glass of water. To be fair Katy had cooked dinner every day during the week and Stella knew she was nervous about making the right impression on Scott. It wasn't as if Katy had sat around doing nothing the rest of the week either. She had arranged a meeting with a small business advisor and had spent one afternoon talking through her business plan with him. The rest of her time she had been working on designs and making up samples to display on a website once it was up and running. She had definitely kept herself busy. If only she could afford a studio to work in so Stella's house could feel like a home again.

"So, what are you going to wear?" she was curious to know.

For a horrible minute Katy had thought that she might have pushed Stella's patience to far what with burning the dinner and everything, but she was still talking to her and not shouting so that was a good sign.

"I'll show you if you like? I really am sorry about the dinner… and the mess in the lounge. I'll clear it up now if you want me to?" Stella was being so good about her staying and supporting her while she started her business, she would make it up to her one day.

"It's okay, I think we can still eat the dinner and we're going to be out this evening anyway so we won't be sitting in the lounge. I might be going out in the morning too with Jo so you can carry on working on your designs then and perhaps clear up a bit for when I get back," Stella smiled trying to reassure Katy that she was not upset.

It was hard sharing a house with someone when you were used to having the space to yourself, especially someone like Katy. She remembered how lonely she had felt when she had first moved in. It was only a matter of getting used to it. Actually, it was nice to have company and have someone to talk to about your day. Katy showed Stella the dress she was planning on wearing. It was a bottle green dress to match her eyes, and was fitted to the thigh before it flared out above the knee giving plenty of room to walk. It had a black lace-work panel at the front and draping sleeves. Her nails had been painted green to match the dress with an intricate pattern on top in black. There was no way Scott wouldn't notice her, but would he like her or was it a bit over the top for him? Stella didn't know. When Stella changed into a pair of comfortable jeans and a blouse, Katy looked worried. "Am I the only one who will be dressed up?"

Stella stopped brushing her hair and thought about the rest of the group, Bryony, Lee and Scott. "Bryony will probably dress up. I think she was going to have a meal at the pub with her husband as her mother-in-law is having the children for the night and they don't get chance to do that often. She will want to make the most of it." It was strange seeing Katy nervous, Stella hadn't seen her like that often as she usually put on a good show of confidence.

Bryony and Lee arrived at the pub first; they were enjoying a night of freedom. Lee's mum and dad were looking after their children until Saturday afternoon, which meant they could relax for the evening without thinking about being woken up early in the morning. They had finished their meal and Lee was getting them another drink when Scott arrived with his sister Lucy. They joined Lee at the bar and once they all had drinks they walked back to the table where Bryony was sat waiting. The pub was beginning to fill up so it was a good job they already had a table.

"I've brought my sister Lucy along, she's staying with me for a couple of nights," Scott told them as he introduced Lee and Bryony to Lucy. "Have you registered our team yet?"

"Yes, we stand more chance of winning today as our team will be bigger what with you bringing your sister and Stella bringing a friend too," Bryony told him.

Scott was surprised that Stella was brining someone and was glad he had his sister with him. If Stella was bringing a new boyfriend he didn't want to feel like a gooseberry between two couples. Scott had his back to the door and didn't see when Stella came in with Katy. They made a striking contrast, one tall, one short, one dark haired and one fair and drew several admiring glances as they made their way to the bar. While Katy ordered the drinks, Stella scanned the crowd to see if she could see the others. Bryony spotted Stella first and waved her hand madly in the air to attract her attention. When Stella saw her she smiled, and she and Katy grabbed their drinks and pushed their way through the rowdy crowd to the table.

There were two seats left between Lee and Scott so Stella took the seat beside Lee, giving Katy the one beside Scott. Katy threw her a glance that said 'thanks' in a panicky, sarcastic way. "Hi everyone, this is my friend Katy, Katy this is Lee beside me, his wife Bryony and..." Stella stopped when she got to Lucy, noticing her for the first time. She hoped that the young woman beside Bryony and Scott was a friend of Bryony's and not a new girlfriend of Scott's. When Scott suddenly announced that the woman's name was Lucy both Katy and Stella's hearts fell. Scott had turned a nice shade of pink so it was obvious Lucy was his girlfriend. All the enthusiasm for the evening had left Katy as quickly as if a bucket of cold water had been thrown on her. She sat beside Scott aware of how close he was but suddenly feeling a million miles away.

'Shit' she thought, why do things like this always happen to me. Determined that no one would guess how disappointed she was, she plastered a smile on her face and joined in the conversation. Scott was very quiet all of a sudden too. He didn't know what to say, he had hoped to meet the woman he had seen in the school again but now he had, and knew that she was a friend of Stella's he felt tongue tied. He could smell the scent of her perfume as she moved and her voice, which was like an accented husky purr, made the hairs on the back of his neck stand up. Somehow he had to get through the evening without making a fool of himself. He took a sip of his beer to moisten his dry mouth and tried to focus on what was being said. He wasn't sure whether her sitting next to him was better or worse than if she was sat somewhere where he would have to look at her.

"Attention please," Simon the barman called over the top of the noise. The pub began to quieten down and he announced that they were ready to begin the pub quiz. "Have your paper and pencils ready and don't forget no shouting out the answers."

Bryony found the sheet of paper she had been given and handed it to Scott who had a pen.

"Are we all ready?" Simon asked glancing around the pub. There was a general murmur of 'yes, get on with it' so he took out his list of questions from his pocket and began.

"Question 1, a nice easy one to start you off. Which sign of the zodiac would you be if you were born on the 11th of October?"

"Oh I know this one!" Bryony said excitedly. "My birthday is on the 1st so it will be the same as mine, it's Libra," she whispered. Scott wrote the answer down. They could hear mutterings as the people at the other tables discussed the first answer then it went quiet as they sat waiting for the next question.

"Question 2, in UK TV's Noel Edmunds *House Party* which village was the fictional 'House' situated near?"

"You should know this one too," Lee teased turning to his wife "It's Crinkly Bottom." Bryony slapped Lee playfully on the arm and the rest of the group laughed.

"Question 3, in which film did Roger Moore first play James Bond?"

"Well?" Bryony asked looking at Lee and Scott, "One of you must know". Scott and Lee leaned forward to confer.

"Was it *The Spy Who Loved Me* or *Live and let Die*?" Scott whispered.

"I'm not sure. I know *The Man With The Golden Gun* was one of his earlier Bond films but I'm not sure about which was his first one. I'll leave it up to you."

"I'm sure it's *Live and Let Die,*" Lucy interjected leaning closer to Scott so she didn't have to speak loudly. Stella watched them discuss which film was the right one with their heads nearly touching and felt awful for putting Katy through the evening. She could tell by how stiffly she was sitting that she was trying hard not to let on how she was feeling.

"Question 4," As Simon called out the fourth question Scott quickly wrote down *Live and Let Die* for the answer to the third question. By the time the quiz was drawing to a close they had all managed to answer several questions each and were quite confident that they had done well.

"Right," said Simon. "Now for the last question, are we ready?" He paused to build up the tension and someone shouted out 'get on with it'. "Which musical featured the song, *They Called the Wind Mariah*?" Everyone looked blank except for Katy. She had made the costumes for that very musical only the year before and remembered the song. As she was the only one who knew the answer she had to move closer to Scott to tell him without the other teams hearing. The smell of his aftershave tickled her nose and she suddenly felt very hot. 'Bloody hell' why couldn't someone else know the answer?

"It's *Paint your Wagon,*" her heart was hammering away in her chest as she leaned closer to him. She was aware of the rest of her team watching her and hoped they couldn't see how flushed her face had become.

"What was that?" Scott had his pen poised on the paper. He had been so distracted by her leaning towards him that he hadn't listened to what she had said. Now he was going to have to go through it all over again. Katy sat forward in her chair and leaned her elbows on the table close to where Scott's hand held the pen. As she turned her head towards him she could see streaks of light and dark blonde hair where the sun had lightened it.

"It's *Paint your wagon,*" she repeated.

He wrote it down and chanced a look at her. She had been watching him write the answer down but now as he glanced up their eyes met and held for what seemed like an eternity. He felt mesmerized by the intensity of her green eyes and her thick black lashes, he couldn't look away, he swallowed hard willing his head to turn and look the other way but unable to make it obey his wishes. Lee grabbed the paper off the table and headed over to the bar where the barmaid was going to check the answers. The spell was broken. Scott grabbed his pint of beer and took a big slug so he didn't have to make conversation until he could get his brain back in gear. Katy picked up her wine and sipped it feeling confused. How could he look at her like that when he was sat at the table with his girlfriend? 'Men, they're all bastards' she thought, putting the glass down harder than she had intended in her anger.

The trouble was it didn't stop her liking him and nice though Lucy seemed to be, Katy felt like slapping her for finding Scott first. She wanted to hate her but she couldn't. She was very sweet and bubbly; it wasn't her fault that Katy liked her boyfriend. First, she had thought that Stella was going out with him and he was off limits and now when she had thought that he was single it turned out that he was seeing Lucy. She wished she hadn't bothered to dress up now. "I'm going to get another drink anybody want one?" She asked getting to her feet.

"It's alright I'll get them, same again?" Scott offered also rising to his feet, when everyone nodded he turned to Katy who was still standing "I might need some help to carry them back though?" Scott didn't want to lose the opportunity to speak to her on her own.

Katy had gone off the idea of getting the drinks now but she couldn't refuse to go or it would look rude. She smiled although her legs were now feeling like rubber, and followed him through the crowd to the bar. It had been an impulsive decision to ask Katy to help him carry the drinks, and now they were on their own at the bar waiting to be served he wasn't entirely sure what to say.

"How long are you going to be staying with Stella?" If she was only going to be staying for a short time and then heading off back to Spain or wherever she came from, there would be no point getting his heart broken.

"I'm hoping to move to the area and start my own business. I'm staying with Stella until I can afford a place of my own, or she gets fed up with me. I can be quite messy," Katy admitted making Scott laugh.

"I must admit I'm not the tidiest of people myself but as long as the place is clean, I can cope with a bit of clutter."

Katy's heart thumped harder. He was perfect for her, why did he have to have a girlfriend already? Life was so unfair. "So, what business are you going to start up?" he asked genuinely sounding interested and not just making polite conversation.

"Well I was a costume designer until I quit my job, so I thought I would make costumes for parties and sell them on line and at car boot sales or a market stall. Hopefully when I've made enough money I might be able to rent a shop".

"I've got a friend who works in the indoor market in town, he might let you set up a rail in his section for a commission on whatever sells. If you're interested I could give him a call and ask?"

Katy felt torn. Of course she was interested, it was exactly the opportunity that she needed, but she felt awkward because of the way she felt about him and she could sense a connection between them. There was no way she could be the other woman in a love triangle. Not after what had happened to her, and to make matters worse she actually liked Lucy. She felt torn because she really wanted the chance to get to know Scott better, but it would be awful to keep seeing him and know there was no chance for them to be a couple.

Practicality won in the end, the opportunity he was offering her she couldn't afford to refuse. There was always the chance he might leave Lucy she supposed, or she might decide she didn't fancy him after all. Accepting the offer wouldn't necessarily mean that she would see him that much, she didn't know why she was even hesitating, she had to go for it. 'Take your chances in life while you can', her brother Diego would say. Not that that had ever done him any favours, but that was because he couldn't say no to anything.

“That would be great, thanks,” she replied at last. Scott’s boyish, irrepressible grin had her stomach doing somersaults that an acrobat would be proud of. ‘Shit what had she done’. She could be about to get her heart well and truly smashed.

“Do you want to give me your mobile number so I can let you know when I’ve spoken to him, or shall I pass a message on through Stella?”

“You can let Stella know I think.” She wasn’t being a coward she told herself, merely being sensible. If she gave him her phone number it would give him the wrong impression sadly, or the right impression but at the wrong time. She would really have liked to give him her number. If only he had been single.

Chapter Twenty Seven

"I'm so sorry about this evening Katy, I had no idea he had found himself a girlfriend. I wouldn't have agreed to go if I had known," They were sat in Stella's car on their way back home. It had started to rain and the windscreen wipers were squeaking as they brushed away the rain, and the light from the street lamps sparkled orange on the wet glass. Katy sighed and watched a large raindrop sliding down the side of the window.

"It's not your fault and besides, Scott said he would ask his friend if I could hang a rail of costumes at the indoor market." The traffic lights were red, so Stella chanced a glance at Katy to see if she was really alright. With an offer like that she would normally have been very excited and full of enthusiasm but she seemed lost in thought.

"When's he going to let you know?"

"I told him to tell you, and that you would pass the message on," Katy paused then put her head in her hands. "It's not fair Stella, why did he have to find a girlfriend now of all times? He's perfect for me I know he is. He even doesn't mind a bit of mess as long as it's only clutter."

Stella concentrated on her driving while she tried to think of something she could say to cheer Katy up. It didn't seem right to hope that the relationship might not last, because Scott was a nice guy, he deserved to be happy. On the other hand, he had shown an interest in

Katy, but then Katy was lovely, he would be mad not to notice that. Stella had seen the moment when their eyes had met. You could very nearly see the sparks between them. She only hoped his girlfriend hadn't seen it. Sadly for Katy it was one of those situations when you have to wait and see how life unfolds. If Lucy had seen the spark of interest between Scott and Katy it might make her decide he wasn't worth staying with, after all they couldn't have been seeing each other long. If that was the case Katy would still have a chance. Or, on the other hand there was always the chance it would make her want to fight for him, and Katy definitely didn't need that right now. Life could be very complicated at times. Stella pulled up outside her house. If only Katy could have met Scott sooner.

* * * *

Stella was up and dressed at nine o'clock the next morning, ready to take Jo to her reflexology appointment if she was up to going. She was sitting at the kitchen table eating breakfast when Katy emerged still looking half asleep. Her hair was all tangled, and her overlarge pyjamas were scrunched to the elbows and the bottoms fell over her feet, she looked like a waif wearing an adults cast off clothes.

"I didn't sleep well last night," she yawned as she padded bare foot across the floor to fill the kettle again. "I've got too much going on in my head, plans for my business, Scott, designs I want to make, Scott."

"You said Scott twice," Stella pointed out.

"I know I can't help it. I keep thinking about him and when I started trying to distract myself with work he kept popping up then too. Plus, Alex sent me another pleading message last night, and when I didn't answer he sent another one that was basically just a swearing rant so I turned my phone off." She suddenly noticed that Stella was already dressed. "What time are you going out with Jo?"

"Well if she's feeling better today, it shouldn't be long before we go. She hasn't said she can't go so I assume she must be okay." No sooner had she finished speaking than there was a knock at the front door.

"Right on cue." Stella got to her feet. "Are you going to be alright here by yourself?"

Stella was in a difficult position because Jo didn't want anyone to know where she was going so Stella couldn't offer for Katy to go with them, but she felt bad about leaving Katy on her own when she was clearly feeling down.

"I'll be fine," Katy reassured her, "I'm going to sew some of the costumes together that I cut out yesterday. I will be ready then if Scott's friend agrees to me using some of his space to display them".

Stella gave Katy a quick hug. "It will all work out for the best. Nothing knocks you down for long."

Katy smiled, Stella was right. She always managed to bounce back somehow. Right now she had to concentrate on making the costumes to display, and designing a business card. When Stella opened the door to Jo she could see she was still quite pale but at least she was smiling and eager to go. Sebastian had already left for work in his car so Jo was glad of the lift. As they drove out of the village both Stella and Jo couldn't help a quick glance at the church and the churchyard to see if they could see Jack.

"I wish I could meet your friendly ghost Jack," Jo was intrigued as to what it would be like. "Do you think you're the only person in the village who can see him? And if you are, I wonder why that is?" Jo pondered.

Stella hadn't given much thought to why she could see him if other people couldn't, and now that Jo had asked the question she found herself wondering the same thing.

"I don't know," she said at last, "it is a bit odd, isn't it? I was very upset the first time I met him, perhaps that had something to do with it."

As she continued to drive towards the turning that would lead to Kingsclere she couldn't help going over it all again in her mind. 'Why *was* she able to see Jack? Was it simply because he allowed her to?' That was a possibility of course, but now Jo had asked the question she began to feel unsettled by it. She had been so caught up with her feelings for him that she hadn't thought about why she could see him if others couldn't. Something didn't seem quite right about it. Or was she just getting paranoid?

She pulled up outside the big old Victorian building, the car wheels crunching on the gravel. It was amazing to think that at one time it would have belonged to one family who would have lived in it, and that it would have been their home. It was so big. Now it was a spacious spa come alternative therapy's centre. It was the same lady sat at the reception desk that Stella had spoken to on Jo's first visit. She smiled pleasantly in welcome as they approached the desk.

"Hello again Mrs Loxley, if you would like to take a seat Mrs Clarke will be with you shortly". They found an empty seat each, close to the window. "How was the quiz night? Jo whispered not wanting to break the relative silence of the room. Most of the other people waiting were reading old magazines or scrolling through messages on their mobile phones.

"We came second actually, so Bryony and Lee were pleased. We got a bottle of wine as a runner's up prize, they took it home with them to round off their evening."

"What about Katy? Wasn't she pleased to spend the evening with Scott?"

"She might have been if Scott hadn't turned up with another woman. She was smitten her first day here when she met him at the school. It was the day she came to find me and got Sophie all het up coz she couldn't find out who she was. The trouble is I feel guilty now for taking her along. It was a nasty shock because I had told her he was single, which to be fair I thought he still was."

"Poor Katy what did she do?"

"Luckily as the others had only just met her they couldn't tell that there was a problem. At least he did offer to ask his friend at the indoor market if she could display some of her costumes there, so if nothing else it might help her get her business up and running." The door that had been left ajar opened wider and Gabriella Clarke scanned the room until she spotted Jo.

"I'm ready for you now Jo," she called. Jo picked up her handbag and crossed the room to follow Gabriella up the stairs.

In Gabriella's treatment room Jo sat herself in the chair and removed her shoes. Gabriella picked up one of her feet and began to inspect it.

"Is there anything you would like to tell me?" she asked smiling broadly.

"What do you mean?" Jo looked at her foot frowning, what had Gabriella seen? Her stomach began to churn nervously.

Gabriella pointed to the uterus reflex on her foot. "It's puffy," she explained "that's what happens when you're pregnant. So... are you?"

Jo looked at her foot – as far as she could see it looked the same as usual, and then back at Gabriella. She felt a sudden rush of excitement and her stomach lurched. Could she really be pregnant? Was that why she had been feeling so tired and off colour.

"I don't know. I mean I haven't checked... I just didn't expect..." Her voice trailed off. She was afraid to believe it in case Gabriella was wrong. She couldn't face the sudden disappointment after having her hopes raised. "Is it still safe to have the treatment?" she asked.

If there was the slightest possibility that she was pregnant she didn't want to risk losing it. Not after all the months of despair at each failure. Gabriella studied the conflicting emotions darting across Jo's face as first the flare of hope appeared, and then the doubt and anxiety.

"I think we should postpone today's session until you can find out one way or the other. If you are pregnant I would prefer not to carry out another treatment until you are through your first trimester. Reflexology can be very useful in pregnancy, helping to relieve heartburn, sleeplessness and backaches but under the circumstances I would rather not treat you at the moment."

Jo sat up and slipped her shoes back on. The possibility that she might already be pregnant had her catching her breath with excitement as she walked down the stairs. It was only just beginning to sink in. Stella looked surprised to see Jo re-enter the waiting room so soon. She got to her feet quickly and hurried over to the door where Jo stood waiting. She looked faint and Stella wondered if the reflexologist had sent her away because she suspected a serious health problem that she couldn't treat.

"What's wrong?" Stella took hold of Jo's arm in case she was going to collapse.

"Let's go, I'll tell you in the car." Jo indicated the room full of patients who were now subtly trying to eaves drop their conversation. A man in a suit was watching the exchange over the top of his newspaper, openly curious.

"Well?" They were now sat in the car, safely away from prying eyes and Stella was desperate to know what had happened.

"She asked if I was pregnant," Jo told her making Stella gasp.

"What did you say and what made her think you are?"

"She said it was something to do with my uterus reflex being puffy. I don't know what to think, Stella I'm scared." She turned tear filled eyes on Stella. "I don't want to get my hopes up because if she turns out to be wrong, I will be devastated. I want this so much!"

Stella reached out and grabbed her hand to give her support.

"Let's go into town and buy a test. The sooner you find out the better."

"Okay," Jo nodded gently squeezing the hand she held. They were both quiet on the drive into town. Stella had to stop at every traffic light on the one-way system, drawing out the time before they could find out and stretching out the tension. They finally drove down the ramp to the car park and looked for a space to park.

"I feel so shaky, I'm excited and nervous all at the same time. I think my legs have turned to jelly."

"Take a deep breath and relax. We will know the answer one way or the other soon." Stella calmly told her. "Are you ready to go?"

Jo nodded and they set off. It was a Saturday morning and the town was busy. They had to wait quite a while for a lift to finally arrive that was going up. Jo didn't think she could manage the stairs, as her legs were still feeling weak with nerves. Superdrug was the first shop they came to that would sell pregnancy tests, so they went in and started looking for the aisle that would contain what they were looking for. They had just found the right place beside the sanitary towels and baby's nappies when they heard a familiar voice.

"She's living with Stella Martin at the moment. I've seen her going in and out and that car of hers is parked outside." Sophie was busy telling one of the mums from School about Katy staying with Stella. Jo and Stella both looked at each other at the same time and hurried out of the shop.

"There's no way I'm buying a test like that with Sophie in the shop. It will be all around the village before the end of the day. It would make it even worse for me then if Gabriella turned out to be wrong, and people would know we were trying and not having any luck. I can't face that."

"Don't worry we can go to Boots and get one. I could do with some more toothpaste and a nail varnish, we can get them at the same time so it isn't as obvious". Boots was a little further up the high street, just passed Starbucks.

"Let's go for a coffee after we've bought it, I need to sit down and prepare myself." Jo's voice sounded shaky as she pushed open the door to Boots.

It was easy enough to find what they were looking for and they were soon stood in the queue at the till. Stella was holding the basket while Jo scanned the shop making sure there was no one they knew nearby. Her heart was thudding painfully against her ribs and she almost felt light headed. She imagined it must be how a shoplifter felt when they were stealing something. She felt as if all eyes were on her, watching her shifty behaviour. Except they weren't shoplifting they were only buying a pregnancy test. Jo felt her stomach churning nervously. It was because they were trying to keep it a secret, checking that no one they knew would see them that made it seem furtive. After everything she had been through, if it turned out to be negative she was going to cry.

At last they were at the front of the queue, Stella placed the items on the counter and the lady scanned them through the till, putting them safely out of sight in a carrier bag. Jo let out a sigh of relief as Stella paid, at least no one could see what they had bought now.

The lighting in Starbucks was much darker than in Boots and although it wasn't yet lunchtime it was quite full.

"Do you want to go and find us a seat while I get the drinks?" Stella asked handing over the Boots bag.

"Okay can you get me a hot chocolate and I will pay you back for it when you sit down, and what you bought in Boots for me." Jo found a seat on a big squashy brown sofa at the back of Starbucks tucked around the corner out of sight. She peeped in the bag trying to read the instructions on the box without taking it out, which wasn't easy. Stella arrived and stood the tray with the two tall glasses of hot chocolate topped with cream and marshmallows on the table in front of Jo. Sitting at the other end of the sofa she put her handbag down on the seat between them.

"Are you going to do the test now in the toilets? It only takes a minute to get the result". Stella was nearly as eager for the answer as Jo had been when Gabriella had first suggested that she might be pregnant.

"I don't know. I'm scared to find out the answer in case it's negative."

"It will be better to find out though, otherwise you might convince yourself that you are and it will be even more upsetting if you're not."

Jo knew that what Stella was saying made sense but it was nice to believe that she actually was pregnant, even if it was only for a little while. She knew she was setting herself up for a fall if she turned out not to be, but it was nice to dream. It meant so much to her that she was putting the moment off in case it made her cry. Besides, if it was negative and she found out before she had her hot chocolate she knew she wouldn't feel like drinking it after.

"I'll have my drink first, then I'll go and do it."

"Good idea," Stella knew she was only delaying the moment because she was scared of the answer, but she let it go and they changed the topic to give Jo time to prepare herself. Stella finished her drink first and waited patiently for Jo to pluck up the courage to finish hers and take the packet with the test inside, into the toilets.

"Good luck" she said as Jo couldn't put it off any longer and finally stood up ready.

She walked slowly to the ladies' toilets and disappeared. Stella glanced at the other people sat drinking their fancy coffees, wondering if any of them were hiding secrets or dramatic events in their lives. She saw a couple huddled together in the corner completely absorbed by each other's company, their legs occasionally touching under the table. She wondered if they were an item, or if they were having an illicit affair. They certainly didn't look married, even the most amorous of couples didn't behave like that when they were in public, especially if they had been married for any length of time. As the woman leaned in closer to whisper in the man's ear Stella turned away embarrassed. She decided it was safer to check her phone for messages instead.

Katy had sent one telling her that she was off to a material warehouse for some more material. She wasn't going to be back until six as it was on the outskirts of London. Stella hoped she had done some tidying up before she had left. She didn't want to make a fuss about the mess, as she knew how she had felt when Gary had complained about her leaving things in the wrong place. She didn't want to become like him, but it would be nice for the house to look a bit tidier. Lived-in was fine, clutter everywhere was too much. If Katy had moved in with her while she had still been with Gary he would have had a fit. It would have probably given him a heart attack due to stress. It wasn't really funny but she couldn't help a little chuckle at the thought.

Inside the ladies' toilets Jo checked out the cubicles to find the one that looked the cleanest. One was very definitely unclean as someone had either forgotten to flush or the flush hadn't worked. She decided to stay as far away from that one as possible. Inside the cubicle she had claimed as her own, she tore open the box that she had stashed in her handbag and which was now hanging on the back of the door. She pulled out one of the cellophane covered sticks. There were two in the box, one was in case the first didn't work or it didn't give you the answer you wanted. You got two tries to find the answer you did want.

She ripped open the cellophane of the first stick with shaking hands then quickly read the instructions. She realised that it would have been better to read them before opening the packet but having come this far she was impatient to get on with it. Once she had read the instruction to *'pee on the stick'*, she stuffed the instructions back in the box and prepared herself. Then, when she was done she stood in the cubicle waiting for the little blue line to appear to show that the test had worked. If she was pregnant a second blue line would appear in the next box. Her hands were shaking as she held the stick and waited.

The first blue line appeared so she knew that it was working. There was nowhere to stand the stick while she straightened her clothes so she just had to struggle with one hand. The hand that was holding the stick was shaking so much, she nearly dropped it down the toilet. She didn't fancy putting her hand down a public toilet to fish the thing out, luckily, she still had a hold of it and she would soon have her answer. The packet said that it was able to tell from the day your period was due, and that it was ninety-nine percent accurate. If it was negative she would have to wee on the second stick that was in the box when the hormone was supposed to be stronger, but that would mean having to wait until Sunday morning. She rested her head against the cubicle door and crossed her fingers.

"Please let Gabrielle be right," she thought over and over in her head. The waiting was agony but she didn't want to look too soon and be disappointed. She wanted to enjoy the possibility for as long as possible, however painful it was.

When the door to the toilets opened and Jo stepped out she looked very white. She walked slowly back to where Stella was waiting on the sofa with tears beginning to fill her eyes. Stella swallowed hard, it didn't look good but she had to ask just to be sure.

"Well?"

Jo sat down and began to cry softly into her hands. Stella put her arm around her shoulders. She didn't know what to say. She was annoyed with Gabriella for getting Jo's hopes up. Jo was still clutching the Boots bag in her hand.

"I can't believe it," she said at last in between sobs "I'm actually pregnant. Two lines appeared in the little windows. I'm so ha... hap... happy". Jo stammered. Stella gasped, had Jo just said she was pregnant.

"Oh my god, I thought you were crying because it was bad news. Oh wow Jo, that's great! You'd better tell Sebastian."

"I still can't believe it. I need to give myself a moment to let it sink in. Will you check the stick just to make sure I'm not hallucinating?" Jo put her hand in the bag and held the little white stick near the top of the bag so Stella could read it. There were definitely two blue lines, one in each window.

"Yep you're pregnant alright. Do you want me to stop at the garage on our way home so you can tell Sebastian the news, or wait until he gets home?"

"I don't think I can wait. I want to tell him straight away."

When Stella pulled up outside the garage Sebastian was nowhere to be seen. Jo found Geoff in the office with the door wide open doing some paper work. Geoff was Sebastian's boss.

"Hello Geoff, do you know where Sebastian is?"

"He's under that black Fiesta doing some repairs, do you want me to get him for you?"

"No, it's okay thanks, I'll do it."

Jo left the office and bent down by a pair of feet that were sticking out from under the car Geoff had pointed to.

"Seb it's me, I need to talk to you."

When Sebastian heard Jo's voice he panicked. He had their car at the garage with him, which meant she would have had to have a lift to visit him at work, and that had to mean it was something important. He slid out from under the car and began wiping his oily hands.

"What's up?"

Jo began to cry all over again. Sebastian pulled her into his arms fearing the worst and made soothing noises until she calmed down. "Tell me what's wrong?"

Was she ill? Was it his dad? He had complained about chest pains the last time they had visited but he had assured them that it was only heartburn. Jo wiped her face with a tissue that Stella had produced from a box in her glove compartment and sniffed back her shuddering breaths.

"I'm pregnant Seb. I did a test and it's positive. I'm so happy I just can't believe it."

"You're pregnant?" had he really heard her right. When she nodded he let out a whoop of joy and swung her up into his arms. When her feet were back safely on the ground he gave her a hug.

"I hope those are tears of happiness because I am over the moon."

Jo nodded, she was so choked with emotion she couldn't speak any longer.

Geoff came running over to them, "Do I detect some good news?" he asked.

"You certainly do, Jo is pregnant. I'm going to be a dad!"

Stella couldn't help a grin spreading across her face watching the delight and pride on Sebastian's face. It even brought a tear to her eyes. It was an experience she would never have herself if she stayed with Jack.

Ghosts couldn't have children. Although the thought of not being able to have Jack's children made her feel sad, it was something she was prepared to give up to be with him. She grabbed another tissue out of the box and wiped her eyes. At least Jo had got what she wanted at last.

Chapter Twenty Eight

Stella had left Jo at the garage with Sebastian. Geoff had let Sebastian finish work early so the happy couple could go and celebrate. Stella couldn't help the little glow of happiness she felt. She was pleased that she had been able to share in their moment of excitement. The little glow lasted until she walked into her lounge and found patterns and material spread all over the floor. She had hoped that Katy would have tidied up the mess before she had gone out. With a sigh she shut the door on it all and walked out to the kitchen. At least that was fairly tidy. The only thing Katy had left out of place there was the hardback book she had borrowed from the box Sophie had donated for the fete. It was on the kitchen table wide open with the middle pages sticking up in the air. Stella found a taxi companies business card to use as a bookmark, and put it in the page that had the corner folded down.

She guessed that Sophie probably wouldn't like it if she saw how Katy had treated the book, folding down the corners and spoiling its otherwise pristine condition. Picking the book up to take to Katy's room, she turned it over curious to read the blurb on the back. Her heart suddenly missed a beat. There on the back smiling up at her was a picture of Jack; only it wasn't Jack. The writing underneath clearly said the picture was of the author, and his name was Nathaniel Morgan. Stella's fingers turned to ice and the book slipped back onto the table. Jacks secret wasn't that he was a ghost at all, and his name wasn't really Jack Davenport.

Stella slumped in the chair and picked up the book again with trembling fingers. Surely she had made a mistake, it couldn't be Jack! Had he lied to her? All this time she had been thinking that she had fallen in love with a ghost, that she would never be able to have a normal life with him, and all that time he had been lying to her. His real name was Nathaniel and there was no reason for him not to have a mobile phone. That had been another lie. Stella put her head in her hands; she had been willing to give up everything for him but it had all been one lie after another.

He probably found it funny, their secret meetings in the churchyard, never taking her out anywhere that other people might see them together. She had been gullible enough to willingly go along with it. Well she had found out about his little deception and she wasn't going to take him making a fool of her any longer.

Picking up her keys she stormed out of the house and walked furiously towards the church. She didn't know why he always seemed to be there but as that was the only place she had ever seen him, then that was where she was going to go. Eventually he would turn up and she had a few things she needed to get off her chest. She was walking so fast that her chest began to feel tight, and as the shock began to fade it was replaced with humiliation, anger and pain. Anger that he had lied to her telling her that his name was Jack, and pain that the love she had felt had all been a sham. Perhaps it was his way of researching a new book.

A lump formed in her throat as she stifled a sob. How could he have done that to her? She had thought that what they had was special, he had seemed so sincere, always managing to say the right things to cheer her up, but it turned out that it was just pretend. At the church she pushed the gate roughly open and it swung noisily on its hinges, hitting the post and swinging back hard. Marching across the grass beside the church she went through in her mind what she wanted to say. She hadn't considered what she would do if he wasn't there, so turning the corner and finding the space empty made her want to scream with pent up fury. She flopped down on the step to the vestry and cried with frustration and disappointment. She wanted to be wrong, she wanted to find Jack there waiting for her like he had before. How could she have let him deceive her so easily? A part of her wished she had never found the book but then he would have gone on lying to her.

"Are you alright?" Stella's heart lurched painfully and her head shot up. Although she could hear that it wasn't Jacks voice a part of her had hoped that it would be. The vicar stood before her looking concerned. Stella sniffed hard and fished in her pocket for a tissue.

"I'm fine" she stood up wiping her eyes and preparing to go. She didn't want anybody else to see her looking the way she did. If she couldn't say what she had come to say then she wanted to curl up on the sofa at home and eat chocolate. She realised she would have to wait to speak to Jack... Nathaniel, at the time they usually met on Sunday.

"There must be something wrong for you to be sitting here crying. You didn't even hear me approach," the vicar persisted kindly.

"I'm fine really." Stella was about to walk away when the vicar spoke again.

"Were you looking for someone?"

There was something in the tone of her voice that stopped Stella in her tracks and made her face the vicar.

It was as if she knew why Stella was there. Stella felt the colour flooding her cheeks.

"Are you Stella?"

Stella couldn't help a little gasp of surprise escaping, which was confirmation enough for her astute companion. "I thought so. Do you want to tell me what has happened to cause you to be upset?" Stella shook her head.

"No thank you." As she made her way out of the churchyard the vicar walked silently at her side. Several times Stella could see that she looked like she was going to say something and then changed her mind. Stella was curious how she had known who she was. Sophie could have pointed her out she supposed, but it didn't seem likely. Stella had only gone to the church service once and she had slipped away quickly afterwards. There was only one other person she could think of who might have told the vicar, and that was Jack. Only he wasn't really Jack, was he? He was Nathaniel Morgan.

A fresh wave of anger hit her followed by a feeling of embarrassment. If Jack; she wasn't quite ready to think of him as Nathaniel yet, if he had told the vicar about her, that made her feel even worse. She felt so humiliated for accepting his lies and not questioning him further. Of course, it was stupid to think he was a ghost. The vicar stopped at the gate as Stella opened it to leave.

"If you change your mind and want to talk, come back to the vicarage. I'll be happy to listen, whatever it is that has upset you. And I won't tell a soul, I promise." She smiled sympathetically and for a split-second Stella was tempted to ask how she knew her name. In the end she decided that it might lead the vicar on to asking her questions that she didn't want to answer, so she returned the smile with a sombre one of her own and left.

The vicar watched thoughtfully as Stella walked slowly down the road. Her head was bent low so she could avoid eye contact with anyone she passed. When Stella was out of sight she too left the churchyard, but instead of heading across the road to the vicarage, she entered the long driveway of the big old house that stood beside the church. She wanted to have a word with her brother because she was sure that he was to blame for her finding Stella in the churchyard upset.

The house was well hidden from the road by large ancient yew trees and tall hedges. It was a bit like sleeping beauties castle, which was why Nathaniel had asked her to buy it for him several years earlier. When she had found out that the Fosters were going to sell up and move abroad, she had told Nathaniel about the house and he had jumped at the chance to buy it. It was exactly what he had wanted. A secluded detached house on the far edge of the village. Close enough to his only surviving family to not be completely isolated. He was already a well-known author by then and hadn't wanted the rest of the village to know who had bought the house, so she had discretely bought it for him.

It wasn't his only house, he had another one in London, and he made a point of never shopping in the village so no one knew he was there. He usually only used the house in the village when he wanted peace and quiet and kept to his own land most of the time, sometimes visiting the churchyard where he had met Stella, for a change of scene.

Since his very public breakup with Anna Bryant two years earlier, he was gradually spending more and more time in Little Welborough which meant that she got to spend a lot of time with him herself. Anna Bryant had been engaged to Nathaniel for six months when he had overheard her telling one of her friends on the phone that she found him boring, sitting in his study for hours on end when he should have been taking her out. Never mind the fact that he was in his study working. Of course, if she had found herself a job rather than sitting about waiting for Nathaniel to entertain her, she wouldn't have been bored. But Anna hadn't wanted to work once she had met and got her claws into Nathaniel.

She wanted to live the life of a celebrity, with all the trappings that went with it. The only reason she was staying with him, she had gone on to say to her friend, was because she liked the lifestyle that he provided. She had enjoyed the red-carpet film premiere's, the money that he gave her to spend on designer outfits for each event they attended, and being taken to chat shows where she got to meet other famous people in the green room. Nathaniel had been hurt even more by her callous attitude when he had confronted her, and again when she had sold her side of the story to the papers. At least he had found out what she was really like before he had married her, Jess consoled herself, but it had left Nathaniel afraid to trust people.

As the house came into view she was struck as always, by the charm of the pretty Georgian farmhouse. It was a shame that at that moment it looked dark and uninviting. The tall trees were casting long eerie shadows on the white walls, and the curtains were drawn tight obscuring any light from inside and therefore shutting the village out. It was as if it were sleeping, just like sleeping beauties castle, although there was no sleeping beauty inside, only Nathaniel.

Nathaniel had gotten over Anna some time ago but it had left him afraid to trust people. He kept his life in the village secret from all but his agent and his sister Jess.

Jess had been pleased when he had first told her that he had met someone in the churchyard. He had seemed a lot happier and more like the Nathaniel she had known before Anna. Then she had found out that he was deceiving Stella by giving her a false name, and she had known it would end in tears. She had tried talking to him, trying to convince him that he should tell Stella the truth, but he hadn't listened.

She sighed wearily, the time had come when if he didn't talk to Stella and admit who he was, she was afraid he was going to lose her. That was assuming that he hadn't already lost her. She reached the end of the drive, there was no point knocking on the front door because she knew that he wouldn't answer it. Instead she made her way through the garden to the back door, which she knocked on loudly, and then without waiting for a response that invariable didn't come, she opened it and walked in.

"Nathaniel, it's me," she called into the silence. She filled the kettle at the kitchen sink and switched it on before slipping off her muddy shoes. Then she made her way down the passage to the study which was at the side of the house, and where at least the windows would let in some natural light. The thick carpet muffled the sound of her footsteps so all she could hear was the rapid click, click, click of the keys on the computer keyboard being tapped. Nathaniel was working on his next novel. The door to the study stood ajar, she pushed it open wider and waited for him to pause in his writing before she spoke.

"How's it going?" she asked as he stopped and gazed out of the window deep in thought.

"Hmm?" He turned to face her and it was as if he had suddenly woken from a dream. "Oh hello, how long have you been stood there?"

"Not long," she smiled. Anna Bryant was a fool not to appreciate her brother. He was kind, clever and thoughtful, not to mention good looking, or so the papers claimed. It was hard for her to see her brother as anything other than the person who had used her Barbie dolls as extra soldiers in a game of war, or the person she had teased when he had first had his brace fitted, but she had to admit with his dark hair and deep blue eyes he was alright to look at.

"I have put the kettle on by the way. I expect it will have boiled by now and I need to talk to you."

Jessica left him in the study and went back to the kitchen to make them both a drink. Nathaniel arrived just as she was putting the milk back in the fridge.

"So, what's up? You don't usually come to see me at this time of day," he picked up his Spiderman mug, which she had filled with tea and began to stir sugar into it.

"I found Stella in the churchyard earlier and she was upset," Jessica told him without preamble, and saw the way Nathaniel hesitated in the process of putting the used spoon in the sink. He turned without saying anything and waited for her to tell him what had happened. He looked tense all of a sudden, and she knew he was worried that she might have said something to Stella about who he really was.

"I didn't tell her who you are so don't look at me like that. I keep my promises, you know I do. Even if I do think what your doing is wrong, and before you ask, I don't know what had upset her but I suspect that she has discovered who you are and she's not happy that you didn't tell her yourself."

"What makes you think she knows?"

"It was the look on her face when she realised I knew who she was. I could see her trying to work out how I knew her name."

"You shouldn't have let on that you knew who she was then," Nathaniel put the cup down roughly on the worktop and stuffed his hands into the pockets of his black jeans, trying to decide what he should do.

"I had to find out if it was definitely her or I wouldn't have been able to tell you that she was upset would I?" Jess countered reasonably. "I'm not going to be dragged into your deception anymore, even if I do understand your reasons for doing it in the first place!"

Nathaniel paced the spacious kitchen wondering what he should do. If Stella had found out who he was he would have to talk to her and explain. The trouble was, what if she wasn't upset for that reason? She might have been upset over something else entirely. If he suddenly told her he hadn't been honest with her now, and she was upset about something else, it might make her reaction to him different to how she would respond if he had told her when she was okay. Jess was right, he should have told Stella before, but it had felt good to know that she wasn't enjoying his company just because of who he was. The first time they had met he had felt drawn to her, had felt that she was the one. He had understood the conflicting emotions she had felt when she had found out that her ex-husband was going to marry someone else, and he had felt pleased that he had been able to help.

When she had asked his name he had panicked and used the first name he could think of. The name Jack Davenport had been on the gravestone in front of him and it had been a spur of the moment decision to use it. When she had turned up at the church again a week and a half later, on the Sunday he had enjoyed the time he had spent with her, and knowing that it was his company and not who he was that put the smile on her face made it even better. He hadn't wanted to spoil it by telling her who he really was. He had spent all the following week thinking about her and was pleased when she had turned up again and found the note he had left for her. He had always intended to tell her the truth but had never found the right time. From the moment he had met her he had felt that there was something special between them and had become frightened of ruining it. He hadn't expected to fall in love, but it had happened. He had felt an instant attraction the very first time he had spotted her gazing dreamily at the church.

Their eyes had only met briefly before she had looked away to wave at someone passing by in a car. In that moment when she had been distracted he had panicked and jumped over the wall into the safety of his own garden. He had cursed himself for days afterwards for not having the courage to stay and talk to her. When he saw her again sitting on the bench looking sad, he had decided that he would not waste another chance to get to know her. They had been seeing each other at least twice a week, sometimes more often, for several weeks now. The time had definitely come for him to be honest with her about who he was. He needed to speak to her, but if he went into the village and was seen then his little hideaway would no longer be the peaceful haven it had always been.

He glanced at Jess who was leaning against the worktop waiting for him to decide what to do. He wondered if he could persuade her to put another note through Stella's door asking her to meet him, or whether it was better to wait until Sunday when they had arranged to meet anyway.

Running his fingers distractedly through his hair he asked, "Do you think I should send her a note asking her to meet me? Even if she hasn't found out who I am, I want to know what has upset her and see if I can help".

It was all such a mess. All he had wanted was to meet someone who liked him for who he was, not telling her his real name had seemed the obvious way for him to be sure of her feelings. Now the thought of losing her scared him. He had to face telling her who he was and hope that she would forgive him for not telling her the truth straight away.

"Why don't you just go and see her? You know where she lives, I can take you in my car if you like."

"I can't. What if she isn't upset because she's found out who I am? I don't want to suddenly dump that on her as well and upset her even more. Then if I don't tell her, and I get seen by a neighbour they might say something before I get a chance to explain."

Jess frowned. Although it was true that Nathaniel should be honest with Stella and tell her who he was, she could see his point. If Stella was upset about something else the last thing she needed was to have a bombshell like that dropped on her.

"Okay I will deliver a note to her again if that's what you want, but only because I don't want to see either of you getting hurt."

Nathaniel tore a sheet of paper off his writing pad and scribbled a quick note on it before handing it to Jess. Jess slipped it into her pocket and left. She hoped for both their sakes that they would get the chance to talk, and Nathaniel would be able to explain.

Chapter Twenty Nine

Stella found a space on the sofa among the rolls of fabric and Katy's homemade patterns, and curled up with a cushion. She could feel a headache coming on and wanted to close her eyes. With her eyes shut she could picture every time she had spent with Jack, all the things he had said, how he had made her feel and the bittersweet memories threatened to make her cry all over again. Being with Jack had felt so right despite her anxieties for their future. How could something so good, suddenly go so wrong? She hadn't felt this miserable when she had realised her marriage was over. Jack had really got to her, made her feel whole for the first time in her adult life. But the whole relationship had been built on a lie.

She heard the sound of someone pushing something through the letterbox but she couldn't be bothered to get up and have a look. Whatever it was it could wait. She didn't feel like moving, she didn't even feel like eating the chocolate she had in her handbag. She felt so miserable and lost. It was only a few hours earlier she had been all aglow with Jo's good news. Sadly, she didn't think anything a reflexologist could do would make this situation any better. Eventually she must have fallen asleep sat on the sofa because she awoke feeling stiff and cold when Katy opened the front door. Her eyes felt like piggy slits where they were puffy from all the crying she had done.

"I'm back!" Katy called cheerfully. She stumbled into the lounge carrying an armful of rolled up material.

The smile on her face faded as she saw Stella curled up on the sofa with a blotchy face and red eyes. It was obvious that she had been crying.

"What's up? What's happened?" She dumped the material and rushed over to Stella, kneeling on the floor in front of her. "Is it because of the mess? If it is, I promise I will clear it away. I meant to do it before I left but I ran out of time. I wouldn't have had time to get to the warehouse before it closed if I had tidied up first."

Stella thought she looked so apologetic it nearly brought on a fresh wave of tears.

"It's not the mess it's Jack," she sniffed.

"Jack! What's he done the bastard?" Katy was so defensive on her behalf that Stella whose emotions were all over the place nearly started laughing hysterically before she remembered why she was so upset.

"He lied to me, all this time he's been telling me..." Stella was interrupted by Katy's explosion. She stood up quickly making her paper patterns fly into the air.

"I knew it, he's married isn't he? The lying, cheating son of a bitch. When I get my hands on him I'm going to..." She was pacing angrily about the room.

"Katy stop, he's not married."

"He's not?" Katy stopped pacing and put her hands indignantly on her hips wondering what other heinous crime he had committed and lied about.

"No. He lied about who he was. He told me his name was Jack Davenport but I found out today that he's... he's..."

Katy dropped down in front of Stella again and took her hands. To be so secretive and give a false name he must be some kind of criminal, or even worse a prisoner on the run. Stella never went properly out with Jack, she always seemed to go to his place wherever that was.

Stella took a deep breath before at last saying, "He's Nathaniel Morgan," Katy's mouth dropped open. Of all the things she had prepared herself for Stella to say that had not been on her list at all.

"You don't mean..." there was a pause as Katy tried to take it in. "You don't mean the writer Nathaniel Morgan, do you?" Stella nodded.

"Wow this is great. Can you get me his autograph? I'm a big fan." The look on Katy's face had completely transformed.

"He lied to me Katy! The whole time we were together he let me believe he was a ..." Stella stopped. She hadn't told Katy that she had thought he was a ghost. It all seemed so ridiculous now that she felt a fool to say it out loud. The only person who would understand how she had been deceived would be Jo, but there was no way she was going to spoil her day, not after what she had been through to get to where she was.

"He let you believe he was what?" Katy urged her to finish her sentence. Stella kept her eyes averted, systematically tearing the tissue she held apart.

"He let me believe he was someone else. He was just toying with my feelings, it didn't mean anything to him at all." Katy was torn between being awestruck that Stella had been slipping off to meet Nathaniel Morgan – the reclusive hunk who wrote exciting novels, made the odd appearance on chat shows and occasionally turned up to red carpet affairs, and being angry that he had lied to her friend.

Friendship won, "The bastard, I'm going to give him a piece of my mind. Where does he live?" Katy couldn't believe she was about to get the chance of meeting a hero of hers even if it was to yell at him. She wondered if he would still give her his autograph after she had finished yelling.

"I don't know where he lives," Stella confessed. Katy thought that Stella was trying to prevent a scene by not telling her.

"Of course you do, you go there to see him every week," She watched Stella's face turn an interesting shade of red. Stella wasn't telling her everything. "Where do you go when you meet him?"

Stella buried her face in her hands. She felt so stupid. Katy pulled her hands away and tried to look her in the eye, wondering what was going on. "Where have you been meeting him Stella?"

Katy suddenly had images of them meeting in dark lanes in his car but the image didn't really fit Stella's personality. A quick romp in the backseat of someone's car wasn't really her thing.

Stella glanced up red faced and said quietly, "The churchyard".

"The churchyard!" Katy was stunned, "Why in the churchyard?"

Was Nathaniel Morgan some kind of pervert, she wondered? Was that why Stella was looking so shamefaced? Katy didn't know what to say to that.

"It's not what you think," Stella was quick to put her straight. She could see the way Katy's mind was working. "It's complicated."

Katy decided to leave it at that for the moment.

"How did you find out? Did he tell you?"

"No, I haven't spoken to him. I was going to take that book you were reading up to your room, and I saw his picture on the back. I recognised him straight away. It's a very good photo."

For a split-second Katy felt guilty. If she hadn't left her stuff lying about the place, Stella wouldn't have picked the book up and she wouldn't be feeling miserable now.

On the other hand, if she hadn't found it Nathaniel would still be lying to her, and calling himself Jack. So, all things considered maybe she had done her a favour.

"Why don't you ring him and talk to him, see if you can sort things out?" Katy suggested.

"I can't," Stella admitted, "I don't have his phone number".

"What do you mean you don't have his number? Surely you asked him for it."

"Of course I did, but he told me he didn't have a phone."

"And you believed him? Everyone has a phone these days," Katy couldn't believe what she was hearing. Sensible Stella had been seeing Nathaniel Morgan for weeks and she didn't know who he was, had not found out where he lived or what his phone number was. She shook her head. Stella really had it bad to go along with all that.

"What are you going to do then?" She asked.

Stella shrugged her shoulders and buried her head in the cushion she had picked up. Katy suddenly remembered seeing a note on the doormat when she had staggered in earlier. She rushed out to get it and handed it to Stella. "I think he's sent you a note".

As Stella looked at the note on the now familiar cream paper she knew that Katy was right, and her treacherous heart still did a somersault of joy. A part of her was still hoping that she was wrong, and that when she spoke to Jack he would laugh and tell her it was untrue. She took the note that Katy held out to her with cold fingers and began to read.

Can you meet me tonight at six, same place?
I need to talk to you.
J

That was it then. The vicar knew who he was and had told him that she had seen her, and that she was upset. That meant that she had been right about the vicar knowing about her too. She looked at her watch. It was just after seven. Too late to meet him now anyway, he would have given up on waiting for her by now. If only she had gone to find out what had been pushed through the door earlier, she would have made it in time. He probably wouldn't turn up tomorrow now either. It was over; she had lost Jack and her chance at happiness.

* * * *

Nathaniel paced the churchyard behind the church. It was nearly seven o'clock he had been waiting for over an hour and she hadn't turned up. His nervous stomach churned uncomfortably. He had blown it. The one relationship that had really mattered to him and he had thrown it away by being a coward. He sat down heavily on the step to the vestry. The same step he usually sat on with Stella. He wondered what she was doing. There was always the possibility that if it wasn't his deceit that had upset her, that she might not have got the note. She could be visiting a sick friend in hospital and not seen it yet, but in his heart, he knew that it was because of him. If it was anything else she would have left him a note to find.

The sun was no longer shining although it was early summer, and the cloudy sky reflected his sombre mood. He wasn't ready to give up yet, he would give her another half an hour and then if she hadn't turned up he would go. If only he had told her himself who he really was. He had already realised that it was him she liked and not who he was. He could have explained his reasons for keeping his identity a secret and he wouldn't be in this mess now. Jess had been right all along, he should have trusted Stella and told her. The trouble was it was easy to see that with hindsight. Unlike writing a book you couldn't backspace and change things. In a book if you wanted to change a decision you had made you just went back and rewrote it. Sadly life wasn't like that. Once something was done it was done. There was no turning the clock back. He checked his watch again; it was seven thirty-five. She wasn't coming.

Standing up reluctantly he walked slowly over to the wall. Once he jumped over it he would be back in his own garden. He would try again tomorrow evening. She might turn up at the time they usually met on a Sunday he hoped. He glanced back one more time hoping to see her coming around the corner, but there was no sign of her. Putting his hands on top of the wall he heaved himself over onto the other side, dropping down with a silent thud. At least his shoulder had stopped hurting now. One time when he had been clearing up the picnic he had brought for himself and Stella to share somebody had turned up to cut the grass, he had been in such a hurry not to be seen that he had pulled a muscle in his shoulder trying to escape. The adrenalin had been pumping through his veins so hard that he hadn't noticed the pain until he had been safely inside his house, with the door locked securely behind him. It had been so painful he had not been able to write anything for days, relying on an old Dictaphone to record his thoughts until he was able to type them up properly. It hadn't stopped him seeing Stella though. Somehow he had still managed to climb the wall so he could spend the evening with her.

His house, which was usually his haven, no longer felt as cosy and inviting as it normally did when he returned. It felt empty and cold, like his life would be again without Stella in it. Even though there were plenty of trees at the front of the house to shield him from people passing by he always kept the curtains drawn, which now added to the sense of gloom and despair that he felt. He decided that he would wait for her again tomorrow evening; he wouldn't give up on her turning up until then. He couldn't give up on her. Somehow, he had to see her and explain why he had done what he had done, make her understand it from his point of view. She was too important to him to lose, if she wouldn't come to him then he would have to take the chance and go to her. If people saw him then they did, he didn't care anymore. If it was all over with Stella he knew he wouldn't be able to live in the village any more knowing that she was close by, and that she wouldn't forgive him. It would be too painful if he ever saw her, and even more so if he saw her with somebody else.

Nathaniel saved the work he had done earlier and shut down the computer. There was no way he could concentrate on it anymore today. His heart wasn't in it. The peace that he had once loved now felt stifling. It was like being an animal in a cage, unable to relax and nowhere to go.

Chapter Thirty

Stella didn't sleep well on Saturday night, the sun was already beginning to come up when she finally dropped off, and the birds had begun to sing. On Sunday morning Katy looked in on her on her way down stairs and left her to sleep. She hoped that it would help her to deal with Jack/Nathaniel when she saw him later. That was of course if she did see him later. Stella was convinced that he wouldn't turn up after she failed to meet him as he'd asked her to in the note. If he was serious about Stella, Katy thought he would turn up. Most of what she had read about him in the press had been good, declaring him to be a genuinely nice man. Interviewers were always singing his praises, but then they weren't having a relationship with him.

She remembered there had been a bit of scandal some years before when his engagement to some woman had ended badly, the woman had sold her story to the national newspapers. As it was the only bad thing she had read about him she wasn't sure how much of it was true, and how much of it was just sour grapes. She had hoped that he would turn up at the house to speak to Stella, mostly because she hated seeing Stella upset, and partly so that she would get to meet him herself.

She yawned and hunted in the fridge for something to eat. She guessed that it was probably because of people like her wanting autographs that he didn't wander freely about the village. Especially with Grace and Sophie about, she was surprised that they hadn't found out about him themselves by now. Katy grabbed some bacon, sausages and eggs. A good breakfast would set her up for the day ahead. If Stella was still asleep when she had finished she would tidy up the lounge, make it a bit more comfortable to sit in. After all, if Nathaniel Morgan did turn up they would need somewhere to sit and talk.

Katy put the radio on quietly to keep her company while she cooked. If only she knew where Nathaniel lived she would go and give him a piece of her mind. Stella didn't deserve to be conned and have her heart broken. Men were all bastards she decided, you couldn't trust any of them. Apart from Sebastian next door, he seemed okay and of course Scott hadn't technically done anything wrong either. She was just annoyed that he had started seeing Lucy before she had properly met him herself. That wasn't his fault; he didn't know that he was about to meet the woman of his dreams. Namely her, and she wasn't the sort of person to steal someone else's man. She would concentrate on getting her business up and running so she could start earning money again.

Next door Jo had gradually come to with Sebastian snuggled up protectively against her back. The memories of the previous day had rushed into her thoughts like a tidal wave. She was going to be a mum at last. She felt her stomach; it didn't feel any different yet. It definitely wasn't flat but then it never had been so there was no change there. Climbing carefully out of bed so she didn't wake Sebastian up, she stood sideways on in front of the mirror and looked at herself. How long would it be before it began to show she wondered? She felt an excited flutter, it was hard to believe it was actually happening at last. She would have to make an appointment on Monday to see the doctor.

They had decided not to tell anybody else until it was confirmed properly, and then only when the first three months were over. She wasn't going to do anything to tempt fate. She wasn't sure that she would actually be able to keep the secret to herself for that long but she would try. She was already bursting to let her mother and her sister know, but for now she would keep it quiet. Jo frowned, she would have to ask Stella not to say anything and hope that she hadn't told anyone already. Sebastian rolled over smiling and reached out for her.

"Come back to bed, I need to make the most of having you to myself."

Jo smiled and crawled back into bed snuggling up again to Sebastian. Life didn't get much better than it was right now.

* * * *

Stella decided to drive to the church on Sunday evening, partly because it had been raining on and off all day, and partly because she didn't want to take the chance of being spotted by Grace or Sophie. Having to hide from them once was bad enough, she certainly didn't feel up to doing it today. The thought of confronting Jack was tying her stomach up in knots. She didn't want to lose him but she didn't want to be lied to, or made a fool of. By the time she parked her car in the space outside the church she was beginning to feel sick. Katy had offered to come with her but this was something she had to do on her own. Taking a deep breath, she climbed out and locked the door. Checking that there was no one she knew about, she hurried through the gate and made her way nervously to the back of the churchyard. As she rounded the corner of the church her breath caught in her throat, her heart started thumping so hard in her chest she could hear a whooshing sound in her ears. Jack was standing waiting for her. Neither of them moved. Jack was regarding her, trying to work out if she knew who he really was. Stella wanted to rush forward and throw herself into his arms and cry, but this was the man who had lied to her, who would still be lying to her if she had not found out his secret. Slowly she walked further into the clearing.

"Why didn't you tell me who you were?" Stella demanded.

"I wanted too but..." Jack/Nathaniel began, but Stella cut him off, "If you really wanted to you would have. Instead you told me the name of a man who had been dead for years and let me think you were a ghost. Have you any idea how stupid that makes me feel?"

"I didn't intend for you to think I was a ghost, but it was the first name that came into my head. I had just seen it on the gravestone as you asked me what my name was. I couldn't tell you who I really was because I didn't want anyone in the village to know I was here. I wanted to be able to live here in peace". Nathaniel tried to explain. "I have never thought you were stupid."

"Okay maybe I can understand why you would do that to begin with, but when you realised how I felt about you, you could have told me the truth then. But you didn't did you? You left me believing you were someone else. Our whole relationship has been built on a lie."

"I'm glad you know who I am, I've wanted to tell you for so long but couldn't find the right moment."

"That's just an excuse. It's easy to say that now that I've found out. Relationships have to have trust. If you had really loved me you would have wanted me to know who you are. How could I ever trust you now? If you can lie once you could do it again, and you could always find a good reason for doing it. I thought what we had was special but I was wrong."

Nathaniel tried to take her in his arms, "What we have is special. I wouldn't lie to you again I promise".

Stella pulled away before she was tempted to give in.

"But how would I ever know? I want to believe you but I can't. You hurt me and I can't trust you. If I can't trust you we have nothing," Stella was trying hard not to cry. "You had plenty of chances to tell me who you were, but you chose not to. How do I know that you would have told me if I hadn't already found out? For all I know you were just having a bit of fun at my expense, and now you could be trying to keep me sweet to stop me telling the rest of the village about you."

"I'm not; I swear it. I love you!"

"I wish I could believe you but I can't. It's over Nathaniel, I don't want to see you again," Stella turned and ran from the clearing before he could see how upset she really was. Tears were already beginning to blur her vision.

"Stella wait! Let me explain," She could hear him behind her but she had had a head start and was already at the gate. A light flashed on her car to show that it was unlocked. She climbed in quickly and locked it again as Nathaniel was coming through the gate. She had to hand it to him he looked nearly as miserable as she felt, but that might be fear that she would expose his whereabouts to the press. It didn't prove anything. Before he could stop her, she had reversed her car and was pulling away. Rather than turning the car around which would delay her getaway she drove in the direction of the town. When she was far enough out of sight she found a convenient place to pull over and let the tears fall.

Right up to the moment she had seen him in the clearing she had hoped that she had been wrong about who he was. One look was all it had taken to prove that he really was Nathaniel. The thought of never seeing him again was painful but surely it was not as bad as spending her life wondering if he was keeping something from her. The ironic thing was that she had been able to completely be herself when she was with Jack. She hadn't needed to try and impress him; he had accepted her as she was. Eventually the tears began to subside and Stella became aware that her phone was ringing. For a split-second hope flared in her heart. Perhaps he was ringing to tell her he could prove that he would never lie to her again, that they could start afresh, but then reality hit her. Of course it wasn't him, he didn't have her phone number for a start. Not having a phone of his own had been another lie, ghosts might not have phones but everyone else did. If only he had told her who he was when they had started seeing each other properly, surely he would have if he had really cared about her.

By the time Stella had retrieved her phone from her bag it had stopped ringing. Moments later a text alert appeared on the screen. She opened the message and read it. Katy was worried about her and wanted to know how the meeting had gone. Stella rested her head on the steering wheel while she considered whether to reply or just head home. There was no point sitting where she was. Knowing her luck Sophie would drive passed and think that she had broken down. Then knowing what a helpful soul Sophie was she would stop to help, and that would mean that Stella would have to explain why she was sitting there crying. The thought of having to face Sophie was enough to make her restart the car and return home. At least she could suffer in relative privacy there. Driving passed the church Stella kept her eyes firmly on the road. She didn't want to see Nathaniel if he was still there.

Her phone beeped again, Katy was still waiting for her to reply. She would be back soon, she would tell her then. Pulling up outside her house she could see Katy looking anxiously out of the lounge window. She could see the relief on her face as the curtain she had been holding dropped back into position. Katy was already at the door waiting for her as Stella slowly climbed out of the car and walked the few steps to her front door. Seeing her puffy red eyes and tear stained face Katy guessed that it had not gone well. She pulled Stella into a hug and without saying anything took her through to the kitchen where she made her a hot sweet tea. It was supposed to be good for shock or stress, one of the two. Whichever it was Katy thought it might help to have something warm inside her. Stella had hardly eaten all day. She flopped down in a chair and rested her head in her hands.

"It's over Katy," she told her in a quiet deflated voice. "I can't trust him so I said it was over." She looked up hoping for reassurance that it was the right thing to have done. Katy nodded.

"You have to be able to trust each other," Katy agreed, sitting down at the chair to her left. "Bloody men, always causing trouble!"

Stella couldn't help going over the conversation she had had with Nathaniel in her mind. Torturing herself with the memory of his face as she had driven away, and fresh tears began to fall silently down her cheeks.

Why did it hurt so much if she had done the right thing? Automatically she took a swig of the tea that Katy had put in front of her and grimaced at the taste.

"God that's awful, what are you trying to do to me?"

"Sorry I thought it might help," Katy replied.

"It won't help my teeth I know that. How many sugars did you put in it?"

"Five."

"Five! Are you trying to turn me into a diabetic?" The sweet tea might not have had quite the affect that she had intended but at least Stella had a bit of colour in her otherwise pale blotchy skin.

"Do you want to talk about what happened?" Katy asked gently.

Stella shook her head, "Not yet, maybe later. I'm going to organise the books I brought home for marking, hopefully it will take my mind off my misery". Stella took her sugary tea over to the sink and tipped it away. Somehow, she had to be able to turn up for work in the morning as if nothing had happened. She couldn't afford to let it affect her work. At the moment she wasn't sure how she was going to manage, but manage she would.

* * * *

When Jess arrived at Nathaniel's house late Sunday evening it was to find him packing a suitcase.

"Where are you going? What happened with Stella? Did you speak to her?"

"Yes I spoke to her, but it's over. She says she can't trust me," Nathaniel flung the lid of his case closed and sat down on his bed with his head in his hands. "I messed up Jess, she doesn't want to know me."

"She's hurt Nate, of course she feels like that at the moment. Give her time to calm down and then try speaking to her again. Did you explain why you didn't tell her who you are?"

"She didn't give me a chance."

"Well then. If she really means as much to you as you say she does, give her time and then she will listen I'm sure of it. You do want her back I take it?"

"Of course I do," Nathaniel stood up and walked over to the window, moving the curtain slightly so he could see the dark shapes of the trees outside. "But I don't know that she will listen. If only I could go back and change things like I can in one of my stories if it doesn't go the way I want it to."

"This is real life Nate it doesn't work like that. If you love her then you have to prove it to her. We all make mistakes in life but you won't know whether you can put this right until you try, will you?"

Jess was usually very patient but he could hear her voice beginning to rise out of frustration on his part. He let the curtain fall back into place. He had never wanted to put something right as much as he did at that moment. The question was how could he prove to Stella that he was telling the truth when he told her that he loved her, and that he had always intended to tell her who he was? Jess was right about one thing. He couldn't give up on her without at least trying.

Chapter Thirty One

Joyce had always told Stella, 'You can hide misery but you can't hide happiness'. As Stella watched Jo from her lounge window walking to work with a smile on her face, she realised how true the saying was. Jo positively glowed with happiness, whereas she on the other hand thought if she put a brave face on her misery she would probably just about get away with it. At least it was the last week of the term. Once she got to Friday she could hide away in her house if she wanted to. Having Katy to stay also meant that there wouldn't be room for her mother to stay, so she wouldn't have to think of an excuse to stop her visiting. She couldn't face having to explain the situation to her mother yet. Stella picked up the books she had left by the window and put them in her bag. It was time for her to leave as well. Katy was still in bed, having a lie in. She often stayed in bed until Stella left so they weren't competing for the bathroom.

"I'm off," Stella called up the stairs as she gathered all her belongings for the day. Swinging her handbag over her shoulder and carrying the larger, heavy bag of workbooks she followed the same path she had seen Jo take earlier. She was glad that everything had worked out for Jo. At the kerb she waited for Tim and Rory to pass on their bikes before crossing the road. They said a quick good morning to her as they slowed up to check for cars, then when it was clear they shot off in the direction of the town. Stella's stomach momentarily knotted as she thought about them passing the church. Every time she thought of the church it reminded her of Nathaniel. Her heart betrayed her by fluttering wildly before logic kicked in and she remembered what he had done and a lump lodged itself in her throat. She had to put it out of her mind or she would never make it through the day.

It didn't take long for the school to come into view, the old-fashioned exterior masking the modernised interior. It was hard to believe that she had nearly finished her first half term teaching there. In some ways it felt longer. She had got to know the staff well in that time and on the whole they were very friendly, it was a good place to work. On the other hand, the time had seemed to go by very quickly. Scott pulled up in the teacher's car park as she pushed open the gate into the playground. He waved when he saw her and waited for her to catch up. It didn't seem possible that it was only two days ago that they had taken part in the pub quiz. So much seemed to have happened and changed in a relatively short space of time. Trying to appear normal and not show her inner misery, she asked how Lucy's concert had gone.

Scott half smiled and half grimaced, "It went okay. To be honest it's not really my kind of thing but I couldn't hurt her feelings by not going".

Scott opened the door and they both went inside. "You wouldn't believe how uncomfortable the seats were either, after an hour and a half of sitting on hard chairs that were obviously designed by a sadist, I was more than ready to leave I can tell you".

Stella smiled. It wasn't his fault that he had met someone new in the very week that she had tried to play matchmaker to him and Katy.

"By the way, I spoke to my friend Dave about Katy displaying some of her costumes in his space in the indoor market."

"And? What did he say?" They were stood outside Stella's classroom; Scott's was further down the hall. At the moment it was quiet but it wouldn't be long before the bell went and the hallway would echo with the sounds of children's eager chatter as they discussed their weekends on the way to their classrooms.

"He said he thought it would be okay, but he wanted to meet her and see some of the pieces before he definitely agreed."

Scott didn't let on that he had had to twist his arm to get him to agree to that even. Scott had listened to him going on about space being precious and that he had his own stock to display, table decorations, novelty gifts and various other items you might need to host a party. Personally, Scott thought the idea of displaying costumes alongside Dave's party supplies was a good one.

"When does he want to meet her?" Stella was fishing in her bag for her diary so she could write down the details. Scott suddenly looked embarrassed.

"I told him I would take her to see him on Friday after school if that's alright? I thought it would help to break the ice if I was there as well."

Dave would find it harder to change his mind if Scott was there, not that he would admit that to Stella, and he hoped it would give him chance to get to know Katy a bit better too. Stella looked at him perceptively.

"He is okay with the arrangement, isn't he? I don't want Katy getting carried away for nothing."

"Yes, it's actually a great idea, it should help both their businesses." Scott was careful not to actually lie. It would be good for Dave as well he was sure of it.

What's more he was sure that Dave wouldn't turn Katy down once he saw her, which was another good reason for him to take her to meet Dave. Scott didn't want Dave asking her out before he got the chance himself. At least he wouldn't have Lucy watching his every move this time. When they had left the pub after the quiz night, she had teased him mercilessly about how flustered Katy had made him. He had been mortified in case the others had noticed as well, but Lucy had eventually convinced him that she could only tell because he was her brother, and she had known him for a long time.

Stella looked tired he noticed, but if Katy was staying with her they probably spent hours sitting up talking, that's what his sister had always done when she had a female friend to stay. The bell rang to announce the start of school and Scott left Stella to head off to his own classroom. The prospect of spending some time alone in the car with Katy on Friday had brightened his day already.

When the bell rang at three thirty to announce the end of the school day Stella was fighting off a headache. It had been tiring to hide the misery that she felt at times. It was alright when she was occupied teaching the class and helping them with their work, but at lunchtime she had struggled to pay attention to the conversation in the staffroom. What she needed was some fresh air, but the idea of going for a walk just made her think about Nathaniel. That was how she had first met him. Hopefully the walk home would help to ease the pressure that was building behind her eyes. She gathered her bags, eager to escape without having to stop and talk to anyone. She made it across the playground and was about to shut the gate behind her when a familiar figure appeared. Stella jumped, Jo was waiting to talk to her.

"I popped round to see you yesterday but Katy said you had gone out and I didn't want to leave a message." She explained. "Were you seeing Jack?"

Stella sighed, Jo didn't know what had happened yet. "You look terrible by the way, are you feeling okay?"

"Not really Jack and I split up," as Jo gasped Stella continued, "if you're walking home I'll tell you about it on the way".

Jo fell into step beside Stella, a look of concern on her face.

"What happened, you were so happy?"

"I found out that Jack isn't really Jack at all, his name is..." She stopped herself from saying his name when it was possible that other people might hear.

"Let's just say his name isn't really Jack, he lied to me Jo. How could I ever trust him when I know that he has lied to me to suit himself?"

"That's awful did he tell you why he lied?" As another thought occurred to her Jo added, "Oh my god is he married after all?"

"No, he's not married, so at least I'm not the other woman," Stella reassured her.

"Well I don't understand, why did he lie to you then?" They had reached the corner of Lovedon Lane. A few more steps and they would be outside Stella's house.

"You had better come in. I can't tell you the rest out here in case we are overheard" Intrigued Jo followed Stella down her garden path before she remembered her reason for trying to catch Stella while she was on her own.

"Before we go in there's something I have to ask you," Stella paused midway to unlocking the door.

"What is it?"

"Please don't tell anyone about ... you know, our news," she whispered the last part of her request, while nervously checking behind her that she wasn't going to be overheard. "We want to wait until we have had it confirmed with a doctor, and we want to get through the first three months if we can before we let anyone know. Personally, I don't know that I will be able to contain the news for that long, but I am going to try."

"Of course, I won't say anything if that's what you want. I haven't told anyone yet luckily so don't worry, your secret is safe with me." Stella unlocked the door and they both went inside.

"Good timing I've just this minute put the kettle on," Katy told them as she poked her head around the kitchen door. "And I bought lots of chocolate to cheer you up after your day. How was it?"

"It was okay, I was about to tell Jo what happened." When Stella saw the pile of chocolate on the table she couldn't help adding, "I'm sure you're trying to turn me into a diabetic." She turned to Jo, "Yesterday she put five sugars in my tea".

Katy was unrepentant. "Sugar is good for shocks, and treats are good for cheering people up."

Stella picked up one of the bars and unwrapped it. She was lucky to have friends who cared about her, and at least she had a comfortable roof over her head too. Katy made them all a drink while Stella told Jo how she had found out who Jack really was, and what had happened.

"I can't believe you were seeing Nathaniel Morgan and didn't realise who he was!" Jo exclaimed, "Haven't you seen him on talk shows or at the premiers of his films? The last one he attended he took some super model with him with legs up to her armpits. Wow! And he was really in this village?"

Stella put her head in her hands, listening to Jo talk about him made her feel even more stupid. It was obvious that he was only toying with her affections. If he could get dates with supermodels why would he even look at her? She had to accept that she had made a fool of herself and put it behind her. The humiliation had her picking up another chocolate bar and eating it before she had time to realise what she was doing. At least the only people who knew about how foolish she had been were Jo, Katy and Nathaniel himself so she wouldn't have to face other people knowing what an idiot she had been. Nathaniel didn't seem to venture into the village either, so she wouldn't have to worry about bumping into him and feeling awkward.

"I know I've been stupid," she said at last. "But I don't watch celebrities attending film premieres and I haven't read any of his books so I didn't know who he was okay, if I had, I would have invited you both along to get his autograph," she added sarcastically. She hadn't intended to be mean but it just slipped out. She was feeling sorry for herself and both Jo and Katy had been disappointed that they hadn't got the chance to meet him themselves, never mind her upset.

Jo put her arm about Stella's shoulders. "I'm sorry I didn't mean it to sound like that, I was just surprised that you didn't recognise him that's all. He is kinda well known."

"He must have really liked you because otherwise he wouldn't have kept meeting you, you could have given his whereabouts away at any time, but you didn't did you? He was willing to take the risk for you. That makes you special," Katy told her stooping down in front of her chair.

It would be lovely to be able to believe what Katy was saying but the reality was that he had lied to her, and that meant that she couldn't trust him. If he had really cared about her the way Katy said, he would have told her who he was before she had found out for herself, he had had plenty of opportunities. Stella picked up her cup of tea, she didn't want to think about it anymore. She wanted to change the subject. She suddenly remembered that she had a message for Katy from Scott.

"Let's change the subject now. When I saw Scott today he told me that he had spoken to his friend and that he will take you to meet him on Friday after school if you like? His friend wants to see some of the costumes before he makes a final decision."

Stella could see the flush rising up Katy's neck at the mention of Scott's name.

"Oh okay. Why can't you come with me to meet him? Surely if we go to the indoor market and ask for whatever his name is we will find him? We don't need Scott to come too."

"Don't be a coward, Scott has offered to take you because it is his friend. Besides this is your chance to find out how serious he is about Lucy, you might as well make the most of it." Katy picked up a chocolate bar and bit hard into it making Jo laugh.

"If you want something you have to go for it, and you want your business to work don't you?" Jo asked. Katy nodded and looked thoughtful.

"I suppose he might not be serious about Lucy, I won't know for sure unless I talk to him but..." She waved her half-eaten chocolate bar at them to emphasise her point. "If he is serious about her I'm not going to try and change his mind, that wouldn't be fair."

Stella hoped for Katy's sake that Scott realised, that although Lucy was very nice, if he was still looking at other women like he had looked at Katy, he couldn't really be sure of his feelings for Lucy. It would be better to let her down now rather than later.

Chapter Thirty Two

Katy had changed her outfit four times before she was finally happy with the way she looked. It was two forty on Friday afternoon, school would finish in less than an hours' time, and at some point after that, Scott would arrive to take her to meet his friend Dave from the indoor market. She checked her reflection one last time in the mirror. She wanted to appear business like, but she also wanted Scott to notice her. As she wasn't the smart suit type of person, she had opted for black trousers and a green and black fitted blouse that looked a bit like a corset with flowing sleeves. The colour of the blouse matched her eyes exactly, and she knew that it suited her, which helped her to feel more confident. Power dressing, that's what her mother would call it. Whenever her mother was called into the school to speak to a teacher about one of her sons, she had dressed herself to the nines explaining that if she felt good no one could make her feel small, no matter what they might say about how badly her boys behaved. Her mother had been to the school dressed to the nines on many an occasion. Katy's brothers weren't bad her mother had often told people, but high spirited. The fact that there were so many of them didn't help;, she had five. Five boys and two daughters, it was a busy household.

The costumes she had chosen to take to show Dave were hanging in special bags like the ones your clothes come back from the dry cleaners in. She was ready, now all she had to do was wait. Katy paced the room restlessly, if Dave agreed to display and sell her costumes she would be up and running as a business. She had had some flyers made as well that she hoped he would hand out to anyone who showed an interest in the costumes. The flyers offered made to order costumes for special events. Katy was nervous, she needed to get Dave on side and then they would have to come to some arrangement about prices, and a commission for Dave. She had jotted down her ideas but she was prepared to be a little bit flexible. What made her even more nervous was the prospect of sharing the car with Scott. If only she didn't fancy him it wouldn't be so bad. She would have to keep reminding herself that he had a girlfriend.

She checked her reflection in the hall mirror, one of her earrings had caught in her hair. She carefully managed to untangle it and shook her head gently from side to side to make sure it was able to swing freely. Satisfied that it was as it should be, she checked her watch again. School would be finishing any minute. She wondered how long after it had finished Scott would turn up. Stella often liked to get her marking done before she came home so sometimes she would stay on for another hour or two after the children had left. The thought of having to wait another couple of hours with nothing to do but fret about Dave's reaction to her costumes, and more importantly how uncomfortable the car journey might be, had her stomach tying itself in knots.

She looked about the lounge for something to do but she had already tidied it up earlier in the day so it was homely when Stella got in. There was the book still waiting for her to finish reading but she felt disloyal for even considering it after what Nathaniel Morgan had put Stella through. She was putting on a brave face but

Katy knew that Stella was still very upset. She had heard her crying herself to sleep during the week and had been tempted to visit Nathaniel herself to give him a piece of her mind. She would have done too if she had known where to find him, but the bastard hadn't told Stella where he lived. She looked longingly at the book that was now sat temptingly on the arm of the sofa. She had been really enjoying reading the story too. She had just convinced herself that Stella would never know if she was reading it if she didn't see her, when there was a knock at the door and she dropped the book guiltily back where she had found it. With her heart thudding madly in her chest she opened the door to find Scott looking as handsome as she remembered him, wearing a navy-blue suit and a mischievous twinkle in his eye that made her feel weak at the knees.

"Hi, are you ready to go?" he asked.

"Yes, I'll just grab the costumes and my bag and we can be off." On shaky legs she hurried back inside and picked up the costumes in their coverings. 'Damn,' she thought why did he have to have that effect on her? She would have to get a grip before they met Dave or she wouldn't be able to concentrate, and her business was important to her.

"Here let me carry some of those for you," Scott reached out and grabbed some of the costumes that were obscuring Katy's view. As he took them his hand brushed against her arm where the sleeve had fallen back, and she felt a shiver of excitement that had her feeling hot all over. Mentally she conjured up a picture of Lucy in her head to remind her that he was someone else's boyfriend, and pulled the front door shut behind her. She had worked with actors long enough to know that when you were nervous the most important thing was to not let others see it. Pretending to be confidant and in control could help you believe that you were confidant and in control.

With the advice of her mum for power dressing, and the mantra of her former work colleagues *'I am confident and in control'* going through her head, she was about to find out if they were right. She strode casually over to Scott's car as if his touch had meant nothing, and waited for him to open the back door so she could lay the costumes on the back seat. Scott's voice had deserted him the moment he had accidentally touched Katy's arm, he opened the door in silence. Usually he found it easy to start a conversation but at the moment his mind had gone blank. Once everything was safely in the car and they were on their way Scott began to relax. Concentrating on turning the car around in the narrow road and then the familiar, mundane task of keeping the car moving helped.

Katy who had managed to portray a fairly convincing image of self-belief was trying to think of a way of finding out how serious his relationship with Lucy was. They were both so lost in their own thoughts that it was a while before either of them spoke, and then they both started to speak at the same time.

"So, what have you been doing this week?" Scott asked at the same time as Katy asked, "Are you doing anything nice now you're off for two weeks?"

They both laughed nervously. There was a pause as they both waited to give the other chance to speak. It was Katy who finally broke the silence again.

"Thanks for organising this," She decided to start again with something less likely to cause her any anxiety. If Scott told her he was off to Paris or something with Lucy she would only feel disappointed, and she didn't want to meet Dave for the first time feeling like that.

"That's okay, I'm glad I can help. I think it will be good for both of you from a business point of view. Dave sells party paraphernalia, so stocking your costumes is adding to the whole party experience that he can offer. People who turn up for party plates might decide to have a themed party and buy a costume as well."

Katy considered his idea carefully, she hadn't realised that Dave sold things for parties, she had assumed that it would be clothes. It made sense to sell costumes and party plates together, as one would attract custom for the other.

"Well I am very grateful, getting my own business started is harder than I thought."

The façade of outer confidence had slipped slightly, revealing a vulnerable side to Katy that made Scott suddenly feel protective towards her. Dave had better keep to his word and give her a fair hearing. The initial thrill of attraction had knocked him sideways; it wasn't just her looks, although she was stunning, it was the air of mystery that she exuded, a subtle mix of confidence, fun and vulnerability. It was a heady combination. At first he had thought that she was cool and confident, which was why he had found himself a little in awe of her.

Now seeing that she was not as confident as she had first appeared made him feel easier in her presence, and not so tongue-tied. It also endeared her to him a little more. Out of the corner of his eye he could see her twisting the strap of her handbag, a sure sign of nerves. Getting Dave to stock her costumes was obviously very important to her. Scott found he was able to chat with her casually about his week at school, and the upcoming fete that would be held on the first weekend back. The tone of his voice was soothing to listen to as they drove through the canopy of trees towards the town.

Katy let her bag slip onto the floor at her feet and laughed as Scott told her about last years' fete, and how the country dancers had got in a muddle and tangled up the ribbons they had been dancing with. Before she knew it, they were pulling up in the car park and it was time to meet Dave.

When Scott headed over to the ticket machine Katy's phone rang, as she answered it and heard Alex's voice at the other end all thought of nerves left her and she became defensive. No way was he going to spoil her day. She had barred his number from her phone but he had either borrowed someone else's, or he had a new number because it didn't register on her caller list.

"Infierno Sanguinetti! What the hell do you want?" she yelled. Whenever she was particularly angry she always lapsed into speaking Spanish as she was so used to hearing her dad swear in his own language. While she listened to Alex's reply, she kept an eye on Scott's progress, he would be coming back soon with the ticket.

"Charming, I thought I would see how you are, is that so odd?"

"You've got a nerve after the way you spoke to me before, and besides you only call when you want something, so what is it?"

"I want you to come back."

"Well tough you had your chance and you blew it, I'm not coming back so get used to it."

"You can't just leave me like this, you owe me half the money for the rent on my flat."

"No I don't you jerk, you should have thought of that before you started screwing around with your tart, it's your flat, your bill. Sort it yourself". "You're a hard bitch. I don't know what I ever saw in you. I never loved you anyway, you were only ever a bit of fun."

Katy gasped with hurt and outrage, she was no longer watching Scott as she was lost in the conversation with Alex. She didn't see that Scott was on his way back.

"Tonto ollas! Well you can bugger off and if you try and ring me again I'll cut you off so don't bother!" Katy ended the call.

"Is there a problem?" Scott asked from behind her making her jump.

"Bloody hell don't do that to me! Dios mío," She clasped a hand against her chest where her heart was beating furiously from shock and anger.

"Sorry. I didn't creep up on you to listen, your voice was raised and I couldn't help overhearing." Scott apologised. Katy might have a vulnerable side but she could definitely stand her ground when she needed to. She sighed, all the fight had left her as quickly as it had appeared.

"It was an old boyfriend; the bastard only wants me back so I can help pay the bills on his flat. Why would I go back to that scumbag after what he did to me, arsehole!" Her voice now sounded small and hurt. The trouble was, what Alex had said still hurt. Knowing that he had gone off with someone else was a serious dent to her self-esteem. How could she ever consider trying to win Scott's affection when she knew how much it would hurt Lucy? He was off limits, sadly. She had really enjoyed the drive into town, now it was ruined. She dropped her phone back into her bag, the long blood red nails on her hand standing out in contrast to the colour of her skin.

"Are you sure you're okay, I can get Dave to meet you later if you want to leave it awhile?"

"No, I'm as ready as I'll ever be. Let's go."

With her shoulders back, she strode purposefully along beside Scott. Between them they managed to carry the costumes the short distance to the indoor market, and up the wooden stairs to the first floor where Dave's store was housed. Dave wasn't as tall as Scott, or as good looking, but Katy guessed that they were about the same age. Dave had shaggy brown hair and a goatee beard, he was in the process of selling a selection of helium balloons to a middle-aged lady as they approached. They waited for him to finish off the transaction, draping the costumes over an old chair to rest their arms. It gave Katy a chance to have a quick look around. The indoor market sold an eclectic mix of items. One stall was selling jewellery while another sold antique furniture. Across the centre walkway there was a stall selling incense, Tarot cards and various coloured semiprecious stones. Katy loved it, it had a real sense of atmosphere to the place. She would love to have a stall of her own in the place eventually. Dave had finished serving the lady and made his way over to join them. He clasped hands with Scott and they slapped each other on the back in a manly greeting.

"Scott, how ya doin? And this must be the lady you were telling me about." He turned to Katy and held out his hand. "You didn't tell me how lovely she was. I'm enchanted to meet you." His voice was gravelly like Rod Stewarts, his smile was warm, and even though the flattery was a little over the top she couldn't help liking him.

"That's enough of that, we've come here for you to look at the costumes and decide if you can stock them, not for me to set you up with a date." Scott drew Dave's attention back to the purpose of their visit. The last thing he wanted was for Dave to muscle in on Katy before he'd had a chance of asking her out himself.

Dave laughed, Scott was definitely interested in Katy and he wondered how far he could push him before he gave himself away.

"Oh so that's how it is, is it? Stepping on your toes am I? If you fancy her yourself then why haven't you asked her out? Or have you and she turned you down?" he teased.

Katy could feel her face going red. The thought of Scott asking her out made her pulse quicken and sent adrenalin rushing through her veins but he already had a girlfriend, and she wasn't about to be the one who broke them up. Taking charge of the situation, she quickly turned the conversation back to the costumes.

"I believe you wanted to see these," she said picking one up and taking it out of its covering. "I make and design them myself so I can make them to order if there is something particular that is requested, but obviously I would need time to get it done".

The costume she had uncovered was a particularly fancy pirate one with a frilly shirt, a red waist sash and black trousers. She handed it to Dave who looked it over carefully.

"I'm impressed, this is good quality," he glanced at Scott who was standing protectively beside Katy with his hands in his trouser pockets. He was trying to act casual, but Dave knew him well enough to know that he had hit a nerve when he had teased him, Scott really liked Katy.

"So now we need to discuss price and quantity," he turned to Scott, "we don't need you for this why don't you have a wander and come back in fifteen minutes when we have finished talking business."

Scott frowned, he didn't like the idea of leaving Katy with Dave which made Dave smile devilishly. Scott liked that look even less, but he didn't have a good enough excuse to stay so reluctantly he left, giving Dave a warning look, which he hoped he would heed. Once Scott had gone Dave pulled out a couple of battered old chairs, one for Katy and one for himself. Katy felt more at ease without Scott there and between the two of them they managed to come to an agreement on what the price of the costumes should be, and what percentage Dave should take for displaying them.

Chapter Thirty Three

With the business concluded Katy and Dave began chatting about other things, and when Scott returned to find them sat laughing together he felt a surge of jealousy.

"You look like you're having fun, did you manage to get everything sorted out?" He asked, leaning against the counter trying not to show how annoyed he felt with Dave.

"Yes, thanks mate," Dave replied with a twinkle in his eye, then turning back to Katy asked, "How about coming for a drink to celebrate?" Scott visibly tensed and stood up straight, putting his hands in his pockets to stop him throttling Dave as Katy considered the offer.

"That's very kind of you but maybe some other time, my friend has been a bit down lately and I wouldn't want to leave her on her own for the evening."

"Why don't you bring her along too? A bit of company will do her good, Scott can come along too to balance the numbers," Dave coaxed. "You don't mind do you Scott?"

Scott relaxed a bit and shook his head.

"It sounds like a good idea to me," there was no way he wanted Katy to go for a drink on her own with Dave, but if they could go as a four he might be able to manipulate the situation so he was with Katy and Stella, if that was the friend Katy was talking about, was with Dave. "Why don't you ring her and see if she wants to join us in the Royal Oak? I presume it is Stella you are talking about?" He queried.

Katy really wanted to go for a drink with Scott, and Dave had given her the perfect opportunity. The only problem was she would feel uncomfortable about Lucy. She felt torn, should she agree or should she do the right thing by Lucy and say no? They were both watching her, waiting for her to say something. She bit her lip undecided, her brother would say if you want him go for it, but her own hurt made her reluctant to say yes. In the end she decided to see how Stella felt about the idea of going for a drink, if she wasn't keen to join them, then she would assume she wasn't meant to go, and would say no. It was only a drink after all and it had been Dave's suggestion, it wasn't like she had set out to seduce Scott.

"Okay," she said at last, "I'll ask Stella and see what she says but I can't promise anything. She might not feel like socialising at the moment." Katy rummaged in her bag and pulled out her phone. "I'll pop outside to call her so she doesn't feel under pressure to say yes."

It was also so that if she had to try a little persuasion on Stella they wouldn't hear how much she wanted to go. With her phone clasped in her hand she left Scott and Dave at the counter and wandered downstairs. Scott watched her go pondering on what she had just said. He had noticed that Stella had been a bit quiet all week but hadn't given it much thought. His mind had been occupied elsewhere, primarily on Katy when he wasn't dealing with work.

"Do ya think this Stella will agree then if you know her?" Dave asked when Katy was far enough away not to hear.

"I don't know, she has been quiet lately but I didn't realise something was wrong. She got divorced earlier this year, it could have something to do with that."

"So, what do ya think my chances are with Katy then?" Dave grinned knowing what he had said would wind Scott up. Katy was a nice girl but he wasn't seriously interested in her. Scott didn't need to know that however, and it was fun to be able to get his own back on him for all the times he himself had been the victim of Scott's pranks.

"She's not your type, and anyway I saw her first so butt out," Scott warned. Dave merely laughed, the evening could turn out to be a lot of fun if Stella agreed to join them.

* * * *

When Stella got home from work Scott had already picked Katy up and the house was quiet. Stella dumped her bags in the kitchen and made herself a cup of tea before heading into the lounge. She was surprised to find it tidy; Katy had put all her materials and patterns into a neat pile in the corner. At one-time Stella would have been relieved to find the space she needed to sit down but now it added to her feeling of emptiness. It had been hard work getting through the week, trying to ignore the misery she felt inside at the loss of Nathaniel. If only he had told her who he was before she had found out for herself, they may have been able to get over the fact that he had lied to her. She would have known that he was serious about their relationship and had wanted her to know who he really was, but as things were she wasn't sure that he would ever have told her himself. And that meant that she didn't mean as much to him as he had said she did. The worse thing was that being with him had felt so good, so right, how could she ever trust her feelings again if it hadn't been the same for him?

Now she had a whole two weeks off work to dwell on it all. The plus side of that was that she no longer had to pretend to be cheerful. The downside was that she wouldn't have anything to take her mind off her sadness. She would end up brooding on what might have been, and what she had lost if she wasn't careful. Two weeks with nothing particular to do suddenly seemed an awfully long time. At least she would have Katy to keep her company. She wondered how the meeting was going, and if Scott's friend would agree to stock the costumes that Katy had made. Stella was just about to get up and take her empty cup back to the kitchen when the phone rang beside her. It was Katy's number that appeared on the caller display so she picked it up wondering if something had gone wrong.

"Hi, it's me," Katy told Stella as soon as the call connected.

"Hi how's it going? Has he agreed to stock your stuff?" Stella asked.

Katy was sat on a bench outside the indoor market so Scott and Dave couldn't hear her conversation.

"It went well. Dave has agreed to stock my costumes for a commission which we have both worked out so it was fair, and he has also offered me some part time work at his busiest times to help me out financially until my sales take-off."

"That's great," Stella was pleased for Katy, it would help build her confidence again after what had happened with Alex.

"The thing is," Katy continued "Dave has asked me to go for a drink with him and Scott to celebrate our deal, but I don't want to leave you on your own so it's up to you, will you come and join us?"

Stella sighed deeply. She wasn't really in the mood to go out for a drink with people.

"Please!" Katy wheedled when Stella was slow to reply. "It is to celebrate my new business and it will be better than sitting at home brooding about Nathaniel."

She knew she shouldn't push it but she really wanted to go for a drink with Scott, and because it was Dave who had asked she didn't feel so guilty. Dave was the one who had suggested that Scott should join them after all, not Scott. It wasn't a date; it was a celebratory drink with new friends. Stella thought about her options. A lonely evening at home with a takeaway and nothing to think about but her own misery, or an evening out with people to keep her mind occupied. It did have a certain appeal. She had two whole weeks to wallow in her loneliness.

"Okay I'll come," she conceded. "Where shall I meet you?"

"I think Scott said that we were going to go to a place called the Royal Oak, do you know it?"

"Yes, I think it's the pub in the High Street near LK Bennett's. If it's not the right place you will have to ring me again and let me know where it is, or send me a message. Are you going there now?"

"Dave said as soon as he finished work, so I guess it won't be long."

"Okay I'll ring you when I'm in town, bye."

"Bye," Katy had to suppress the excitement that had bubbled up in her chest at the prospect of spending the evening with Scott. She was either very stupid, a masochist or lucky, she wasn't sure which yet. If Scott was still obviously keen on Lucy this evening could be torture. Slipping her phone back into her bag she headed back inside to tell the two men the news. Dave was in the process of cashing up when she made it back up the stairs. Although it was light outside, there were very few windows upstairs in the indoor market and it seemed quite dark having just come in from the early evening sunshine. It wasn't gloomy though, as the store that sold incense across from Dave's stall had various different lights on display in an array of colours. It created a magical slightly Arabian feel to the place. In the far corner Katy noticed a small café, and sat outside was a lady reading Tarot cards. Katy loved the whole vibe of the place and liked the idea of helping Dave out on his stall. There was a really good atmosphere amongst the stallholders too, slightly bohemian and casual but friendly. It was a bit like being back at the theatre in the props department, you could find anything there ranging from the old to the uber modern.

Dave's party wares were definitely modern, but the incense and candles along with the fortune-teller were reminiscent of times gone by. Dave and Scott had borrowed a clothes rack from one of the other stallholders and Scott was setting it up for Katy to put the costumes that she had brought with her on.

"Stella said yes so I told her that we were going to the Royal Oak, she will probably meet us there."

"That's great. Now that Scott has finished putting the rack in position you can hang the costumes on it and we can get going. It should be half past five by the time you finish and I am all cashed up, I just need to tidy the shelves a bit while you are busy."

"If I take the costumes out of the cellophane bags you can hang them where you want them," Scott suggested. Katy dumped her bag on a chair and between them they had soon managed to display the costumes the way Katy wanted them. Children's costumes at one end and the adults' costumes at the other.

"I'll leave the cellophane bags for people to take them away in if you like?" Katy said as she folded them neatly and stacked them under the counter with the bags for Dave's stall.

Satisfied that everything was put away, or at least where it should be ready for the morning, Dave switched off the lights above his stall and pulled down the metal frame that shut his stall off from the others. He locked it in place and with a wave to his fellow stallholders, who were also in the process of shutting for the day he followed Scott and Katy down the stairs. Katy blinked as she stepped back out into the sunshine, her eyes adjusting to the change in light again. As she wasn't sure where the Royal Oak was, she waited for the men to make the first move and then fell into step beside Scott. It wasn't that she had deliberately chosen to walk beside him, it was just that there was more space on his side than on Dave's. It didn't stop the flush of colour creeping into her cheeks in case he thought that she had consciously chosen him.

While they were walking up the high street a text came through from Stella letting Katy know that she was just parking the car and that she would be with them soon.

* * * *

Nathaniel had spent the last five days skulking about the house unable to settle to anything for any length of time. The case he had started to pack still contained the clothes he had thrown in it after his meeting with Stella. He hoped that the time would have given Stella chance to calm down and to think things through before he tried talking to her again. Several times he had sat down in front of his computer to continue writing his book but nothing would come, his mind constantly going over what had happened and how he could put it right. Somehow he needed to prove to Stella that she could trust him, and that he hadn't been lying to her when he had told her that he loved her. He still wasn't sure how he could convince her, but five days was as long as he could stand to wait. It had felt like a lifetime.

Nathaniel's agent had sent him an email to tell him that he had arranged for him to appear on a chat show in London to promote another one of his books that had been made into a film. The film was due to be released at the end of the month and the interview was being filmed tonight and it would be aired tomorrow evening. The lead actor was going to be there as well before he would fly out to LA first thing in the morning. Nathaniel really wanted to speak to Stella before he had to head back to London. He checked his watch, it was nearly six o'clock she would definitely be home from work by now. Hopefully if he could talk to her, if she would only let him explain, she would hear the sincerity in his voice. He loved her too much to give up on her. Picking up his car keys from the table in the hallway where he had casually discarded them over a week ago, he headed out the side door that led directly into the garage.

A week ago, everything had been okay, if only he could turn the clock back and tell her who he was before she had found out. Now that the time had come to face her again he felt nervous, what if she wouldn't give him the chance to speak? What if she still turned him down after he had talked to her? All week he had consoled himself with the knowledge that he was giving her some space before he talked to her again, before he made her see how he felt about her. But now he was about to leave, the scary thought that she might not listen was like a blow to the stomach. Nothing had ever felt so important to him before.

As he pushed a button on a remote control the door to the garage swung open, with his heart pounding hard in his chest he started the car. He was going to see her again and talk to her. He had to stay positive because he couldn't accept anything less than winning her back. Nothing else mattered to him.

Chapter Thirty Four

As Nathaniel's car pulled up outside of Stella's house another car passed by and pulled up further down the terrace. Nathaniel took a deep breath and climbed out the car. He could feel his stomach twisting into knots as he walked the short distance down the garden path and knocked on the door. The house was silent. Holding his breath in anticipation he waited, hoping that any minute he would hear footsteps coming towards him from inside the house, but there was nothing. His breath came out in an anxious shudder. Glancing down the road to see if by any chance he could see her anywhere he tried again. When there was still no sound of movement from inside he took a step back, looking up at the upstairs windows wondering if perhaps she could be in the shower and unable to hear him knocking. He was just about to try knocking for a third time, when the door to the house next door opened and a young woman in a tie-dye top came out carrying some rubbish for the bin. She looked surprised when she saw him standing at the door but the look quickly turned to one of shock the moment she realised who he was, and she dropped the bag of rubbish on the ground at her feet.

"Do you know if Stella Martin has come back from work yet, I thought I would find her here but no one is answering?" Nathaniel asked anxiously.

"She went out about half an hour ago, she was going to meet her friend Katy somewhere. Do you want to leave a message? I can watch out for her and tell her the minute she gets in," Jo told him. "I don't know how long she will be or I would let you come in and wait." Jo had been surprised to see Nathaniel on Stella's doorstep but she hoped it was a good sign, it was a shame that Stella wasn't in to speak to him.

Nathaniel was disappointed, he hadn't considered the fact that she might have gone out. Now he wasn't sure what to do. He really didn't want to leave for London before he had been able to speak to her.

"Have you got her mobile number so I can ring her?" He asked. Jo was tempted to tell him that she had heard that he didn't have a phone, but decided against it in case it caused more trouble.

"Yes, it's programmed into my phone, hold on," she rushed in doors and came out moments later carrying her phone. "Here it is, are you going to type it straight into your phone?" she waited expecting him to get his phone out and type in the number, but instead he produced a small notebook and pen.

"I don't have a phone when I'm in the village," seeing the look of stunned disbelief on her face he explained, "I like the peace and quiet".

It made sense and, Jo thought, it also meant that he hadn't been lying to Stella when he had told her that he didn't have a phone. She read out the number and Nathaniel wrote it down.

"I have to go to London tonight and I might have to be there for a while," he told Jo, "Look, in case I can't get through to her, or... well in case she puts the phone down on me, will you tell her to watch the 'Ben Pargeter show' tomorrow night, it's very important that she sees it." Nathaniel looked so desperate that Jo agreed. He slipped the notebook and pen into the pocket of his jeans and climbed back into his car.

"Don't forget to tell her, it's really important that she watches the programme," he called back before he drove away. An idea had come to him while he was talking to Stella's neighbour, but somehow he didn't think his agent was going to like it.

* * * *

Tim and Rory had bought a takeaway to get their weekend off to a good start and were about to sit down and eat it when someone knocked on their front door.

"Why do people always turn up or ring when we are about to eat?" Rory complained as Tim got to his feet and went to see who it was.

"Don't worry I'll get rid of them as quick as I can, why don't you pour us out a glass of wine to go with the curry while I see to the door?" Tim hurried along the passage and opened the door, his habitual greeting already forming on his lips. When he saw who was standing anxiously on the doorstep the words dried in his throat, his smile frozen in place. Rory's mum stood rubbing her hands nervously together, and behind her stood Rory's father. Tim wasn't sure if them turning up was a good or bad thing, so he waited for one of them to speak first. If they were here to cause Rory more upset there was no way they were stepping over the threshold, it didn't matter that Rory's dad was a soldier and ten times stronger than he was, they wouldn't get in.

"Well are ye gonna let us in lad or not?" Rory's dad asked when it was clear that Tim wasn't going to step aside.

"That depends," Tim told him keeping a firm hold on the door, "On what you intend to say to Rory, you've hurt him so much already," Angus was impressed with how protective Tim was over Rory. He may not like the fact that Rory had chosen this man as his partner but at least he really seemed to care about him. After what had happened to his friends' son recently, he wasn't about to lose his own son over something that now seemed trivial in comparison. He was still disappointed, he couldn't help that and a little uncomfortable if he was honest, but Rory was his son and he would have to get used to the choice he had made or he would lose him forever.

"We've come to clear the air. We don't want to lose our son," Rory's mums' voice trembled as she spoke. Tim could tell that she was struggling not to cry. Tim reluctantly stepped aside to allow them to enter, he would reserve the welcome until he was sure they deserved one. Leading them down the passage to the kitchen he pushed open the door. Rory was stacking the foil trays that had held their dinner, and was putting them in an old carrier bag to throw in the bin later. He had his back to the door and was unaware that Tim had company.

"Who was it?" he asked as he turned around. The look of delight, and then shock that appeared on his face was almost his mothers' undoing. She rushed forward and threw her arms about him, hugging him tightly. Rory hugged her back while glancing nervously at his father who was still stood framed in the doorway. It was the brief smile and nod that his father gave him that finally allowed him to relax and believe that everything would be alright. Tim stood anxiously to one side, allowing Rory and his family some space. Once Lily had relaxed her grip on Rory, Angus stepped forward and shook his hand. Noticing the food on the table he said, "If I pop out an get us a wee takeaway are we welcome to eat with ye?" Rory nodded,

"Of course." Sensing that Angus was not about to give Rory a hard time Tim offered to go and get some chips from the chip shop.

"I can go if you like? It'll give you chance to talk in private." He looked to Rory to see if he agreed, or if he would rather that he stay. Rory smiled gratefully and Tim found his shoes. As he left the kitchen he waited by the front door listening for a while to make sure that the conversation didn't become heated, once he was satisfied that there wasn't an argument brewing he set off. The chip shop was only a short walk away so he knew he could get there and back fairly quickly.

The atmosphere in the kitchen felt a little awkward to start with. No one wanted to say anything that might cause someone else to get upset. Rory offered his parents a glass of the wine from the bottle he had opened just before they had entered, and they sat down at the table.

"I'm glad you came," Rory said at last to break the ice. Lily grabbed Rory's hand and glanced anxiously at her husband. It was important to her that he clear the air. Angus looked Rory straight in the eye and spoke.

"Och well, we missed ye Rory lad. I can't say I approve of ..." Angus paused finding it hard to express his feelings. Lily could feel Rory tense at his father's words but rubbed his hand reassuringly as Angus continued, "Well let's just say I don't understand it, but I'm willing to accept your... relationship. Your happiness is more important to us than whether I agree with the way you choose to live your life. Mebe I'll get more used to it with time."

Rory knew how difficult it had been for his father to say what he had said, and it brought a lump to his throat. It meant such a lot to him to have his father's acceptance. It was like a great weight had been lifted off his shoulders. He felt lighter than he had felt in weeks. Then the anxiety returned as he realised that his parents still didn't know yet that he and Tim were going to become civil partners. Should he tell them now he wondered, or allow them all a moment of peace before he brought it up? Standing to his feet he paced over to the cooker, which was furthest away from where his dad was sitting, his hands stuffed into his pockets and his shoulders hunched.

"I'm really glad that you have come because..." Oh God he thought am I really going to do this now? He heard the front door opening and knew that Tim had returned with the chips. He hoped they weren't about to be wasted.

"The thing is, Tim and I are going to have a civil ceremony to make our relationship legal."

His words rushed out in one go and he held his breath waiting for the explosion. Angus pushed himself to his feet as Lily grabbed ineffectually for his arm to restrain him. His hands clasped and unclasped as he struggled to control his emotions, but as Tim stepped into the room with the bag of chips he held out his hand towards Rory. Rory stepped forward and clasped his father's hand.

Angus's voice was quiet as he spoke, "Congratulations lad."

Lily breathed a sigh of relief. Like Rory, for a minute there she had thought that the truce was about to fall apart. Tim put the bag of chips on the table.

"Well it looks like we have something to celebrate at last," he said picking up the glass of wine that had been left for him on the side. "Cheers!"

Chapter Thirty Five

Stella arrived at the back of the Royal Oak as Katy appeared through the doors to the outside seating area. Stella spotted her over the low wall and made her way to an empty table. The sign above the door proclaimed it to be the oldest pub in the country. Although she had never been inside to see what the interior was like, it certainly looked old from the outside with its black Tudor frame and leaded windows. Katy had a glass in each hand, one of wine and one of orange juice.

"One of these is for you. I don't mind which one you have it depends whether you want me to drive us home, or whether you are going to drive?"

"I'll drive as it's your celebration, your first big step towards being self-employed." Stella took the glass of orange juice that Katy held out to her and sat down, tucking her bag in the gap between her leg and the table's leg. Scott and Dave appeared moments later carrying their own drinks and a couple of menus. Scott introduced Stella to Dave and took the seat beside Katy.

"We thought you might like to eat here as well, if you're not in a rush to get off anywhere?" Scott told them dropping the menus down.

Stella noticed how Scott had made sure he was sitting beside Katy and decided that she would remind him that he was already involved with Lucy, and that she wasn't about to let her friend be used. "So Scott, what is Lucy up to tonight or is she joining you later?"

Katy suddenly sat very still, her heart tripping over itself as it began beating erratically and she listened carefully to his reply. Part of her didn't want to hear what he said, but the other part of her was curious all the same. She liked Lucy, but she liked Scott more and desperately wanted to hear him say that they weren't seeing each other anymore. Stella noticed that Scott didn't seem to be perturbed by the question. She had expected him to at least look a bit uncomfortable.

He took a quick sip of his drink before casually replying, "I've no idea, she's gone back home now. I don't expect I will see her again for a while," he explained.

It seemed like a very casual relationship to Katy, which was a good thing because it meant that she might still stand a chance. On the other hand, if that was the sort of relationship he wanted then he wasn't quite what she thought after all, it was all very confusing.

Seeing the puzzled look on Katy's face Scott added, "She was only staying with me for the weekend as she was singing in the cathedral, and being the kind big brother that I am, I said she could stay."

As the realisation struck Katy that Lucy was actually Scott's sister and not his girlfriend, relief and joy flooded through her. She could have kissed Stella for asking the question she had been avoiding ever since Scott had picked her up in his car. If only she had asked him earlier she wouldn't have had to feel guilty about fancying him... again! It was the second time she had mistakenly thought he was going out with someone and been wrong, Stella had been her first error. Katy couldn't help a small smile from appearing on her face, she suddenly felt very light-hearted. Now she could enjoy a guilt free evening getting to know him better.

Stella laughed, "We thought she was your girlfriend, didn't we?" Stella gave Katy a pointed look that was clearly saying 'now's your chance'. Katy could feel her cheeks turning a rosy shade of pink.

"So, do you have any other brothers or sisters?" She asked to hide her embarrassment, and move the conversation along.

When Scott turned his full attention on her, looking her straight in the eyes, she allowed herself to enjoy the quiver of excitement that had her stomach leaping for joy. When he smiled at her with his blue eyes twinkling mischievously, obviously enjoying the fact that they had spoken about him, he sent her pulse into a flutter. 'How could I ever have thought I could resist his easy charm' she thought as she gazed back.

"No, Lucy is my only sister, what about you?"

"I have got five brothers and a sister, I'm slap bang in the middle" Katy told him. "My fathers from a big family, although most of the older generation, his parents and my aunts and uncles still live in Spain".

Stella listened to them talking for a while and then realised that Dave was asking her what she would like to eat. He seemed like a nice man and they chatted politely, but Stella couldn't help feeling awkward. It was great that Katy and Scott were getting on so well but it added to making her feel more alone. Chatting with Dave just reminded her of how much she was missing Jack – she still found it difficult to think of him as Nathaniel, and how special what they had together had felt. She wished she could go back and have her last conversation with him again. Perhaps she had over reacted. If she had given him more time to explain his reasons maybe it wouldn't have seemed so bad. The trouble was, although a part of her wanted him back there was always the 'would she ever be able to trust him' question?

Not that it mattered now, he hadn't tried in the last week to change her mind, she had blown it completely by telling him it was over. She obviously hadn't meant that much to him after all. She sipped her drink remembering what Jo had said about the models that he usually dated, he couldn't really have been interested in her anyway, not when he could go out with models. When she had been with him though, he had sounded so sincere, so kind and thoughtful. Her thoughts were constantly going around and around like they had all week. She had been finding it difficult to sleep, spending her nights going over in her head the romantic meals they had shared, the things they had said to each other, and it had often left her feeling tired and lethargic the following day. Some nights she had cried herself to sleep, silently sobbing for what she had lost. Belatedly she realised that Dave was talking to her again and tried to focus on what he was saying, it wasn't his fault that she was suffering from a broken heart after all. The least she could do was to be polite and try and concentrate on what he was saying.

* * * *

It was quite late when they eventually got in. Katy almost skipped through the door she was so happy. Scott had asked her out on a lunch date for the following day. She drifted up the stairs to her room telling Stella as she went, that she wanted to search her wardrobe for something to wear before she went to sleep. "Otherwise I will lay awake all night mentally going over what choices I have in my wardrobe. It's better to do it now," she said, "If we are meeting for lunch I will only have a few hours to get ready in the morning".

Stella was pleased for her; at least someone's life was working out well. Scott and Katy would make a lovely couple. Katy was definitely more his type than Stella had ever been.

Stella dumped her bag on the kitchen table and was just about to put the kettle on when she heard a knock at the front door. She checked her watch; it was a bit late for visitors, which meant it must be an emergency of some kind. She hurried along the passage, her heart pounding hard in her chest, while her mind raced through the possibilities. Had her mother had an accident? Was it the police? Suddenly she felt sick and shaky, imagining the police at her door. It reminded her of the moment she had opened the door to the police all those years earlier. She could still remember it so vividly; the shock of discovering that her father had been killed in a car accident. The image was permanently ingrained in her subconscious and caused her to panic whenever someone knocked on her door late at night. Her skin felt clammy as the feeling of dread lodged itself painfully in her stomach. She couldn't go through it again, not now. With cold shaky hands she opened the door and peeped out. Instead of a policeman, Jo stood fidgeting on the doorstep impatiently waiting for her to answer.

"Thank god you're back, I've been watching for you for hours!" she exclaimed darting through the door and shutting it carefully behind her.

"What is it, what's wrong?" Stella asked feeling a little faint with relief. If it wasn't the police there couldn't have been an accident, or could there? Had they tried her door and when they had found that she was out, had they popped in to get Jo to give her the news? Would they do that? Her stomach began to knot itself up with tension again.

"You had a visitor earlier," Jo told her brightly.

The colour drained from Stella's face, the fact that Jo was smiling hadn't registered yet.

"Oh, god who was it? What did they want?" Jo noticed how pale Stella had become, and took her arm guiding her into the kitchen where she could sit down. Katy followed them in. She had heard the knock on the door and then the voices and was curious as to what was going on.

"Nathaniel Morgan was here earlier. He wanted to speak to you, he looked desperate actually," Jo told her.

"Well tough, he deserves to be desperate after what he's put Stella through," Katy sat beside Stella and put her hand protectively on her shoulder. "He's probably worried she's going to tell the press his whereabouts."

"I don't think so, he looked really upset that he had missed you, I think he really does care about you Stella."

Stella looked up with tears in her eyes, the relief of knowing that there hadn't been an accident had been replaced with disappointment, if only she hadn't gone out she could have spoken to him herself. She had missed him so much over the last week, it was like a physical pain.

"Anyway," Jo continued, "He left you a message. He asked me to tell you, that he's had to go to London for a while and that you should watch the Ben Pargeter show tomorrow night. He said it was very important. He wanted your phone number too. I hope you don't mind that I gave it to him?"

"He has a phone now then I take it?" Katy said sarcastically. She was still cross with him for the way he had treated Stella. She hadn't even finished reading the book he had written yet, because every time she picked it up it made her feel guilty for enjoying it and then that annoyed her and she ended up putting it down again.

"No, he didn't have one on him or I think he would have rung you there and then," Jo told Stella. "I asked him if he wanted to programme it into his phone to see if he had one, but he said he didn't have one when he was staying here because he liked the peace. Then he wrote your number on a piece of paper, so he was telling the truth when he said he didn't have a phone."

Stella rummaged in her bag for her phone to see if she had any missed calls from an unknown number. She hadn't heard her phone ring but then she didn't always hear it when it was in her bag, especially when there was a lot of noise going on around her as there had been in the pub. Katy and Jo watched as she opened the wallet that held her phone and checked the screen.

"I haven't got any missed calls so he obviously hasn't rung me," she put the phone on the table rather than back in her bag so she would hear it if it rang.

"I suppose he would have to get to wherever he's going before he tries to ring you, and we don't know how long that will take," Jo reasoned. "You mustn't feel disappointed yet, he could still ring you tonight". They all looked at the phone, willing it to ring but it stayed stubbornly silent.

"I'll make us a drink, shall I?" Katy suggested getting up and re-boiling the kettle that had been forgotten since Jo's arrival. "Are you staying for a drink Jo?" Katy asked as she grabbed a couple of mugs from the cupboard. Jo looked at her watch, it was nearly eleven o'clock.

"No, I'd better not. But if he rings you tonight, you have to come and tell me what he says first thing in the morning okay," She rested her hand on Stella's shoulder as she got up out of her chair and Stella nodded. *'If he rang,'* and that was a big '*if*'. So far he hadn't rung and he must have found somewhere with a phone by now. Katy went to the door with Jo to see her out and then locked it behind her, they weren't going to go out again tonight. Stella had made the hot chocolate by the time Katy had returned to the kitchen and was scrolling through the messages on her phone hoping to see one that she might have missed. A watched clock never ticks her mum would say, all while she was sat waiting for the call it was bound to not come. With a big sigh she put the phone down and forced herself to think of something else. She hoped pretending she wasn't waiting for the call would still count, because now she knew he had her phone number it would be impossible not to wait for it.

* * * *

Nathaniel had been driving for what seemed like several hours but in reality, had only been an hour and forty minutes. Time always dragged when you wanted to get somewhere quickly, and he was desperate to get to the studio where the interview was to be recorded so he could find a phone. The journey wasn't going well, nearly everything that could hold him up had. First there had been an accident on the motorway, which had caused a delay, and then once he had arrived in London there had been a detour due to road works. He eventually found a space to park his car in a side street off Wood Lane and walked the short distance to the Television Centre. Hopefully there would be time once he was inside to phone Stella before they wanted him in the studio.

Nathaniel hurried across the small car park that was, as he expected full, and passed the tall grey pillars holding up a large porch way where the double doors would lead inside. Although it was quite dark outside because it was late, inside was very bright. Amongst the people milling about doing their jobs was Nathaniel's agent, Mike.

Mike rushed forward as soon as he spotted Nathaniel coming through the door, "Where have you been I thought you weren't going to make it on time?" Mike was a terrible worrier, he stressed out about everything.

"Relax, I didn't think they were starting the recording until nine thirty, it's only...." Nathaniel checked his watch, trying not to let Mikes' air of fraught anxiety fuel his own concerns about Stella's reaction when he phoned. "It's only half past eight"

"It's nearly a quarter to nine and they want to run through the questions they're going to ask before the recording starts. You need to get into make-up so let's get moving". Mike ushered Nathaniel towards a lift where he pushed the button to take them to the second floor where the green room was located. Mike fiddled nervously with a cigarette that he would desperately love to have lit at that moment, but couldn't.

"I need to make a quick phone call before we start" Nathaniel told him. To be honest he wasn't sure that the call would be quick, but there was no point worrying Mike any more than he was already by telling him it might be a long call, especially as Stella might put the phone straight down again when she knew who it was on the other end of the line.

"There isn't time for that now, you have to get to make up as well as go over the questions Ben Pargeter is going to ask. If there is time after that you can make your call. Who's it to anyway?"

"Someone I met quite recently, there are some things I need to straighten out with her."

"Well if it's only a woman she can wait, this recording is more important. Don't forget it's to promote the book that you wrote, that they have just finished making into another film. This is going to bring us in a lot of money again".

The lift had stopped, Mike stepped out and waited for Nathaniel to follow him down the corridor. Nathaniel was tempted to stay in the lift and let it go back down to the foyer where he would find a phone, but a lady with a clipboard approached him telling him how pleased she was to meet him and would he please follow her to make up where she would go over the shows agenda with him. Reluctantly he followed her along the brightly lit corridor, passed several doors where he could hear people talking and laughing. He checked his watch; if they got on with it all he would still have time to phone Stella before the recording started.

Chapter Thirty Six

Stella and Katy had sat up waiting to see if Nathaniel would ring until nearly one o'clock in the morning before finally giving in and going to bed. The fact that he had turned up at the house and had told Jo that he would ring, and then hadn't was worse somehow than if he hadn't turned up at all. If only she hadn't gone out, if only she had given him a chance to prove to her that he had meant all the things he had told her. With her thoughts chasing themselves around her head it was exhaustion that finally made Stella fall asleep as it was just starting to get light. She was still sleeping when her mobile phone suddenly sprang to life playing a heavy rock song to alert her to a call. Stella jack knifed into a sitting position with her heart hammering away in her chest as if she had run a marathon. Panic made her hands shaky and as she clumsily reached for the phone, she knocked it off the bedside table and onto the floor. Quickly she scrambled over to the side of the bed and picked it up just as it stopped ringing.

"Damn!" Stella flopped back against the pillows with the phone clutched in her hand. She checked for the number of the missed call, her heart still pounding erratically in her chest. It was an unknown number, could it have been Nathaniel? Katy knocked on the door, "Did I hear the phone ring? Was it him?"

"I don't know," Stella snapped. "Whoever it was rang off before I got chance to answer it," she dropped the phone carelessly on the duvet cover. Her heart was still pounding so hard she thought she might have a heart attack any minute.

"Bloody hell isn't that typical? I hate it when that happens," Katy plonked herself on the end of the bed. "At least you can check the number, it must register on your missed calls list."

"It does but I don't recognise the number and before you ask no, I'm not going to ring it back and find out who it is. It might be a sales person trying to con me into buying something I don't want."

"Well if it was him he will try again won't he?" Katy replied reasonably tucking her knees up against her chest and clasping her ankles. Stella picked up the phone and willed it to ring again. When Jo had told her the night before that he had called around to see her she had been disappointed that she had missed him, now she had potentially missed his call as well, how unlucky could she get. As the phone suddenly began ringing again Stella nearly leapt out of her skin, dropping the phone on the bed with shock. Quickly she picked it up and answered it a little breathlessly. "Hello."

Katy watched, eager to see Stella's reaction.

"Hi, Stella, did I disturb you? You sound as if you have been rushing, is it a good time for a chat or shall I ring you back later?" It was Joyce, Stella's mum.

"No, it's fine mum, I only woke up a while ago and the phone ringing made me jump that's all." Katy got to her feet and left Stella to chat to her mother while she got herself washed and dressed. If they were still on the phone after that she would make breakfast. She wished Stella would ring the missed call back, Katy hated not knowing if it was Nathaniel or not.

* * * *

Nathaniel couldn't settle to anything in his London home, he paced the sitting room like a caged animal before pulling out his mobile phone and trying Stella's number for the second time that morning. The first time he had tried ringing he had waited with his heart in his mouth for her to answer, but she hadn't, it had gone to voicemail. Rather than leave a message he had hung up, preferring to try again himself later. He stood in front of the window that looked out onto a wide, tree-lined street and selected the number to redial. People passed by outside without him taking notice of their existence as he was contemplating what he should say when she eventually answered. After several seconds he heard a voice telling him that the line was already busy and to call back later. 'Typical' it was funny how people who were selling things or who wanted you to claim back your PPI always managed to get through, but when it was something personal there was always a problem, the line was busy or there was no signal.

When he had eventually been able to ring Stella the night before, there had been no signal and then it had become so late after the recording was finished that he had been reluctant to ring in case he had woken her up. It wouldn't exactly have put her in a good mood if he had disturbed her when she had fallen asleep, so he had decided to wait until this morning. Now he still couldn't get through. He tossed the phone onto the sofa and stared out the window deep in thought, wondering what he should do. He had several meetings to go to and the sort of conversation he was likely to have with Stella was not one that he wanted to have in a public place or with people listening. He might get a chance to ring again in the afternoon but it was unlikely. If he could get everything done quickly he could possibly leave London again and return to Little Welborough, where he could speak to her in person. If he did that he had a better chance of being able to convince her that he meant what he said, and at least he could keep trying until she did believe him if he was in the same village.

* * * *

Stella appeared bleary eyed at the table and put her head on her hand as Katy pushed a plate of scrambled eggs on toast in front of her.

"So, what did your mum want?" Katy asked.

"The usual, am I going out enough, how's Scott, that sort of thing."

"Yikes, what did you tell her about Scott? I don't want her thinking I stole him off you." Katy handed Stella a mug of tea and sat down opposite her at the table.

"I told her that Scott and I are just friends, I didn't say anything about you seeing him yet. I'll let her get used to the idea of him not going out with me first." Stella took her first reviving sip of tea, warming her hands round the cup for comfort.

"I guess she's not happy with you only being friends, did she give you a hard time?" Katy knew only too well how desperate Joyce was for Stella to settle down again so she would have some grandchildren in the not too distant future. She could imagine how disappointed she would have been to find out that there was no great romance between Stella and Scott.

"She could tell that I was upset and thought that Scott had dumped me, she was quite sympathetic actually." Stella thought back over the conversation she had had with her mother. She had been like a mother tiger defending her cub, so much so that Stella was glad that Scott wasn't around to hear what her mother had to say about him. To be fair to him, in case her mother ever saw him again she had confessed that it had actually been her decision that they should just be friends.

Joyce had then assumed that Stella was down because she was lonely and had been lovely about it, telling her not to let it get her down and that there were plenty more fish in the sea, the usual spiel after a break up. It was a good job that her mother didn't know the real reason she was feeling so low or Stella was sure she would track Nathaniel down and demand an explanation. He wouldn't get away with any rubbish about not having a phone with her mother around. Stella pushed her plate away untouched. The one man she had truly fallen in love with was Jack and he wasn't real, what a mess. The trouble was she missed him so much and she felt guilty now for not letting him have the chance to explain why he had behaved the way he had. She was such a sucker, she should have realised from the start that something wasn't right, not allowed herself to believe he was a ghost. She had trusted him and he had let her down. God her head ached, her thoughts constantly went around and around, should she have given him a chance to explain or would he have just told her more lies? The truth was all she really wanted was to have him back, it might be pathetic but it was how she felt. The thought of spending a day waiting for the phone to ring was not an appealing one. She needed something to occupy her mind but what?

"Don't forget, Nathaniel told Jo that you have got to watch the Ben Pargeter show later," Katy reminded her. "I wonder why it is so important that you have to watch it?"

"I have no idea, but it's not on until this evening and I have to get there first without going mad, what can I do that will take my mind off him?" Katy was meeting Scott for lunch so she wouldn't even have her chattering to keep her occupied.

"You can come to lunch with Scott and me if you like?" Katy offered.

"No don't be silly, you don't want me going on your first date with you, we're not teenagers anymore," Stella smiled, "thanks for the offer though". When Stella and Katy had been at school, they had often gone on dates together to give each other moral support, but those days had long gone. "I can always cancel the lunch date and go another time if you want me to stay with you?" Katy offered.

"No! Don't you dare, I don't want to be responsible for wrecking your love life as well as my own, you go," Stella insisted. Katy squeezed Stella's hand affectionately before heading upstairs to finish getting herself ready for her lunch date. Stella picked up the book that had been discarded on top of the box for the school fete and turned it over so she could see the back. It was Nathaniel's book, the book that had ruined Stella's happiness, but she couldn't put it down. She gazed sadly at the picture of Nathaniel, there was a hint of a smile on his handsome face that didn't quite reach his eyes. Eyes that until recently she had been able to look into for real, she had seen the happiness on her own face mirrored in them she had thought. She traced her finger over the outline of his lips and remembered the first time he had kissed her. Opening the book, she saw on the inside cover there was a bit of writing about the author, Stella began to read what it said about him.

'Nathaniel Morgan was born in Hillingdon, London. He and his sister were brought up by their grandparents in Hamondsworth following the death of their parents in a plane crash. Nathaniel Morgan's father was a pilot, and was flying the plane at the time of the crash, his mother was an air hostess. Nathaniel started writing as a way to help him express the emotion that he often kept bottled up inside and gradually began writing stories where he could control the outcome of his characters' lives. His sister turned to religion to help her deal with her loss but despite their very different careers the two have remained close.'

The small insight into Nathaniel's life was enough to make Stella want to weep all over again. It also made sense of how the vicar knew who she was when she had found her in the churchyard upset. The vicar was obviously Nathaniel's sister. That was why she had been so keen to reassure Stella that she could talk to her if she wanted to, and that was why when she had first seen her from behind in the vicars' robes with the sun in her eyes she had thought it was Nathaniel, or Jack at the time. Stella felt her heart lift a little, if the vicar was Nathaniel's sister she might be able to help her to understand why he had lied to her, and if nothing else talking to her would allow Stella to feel close to him in some way. Stella finished off the tea Katy had made for her, which had by now turned cold and went upstairs to get dressed.

Chapter Thirty Seven

Stella hurried along the road that led to the vicarage, now she was on her way there she suddenly felt nervous. She wasn't quite sure what she was going to say, she bit her lip as she considered her options, each one making her stomach turn over with anxiety and causing a slight burn. Should she start off by asking her outright if Nathaniel was her brother? She would look pretty silly if the vicar asked who she was talking about. Her stomach rebelled again; perhaps she should have had some breakfast after all. What should she do if the vicar wasn't there? For a split second this thought brought her a sense of relief before she remembered that she actually wanted to talk to her about Jack/Nathaniel.

It was a warm day and by the time she could see the vicarage she felt hot and clammy, she was warm from the walk but her nerves had the blood draining from her skin leaving her in a cold sweat. She stopped at the entrance to the front garden and wiped her hands down her jeans. This was silly she told herself, she was only going to find out if she was Nathaniel's sister, it wasn't like a test or anything. 'But what if she doesn't know who you're talking about and she thinks you've gone mad?' the voice in her head fretted. Stella was on the verge of turning around to go back when she saw Sophie heading along the road towards her. It was enough to make her hurry along the path and knock rapidly on the door. Her heart hammered loudly in her chest, 'please open the door before Sophie sees me' she begged silently. Then, glancing over her shoulder she checked that Sophie wasn't about to join her on the doorstep. The very thought of it had Stella's stomach tying itself in knots all over again. What if Sophie was on her way to visit the vicar as well? Panic nearly had Stella fainting with relief on the spot as the vicar opened the door. She looked surprised to see Stella, but smiled warmly and invited her in. Stella checked one last time behind her to make sure that Sophie was nowhere in sight before she stepped over the threshold and into the sunny passage way.

"I was just about to make myself a drink would you like one?" Jess asked, leading Stella towards the kitchen at the back of the house.

"Yes thank you, that would be lovely" Stella replied "Unless you're expecting someone, I could come back another time if it's inconvenient," she added. If Sophie was about to join them she would rather not stay, she couldn't think of a plausible reason to be there that would satisfy Sophie's gossip antenna.

Jess shook her head, "No I'm not expecting anyone".

She put the kettle on and gestured Stella towards a seat. It was a large kitchen but not modern. The cupboards looked like they had been put in in the seventies and the Formica worktops were well scrubbed and faded from use. The wooden table and chairs were an odd assortment, some dark, some light that were scarred from all their years of service, but the homemade cushions gave the room a homely, welcoming feel. When Stella sat silently at the table fiddling nervously with the strap of her handbag, Jess decided to broach the subject of Stella's appearance at her home.

"Is this about Nathaniel?" she queried, watching for Stella's reaction. When Stella's head shot up and she nodded, Jess carried on. "I know he's made a terrible mess of things but he really does love you, you know?"

"Then why didn't he tell me who he really was? Why did he leave me to find out for myself?"

Jess sighed, she had asked Nathaniel that herself many times. "The trouble is he has been hurt in the past. You probably know by now that he was engaged a few years ago but it didn't work out?"

At Stella's nod Jess continued. "Well it turned out that Anna, that was his fiancé's name, was only interested in him because of his celebrity status. She wasn't interested in Nathaniel as a person; she even made up stories about him to sell to the press when they broke up so she could make some money out of the split. There was nothing too dreadful written because she wouldn't have had a leg to stand on if it was too obviously made up, but enough to cast him in a bad light. She told them he used her as a trophy to parade at events but ignored her when they were alone. The truth was she got bored when he was working and she wasn't the centre of his attention. So, after all that when he met you and realised that you didn't know who he was, and that you enjoyed his company anyway he didn't want to spoil it. He wanted a chance to get to know you properly before he told you, and then he started to worry about telling you because it had gone on too long."

"Why didn't he explain that to me when I confronted him?"

"Would you have listened?" When Stella remained quiet and Jess saw the colour flare up on her cheeks, she knew she had hit a nerve. "I think he wanted to, but understandably you were upset at the time and I'm not sure you would have believed him then anyway."

Stella hung her head, Jess was right she wouldn't have believed him, at the time she had felt so humiliated and hurt that she wouldn't have listened. Jess grabbed Stella's hand and gently squeezed it to show there were no hard feelings. She could see how much Stella was suffering, how betrayed and hurt she had felt, and she wanted to help. Stella was a lovely person. Jess had heard a lot of good things about her since she had moved into the village and started working in the school. She also knew that Stella was what Nathaniel needed. As soon as they could sort out the mess he had created she was sure they could work out a way forward.

"I knew he had been engaged but that it hadn't worked out," Stella conceded, "I didn't realise why it had all gone wrong though, I feel awful for not listening to him now! Has he been living here with you? Will he come back?"

Jess looked at Stella thoughtfully, she was contemplating how much she should tell Stella. She could answer her honestly enough by just admitting that he had his own house or she could trust her with the secret that he lived beside the church. Which would Nathaniel want she wondered?

"He has his own house in the village," She said at last pausing briefly before, with her fingers crossed and a lot of faith she added, "It's the house beside the church, he often hops over the wall rather than going through the gate so people don't see him. He likes the peace and quiet of anonymity to write".

As Jess finished speaking Stella realised how it had often seemed as if 'Jack' had disappeared, he had obviously jumped over the wall back into his own garden. He hadn't deliberately tried to deceive her, she had done that herself. Part of her had enjoyed the romanticism of a ghostly gentleman who would turn up especially for her, someone only she could see. But Nathaniel was still a kind caring man who she had misjudged, slightly. She couldn't completely ignore the fact that he had deceived her, but she could now understand his reasons for it a little better. The trouble was, she wasn't sure if she had blown her chances with him by refusing to listen to what he had to say.

"When he comes back... if he comes back, will you tell him I'm sorry for not listening to what he had to say?" Stella picked up her bag and stood ready to leave.

"He'll come back don't worry," Jess reassured her, "and of course I will tell him that you are sorry, but I expect he will want to talk to you himself."

Stella wasn't so sure about that but she kept her thoughts to herself as she walked back down the passage to the front door. At least now she understood why he had behaved the way he had. She stopped once she reached the door and thanked Jess for listening to her and for explaining why Nathaniel had told her his name was Jack instead of his real name.

"You know he's on the Ben Pargeter show tonight don't you?" Jess asked as she opened the door for Stella to leave.

"Yes, he told my neighbour yesterday, he called at my house but I was out," Stella explained.

"Are you going to watch it?" Jess wanted to know. She was glad that he had tried to talk to Stella again before he had left, and was pleasantly surprised to hear that he had spoken to her neighbour.

"Yes, I expect so, apparently he wants me to see it."

Stella walked slowly back to her house thinking about the conversation she had had with Nathaniel's sister. Jess was very easy to talk to, like Nathaniel it would seem. It was strange that she had never noticed the resemblance to him before when she had met the vicar. They had the same deep blue eyes and easy smile. Nathaniel's hair was definitely darker than his sisters, but now she knew they were related the similarities between them were obvious. She could understand why Nathaniel wouldn't want people in the village to know where he lived. Sophie would be forever dropping by to invite him to do talks for her reading group, or opening fetes. His life wouldn't be his own. She was still upset that he hadn't told her himself what his real name was, but she could understand his reluctance initially. Jo was stood at Stella's door when she came around the corner, and as Stella was deep in thought it made her jump.

"There you are, I wondered what had happened. Did he ring you last night in the end?"

"No but I have just been talking to his sister."

"His sister; how did you meet her?" Jo asked, then before Stella could answer she suddenly added suspiciously, "was it definitely his sister and how do you know?"

Stella laughed, she couldn't help it. That was a lot of questions in a short space of time Jo had hardly had time to draw breath before she had asked the next one. Stella unlocked her front door and pushed it open,

"Come on in and I will tell you over a cup of tea, which come to think of it, I never got around to having earlier." She had been so busy talking to Jess that they had never had the drink that Jess had offered to make.

* * * *

Katy arrived back at six carrying a Chinese take away.

"You have to eat this because I paid for it out of the money from my first costume sale," she informed Stella. She was determined to get Stella eating again and if it took a little emotional blackmail then so be it. Stella was feeling a little more cheerful since her talk with Jess, and the smell of Chinese food made her stomach rumble.

"That's great about the sale, I'm really pleased for you. I'll get the plates," she told Katy as she headed into the kitchen.

Katy followed on unable to hide the smile on her face. She had had a really good day. Her date with Scott had gone really well. They had spent hours talking about anything and everything and Scott had a great sense of humour. After lunch they had gone bowling and she had won, it was pretty close but she had beaten him on the last ball. Of course, that might have had something to do with the fact that Scott's phone had rung while he was preparing his last shot, sending it into the gully at the side. The phone call had been from Dave to tell them that he had sold Katy's first costume, and that he would definitely be wanting more as there had been a lot of interest in them. Her day couldn't get much better, but as she got closer to home she had started to feel a bit guilty as she knew how unhappy Stella had been. Seeing the Chinese takeaway on the drive home, she had stopped to get a selection of dishes to cheer her up and to encourage her to eat.

Seeing Stella dishing herself up some of the food, she was glad she had thought of it. She wasn't silly though, she realised that something else must have happened to have cheered her up because Chinese food might be lovely, but it usually took more than that to perk her up when she was feeling down. Over the food Stella told Katy about her visit to see the vicar, Jess; who she had found out was Nathaniel's sister. By the time they had finished eating and had washed up, it was nearly time for the Ben Pargeter show to start. They were on their way to the lounge when someone knocked on the door; it was Jo.

"I thought I would come and watch the show with you as Seb has gone to help his dad put up some shelves," She told Stella once the door was open. "I hope that's okay? You are going to watch the show, aren't you?"

"Yes, come on in we're about to switch it on," Stella led the way into the lounge. Katy had already turned the television on and was sitting crossed legged on the floor with a box of chocolates on the coffee table beside her. Stella and Jo sat on the sofa behind Katy and selected a chocolate from the box. The show began with Ben Pargeter announcing his guests for the evening to the applause of a studio audience. His first guest was an old rock star who was making a comeback tour. Stella was surprised that he could still hold a conversation let alone sing as he slurred his way through the questions Ben fired at him. How much of that was age and how much was down to alcohol abuse she wondered. The soundman had to bleep out several of the replies, as they were inappropriate for the time slot that the show was being aired. There was a short break for adverts following the rock star who had just about managed to stay alert through the interview and Stella wondered if he had done his tour more harm than good by appearing on television like that.

When the show came back on Stella's stomach began to flutter nervously. Nathaniel would be on next, along with the star who was to play the hero in the latest film adaption of one of his books. The thought of seeing Nathaniel again and hearing him talk was unsettling. She wasn't sure how she felt about the whole thing.

She knew that it would probably add to the pain she felt of losing him, the feelings of love would all come flooding back and remind her of what she had thrown away so carelessly, but at the same time she couldn't resist the chance of catching a glimpse of him. She picked up a cushion so she could hide behind it if it made her want to cry, and listened as Ben announced Kurt Connell the latest heartthrob to storm Hollywood, and then the writer of the 'epic tale', Nathaniel Morgan.

The two men walked on together to thunderous applause and Stella felt her heart sink even further. Why would Nathaniel want to come back to her when he could choose from any of the women in the studio who were screaming and cheering for the attention of the two men as they waved and sat together on the hideous purple and orange sofa? He could have anyone he wanted, models, actresses, how could she even think that she could compete with them? Stella could feel a sob forming a lump in her throat. Kurt Connell might be a Hollywood heartthrob but she couldn't help thinking that Nathaniel was better looking. Kurt's blonde, boyish charm and fake tan couldn't compare to Nathaniel's brooding dark looks that had first made her think of him as a pirate. She could feel her insides melt at the first sight of him and she found it hard to hold back the tears that were threatening to fall. Nathaniel sat silently on the far end of the sofa, waiting patiently for his moment to speak. Kurt chatted away to Ben like an over excited puppy, full of enthusiasm for his part in the film.

Finally, Ben turned to Nathaniel, "So how do you keep coming up with all these amazing plots for your books, and how did you get started in the first place?" Ben asked, sitting forward in his chair and fixing a polite smile on his face.

Nathaniel's voice sounded deeper than Stella remembered it as it resonated in the studio microphones, although it still had the slightly husky softness to it that Stella was used to. She could feel her heart hammering erratically in her chest. Nathaniel explained to Ben how he had started writing to escape the pain of his parent's deaths, and that ideas for stories came to him from news stories and whatever was going on around him.

"And talking about what is going on in your life, I know you are normally a very private person, but I believe there was something you wanted to add on that subject wasn't there?" Ben prompted.

"Yes, that's right Ben," Nathaniel turned so he was looking directly at the camera and said, "I recently met someone who is very special to me and unfortunately we had a bit of a misunderstanding, if she is watching I want her to know that I meant everything I said and I hope she will give me another chance so I can put things right. Because despite what she thinks, I really do love her."

As Stella felt all the air leave her lungs and heard a whooshing sound in her ears, the audience gasped collectively before a combination of cheers and wails could be heard. Jo and Katy, who had turned to look directly at Stella were sat open-mouthed watching for Stella's reaction before hurling themselves at her exuberantly.

"Dios mío, I can't believe it, he's just announced on national television that he loves you, you can't doubt that he means it now," Katy told her taking hold of Stella's hand which had turned cold from shock. "What are you going to do?"

The sound of the television continuing its programme in the background was forgotten as Jo darted of to the toilet. The mixture of baby hormones and excitement was playing havoc with her bladder. As she came back downstairs the doorbell rang. Stella and Katy didn't seem to have heard it, so as she was passing she answered the door. She couldn't believe it when she saw Nathaniel stood on the doorstep with the late evening sun shining on his dark hair. He was surprised when he saw Jo opening the door and stepped back to check the number screwed to the wall was the right one, thinking that he had rung the wrong doorbell.

"I thought this was Stella's house" he stated, a puzzled look on his face.

"It is," Jo told him grabbing his jacket and pulling him inside. There was no way she was going to risk him leaving. "She's in the lounge with her friend Katy. We've just been watching you on the telly actually. I presume you were talking about Stella?" Jo knew that she was gabbling but she was very excited, it was so romantic. She might even have to cry in a moment, her emotions were all over the place because of her hormones. As she opened the door to the lounge and stood back for Nathaniel to proceed her into the room, she could feel her eyes welling up. The look on both Stella and Katy's faces was a picture. Stella looked as if she might pass out and Katy looked as if she were dying to ask for his autograph but knew that now was not the time. Nathaniel's presence seemed to fill the room, he was tall and broad shouldered but it was more to do with his personality, and the raw emotion that radiated from him that made the room suddenly feel small.

"Could I have a word with Stella on her own do you think?" He asked both Jo and Katy. Katy leapt off of the sofa and sidled passed to join Jo who was hovering anxiously by the door.

"Of course, we'll be in the kitchen if you want us," She told Stella as they left, shutting the door behind them.

"I wish we could listen in," she whispered to Jo as they settled themselves at the kitchen table. "I can't believe Nathaniel Morgan is actually in this house," she exclaimed, "right now, as we speak" she added as if Jo didn't already know.

"Do you think it would be wrong to ask for his autograph before he leaves?" At Katy's question, Jo laughed and Katy couldn't help but join in. It was so bizarre having her favourite author in the house, it didn't seem real and to think that Stella had been seeing him for a couple of months without even knowing who he was.

When they were alone at last Nathaniel took a deep breath and spoke. "I know you saw the interview I did on the Ben Pargeter show, Jo told me when she answered the door. So, will you give me the chance to prove that I meant all the things I said to you when you thought I was Jack?"

Stella had missed him so much, and she knew she had been unfair not giving him a chance to explain his reasons for doing what he had done, so biting her lip to stop herself from crying she nodded. Nathaniel moved forwards slowly, unsure as to whether she would let him sit beside her on the sofa, but taking the chance anyway. He sat with his body turned towards her and gently lifted her chin, then looking deeply into her eyes so that she could see that he meant every word he was about to say he continued.

"Every morning when I wake up I think of you. When I am with you I feel good, better than I have ever felt in my life. It's as if I am complete at last and I know that we belong together. I love you!"

Stella could hear the catch in his voice as he spoke, there was so much emotion that she knew that he meant what he was telling her. She had known that she had misjudged him after she had spoken with his sister. She regretted her impulsiveness when she had told him that it was over between them, but she had felt so hurt and humiliated then. With tears of happiness now running down her face she managed to say, "I love you too," before she found herself wrapped in Nathaniel's arms and sobbing softly against his shoulder.

"I knew you were the one for me the moment I first set eyes on you and it scared me half to death." He confessed. "Then when I saw you again in the churchyard upset after reading your letter, and I couldn't resist talking to you. I needed to make you feel better. I'm sorry I deceived you, I really am it's just... I needed to know that it was me that you loved and not the job that I do".

Stella pulled back enough to be able to see the expression on Nathaniel's face, she could see the turmoil he had been through and understood his reasons for what he had done.

"So, will you give me another chance?" His voice was barely a rasp.

"Of course I will, I've missed you so much," Stella managed to say through the lump in her throat. Nathaniel wiped a solitary tear away as it rolled down her cheek. Then he slowly lowered his head for a long lingering kiss that sent the blood thrumming through her veins. As her eyes drifted shut she was lost to everything but Nathaniel and the feel of his arms around her. He was definitely no ghost; a ghost could never make her feel what she was feeling at that moment. Moving to Little Welborough had been the best thing she had ever done.

* * * *

The bell over the door jangled as Stella entered the village shop in search of chocolate for the journey to visit her mother. Both Grace and Sophie stood behind the counter each holding a mug of coffee and speculating wildly on who the celebrity was who was going to open the school fete. Grace had heard the headteacher talking on her mobile phone to one of the other members of staff while buying her paper, telling them that a celebrity had agreed to open the fete. As the two women realised who had unwittingly entered the shop a sly smile of triumph spread across Sophie's face. Stella picked up a couple of chocolate bars and placed them down on the counter warily. There was something on the look of Sophie's face that unnerved her. She had the look of a spider who had just trapped a fly.

"Stella how lovely to see you. Are you all ready for the start of the summer term?"

Stella smiled tentatively wondering where the conversation was going. "Yes thank you".

"I hear they have found someone to open the fete isn't it wonderful?" Stella was surprised that they had found out so quickly. Nathaniel had only agreed the previous evening. Then it dawned on her, they were fishing for answers, they didn't know who it was yet.

"So what do you think of the choice?" Grace prompted hoping Stella would let slip who the celebrity was.

"Uh... well," Stella was wondering what she should say when the bell over the door jangled again and another customer came in, and having scoured the choices in the buckets by the door picked up a bunch of flowers. Sophie's jaw dropped and the mug of coffee she had been holding fell from her grasp clattering onto the counter top and spilling the contents onto the floor.

"I thought it would be nice to get some flowers for your mum as I'm meeting her for the first time, what do you think of these?" Nathaniel asked Stella holding a large bouquet up for her inspection; unaware of the effect he had had on the other occupants of the shop. The cat was out of the bag now, the news would be all around the village in no time.

Stella smiled warmly at Nathaniel. "She will love them", *and you*, she added silently in her head. Nathaniel paid for the flowers and the chocolate before Grace or Sophie had recovered enough from the shock to ask any questions. Then with his arm about Stella's waist they left the shop leaving neither, Grace, or Sophie in any doubt as to who would be opening the school fete or to the relationship he had with Stella. Stella felt her heart swell with pride and love for the man she had once thought was a ghost. The kiss he gave her before she climbed back into his car was full of passion and had her longing for the visit to her mother to be over so they could spend the evening alone together. The ghosts of the past were forgotten for both of them as they set off on the journey that lay ahead.

Lightning Source UK Ltd.
Milton Keynes UK
UKOW04f0626160118
316236UK00001B/4/P

9 781786 231048